maıɼe

MAIRE

Book One of the Fires of
Gleannmara series

Linda Windsor

Multnomah•Publishers *Sisters, Oregon*

MAIRE
Published by Multnomah Publishers, Inc.
© 2000 by Linda Windsor

International Standard Book Number: 1-57673-625-3

Cover design by Uttley/DouPonce Designworks
Cover image by Kirsty McLaren/Tony Stone Images

All Scripture quotations, unless otherwise indicated, are taken from
The Holy Bible, New King James Version (NKJV)
© 1984 by Thomas Nelson, Inc.
Printed in the United States of America

FOR INFORMATION:
Multnomah Publishers, Inc.•Post Office Box 1720•Sisters, Oregon 97759

Library of Congress Cataloging-in-Publication Data
Windsor, Linda.
  Maire: tame the heart/by Linda Windsor.
    p. cm.—(Multnomah fiction)
"Book one of the Fires of Gleannmara series."
  ISBN 1-57673-625-3
1. Women soldiers—Fiction. I. Title. II. Series.
PS3573.I519 M35 2000
813'.54—dc21   00-009334

00 01 02 03 04 05—10 9 8 7 6 5 4 3 2 1 0

To Jim, Jeff, Kelly, and Mom—
my wonderful family and one of God's greatest blessings.

I couldn't have done this without your support—
cooking, cleaning, laundry, encouragement, and love.

A foreword,
as 'twere, from Erin's heart...

Gleannmara. Ah, the sound of it warms me to me earthy core. 'Tis one of me favorite spots, nestled as it is between me mist-shrouded Wicklows and the Irish Sea. The Romans, you see, once dubbed me island *Scotia* and me people the *Scots,* which is why some of me children took that name to Scotland later on...but I digress.

I am the Emerald Isle of Ireland—Erin, for short.

Since creation, I've had all kinds of names—Hibernia bein' the first on record—and sure, I've seen all manner of mankind come and go. Before the Great Flood were some Greeks, and after? Well the list is considerable. Descendants of Noah's sons—Japheth and Shem were the first, the former a settling group and latter a troublesome lot of pirates. Aye, at the base of me bloodlines are the Hebrews. Then came the Greeks, Parthelan at Tallaght—the graves are there to this day—and Nemedh, whose people fled the pirates from the North, for Greece and to Britain, which is named for one of the leaders, Briotan Maol.

But the love of my God-graced green mountains and plains was never forgotten, and my children came back, like hungry babes to a mother's breast. The Firbolgs returned first from Greece, then later the Tuatha de Dananns from the North. After a terrible clash, the latter emerged triumphant, what with their superior powers.

Now there's them that believed this group to have the powers of magic. I meself think the Tuatha de Dananns were not magicians, but the forefathers of today's scientists. They were gifted with an intimate knowledge of God's earth and its workin's. A more primitive people could have easily mistaken such advanced learnin' for magic power as opposed to God-given knowledge.

No matter how much they knew, tho', the Dananns were no match for the coming of the sons of Milidh, and me last colonization at about thirty-five hundred years before Christ. These Milesians come by sea from what's now Spain, no small feat for that time. Here, as in the days of my creation, I saw the work of the Almighty's hand, for the Milesians' ancestors were none other than Phoenicians, a sea-lovin' race blessed by the Almighty for a deed of their Scythian forefathers back in the time of Moses.

Josephus wrote of how these Phoenicians were from a Red Sea settlement called Chiroth and how they gave aid and supplies to the Hebrew children fleeing Egypt with Moses, thereby invitin' the pharaoh's wrath. 'Twas no escape but by the sea, so the good Lord blessed their ships. He sent an east wind to carry them to the Iberian Peninsula where they later became the greatest navigators of the ancient world—the Phoenicians.

'Twas no wonder that their descendants, the Milesians, were able to sail to my shore and defeat the Dananns in battle, despite a tempest that some say the Dananns conjured with their mysterious powers. How could even those as learned as the Dananns know these were a seafaring people blessed by the hand of the Creator centuries before? To this day, some folk think the conquered Dananns shape-shifted into spirits and now live in the Other World as faeries and such. I was even called *Erienn* after one of their queens.

Me own account, howsomeever, is that the Dananns what got away hid themselves in the hills, where they lived as hermits and continued their studies of the earth and stars. For all that, they remained as much in darkness as their victors, still worshipin' the creations instead of the Creator...that is, until the comin' of the Gospel Light.

It's thought the apostle Paul referred to me in his letters as "the green island to the north" lightin' the first spark, which gradually was fanned into a Pentecostal fire by the teachers of the truth who followed. This is further verified by the pagan druid history of the Star of Bethlehem and of the darkness on the day of Christ's crucifixion. Some think the Magi themselves might have been druid astrologers and kings who knew by the signs that something was amiss.

The way me children embraced that Gospel Light made me proud enough to bust. Druids and kings who sought truth and light gave up their wealth and prestige to become servants of the one God. No other country in the history of the world produced more missionaries than me own fair land. And if I might say so, 'tis meself whom man credits today for saving civilization when the rest of the earth sank into the dark age of the barbarians.

Now the tale I'm fixin' to tell is about the comin' of God's Word to the hills and vales of *tuatha* Gleannmara. The spark of the gospel kindled there burns this very day in the hearts of its children, despite the tribulations of corruption and invasion spawned by the prince of darkness his own self.

Make yourself comfortable and read the story of Rowan, whose heart is as noble as it is brave, and of Maire (that's MOY-ruh to them what has neither the eye nor the tongue of a Gael), the pagan warrior queen who found love in his arms.

ONE

Growling with battle fury, Rowan of Emrys wrenched his sword from the rib cage of the tattooed barbarian. There was no time to study his vanquished foe's sightless, staring eyes or dwell upon the carnage their brief encounter wrought upon his body. The heathens swarmed like angry hornets over the walls of the frontier guard post, stinging with primitive yet deadly weapons wielded with a skill that Rowan had to admire.

Beyond the pile of bodies that evidenced Rowan's own training, one of his comrades now struggled, outnumbered two to one. As Rowan started to his aid, a hideous, otherworldly scream clawed through the air, plucking with icy fingers at the hair on his arms and raking up his spine. A spear of fire plunged into his back, spreading to sear the muscle of his well-developed torso, jerking him into an arch over it.

Blind with pain, he pulled himself together with sheer instinct and brought his blade around full circle, swinging at the source. It was then that he saw the shrieking banshee. Her hair was a wild tangle of lime; her painted face as grotesque and fierce as that of any man the mercenary had ever met on the field. No doubt the blood staining Rowan's sword belonged to her mate. Yet it was not her wildness or her fierceness that made Rowan flinch. It was the sight of his sharp blade slicing into her middle—a middle swollen with child.

With wide eyes black as sin, she dropped her weapon and grabbed at her belly in disbelief. Bile rose to the back of Rowan's throat at what had transpired before his very eyes, at what he could no more stop than the battle raging around him. He—the most decorated and youngest captain of the border guard—was going to be sick. Sick at what he'd done, sick at the pain viciously gnawing its way through him....

Rowan ap Emrys tossed on his bed, scattering the fine linens, but the bloody vision of battle and that of the last victim he'd struck down wouldn't leave. Not yet. Nor would the pain that burned into the scar on his back.

The dream was so real. His stomach lurched to no avail, except to add to agony.

Just when he could bear it no more, the bloody visage shape-shifted into a whole woman again. She was a warrior, with a wild mane of red hair and fierce green eyes that could warm a stone—or shatter it. A torque of gold about her neck betrayed her royal status. With the grace of the willow and the strength of the sacred oak, she extended her hand to Rowan and—

"Master Rowan!"

She was gone.

Rowan came up from his bed, wiping the perspiration from his brow. He squinted in the early morning sun at his steward. "What is it, Dafydd?"

He couldn't be angry with the man for sending the beauteous creature away. Like a faerie, she always vanished before Rowan managed to touch her.

"The Scots have landed at the village. There's smoke rising over the ridge as we speak!"

Smoke. There'd been resistance. Rowan swore. "I warned those fishermen that if the Irish raided, to stand aside and let them take plunder rather than lives! Gold can be replaced; loved ones cannot."

"Lady Delwyn is seeing to our valuables, and I've already sounded the alarm."

Rowan pulled on a coarse linen robe over his naked flesh. The remnant perspiration from the dream hampered the material as he shook it down over his considerable frame. The rough scrape of the material against his skin was a stark contrast to the fine sheets of his bed. He hadn't heard the horn's blast. All he'd heard was that horrible scream…

Well, like as not, it was too late to help the villagers anyway.

"Assemble the men. I'll meet them outside the courtyard. We'll make a stand here."

"Aye, it's too late to do the village much good."

As the steward dutifully hurried off, Rowan struggled on with his boots. The noise of battle still filled his ears, though the village was too far away for it to travel. The nightmare never released him easily. Upon strapping his sword at his waist, he was surprised that it didn't feel strange though he'd not used it since that day of battle, long ago. He'd prayed he'd never have to use it again, but that didn't seem to be the case today—not if his parents' estate and the lives of those who lived here were to be spared.

He ran through the chaos of the household preparing for the raid. Stepping outside, he shook the last of the banshee's yell from his beleaguered brain. There was no time to console his mother or to see his invalid father safely moved to the chapel of the villa. Like the house and buildings itself, his parents belonged to another time—one of a peace protected by Rome. The passage of time since the last of the legions withdrew had eroded the villagers' youth—as well their ability to protect themselves from the barbarian attacks that ensued.

Like heralds of destruction, spirals of smoke drifted toward the villa from the nearby village on the sea. Dafydd stood speaking with a young lad Rowan recognized from the village. It was Dafydd's brother's son.

"Some of the villagers thought they could stop them," the breathless youth was saying. He shot Rowan an apologetic look. "Father and Justinian tried to tell them not to fight."

"It's natural to defend one's home. Just not wise in this case," Rowan answered. "How many are dead?"

"Six that I know of. Justinian is gathering the wounded at the wood near the village's edge."

The Celts found no honor in slaughter; only a good fight made their blood boil.

"And Justinian himself?"

"Well; but sore that they set fire to the church even after he gave them what they demanded."

Rowan could well imagine how his usually mild mentor and teacher of the Word had ruffled at such an insult. With the same fervor that the priest now embraced the teachings of the faith, he once had embraced the life of a pirate and rogue. Not much different from Rowan himself, save Rowan's rowdier days were sanctioned by the law. Justinian's had not been. "And your father?"

The boy shook his head. "Mad as the priest over the fire. He can't blame the Scots for fighting with those who resisted."

"Well, I can!" Dafydd's words came hot and fierce. "Cursed heathens that they are, they should all be put to death for killin' innocent folk."

"Whether their swords drip with innocent blood or not, they're coming this way now," Rowan said to no one in particular. And then his own sword would drip blood for the first time since—

He turned abruptly from the thought and assessed the chaos in and around the villa. Dafydd had done well—exactly as Rowan had trained him to do in the event of a Scotti raid. Servants rushed to prepare as they could, joined by the chaotic influx of families who flocked to the villa at the sound of the warning horn.

God willing, these precautions will not be needed.

Pray God, no blood would be drawn, nor fire set to the place his parents had so lovingly built. It was a rare symbol of a better time before Gaelic replaced Latin as the common tongue and the villas gave way to roundhouses on the landscape. Still, Rowan would fight if need be to preserve his family home, just as his father, a much decorated Roman general, had done many years before.

"Rowan."

The sound of his mother's voice was like a gentling calm on the roar of his blood, which was gradually stirring to a tempest by the prospect of impending battle. Despite his adoption by a Romanized family of Wales, his blood was the same as those who came to plunder them. God help him, there was still a part of him that flushed with excitement at the prospect of battle.

He felt his fierce features soften into a smile as Delwyn ap Emrys laid a jeweled hand upon his arm.

"The valuables are buried, but I dread seeing the house torn asunder by the raiders' pillage."

The adoration of the sun's fingers on the artistically crafted gold setting of her ring, in which were nestled some of nature's most precious stones, snagged his distracted attention.

"All valuables buried? Not your ring, I see." Heathen raiders or not, his mother would never take off the wedding ring Demetrius had given her when she was a bride of sixteen. The gems and metal were forged by the hands of time, as was his parents' love for each other.

"I just can't bring myself to take it off," she apologized with a reticent twitch of her lips.

And she would not have to give it up, God willing, Rowan thought. "I promise to do all God would have me do to avoid that. I've a plan."

Lady Delwyn's face brightened momentarily with pride before a loving concern shadowed it. "You'll not risk harm."

"Not if I can help it."

He had discovered how precious was the life God had given him, unlike the day he'd been brought to this place from the Pictish frontier, a wounded and broken warrior wanting death.

But well he knew that second chances at a good life did not

come without a price. God had given him time to heal and blessed him with abundance. Despite his prayers to the contrary, he must now take up the blood-sullied sword of his past to save all he cared about. Hopefully, it was God's plan that was forming in his mind as he assessed Emrys's situation in the path of the raiders.

Rowan didn't want to worry his mother with his bold plan. He hoped the belligerent Scotti would weary of bloodshed by the time they reached Emrys and agree to his idea for determining the outcome of their trespass on Welsh soil.

"I'll try the voice of reason first."

His mother's brows arched. "Reason with heathens?"

"God will lend weight to my words, Mother. Meanwhile, gather the women into the chapel to petition Him to do so. 'Tis His hand, not those of these farmers, that will save us."

Rowan glanced meaningfully to the men who assembled by the moment to stand with him against the Scotti. They were men of soul, not iron.

"Tell Father I'll not leave our people to Scotti mercy."

"Demetrius believes in you as I do," his mother assured him. "God will be with you, son."

Bedridden with the ills of age and a weakening heart, Demetrius ap Emrys had long since turned the running of the villa over to the Scot slave boy he'd adopted twenty years before. Rowan had resembled a son lost to illness and counted his fortune well found in his new situation, although he still remembered the humiliation and horror of being sold by his own brother; Britons sold their kin into slavery, not the Irish Celts!

There was no doubt in Rowan's mind that this underlying resentment had carried him with bloodlust onto the frontier battlefields, where he'd cut down those who had caused a young boy so much grief. Then Rowan had been brought home, burning with fever and infection from wounds received in a barbarian raid. Death had not come as he, in his lucid moments, expected…even prayed for. God had other plans for him and his.

But what, Father?

"I pray I will live up to the general's expectations," he said, hearing no answer to his furtive inner question.

"You have never let us down, son." His mother's assurance snatched him from the past. "Never."

She held his gaze long enough for Rowan to recognize she knew where he'd been and what he was thinking at the moment. Her intuition never ceased to amaze him. With a brush of her lips on his cheek, she turned in a swirl of gold-threaded skirts to enter the villa.

Lady Delwyn was still beautiful, Rowan thought. The glow of her kind heart dimmed the ravages of time on her face. Demetrius gave her credit for his inspiration, and indeed it was her influence that had led Rowan to study the gospel during his recovery.

"We're ready for the fiends, Rowan. Better to die than have 'em overrun our fields and ruin what little chance we have for survival this winter."

Rowan shook his head as Dafydd, his sturdy, stocky bailiff approached. "Only as a last resort."

Dafydd's face was flushed at the prospect of a fight. While Rowan understood the Welshman's outrage at this affront to their families and land, Rowan had to be careful not to let it affect his judgment. Even as his palms grew damp with dread, an old, involuntary excitement at the prospect of combat plagued his mind. With it came a haunting flashback of the battle that had ended his military career.

Father, please, not now! Rowan swallowed the bile rising in his throat. Had the dream been a foreshadowing? Thankfully his voice gave no hint of his inner turmoil.

"I hope that won't be necessary, Dafydd. I intend to appeal to their fierce sense of honor first. The Scotti hold that dear, despite their heathen ways. Perhaps we'll settle the outcome with cunning rather than with lives."

"Honor!" Dafydd let loose with a curse in his native Celtic tongue, something about the worth, or lack thereof, of a pagan god's dung. The steward might worship his maker as earnestly as any man in the true faith, but he did not hesitate to use the gods of his forefathers to sully what riled him. "There's no honor in them that pillage and burn a church. Like as not that robe you're wearin' will only make them laugh at you."

Rowan ignored the outburst. "Have the men form a line between me and the villa and hold it while I go ahead to meet the raiders." Self-consciously, he fingered the coarsely woven material of his robe. Justinian offered it when Rowan began to study the gospel. Torn between his sense of obligation to his family and that to his God, it was months before Rowan finally donned it. Perhaps its feel against his skin reminded him of humility.

"I'll not let you go out alone," Dafydd argued. "We'll *all* go."

"I go alone." The finality in Rowan's voice ended the steward's protest. "I'll not have the Scotti think we are rallying against them like the villagers."

He was glad Dafydd did not suspect the palm-wetting fear and dread threatening his cool demeanor at the prospect of taking up his sword again. Yet, despite Rowan's strong reluctance to touch the weapon, which had both saved and destroyed him that fateful day on the battlefield, he was not fool enough to approach an enemy intoxicated by bloodlust and victory without it. An undermining cold like a winter brook ran through Rowan's body. The Scriptures said to trust in God, but they also said not to tempt Him.

"Why don't we let God decide whether we have to use our swords or not?"

Dafydd snorted in sheer wonder. "This from the same man who single-handedly turned away a Pictish attack on—"

"My sword was my master then, Dafydd." Rowan had been raised in the Christian faith by his parents, but it had no place on the battlefield, or so he'd once believed.

"And one to be feared, I'll swear by that."

Having sent more than his share of mortals to the other side with the weapon, Rowan couldn't argue. Thankfully, a movement on the newborn, green horizon snatched Rowan from the turmoil—inner and outer—assaulting him. He fixed his attention on a more immediate battle.

"There they are!" Dafydd shouted beside him. "To arms, men!"

"Do exactly as I said and form a line in front of the villa," Rowan ordered, "and remain there until I signal you. If I can work this out peacefully, no one will suffer. Nonetheless, we have to show that we will not give way easily."

Dafydd sneered. "Like the fishermen and the cleric?"

"Those who resisted were foolish. Justinian knew the gold in the church could be replaced. Human life cannot." Rowan glanced at the first of the painted warriors amassing on the hill. He prayed again that the village priest had kept the bulk of the villagers under control during the pillage. The sight of the enemy's war paint and tattoos, which made the Scotti appear as demons sprung from Hades itself, was enough to intimidate the most stalwart enemy. Their cries were worse, though. Inhuman and terrifying. Still, God knew the Scotti bled and died like any mortal—Rowan had spilled enough of their blood to prove that.

One time too often.

Merciful Father, let it be forgotten, just this day! Give me my sword to save lives, not take them. He cast an encompassing look at his troops. Their lives were more important than their worldly goods. He'd worked shoulder to shoulder with these good-hearted fellows, wrestling with the heavy plows imported from Belgae to clear land to feed their families. They were more his family than the blood clansman who'd sold him.

Rowan's eyes glittered, hardening as more and more of the painted heathens gathered on the horizon. If saving his people meant bloodying his sword, then so be it. And yet, as he gave one last order, his words were free of the shared rage and anticipation of conflict infecting the men behind him. He willed his right hand to the hilt at his waist.

"Pray, good fellows. 'Tis a stronger weapon than this."

Rowan believed this in his heart, but he could not feel the assurance of which he boasted. Indeed, his greatest challenge at that moment was not the hordes amassing in the distance, but to practice as he preached: to rely on God to make his plan work.

At the crest of the hill overlooking the villa below, Maire stood with her foster brothers, as spattered by blood as they.

It's real.

Her heart pounded hard enough, she was certain, to loosen the red and yellow enamel decoration of her leather breastplate. The years of slaying wooden posts and sparring with her brothers and trainers were over. Instead of splitting the head of a melon this day, her sword had laid open a human being's skull...and the carnage threatened to explode in her stomach each time she recalled it.

Yet she dared not show her weakness, to let any see that her bones felt as though they were turning to water and her blood to bile. She was Maire of Gleannmara, the princess born to follow her warrior mother's legacy. While other little girls were instructed in the womanly arts of needlework and cooking, Maire had honed her skill in the arts of war against men half again her size. She could better than hold her own with any weapon.

"What do you make of that, Firebrand?"

"They're expecting us," she answered the bearlike man who stood at her side. "'Twill make no difference."

Eochan was the eldest of her two foster brothers. His size and strength were his greatest assets, as well as his liability. A blow from him would send a foe reeling into the other world without warning, but Maire had learned that her speed and agility stood a better chance of dodging the advance, enabling her to strike before the burly warrior recovered his swing. Most of the time, that is. Once in practice he'd broken her rib, then nearly collapsed with contrition. The bear had a tender heart.

"No doubt—" he nodded—"you've won the morning, to be sure."

"Over fishermen, not warriors."

The time had come to prove herself. This very sunrise, when they'd landed on the beach, she'd gone eighteen, the age at which the high king Diarhmott had proclaimed she might become her mother's successor.

But why, in the name of her ancestors' gods, had those fishermen taken it upon themselves to defend the church? Her brothers had anticipated no resistance with the sacking of the village's house of worship. Then suddenly, men with poles and hooks such as they used to make their living, were attacking them. It became a matter of survival to spill blood, although there was no sense of triumph in overcoming men more accustomed to handling nets than weapons. Where were the warriors of the village?

"Well, look at that!"

Eochan pointed to a tall, robed figure striding toward them in the distance. The stranger moved unconcerned, as if out to take in the soft air, which was so thick with mist that Maire's short tunic of coarse cloth hung damp over her combat-lean form.

"A priest with a sword." Maire's curious gaze moved beyond the man to the strange looking rath below.

At least the village priest had a stone tower of sorts in which he'd encouraged some of the villagers to take refuge. No earthen work or even stick fencing protected the odd, rectangular buildings below. The momentum of the Scotti's run down the hill would carry her men through the structure like a boulder of destruction. Natural curiosity made her wish she might see it outside the fierce rush of conquest, for the well-kept garden, around which the massive dwelling had been built, was unlike anything she'd ever laid eyes upon.

Her estimation of her foes' wit dropped, in spite of the beauty they cultivated. A body couldn't live on flower blossoms, no matter how pleasing they were to the eye. But then there was enough cleared land here to afford both food and pleasure to the eye, she supposed. The blossoms were so vibrant Maire could almost smell them across the distance. It was a relief from the stench of spilled blood.

"He's too late to help the village, if that's his purpose. Let's charge, Maire, and see if his studies have sharpened his skill with that sword swinging at his side."

"This is different, Declan."

Instinct told her this as much as anything. Unlike her youngest foster brother, who'd finally caught up with them, she was loathe to start the bloodlust again when she'd scarce recovered from the last. She fingered her warrior's collar as though she might draw on wisdom from its past. The pure, twisted gold circling her slender throat had belonged to Maeve and been witness to many battles.

"He appears to come to us with a purpose."

"Aye, to make a sacrifice with his own blood, by the look of it!" the more impetuous of her foster brothers crowed in disdain.

Declan would challenge the sea itself, she thought. Faith, he'd done just that before they embarked. Knee-deep in the surf, he'd slashed at the continuous flow of waves beating against the beach until, winded and full of himself for his demonstration of skill, he'd finally joined the rest.

Now he wiped the blade of his *cloidem* against his *brat* of four colors. The cloidem was sharp enough to split hairs driven against it by the wind, or so he'd boasted in the shipboard revelry the night before. Like most of the men, he wore nothing else save his cloak of distinction and rank. His fine body was painted, his long, fair hair stiff with lime. With a shout of defiance he shook his sword over his head at the oncoming stranger.

"Best you take heed, pup. The princess has her mother's instincts."

"Brude!" Maire was shocked to see Gleannmara's elder druid coming to the front on a small, shaggy pony. Her face flushed scarlet at the compliment of his presence. Though getting on in years, Brude blessed the voyage with his presence. Still, no one expected the druid to accompany them to the battlefront. With him here to sing a battle song, victory was already theirs.

"And a maiden's blush as well," Eochan teased. "So give us the word, Firebrand. What do we do?"

Maire considered the question amidst the spell cast by the druid's appearance. It was not ordinary for Brude to accompany them on such a minor excursion as a simple raid. It could only be guessed that he'd come to declare Maire equal to the task of ruling her mother's *tuath*. Surely the spirits of victory were with them now.

"Tell me what you think of yon stranger, child," the ancient prompted, his brow furrowed with time and cultivated with the wisdom of his ancestors.

Maire braced herself mentally, knowing this was yet another test. The stranger was closer now. He was tall and broad shouldered. His robe filled with the westerly breeze and flowed about his long legs as if to make him appear a giant.

"Those are not the shoulders of a man who spends his days bent over parchment and quill."

"Good…good," her mother's chief advisor encouraged. Despite the strain of his years, Brude's eyes were brighter than the fires of Beltaine, full of the life force itself.

"Nor is his stride the humble one of a meek worshiper of the Christian God."

The Christian faith was not unknown in Erin. Many high kings and druids had embraced it. Indeed, people flocked to its gentle call. It was through a Christian holy man's influence that pagan and Christian alike accepted King Diarhmott on the throne.

Of course, Diarhmott claimed he'd only used the Christian teacher toward his own end. Like many of his clans, the high king felt at heart this Christian god was too meek for their warlike Celtic nature. Nor was he overimpressed with the god's word as the last few of his predecessors had been. The old laws and gods had served them well enough for centuries. Still, change was good. Change meant growth, though Maire—like every Celt she'd known—was ever wary of its direction.

"What else, child?"

Maire tried to make out the stranger's face. "His eyes are narrowed, sharp like a hawk's. He measures our strength with each step he takes toward us."

"Then he should turn tail and run at any moment now."

Maire dismissed Declan's observation, trying to tune in to Brude's uncanny perception that it might speak to her as well. After all, she was Maeve's daughter. "No, he wishes to talk, I think."

She noted the man's hand resting, unassuming, on the hilt of his weapon. His thumb might be hooked in his belt for all the threat it implied; yet, as he neared, Maire felt the hair prick like cold fingers at the nape of her neck.

"He's a warrior, no doubt," she said with conviction, "but there's more to him than meets the eye."

"What?" Eochan glanced askew at the insinuation of the unseen, first at Maire and then at the druid, who was nodding in agreement. The giant Scot would charge a legion of fighting men on his own, but he had no backbone for spirits. The word of a druid that the spirits were on his side was all he required.

"I sense it too." Brude's pleasure in her perception was clear. "There is a presence beyond the physical with this man. 'Twill take more than skill alone to deal with him. But have no fear," he added, upon seeing the graze of alarm on Maire's face. "That is why I am here."

The older man slid off his pony and produced a small harp as if by magic out of the volumes of his embroidered robe. "There are many concerns to distract my queen without those of hostile spirits."

"Did you hear what he said?" Declan whispered beneath his breath.

Indeed Maire had. Brude called her his queen. She'd thought he'd remained aboard ship, yet he'd seen enough of her courage and skill to declare her his queen. Had he used the eyes of a raven?

Maire had never fully understood the druidic power to communicate with certain animals. Indeed, the bard had a pet heron, which waddled after him like a feathered shadow. She'd seen him speak to the bird and heard the bird answer many times, although not in such language as she could understand.

Even as the elder tested the eloquent strings of his instrument, the men forming about them began to chant her name on the wind. They had heard Brude's words, too. With each repetition, the tribute grew louder and louder. She hadn't expected this until they returned to Gleannmara in triumph. Part of her bade her lower her gaze and tug at the hem of her tunic in embarrassment, but she'd been groomed for this day. Instead, she stood taller with each rousing cheer, until she'd reached the pinnacle of her height at Eochan's shoulder, where a golden broach secured his woolen cloak.

"Come listen to an old man's words, my queen, while your brothers see what this stranger wishes."

"Shouldn't I be the one to find out?" After all, she'd just been acknowledged as queen.

"He is not what he appears, nor do we wish to appear what we are until we discover his purpose. Let the men find it out. Then he shall deal with our queen."

Brude was right. Her mother never initially negotiated with her enemy; although once past her emissaries, her opponents found her as formidable as any man. Why encourage the enemy to think there was possible weakness on the clan's part, with their chieftain being a mere woman? It was only in the combat of weapons that this underestimation was to her advantage—a combat that was imminent.

"There will be no bloodshed," Brude told her as she watched Eochan and Declan meet the tall figure several yards away. "The strings of Macha are not thick with it, but sing clear as a lark's song. The day is Gleannmara's."

Maire was not so certain. Her brothers' swords were unsheathed and driven into the ground beside them, ready should any cause arise to use them. The stranger had yet to remove his from its silver-studded sheath. He greeted the Scotti warriors as if they were long-lost friends, gesturing toward the rath below as though in welcome.

"Perhaps the answer to my queen's problem with Morlach is at hand."

Maire forgot the stranger and her brothers at the mention of the man who'd been appointed by the high king to oversee Gleannmara until she came of age. Morlach was not moved by the spirits as was the wizened Brude, who now pressed his ear to the melody-rich wood of his instrument. No, Morlach's motivation was nothing short of greed. The druid-sacrificer-turned-lord-of-his-own-tuath had made it clear that he'd not invested his time and interest in Gleannmara to have it snatched from him by an upstart princess of barely eighteen. He intended to wed Maire and join the two kingdoms.

After her parents had died in battle, Brude and her foster family raised and protected Maire at Drumkilly. She had not set foot on her beloved home of Gleannmara since Brude took her away, beyond Morlach's reach. But now she'd come of age, which put her beyond the protection of those who loved her. Worse, Morlach exercised his influence over the high king to win royal favor for the union of Rathcoe and Gleannmara. Her destiny though, was in *her* hands, not Morlach's, for Maire had made up her mind to die first.

This raid was to provide the opportunity.

TWO

"The master of these farmers wishes the contest between us settled by champions," Declan said, announcing his and Eochan's return. "I'd like to offer my sword to my queen."

"Nay, Maire. I'm the eldest. 'Tis only right that I should be your champion."

Maire acknowledged neither offer. While her gaze was affixed on Brude, her thoughts raced on, finding voice. "Am I to assume that if he wins, his people and land go unmolested and if we win...what is it he offers that we cannot already take?"

"He says to overrun his lands and destroy his people's livelihood is of far less value to us than a handsome tribute of twenty-five *cumals* to be paid annually."

"A hundred head of cattle or its value?" Maire was astonished. It was a kingly prize.

"Gleannmara's pastures are scant of beef, what with Morlach's bloodletting hand."

Maire met the pale blue gaze of the druid. He spoke the truth. The overseer had taken unfair reward for the duty of his appointment by the king. He professed enriching the soil with the blood of their cattle, but his coffers grew fat from the sale of skins and salted meat while the soil produced no more grain than it had before. At first mention of this raid, the men of Gleannmara rallied to Maire's side, hope in their hearts that she would at long last save them from Morlach's heavy-handed rule.

"Like as not, the priest's people have already buried the

bulk of their valuables," Maire thought aloud. The Britons were known for that, leaving only a showing to satisfy the invaders. This offer of tribute was more than her men could steal and carry back on their small ship. But a tribute from across the sea was more than a notion to enforce. The king of Tara would testify to that, and he had the advantage of his Leinster subjects sharing the same body of land rather than having a sea between them. "And how will I know they'll keep their word?"

"He expects us to take hostages to guarantee his people's fealty to Gleannmara," Eochan replied. "But in exchange, he expects Gleannmara's protection against other invaders."

"Not that *he'll* need it," Declan interjected. "I expect to add his dark head to my trophies."

"His head will be mine, little brother. I am the eldest," Eochan reminded his bantam-tempered kin.

Maire ignored the dispute, trying to deal with the quagmire of emotion clouding her judgment. She'd wanted to prove herself worthy as queen, but she also had planned to avoid Morlach by dying in battle. Unfortunately she'd yet this day to come across an adversary who might defeat her. May her clansmen never become as peace-softened as the fishermen they'd faced earlier—or as the farmers collected below!

Now it seemed her valiant death was not to be. How could she let this stranger win, when the tribute would mean so much to Gleannmara? In an outright fight, her kinsmen would win regardless—or mayhap one of the sodmuckers might get lucky and land a fatal blow against her. Regardless, this stranger had made a good point. Why destroy what might be put to work for her clan? She glanced at the druid, aware that he watched her every expression, perhaps even read her thoughts.

Brude sang out her decision even as she reached it, ending the dispute festering between the brothers. "Gleannmara's queen will fight on our behalf. There's no other choice."

His voice was surprisingly strong for his many years as chief bard and elder druid. No one knew the man's age. It was as evasive as that of the great forest that had adopted him as its own before her mother's birth. As if in chorus, the clan's chanting of Maire's name underscored his point.

"Of course I will." A heady rush at the prospect of winning for her people welled in her blood. This was what she was born for. Still...

"What is the question I see in your mother's green eyes, child? Do you doubt your skill?"

"Do you, Brude?" Maire tossed the challenge back in an effort to deny her real quandary over Morlach.

As if to remove any further doubt regarding her willingness and ability, she pulled off her leather helmet. Her brothers had insisted she wear the worrisome protection on her first foray into battle, while they went bareheaded. They'd pledged no harm would come to her—an irony only Maire seemed to appreciate since she'd bested them more than once in training. Size was Eochan's downfall, and temper was Declan's. It had been simple, once she learned their weaknesses, to defeat them.

Her flame-red hair, battle-streaked with lime like Celtic warriors past, tumbled down her back. Again her name rose enthusiastically from the ranks. She would win for Gleannmara. The spirits of victory were with her. Somehow she'd deal with Morlach and the king later. Her mother's voice echoed in her mind: "Choose your enemy one by one, whenever the gods allow."

Maire stepped out of the cover of her clansmen to study her opponent with single interest. "I'd have a song, Brude. A blood stirring one about Maeve, chieftess of the Uí Niall, conqueror and queen of Gleannmara!"

The bard's song would give her focus and fire her passion even more against her opponent, though she felt she was about to burst with energy as it was. A right ballad to call up the deeds of past heroes and heroines would show this Welshman that her blood was that of the most courageous and victorious of her ancestors. Her late mother had won Gleannmara; Maire would defend it.

"Put the helmet on, Maire," Eochan called after her as she started down the incline to where the robed stranger waited.

She brushed the suggestion aside like an annoying insect buzzing at her ear. Her brain needed to breathe. The distraction of the confining helmet more than offset its merit. She adjusted a band of tooled leather across her forehead. Although her hair had been stiffened enough with lime to keep it from hampering her vision, no precaution was excess in a matter of life and death.

She strode boldly toward the waiting warrior-priest, the leather-coated wickerwork shield of her clan strapped on her left arm as she inventoried her weapons with her right. Her mother's sword; her short, pointed *scían*; the lightweight ax slung across her back; all were within easy reach.

Then there was the wee stinger sheathed between the carved swells of her breastplate, the weapon's hilt disguised as adornment. The blade was but a hand in length and thin as a reed, but it was deadly nonetheless.

Maire smiled as the incredulous expression on her opponent's face gave way to blustering indignation. *Go on, fool. I'll be the last foe you underestimate.*

"I asked for no woman, good fellows. I asked to face a champion."

Her opponent's initial incredulity was exactly the reaction Maire counted on. Except that it went beyond, for suddenly the man stared at her as though she were naught but a spirit, a ghost. Much as she wanted to think she was intimidating, she knew it was neither her boasting nor her appearance that drained her adversary's face of blood and squeezed perspiration from its pores. She'd seen men about to heave up bad ale who had more color than the man facing her now.

And those eyes! By her mother's sword, they devoured her

as though starved for and repulsed by her at the same time. Maire felt some of her own blood slip away from her face. Surely he couldn't know that the blood splattered on her body and sword was her first. Nay, he was just assessing her. She stood taller, defiant to the examination of the gaze capable of peering over the top of her head.

"What I lack in size, I make up for in speed and skill, sir," she declared boldly, ignoring the urge to shrink from him.

He took note of the length of her legs, exposed from the thigh down by her leine so that her hem didn't impair her movement in battle.

When his gaze lingered overlong on the embroidery of stick animals and figures on the garment's edge, she issued a hot challenge. "You've never seen Celtic gods before?"

"Not in such a comely display."

Maire resisted the urge to pull the skirt down to the laced tops of her kid boots. She'd not give the man the satisfaction of knowing he'd put her ill at ease by this strange admiration. "Did you come up here to play the flirt or to fight? Either, I assure you, will result with your heart skewered on my sword."

"If my heart needs be skewered, it would favor your weapon above any of the dozens I've faced in battle."

Her cheeks grew hot, as though the sun overhead had kissed them outright. "Then let's be at it, before your idle flattery turns my stomach." She motioned down the hill toward the villa. Such word play was not an assault she'd been trained for. It stung and stroked her pride with the same hand.

She ignored the bewildering mix of reaction his words and attentive gaze evoked. "Will you not treat your people to the spectacle of losing your head to the sword of Gleannmara?"

The man suddenly looked as though he'd been broadsided with a blade. "Sword of *what*?"

Maire blessed whatever it was that swung the pendulum of discomfiture back to her opponent and lifted her weapon high.

"The sword of Maire, queen of tuatha Gleannmara!"

Behind the bold warrioress, her name rose from her troops like a chant to the sun, but all Rowan heard was *Gleannmara*. He reeled inwardly, as though struck full force by the ax slung across her back.

Gleannmara! The home of his ancestors. The home from which he'd been sold...but not by this clan. In brief seconds, he wondered of the fate suffered by his brother and family. Had they died at the hands of these raiders, who now claimed the green, forested hills as their own? Had he nurtured his bitterness—since he was a child of six, sold and carried in chains aboard a merchant ship bound for the Welsh coast, never to see his home again—for nothing? Had his struggle with his faith—to turn from his desire for vengeance to forgiveness, as had the scriptural Joseph—his thoughts of even returning to preach God's Word to them, been in vain?

The irony was not beyond him any more than that which put him up against a female; the soul's enemy knew his weaknesses and used them without mercy.

Rowan stared at the young woman's face as though he might see the fate of his family. Gradually her delicate features became distinctive beneath the blue paint and lime smeared over them. The proud tilt of her chin, the way her small nose turned up, almost as an afterthought, the fullness of her mouth, now drawn into the most pensive of pouts—all were strangely familiar. Was there no end to this dark battery of distraction?

"Will you summon your clan, man, or shall I cut you down while you stand gawking like a stone-struck fool?"

Four years it had taken to bury his past pain and anger, yet the sight of a pagan female warrior and the mention of his former home resurrected it in a matter of moments. Only God provided the steel of his resolve, for he knew he was incapable of recovering on his own. Renewed, Rowan jerked his head toward Emrys and stepped off the precipice of his faith. Surely God would not have him spill another woman's blood. He would die himself first.

"Come with me, queen of Gleannmara. Let this match take place where all can watch; although I warn you, all your skill will do you little good against my sword."

"Your ego is well matched to your size, sir."

"And yours to your mouth."

Rowan felt the glare of that green gaze burning into his back as he turned away and started down the hill. Soldier sense told him he was a fool for turning his back on an armed opponent; a more spiritual one assured him it was well to do so. From the corner of his eye, he saw her slap her sheathed sword and take double steps to catch up with him. When she did, he could not help but grin. She was game enough, this one, to earn his respect, and not as unwise as her youth might make her.

"My name is Rowan, son of Demetrius, master of Emrys. It does you credit, Queen Maire, that you see value in not destroying that which can produce enough for us all."

"I care not what your name is, or that of this land. I only care what Gleannmara will take home from it. Let them that bury you worry with those details."

"I shall do my best to avoid that," he promised, still unable to wipe the grin from his face. It was a challenge to match wits with this one. Under other circumstances…

"Rowan of Emrys," she murmured aloud. "Rowan…like the tree?"

"And as hard as the blade."

"Or at least as hard in the head. 'Twill take more than one swat, I'll wager, to split it like a practice melon."

"Or like that fisherman's head," one of the queen's spokesmen remarked from behind them. He was the shorter of the two who'd come to speak with Rowan—a fair-haired buck who fairly itched for battle even now. Rowan knew one slight mistake and the entire lot would be out for blood.

Mayhap the protectiveness of the queen's spokesman was a sign of an even closer relationship? If so, why wasn't the Scotti warrior the champion instead of the battle sprite struggling to keep up with him? How could the man allow it? Just the mention of a man's head splitting like a melon had robbed this Maire of at least one shade of color.

Sudden understanding dawned: She'd drawn her first blood today! Rowan nearly stumbled over his thought. Faith, this was all he needed—standing against a novice *and* a female in battle. *Father, show me a way out of this, I beg you!*

"It does you credit that you would avoid unnecessary bloodshed, Emrys; although it takes little more than a blind eye to see you're no cleric, but a warrior in a churchman's robe."

"I merely sought to capture your attention that I might appeal to your clan's honor and spare my tuath by my sword arm. They are good, hardworking people, all of them."

"I suppose we both have our little surprises then." The way Maire's lips curled, her sideways glance—they were not good signs, not the way they ran Rowan through like a hot iron of seduction.

She might have no idea the assault she practiced upon him, but that made it no less deadly.

THREE

T he scent of the grass crushed beneath their feet rose to Maire's nostrils, a fragrance of new life and peace rather than death and war. Bones! Her warrior's resolve wavered like the legs of a newborn colt—for all it was born to do, it was wobbly and unsure of itself.

Realizing that Emrys was a man who cared as much for his people as she cared for hers was like saddling that fledgling colt with a heavy load on its first try to stand. The obvious prosperity of the land and dwellings were a sign that his consideration was returned. A barn in the distance housed livestock in a manner better than that in which most of Maire's people lived. A beloved chief is a prosperous one, her mother once told her.

As he spoke to his people of their bargain, Maire studied the square cut of the stranger's shaven jaw, where a shadow of a beard threatened to sprout. What made him scrape his face clean as a babe's bottom? Even his dark hair was close cropped about his collar, like some of the traders who hailed from the Mediterranean countries. It reminded her of a raven's wing, alive with more than one color of black.

As he turned to indicate he was ready for the contest, he froze for a moment, staring at her. Thought enveloped his blue gaze. They were not a pale and lifeless color, those eyes, but a gemstone hue of many facets. He seemed suspended in another place and time, not really seeing her. What manner of confoundment lured him away from the prospect of the impending battle to the death? What nameless anguish cried out from his eyes, making the two of them seem kindred spirits rather than enemies?

To her astonishment, she found herself once again wishing her visit to the villa and her meeting with its master were not as an enemy. There was something foreign and intriguing about them both; the nature of which she'd never have the chance to know as a guest, only as a conqueror.

Behind him his people clustered, the farmers and domestic servants who still objected to the terms he'd presented them, if not with voices, with grudging looks. Aye, she mused, they'd have to take hostages, as well as send people of her own to defend this peaceful tuath against others who might be tempted to plunder its unprotected wealth.

Of course, sending any warriors from Gleannmara would have to come *after* she dealt with Morlach. One battle at a time. Maire steeled herself against the gnawing fangs of anxiety spawned by thought of the greedy druid.

"The day is yours, my queen," Brude told her, clapping a gentle hand on her shoulder. "Make the best of it for all."

Maire hardly heard him as a woman emerged from the massive dwelling to join the men gathered about the tall warrior-priest. The crowd parted before the woman like water before the bow of a trim craft until she reached Rowan's side. Too old to be the man's wife, Maire guessed. This richly clothed woman was his mother or some other female relative, one who commanded his respect and affection. He answered her worried expression with a reassuring smile, his hand drawing her attention to the amulet he wore on his chest, which was bare now that he'd stripped off the robe in preparation for the combat. The amulet was an intricate design, a vision of gold symmetry enveloping strange lettering.

"What manner of magic does he have in *that,* Brude?" Maire knew if anyone could fathom the power of the amulet or read its message, it was Gleannmara's druid. Beyond his native tongue, he knew the secrets of ogham, the stick writing of those from far memory, and the languages of Greek and Latin.

"It is a symbol of his god, nothing more. I've heard the Christian God espouses nothing but love for one's enemy. It cannot be so harmful. Nothing will come of this day but good for all. I feel that even his God intends this."

With her death or his? Maire wondered as she stepped into the makeshift arena of packed soil, rid of grass and weed by the traffic of villa life. How could this be settled without the bloodshed Brude assured her would not happen? And how could anyone love his enemy? The spiritual world was one Maire left to the druids. Making what she could of this challenge was enough.

Yet her puzzlement would not leave her. What would this man's God have him do? Blow her a kiss before she took off his head?

Maire watched warily as Emrys handed his weapons to a steward and approached her unarmed. Naught but a swath of cloth girded him now, freeing his powerful arms and legs for the fight.

"Queen Maire, know before we start that I wish you no harm."

To her astonishment, he lifted her sword hand to his lips and brushed her knuckles, still wrapped tight about the hilt, with a kiss.

"Nor I you," she managed, heat washing over her at the onslaught of whistles and wolf calls, her own kinsmen's among them. He surely made a mockery of her.

"'Tis a true shame you'll lose that silver-tongued charm along with your head, Rowan ap Emrys." She mimicked the Welsh *p* accent of their shared Gaelic tongue.

"I promise I'll do my best to keep both." The man smiled as though he asked her to dance with him rather than do battle. His grin was like a cascade of pearls, white against a face lovingly bronzed by the sun, rather than tanned like old leather.

Refusing to be thrown off balance by such calculated

foreplay, Maire called over her shoulder to Brude as Rowan retreated to take up his arms.

"Sing this swaggert a song, bard, that he'll know the futility of his fight against the fearsome line of the Uí Niall. 'Twill sweeten the blow of his death for these good people."

Circling cautiously, sword ready, Maire hoped the gold amulet that rested in a smattering of dark hair against Rowan ap Emrys's sweat-dampened chest was no more than adornment. It bore the symbol of a *P* superimposed over an *X*. This was flanked on either side by letters, the whole being encircled by a skillfully worked wreath.

Adornment or nay, it served to distract her so that when the man launched his first attack, she narrowly fended it off. Spinning, she caught his returning blow, blades striking, sliding, and locking at the hilts.

"It's a Chi-Rho," Rowan explained, his voice as tense as the muscles that held the weapons suspended between them. "A symbol of our faith in the God who will decide the outcome of this test."

Struggling to hold her own, Maire's face was all but pressed against it now. She cowed down as if swaying beneath his strength and then shot up, pushing him away and dancing out of the range of his blade.

"I will accept the favor of any god," she conceded. "Yours included."

There was a gash above the amulet now, which Maire had managed with the dagger in her left hand as she shoved away from him. Her nostrils were white from breathing clouds of dislodged lime beaten from her shield, which now lay discarded at the edge of the crowd. There was no room for defensive armor in this fight. She needed deadly weapons in each hand against the considerable strength and skill of her opponent.

The sun, what there'd been of it that day, had reached its pinnacle at the start of the contest. Now it dove like a phoenix of fire in the shadowed sea behind the western hills to the clashing cadence of weapons. Darkness was all but upon them and still Maire had gained little more against her opponent than a few scratches. Rowan ap Emrys had scars on his body bigger than the wounds she'd inflicted, and her strength was wearing down. Time and again, the God of the amulet managed to turn her opponent's flesh to air before her quickest thrust.

Not that the forces conjured by Brude's song had not done the same for her. Twice she'd felt the wind of Rowan's sword as it narrowly missed her neck, once nicking the adorning gold of her protective collar. Her breastplate bore evidence of a steely slice that would have cut her in half had more than the tip of his weapon grazed her. Her agility and speed were all that saved her, allowing her to dodge his powerful blows better than block them. No, it was not Brude's gods Maire doubted now, but herself. Her strength was fading like the sun.

The druid might sing of her ancestors' skill and courage till his voice gave out. Her clan might chant her name to the heavens in encouragement, but Maire knew her burning limbs were becoming dangerously slow. Her return blows weakened in succession. If she could get close enough to lock swords, just one more time, there was a chance she might slip the thin dagger from its hidden haven between her breasts and plunge it upward into his chest, where Rowan's erratic expansion of breath and sinew tapered to a lightly furred valley. There, perspiration from the chase she gave ran in rivulets through the clinging dust stirred by their fierce dance of death.

She could not be the only one who was tired, Maire thought in an effort to thwart despair. Their lively banter, which had entertained the onlookers as much as the fight itself, had now dwindled down to breathless exchanges between them. Many of which were unfinished. Her adversary's dark hair curled wet about his neck and face—a face mottled with the blood rush of possible triumph.

With a telling grimace, the Welshman came at her as she circled him seeking her chance for offense. Her arms afire with the effort to parry his sudden thrust, Maire spun about with the momentum of her sword to dance to the other side of the arena before he caught her on the back swing. Her legs were willing, despite the aching protest of her muscles, but something went wrong.

The blade of Rowan's sword struck her buttocks hard enough, had not it landed broadside, to cleave them to the bone. Maire went to her knees with the blow, the coarse dirt tearing at her flesh with stinging fingers. She caught herself with her left hand and rolled away, leaving the dagger she had wielded behind. She would need a hand free to loose the stinger anyway. Let him think she'd lost another weapon and was reduced to her sword alone.

"Will you concede, Maire? Unlike your desire to take my head, I've no desire to take yours."

"Our queen has used but half her tricks," Declan boasted behind her. "She toys with you, Welshman."

Her foster brother's dying breath would be one of rebellion to its god. He refused to see the obvious as his still clansmen had. Only Brude continued to sing her on to glory, caught up in the poetry of the past. It was all he had to lean on in his advanced years, and all that was left for her in her last hour.

By the gods who had set her mother on glory's path, she had used all her well-tutored tactics...all but one. Maire gasped for air, her lungs screaming with the effort even as she did so. The last blow had inflicted as much a wound on her pride as her bruised buttocks.

"Give it up, little queen. Surrender your sword and return with your tribe to your home."

"Never!" she managed through clenched teeth. The taste of surrender was too vile to consider.

"I'll not kill you, Maire."

"Then you'll die yourself."

Raising her sword, she lunged at Rowan. His defensive parry felt as though it shattered the bones in her arm. But for a miracle of magic summoned by Brude's poetry, she'd have lost the weapon altogether as she staggered past her opponent. The magic might last, but the flesh was failing.

Maire could not help herself. She leaned on her weapon and tried to catch her wind at the far edge of the circle of onlookers. The yard was now aglow with the light of torches, which infected each ragged breath she took with the unsavory taste of pitch. As Rowan warily approached her, she wondered if she could even raise the blade. The cheers of his people drowned out the thunder of blood rushing past her ears, but the contrary quiet of her clansmen was louder.

Odd, how she'd been prepared for death when she stepped on this foreign soil. They'd have sung about her glorious passing in battle around fires long after she was no more than dust in Gleannmara's hills. Now her plans were reduced to this! If she failed her people, they would go back empty-handed, back to Morlach's harsh dominion. She'd hoped at least to fill their coffers with plunder enough to replenish the pastures with cattle. Instead, the bards would preserve this disgrace for eternity. She'd sullied her mother's memory, disappointed her clan.

"Was the mighty Maeve downhearted? Tho' she be too weary to raise her head to see the brutal attack of her enemy, she fell back beyond the sweep of his weapon and met his body with a deadly thrust of her sword. All around, her minions roared…"

Maire's battered thoughts became one with the familiar words of Brude's song. It took her away to a hall filled with boisterous warriors reveling in her mother's triumphs. Pride nearly bursting from her chest, she was again the young girl watching from the balcony reserved for the women, picturing herself in Maeve's place, fighting valiantly to the finish. Then it would be her they hoisted on their shoulders and drank to, not her mother.

"There must be a way to settle this without separating your head from that comely body."

Emrys's voice shattered Maire's short retreat, bringing her back to the grim presence. Although he offered words of reconciliation, his raised sword belied them. Exhausted and nearly blind from the smoking pitch of the torches, Maire fell back as her glorified mother had once done, escaping the deadly whistling path of his weapon. Summoning all her strength, she thrust her blade upward as the man charged over her and felt the engagement of flesh. Twist as he might, he could not avoid the hungry bite of her steel.

A scraping of metal collapsing against metal registered as his full weight dropped upon her. Stunned by the breath-robbing assault, Maire struggled to gather her senses beneath the felled man. Something was wrong. She felt the warm flow of his wound seeping beneath the armor at her waist as only blood can crawl, yet her sword lay sandwiched between them, instead of protruding from his back. Somehow its blade had been deflected. There was no room to move, much less use the weapon, pinned as she was by his weight.

Was she to die and leave her people to Morlach's dominion after they'd rallied so bravely to her side? Stubbornly, Maire blinked away the acetic glaze spawned by her dismay to meet the gaze of her soon-to-be murderer. At any moment, she'd feel the death crush of his fingers about her neck, and, Maeve help her, she had no strength left to resist.

"I'll surrender my sword, little queen, if you give up the notion of taking my head as trophy."

What? There was not enough breath left for Maire to ask for confirmation of what her ears reported. Surely, he'd not offered his sword to her in surrender when victory was firmly in his grasp! What means of cruel trickery was this?

"I'll go myself as your hostage to prove my word true. My sword will be yours as long as you fight for what is right under my God's eye." His breath was hot against her ear, as ragged as her own. Gradually she felt his body relax over hers, further betraying his weariness.

Maire's eyes widened as Brude's earlier words came back to her: *"There will be no bloodshed."* The druid had indicated this contest would be the answer to all her problems. It would seem the gods were giving the day to her despite her failure.

"You'll swear loyalty to Gleannmara?" she whispered, still in disbelief. His sword would be an asset to the tuath, especially if she were to battle Morlach for it, which she'd do or die trying.

"And to its queen, so long as she asks me to do nothing against my God's will."

If his God hated evil, He would see Morlach put in his place, Maire reasoned, as a strange calm enveloped her. She would need the help of all the gods she could muster.

"And so Maeve took the prince of her hostages to marry as her choice, rather than accept that of the men of Erin for her…"

That man had been Maire's father, Rhian, and the union was a happy one from what she recalled from her short childhood. He'd been at Maeve's side to avenge her death before falling himself. It was all commemorated in beautiful song, their union of love in life and death. It was the kind of ballad that made a red-blooded Celt's heart sing tender beneath his formidable armor of muscle and fierce spirit. Even now, wild roses grew amid the hawthorn about their place of rest, forever entwined.

"As my husband?" The question slipped out even as Maire considered the bizarre possibility. This man had already demonstrated himself to be honorable, if in a somewhat fey manner.

Why hadn't she thought of it before? If she married another, Morlach would have no grounds to press her further in the king's eye. Pursuit of her land would be nothing short of outright aggression and in direct opposition to the king's promise of protection to Maire's mother.

"Aye, as hostage and husband," she decided, seeing this also as a way to ensure the payment of tribute by joining their tuatha. Not that Emrys looked capable of producing a decent fighting force.

Rowan's surprised laugh shook her from her ingenious burst of thought.

"By all that's holy, you ask too much! Why would I take to wife such a painted vixen with sword as sharp as her tongue?"

Again he mocked her. Humiliation boiled in Maire's blood, fortifying her waning strength. She snaked her fingers between their bodies and around the hilt of her secret weapon. In his sudden swell of confidence, the man had relaxed his guard. All she had to do was keep him that way until the blade was free.

"You've admitted yourself that I'm comely enough and—" Maire moistened her lips and silently cursed at the battle grit clinging to them. Coquettishness was not her strength, but she'd seen other women use that ploy to snag the attention of a strapping warrior. No matter how she longed to, even she knew that now was not the time to spit. She swallowed the grime as best she could. "I cannot say in truth that I do not find your person worthy of this queen."

Though she had briefly admired the Welshman's fine physique when he'd stripped off his clerical robe for the fight, she couldn't bring herself to return his earlier compliment. The wrap of cloth about his hips was not unlike what her male kinsmen wore outside of battle, although his was shorter to allow greater mobility. Thankfully, it was more modest combat attire than the Scotti preferred. It annoyed Maire that the mere thought of a more intimate glimpse of her opponent deepened the battle flush of her cheeks with embarrassment.

Regardless of what she thought of him as a man, Maire now had his full attention. She wriggled beneath him, a provocative smile curling on her lips. From the corner of her eye she saw Eochan block Declan, whose fist was tight about the hilt of his sword. If her brother broke the terms of the contest, shame alone would emerge the victor.

The long, thin blade of her stinger came loose and her oppressor was none the wiser. What he mistook as an intended embrace became, with a practiced flash of metal in the torch-light, her triumph.

"We marry in name only, of course." More color claimed her face. If more was to come of the marriage, as it had in her mother's...well, that remained to be seen.

She pressed the razor-sharp blade against Rowan's skin, where a vein swelled with the flow of his life spirit. His wince was barely perceptible, but it told he'd felt a taste of the stinger's deadly potential.

"May I ask why this sudden proposal?" He grated the words out, careful not to strain against the knife in his evident battle between hostility and bewilderment.

The crowd closed in no more than a body's length from them in hopes of hearing the negotiations whispered for each other's ears only.

"I need a husband to be rid of a troublesome suitor. You need your head."

Rowan clearly didn't care for either rationale. Had there been real steel to his cutting gaze, her eyes would be gouged out by now.

"Then I don't see where I have much choice."

"I'd have your word in your god's name," Maire added, somewhat offended by his decidedly reluctant concession. After all, it was *he* who'd admitted aloud she was comely.

"You have my word in the name of God, the Father Almighty, Creator of heaven and earth, that I will take you as my wife."

Maire shook her head. "That I will take you as my hus-band," she corrected, gaining satisfaction at his deepening scowl. Here was a man unaccustomed to a woman's dominion. He'd get used to it, being married to a queen.

"However you wish to put it, milady."

"Then give me your sword...carefully." She kept the stinger pressed against him as he reached over her head to retrieve the weapon he'd dropped to break his fall. "Place it in my other hand."

Her fingers closed about the hilt of Rowan's sword. It was still warm from his grasp. A surge of nearly lost triumph welled in her chest as if to explode like heaven's own thunder. Praise her mother's gods, she'd won!

"You may get off me now, sir."

"Aye, for now."

Maire allowed the taunt to glance off harmlessly, unanswered. It was her moment. It was Gleannmara's day. The bards would sing of this in centuries to come, after all. She was just gone eighteen. She'd beaten a seasoned warrior in battle. She won Gleannmara a tribute fit for a king. Further, she found the answer to Morlach's threat and secured the tribute with the same blow, taking Rowan ap Emrys as husband and hostage. Brude had been right all along.

She flashed the druid a smile as she held up Rowan's sword to the ecstatic approval of her clansmen. Her vigor returned, renewed with each shout of her name and of Gleannmara's. Floating on a cloud of triumph, Maire was unprepared when Rowan suddenly seized her in his arms and kissed her soundly on the lips. His sword fell from her hand, disabled as she was by shock.

As he released her, only the rising heat of embarrassment thawed her frozen state. Indignation grew to a roar in her veins, but before she could land a retaliatory blow on his smirking face, the Welshman caught her wrist and raised her arm along with his own as if they shared the victory.

"Mother and friends, I give you my bride-to-be! God keep us all."

FOUR

With no time to exult in Maire's disconcertment, Rowan sprang from her side to catch his mother before she collapsed on the ground in a full swoon. Lady Delwyn had stood during the contest, refusing the chair her servants brought her. Rowan had heard her inadvertent cry as he'd plunged down toward Maire's sword.

His announcement, however, proved more of a shock than her unselfish love for him could bear.

"Seize him!" the queen's younger spokesman shouted, stepping up to block Rowan's path. "He's a hostage."

"Let him be, Declan." Brude's words were not nearly as loud as the warrior's, but their impact stalled Maire's men in their tracks. When all eyes were upon the druid, he explained. "He is a man of his word and of a noble god. Leave him to make ready for the journey ahead."

The young buck called Declan fell reluctantly aside. Rowan gave Brude an appreciative look and rushed into the villa with his charge. His mother's maidservant wailed in his wake. A glimpse at his mother's pallor assailed his conscience. Of all who watched the contest, it was only Lady Delwyn who had an inkling of the real battle he fought, for it was she who'd nursed him through the fevers. It was she who shook him from the battlefield, where he wretched at the sight of the dying barbarian female, desperately clutching at the unborn babe his sword had slashed from her swollen belly. Only his mother knew the horrible deed that had robbed Rowan of his will to ever lift a sword again.

He'd been so intent on the contest between him and his smug bride-to-be that he'd unintentionally dealt his gentle mother a terrible blow with his announcement. God had been with him. He hadn't had to kill Maire of Gleannmara. In his defeat, he'd triumphed, and the victory impaired his good sense.

His mother stirred as he laid her on the high-back couch in the hall and clutched weakly at her chest. "Tell me it isn't so, son! How can you consider marrying that painted heathen?"

"Mother, I prayed for God to show me His will and save our people from harm. It appears this is the manner in which He chose to answer."

"I cannot believe God would have you marry a heathen. And what will we do without you?"

Rowan helped her as she sat up, her strength returning. Her hand trembled as he released it. Marriage certainly hadn't been Rowan's intent at the outset. All he'd hoped for was to save his people from plunder, and then Gleannmara had been mentioned. He could barely explain himself what had happened. But had any of God's chosen ever understood why the Lord's answer to a prayer was not exactly as anticipated?

No, this was no accidental turn of events. Of that Rowan was certain.

"Mother, Dafydd knows more about running this estate than I. Under his management, we should more than be able to pay the tribute I promised Maire, if she should win. And once word is spread that Emrys is under her clan's protection, you need fear no more Scotti raids. I didn't have to kill her. God spared me."

"Maire, is it?"

The glaze of worry in his mother's pale gray eyes sharpened. Rowan wondered if she saw more than he'd admitted, even to himself. How could he explain that he somehow knew this female? He'd seen her night upon night and again just this morning. At least he thought it was the Scotti queen. Could such a comely creature as had so often visited his dreams lie beneath the Scot's paint and spattered blood? Did the filth of battle disguise her flawless complexion? Were her stiffened and lime-whitened tresses truly silken and fire-kissed?

"Aye, Mother. Maire of Gleannmara." Rowan emphasized the name of the tuath from which he'd been sold long ago.

Recognition registered on her face. With it came a quiver of resignation.

"Oh, I see."

From time to time, Rowan had spoken to his mother about returning to his place of birth and hinted at going as a cleric. It seemed the most logical way for him to do this, now that iron had become his servant as a plow not his master as a weapon. He'd met scholars from Ireland who'd come to Emrys to study. And he'd heard the call.

Rowan often dreamt that Glasdam was searching for him. He and Rowan had been close. But with Demetrius's failing health, Rowan hadn't pushed the issue of leaving Emrys. He'd not wished to cause Lady Delwyn more concern than she already bore.

"Will you seek your brother for revenge?" That was his mother. Straight to the point, often able to see more about Rowan than he knew himself.

"Would God have opened this door for me if that were my purpose?"

His mother's touch was gentle on his arm. "It will break your father's heart."

Rowan was struck, not for the first time, with the ironic reversal of his and his father's roles. Since the day Demetrius had carried Rowan into the chapel to pray for his recovery, the son had watched his father's physical strength wane, while his spiritual strength grew. Demetrius had known this day was coming. It had to, for Rowan to be completely healed of his past.

"He and I have discussed this matter many times. He will

understand, as I know you will when God speaks to your heart."

"Rowan, your side!"

At his mother's exclamation, he looked down, suddenly distracted by the large stain of blood now clotted where the amulet had deflected the warrioress's near-fatal blow. With the speed of a magician's hand, Lady Delwyn snatched an embroidered scarf from the table at the end of the couch and handed it to him without thought to the hours of eye-wearying stitching she'd invested in it.

"'Tis nothing but a scratch."

Rowan tested the gash of flesh before pressing the linen over it. It was nearly sealed with dirt. Even as his momentum carried him onto Maire's upthrust blade, he'd twisted mightily. It had seemed to take forever to complete the fall. He'd had time to call out to God, his silent prayer blending with his mother's heart-wrenched cry for mercy. The answer came with the telltale collision of his amulet against the upward momentum of the steel. He'd barely felt the rip of his side as the deflected metal cut into him.

"It looks worse than it is," he reassured her. He planted a light kiss upon her forehead to soothe the dismay gathered there in soft furrows.

"Emrys, while this sight of a warrior and his maithre is sweet as a robin's trill, we've no time for long good-byes." Maire strode boldly into the room, as though she were mistress of the house, and squared off before him. "We'd best be to the ship and away before morning. We've much to do."

In truth, she hated to interrupt this tender moment between mother and son. Such exchanges had been rare in her orphaned life. But only fools would remain long enough for the countryside to gather an army against them. Brude had already started back for the ship to prepare for a sacrifice to the gods, but not before cautioning her to take no more time than was needed to gather the prizes. Besides, how could she resist the opportunity to raise the color in her adversary's face? It was only fair turnabout after the embarrassing kiss with which he'd staggered her.

Rowan straightened and turned. If he was annoyed, he didn't show it.

"I will speak to my people and tell them to cooperate with yours in regard to fulfilling the details of our arrangement. We'll be wed by the priest at the village on our way to the ship."

"We'll be wed by Brude," Maire corrected. She would not ask the robed men of the church she'd just plundered to marry them. Why give them the chance to curse this union? Better that her mother's gods, who had given her victory, bless it instead.

Rowan exchanged a glance with his mother. He hesitated, a considering look on his face, and then he nodded. "Have it your way, little queen."

A fight won too easily was not necessarily over, Maire thought, wary as Rowan reached for her hand and lifted it to his lips.

"I will council with my people and then gather my things." With an exaggerated sweep of his arm, he bowed. "My house is yours, little queen. Mother, I leave her to your hospitality."

"God's will be done." So saying, she adapted, despite her earlier distress, to the role of hostess with the quiet grace it demanded. "You may call me Lady Delwyn, Queen Maire. May we serve you food and drink? Or would you prefer a bath first?"

"A bath?" Maire echoed in surprise.

After assigning the task of gathering the first portion of the tribute to Eochan and Declan, Maire had searched for Rowan inside the curious lodge, expecting to find the woman pleading with him to change his mind. While that had been his mother's first reaction, she'd apparently acquiesced to his will, or the will of their god. Her noble serenity bespoke a quiet strength and courage equal to that of any warrior. Lady Delwyn was, after all, losing her son as a hostage to an enemy. Even as she stood there, Maire had seen the struggle between dismay and acceptance wage war on her hostess's face; the latter emerging victorious at the mention of her god's will.

Had this god spoken to the woman just then? Maire had heard nothing. Odd that a god would instruct his people so, rather than having learned scholars such as Brude interpret his will for them. Perhaps he was more of a commoner's god— although this family was far from common. Everything about them was refined, from habitat to manner.

"The bath is an old one, but my husband had artisans from Rome restore it, as he did with the rest of the house. Have you ever seen such beautiful wall paintings?"

"We have our own talented artisans," Maire informed her, determined to let her companion know the Scotti were not totally without talent and taste. Still, she had seen nothing to compare with the elegance of this strange house. "But I would see the other rooms," she added, striking her tone with authority to remind the woman that she—the *painted heathen,* as the woman had called her earlier—was in charge at the moment.

Instead of living in separate huts within the compound, the members of Rowan's family and their servants lived in apartments joined together in a large square around a garden. However, this was not a garden cultivated for food. Beauty was its only purpose. In its center was a fountain with a statue of a comely maiden pouring water from an urn into its base. These people had managed to bring the colors of a spring meadow and the babble of a brook into their home.

A pillared and covered colonnade that connected surrounding rooms or apartments formed the perimeter. In place of familiar packed dirt floors covered with fresh straw, there were tiled ones of slate and mosaic laid in beautiful designs. In one apartment, the Chi-Rho of Rowan's amulet was inlaid in the floor with blues, reds, yellows, and greens.

While the villa's hall and dining room were the most elaborately decorated of the rooms, the others were grander than any Gleannmara boasted. Their furnishings were rich— engraved trunks, folding stools, and tables of intricate mechanical design on brass legs—all were fascinating to a girl who'd never been beyond the great eastern sea before. Surely, not even the Sidhe of the other world enjoyed finer surroundings.

Rowan reappeared as Lady Delwyn was showing Maire the master bedroom. In his arms, cradled like a babe, was a frail man of large frame. No doubt the elder had been a sizeable warrior in his own day, before the forces of time had worn and withered what had once been a well-formed torso. Now, like an ancient ruin, fleshy remains clung to the once sturdy frame that had supported it.

As Lady Delwyn's son deposited the elder man on the bed, she flew to the invalid's side and kissed him tenderly upon the forehead.

"God works among us in strange ways, beloved. Would that I understood them better."

"All that is necessary is faith."

"A seizure left my father unable to move his legs," Rowan explained, causing Maire to break her gaze away from the couple. Instead she studied the vibrant blues and pinks of the room's painted panels, which were artfully displayed over a stippled dado base of the same colors.

The renegade skim of emotion that had touched her when watching mother and son resurfaced at the sight of the devotion between husband and wife. Maire vaguely recalled the same between her parents and envied that still evident between her foster parents. Would she ever know such love? A discreet glance at the somber Rowan ap Emrys was not encouraging.

The man on the finely dressed bed studied Maire as his wife tucked a pillow behind his balding head to raise him. Like his son, his jaw was scraped clean of hair. A thin white line on one sunken cheek proclaimed the survival of one near brush with death's blade. No doubt there were other such banners of valor, shrinking away with his age.

"I am Demetrius, Queen Maire, but you needn't feel sadness for me. God has seen fit to turn my sickness into a blessing. He has seen fit to send an able and loving son to do what I cannot. And I have faith that Rowan's leaving, too, shall lead to good. You seem a maid with a heart as tender as her sword is skilled."

For all his failings, the man had eyes like a hawk's, Maire thought grudgingly. No one ever saw her cry. No one! Not since she'd been told of her mother's death.

"Your mother Maeve would be proud."

"You know of Maeve?" Now here indeed was a surprise.

"Your bard's voice carried to the chapel room when the shouting hushed at the climax of the contest. My son says you were a worthy opponent."

"I bested him." How could it occur to the old man that she was anything but? She shifted uncomfortably, recalling that, but for the shock of her proposal, the Welshman had gained the upper hand. Regardless, when all was said and done, she was triumphant.

Maire wiped her cheek against her arm, smearing the blue-ing. It only made her more aware of the contrast of her filthy state to that of the villa and its inhabitants. By now, it had formed a paste with sweat, dirt, and dried blood—the fisher-man's at the village, hers, and that of Rowan ap Emrys. The skirt of her saffron tunic was stained dark from her final blow against him. Part of her wanted to wear the leine as a badge of hard-earned victory, while another longed to accept Lady Delwyn's offer of a bath to be rid of it. She wondered how Maeve had dealt with the plague of such womanly notions.

"Our men have gone to collect the choicest of our herds while the servants pack my trunk. Is there anything you see in the house that you would have as a bride's gift?"

Rowan's question snatched her from her whimsy. The house. That's what Maire wanted to answer, but that was impossible. What a palace it was!

Her gaze flickered over the luxurious bed with its thick mattress and exquisite coverlets. Claw feet of bronze supported it, curving up on each corner to support the head of a lion. No, she couldn't bring herself to oust an invalid from it. Not when there was one just as royal in another apartment, one so long and wide that she could easily stretch out with arms over her head, or to her side, and not touch the edge of the plush mattress. It was a far cry from the narrow carved bed box she used with its cushion of leaves and needles.

"The bed in the westernmost apartment and all its trappings," she decided, giving in to her fancy. She'd earned it, well enough, and woe be to the man who dared taunt her over the frivolous nature of her choice.

"Take it as our gift to our son's bride," the man on the bed told her.

"I gratefully accept, sir."

Maire could hear her brothers' protests now—their ship was barely large enough to hold a few prize livestock and the clan's plunder—but she'd silence them quick enough. She'd come as a sister in arms, but she returned as their queen.

"An excellent choice," Rowan seconded his father with enthusiasm. "It was made to accommodate my height, but there's room for us both."

Maire swallowed a startled gasp. She wondered if the battle paint had worn away enough to reveal the scarlet tide she felt burning her scalp. Crom take the man, he was a veritable mockingbird of thinly veiled affront to her, his conqueror and the queen of Gleannmara!

"Aye, that it would—" she rallied, adding with a slashing look—"should I decide to share it with you."

He let the challenge slide with a goading smile of satisfaction. One would think he'd won the day, not she. The daftness that led him to give away the battle was his weakness, not hers.

"Meanwhile, in the time it takes for our men to round up your tribute, I intend to rid myself of this battle grime and change into something suited to the voyage ahead. Would you care to join me, little queen?"

"And give you the chance to drown me? I think not." What an absurd idea. The man was crazy as a swineherd to think she'd wallow in the same water as he.

"Never let it be said that I was ungallant to my future bride. I would willingly leave the heated bath for you and use the *frigidarium* instead."

"No." Maire gave no hint that she had no idea what a frigidarium was.

"Ah, I should have guessed your kind had an aversion to cleanliness. Do you know what a bath is?"

Maire's temper bristled. *Her kind?* Her clansmen might be more barbaric than his farmers, but by the gods, they were not unclean, not as long as the gods provided nature's own bathing pools. Some were even heated and blessed with healing powers, which was more than this man-made bath could boast.

"Of course I do. And I resent your overblown air of superiority. If you recall, it was I who won this battle, not you or your god."

She turned to Rowan's mother, who watched the exchange keenly.

"Aye, I'd have this bath after all, but with one of my clansmen as guard, lest there be any trickery to this."

"Who knows?" Rowan remarked wryly. "Beneath all that filth, she might not be harsh on the eye at all."

"Rowan, you go too far," his mother gasped. She turned to Maire in apology. "Come, child. I'll fetch the towels and attend you myself."

"I need no attendant." Maire's gaze remained on Emrys's face. "Stay on that course with me, Emrys, and what you see will be through blackened slits!"

With a decided swagger, she turned to follow Delwyn ap Emrys out of the room. And, lest the man decide to push his luck, she rested her hand on the hilt of her sword.

FIVE

By the time the ship was ready to depart, Maire felt renewed by her surrender to the whim of a bath. And what a bath it had been! It was no large wooden tub in which to hunker down, with knees drawn to the chin so that the water reached one's shoulders. This had been a small pool lined in beautiful, blue tiles and large enough for Maire to stretch out her full length. She'd done so gladly to wash the lime out of her hair with the pleasantly scented soap Lady Delwyn had left her.

On the walls of the room were paintings of frolicking sea nymphs and dolphins, but most marvelous was the manner in which the room was heated, not by a fire sooting up the beautiful walls and plastered ceiling as it did in her lodge, but by ductwork beneath the floor, which was fired by strange furnaces in another section of the house.

Maire fingered the equally fine material of the dress rolled beneath her arm, as if to remind herself that the experience had been real and not a dream. The garment had been given to her by Delwyn ap Emrys to put on after her bath. Adorned with gold and silver embroidery, it was more beautiful than any Maire had ever seen. But for the possibility of renewed battle on their retreat, she'd have donned it instead of her old clothes and fighting gear. Instead, she washed out the stain of battle from her tunic and wrung it as dry as she could before putting it back on.

Between disputes among their respective tribes and Rowan's good-byes, there'd been an untold number of delays in their departure, which allowed time for her leine to dry before they left the villa. At the last moment, Rowan insisted on bidding his god farewell, which made no sense to Maire. Didn't the Christians believe their god was always with them?

"Do not fear our God," Rowan's mother counseled her as Maire waited impatiently at the open door of the chapel. "He will speak to you when you are ready to listen."

What the lady had mistaken for fear on Maire's face was but a battle between the young queen's heart and mind. The golden cross on the altar would fetch a fine price. As would the master's bed. Yet, Maire was reluctant to take either one from these people, particularly now that they had names and, for the most part, pleasant personalities to go with them.

Then, though she had defeated Rowan ap Emrys in combat and was forcing him to leave parents he obviously loved, Delwyn ap Emrys hugged her in parting and asked the Christian God to bless their voyage home. For all that the gesture made Maire uncomfortable, it warmed her as well. She'd found Lady Delwyn's command of humility and authority a source of envy and admiration; although Maire knew full well humility had no place in a warrior queen's disposition, except to the gods.

Now, as they loaded the ship, the moon ventured an intermittent peek through the clouds above, bathing the narrow beach of rock and sand in silvery light. The loading ramp swung away from the shore, where Roman ships had once loaded coal from nearby mines now abandoned. The foredeck was crowded with six head of cattle, fatter and sturdier in build than those that pastured on Gleannmara. The beasts were calmed by the mixture of herbs and hay Brude had fed them. As further precaution for the three-day return to Erin, they were hobbled and secured in a roped off pen.

Next to them was a pair of horses. Unlike Erin's traditional small and shaggy native breeds, these were of much larger stock. Maire could not peer over the back of either the stallion or the mare. The matched pair nearly caused another full-fledged battle between Declan and Rowan's overseer, Dafydd, a little man with the nerve of a giant. Rowan had specified cattle as tribute, but when Declan saw the splendid pair of horses housed in a barn as comfortable as the huts of the people who tended them, the young Scot demanded they be included. The pair was Rowan's, and—as the last of the clan gathered at the house to await Maire's command—the argument was settled by his quiet order to fetch them from their stalls.

The family of Demetrius had bred the fine steeds for generations. The stock, he'd explained, was imported from the East centuries before for use by the armies and cavalries and for entertainment during Rome's domination. Maire could well imagine that such beasts, whether racing chariots in the arena or on the battlefield, were magnificent to behold.

As were Rowan's pair. Their high-strung natures were somewhat gentled by trusted hands and Brude's concoction, but they stilled pawed the deck. Rowan attempted to soothe them to counter the unfamiliar sounds created by the creaking boards and straining lines hailing the ship's departure.

Maire could hardly believe her fortune. She had a bed and livestock fit for a king, in addition to the plunder and tribute stowed above and below deck. None of her clansmen had been lost, although the villagers had left their share of wounds to vouch that not all had come easily. This was indeed cause for the sacrificial fire Brude would make for both their success and Maire's wedding.

As for her concern about the shore natives regrouping and attacking the men she'd left to defend their means of escape, it had been for naught. The frightened and beaten people had flocked to the small stone church to put out the fire started in the midst of the Scotti pillage, and there they remained until nightfall. At that point, some crept back to their homes and locked themselves tightly in. Even when the ship was well away from the shoreline, not a single light of habitation showed, save those lanterns and torches carried by the Lady Delwyn and the people of Emrys.

"Easy, Shahar," Rowan cooed as the stallion began to toss its head up and down at the snap of the leather sail overhead.

The ship surged forward, catching the rare land breeze. Maire watched her hostage run his hands along the stallion's back and flank, continually reassuring it. Having been brought up in a man's world where such fawning was fine for animals, she almost envied the horse. Her foster parents loved her of course, but they'd been reluctant to show her such love as Delwyn demonstrated for Rowan, for fear of ruining her as a future warrior. The little girl in her had missed that which she saw others enjoy.

Maire twisted her lips in disdain, as though wringing the unbidden longing from her chest. It was a female weakness, this needing to be loved, and one that her brothers would scoff at if they knew. Not that men couldn't love if it suited their purpose. Maire had seen contrived attentions enough to recognize them when a lusty roll in the grass was the prize. Males, it seemed, didn't need to be loved like women. Their need was more that of an animal, one that could be satisfied without the sharing of emotion she'd overheard women confide in whispers amongst themselves.

Yet, Rowan ap Emrys seemed different somehow, appearing to possess a tremendous capacity to love, more so than any man she'd seen. It showed in his treatment of his parents and animals, not to mention the way his servants bade him good-bye—not as their overlord, but as a brother. Even the cantankerous Dafydd had shed tears openly when Rowan grasped his arm in farewell.

Lady Delwyn was not quite so obvious with her dismay. Since her initial alarm, she'd assumed a serenity that forbade it. Her calmness almost glowed from within her, as though she knew this disaster brought on by Maire and her people would result in good. Standing on the beach, she smiled and waved until the mist swallowed her in the growing distance between ship and shore.

Her son had exhibited that same aura of quiet strength and peace as he'd knelt before the chapel altar one last time. Did it come from the spirit of the golden cross or from his medallion? Maire had neither seen nor heard any assurance to this end.

"His God will speak to you when you are ready to listen."

Despite the warmth of her wrap, Maire felt her flesh pebble as Delwyn's words came to her mind. She didn't want to speak to a god. Better to leave that to Brude, who was accustomed to dealing with spirits and such. She preferred to sing and dance in the deities' honor. By her mother's milk, give her beings she could perceive with all her senses!

"You shiver as if it were you who took the cold plunge instead of me."

Maire nearly leapt out of her skin at the closeness of Rowan's voice. How had he left the horses and slipped up behind her without her notice? His god had saved his life, or at least the amulet with his god's symbol on it had, but had he also given the man the ability to walk like a spirit?

But for Brude's intercession on his behalf, and the reluctance of the horses to board the ship on the floating ramp, Rowan would be in chains like any new hostage. But only Rowan could coax the nervous horses aboard and calm them. The invaders had no choice but to let him walk free if the steeds were to go with them.

Emrys had a way with animals, another gift from his god— a god at least as powerful as Brude's concoction, given the druid's expressed respect of the deity. A panicked horse, especially one the size of Rowan's beasts, could kick a ship apart. The ancient songs told how some of the prized steeds belonging to the Milesian forefathers of the Scotti had been slaughtered when they panicked to save the vessels on the long sea journey from Iberia.

"Winter has yet to remove her icy fingers from the sea and

its mist," Maire replied at last, the tragic lines of the ancient epic forgotten. Her thoughts were no longer on horses.

Brude said there was a presence about Rowan ap Emrys, and indeed, she felt it. It bullied her own despite the fact that he gave no appearance of threat. Be it spiritual or fleshly in nature, the force of his nearness set off every alarm in her body. With the length of a hostile sword between them, she hadn't noticed so much.

It wasn't his size, she reasoned. She'd held her ground with sparring partners as big as he and felt nothing like she was feeling now. It was only through sheer willpower that she didn't flee from her isolated spot at the rail to where her men celebrated over a keg of wine taken from the church.

"How does it feel, then, to be made a queen of Gleannmara?" her unsolicited companion asked. "Your man Eochan told me you proved yourself worthy to rule the tuath this day."

"I earned it," Maire declared proudly. She stared off at a window of stars where the heavy drape of clouds had thinned. "It feels good, I suppose, but not as good as beating you in combat."

Rowan didn't rise to the feisty queen's taunt but took it with a smile. "But you are not celebrating."

"I'm about to wed a stranger, a madman, who in the moment of his triumph offers me his sword. I wonder if I'm not as fey as you. Why did you do it? You'd everything to gain for your people and nothing to lose."

"Suffice it to say I couldn't bring myself to remove such a pretty head from its body."

Rowan sensed rather than saw the color warming the girl at his side and was uncommonly pleased. If he could not explain fully to his Christian mother how God had answered his prayers, there was no way this pagan beauty could grasp his reasons. He wasn't wholly certain he fathomed them himself, particularly when Maire had unexpectedly seized the victory from him and demanded he become her husband.

Still, the decision to surrender to her hadn't been a matter of choice. He'd known he could not kill her the moment she'd stepped out of the cover of her troops. Though he hadn't thought it possible, that conviction grew stronger when she announced that she was Maire of Gleannmara. Surrender of his sword was the only option whereby they both might survive to see the purpose of this far from chance encounter.

"So you think I'm fair to the eye, now that I'm rid of the war paint and grit?"

Her question surprised Rowan. His future bride was proud enough without his feeding her pride overmuch…yet it seemed she was vulnerable with the age-old feminine desire to be admired. Surely she'd been complimented by her countrymen before.

"Fair enough, I suppose." The words hardly did her justice, Rowan thought, resisting the urge to stroke her hair as he had the horses' manes. Damp from the bath that scented it, her untamed tresses tumbled like a wave of sunfire over the wrap of her multicolored brat. The ship's lantern light was too poor for him to fully appreciate the gaze that chewed upon his answer as though its palatability were undetermined. He'd seen those eyes ablaze with the passion of combat and found, much to his surprise, emotion of another kind stirred within him.

Not that he'd become so focused on his study of the faith that he'd become immune to the allure of the opposite sex. It was the need for constant nourishment of his animal nature that had changed. Instead of thriving on war and its sometimes carnal rewards, his nature was fueled bright by the studying of God's Word and watching His blessings turn the efforts of the farm workers into fruit more plentiful than any imagined possible. He'd found more pleasure in cultivating the fruits of life than he'd ever known in plundering them.

Maire drew her cloak tighter about her and shifted

uncomfortably, moving a step away from him. The maid was as nervous and high-strung as his blooded horses, as fine a representation of womankind as they were of the equine. *Like a filly that has reached its pinnacle of development, yet remains unbroken,* Rowan mused as he studied her proud profile silhouetted against the dim light.

He'd been right. She was the girl in his dream. The resemblance was too strong to allow for chance when coupled with the fact that she'd come from his homeland.

"You but say the word if this churlish knave bothers you, Maire, and I'll give him a taste of a man's sword." The threat invaded Rowan's contemplation, bringing him about as sharply as the woman beside him.

Maire was clearly surprised to see Declan standing there, feet braced on the deck before them, his manner puffed like a banty cock in full plumage.

"Emrys has been a man of his word to the utmost, brother. I'm in no danger—" she eyed him for a moment, setting that small chin of hers—"not to say that my own sword would not suffice if I were."

The fair Scot nodded with as much concession as the chain and rope riggings gave the leather sails above them. "I did not mean to insinuate otherwise, Maire, but I confess, I cannot help but object to this marriage idea of yours."

"It serves Gleannmara well. Now Emrys's tuath will be ours as well."

"And all that sleepy bit of plow pushers will do is fill your belly. You can't fight with a cow or grain."

Rowan smirked. "Nor can an army fight on empty bellies."

Declan ignored Rowan's wry point and switched tactics. "Come join us, Maire. 'Tis your victory we're celebrating. Mayhap together we can think of an alternative for you."

"You've offered none thus far, brother. This is the best course I see, and Brude agrees. There's much to be learned from the songs of the past."

So that is the lay of things... Rowan studied the younger man. *This Declan considers himself more than brother to the queen.* The lad's anger bellowed through his nostrils like that of a young bull with its herd threatened. The brashness of his nature, it seemed, did not assert itself in matters of the heart. Not that Rowan found fault with that. No doubt the handsome warrior feared she'd cut him down as quickly with her tongue as her sword. Leaning against the rail, Rowan folded his arms, content to watch the exchange with undeniable interest.

"Then share his fancy bed, but know neither his high ways nor his God will protect you against Morlach when he hears of this treachery. 'Twas Brude's magic that won at the last!"

Maire rose to Declan's heated insinuation that she was less skilled than the Welshman. "'Twas *my* stinger. And it was Brude's magic that showed me the answer to my problems, whilst you and Eochan faced them with evasive eyes, shuffling feet, and all manner of *ifs*. This man at least meets his enemy head on and honors his word."

"We'll see how quickly his courage and honor desert him when he faces Morlach instead of a woman."

Maire glanced expectantly at Rowan, as though not sure which of them had the most reason to take exception to Declan's outburst. Rowan sensed her confoundment and disappointment when he let the insult ride. No doubt men in her world had lost their heads over less veiled affronts. Keeping a wary eye on the hand Declan placed on his sword, Rowan merely smiled. "And who is this Morlach you speak of, brother?"

"Evil incarnate," Declan derided, the disdain in his eyes giving evidence that his estimation of Rowan was dropping by the moment at his lack of spine. "Master of the powers of darkness...and I am not your brother."

"A druid? This is the worrisome suitor you speak of?" The chuckle in Rowan's question was not one of mild amusement. He was as deadly serious as the subject they now broached.

"Morlach is guardian of Gleannmara," Maire answered shortly. "The high king appointed him to the task until I came of age. From all I've heard, he's bled my people with his greed, and now he seeks to marry me so that he can continue to feed on Gleannmara's sweat and blood."

"You've not seen this for yourself?" Maire didn't strike him as the sort to let this sort of rumor go without taking some sort of action—to verify it, if nothing else.

"She's been under Drumkilly's protection," Declan told him.

"And Brude's," Maire added. "He feared if I returned to Gleannmara, Morlach might work mischief and—"

"And if your god could not help you win over a woman's sword," Declan interrupted, "Morlach will make fodder of you both!" The idea did not seem to displease the Scot warrior at all. "He certainly didn't protect his church."

As if to prove it, he flashed his bejeweled fingers at Rowan, wriggling one specifically. On it was a gold ring bearing the same letters on the medallion around Rowan's neck.

Justinian's ring! Rowan clenched his teeth until they hurt from holding back his rage. He'd given the cleric the ring as a symbol of their friendship.

"The plague take you, Declan!" Maire swore hotly. "All the prizes were to be collected and divided according to the law!"

"I slipped this on my finger and forgot until now."

Declan, unaware of the silent demon in Rowan chaffing to be unleashed, wriggled the ring again. It was Maire, however, who charged the warrior like a mad badger, apparently determined to knock the haughty grin off his face. Rowan grabbed her, bringing her up short. Her extended punch caught the air beyond Declan's cleft chin. Rowan held the squirming, cursing female, tightening his grasp until there was no breath left to fuel her protest.

"Perhaps this Morlach is the reason my God allowed Maire to best me," he said over her frustrated grunts and thrashing.

Declan sneered. "You grasp at foam like a drowning man, Emrys!"

Maire lunged over Rowan's arm to reach the dagger laced to her leg, loosening his grasp momentarily. "I'll skewer you like a fresh killed rabbit!"

"Be grateful it's not your neck I'm grasping at," Rowan answered her brother, tightening his rein on his captive.

If she only knew how his spine pricked at Declan's flying barbs. But for God's grace itself, he'd snap, releasing his anger like a bow its arrow. 'Twould serve Declan right…but it was not Rowan's place to deal out justice. That belonged to God. Besides, he almost felt sorry for the lad, for of the two of them, Declan was more a hostage than Rowan—a hostage of his own fear.

"My faith is built upon a rock, my friend, not the sands of fear and darkness. I shall sleep like a babe at the prospect of meeting this Morlach, while you squirm in your nightmares. 'The LORD is my light and my salvation; whom shall I fear? The LORD is the strength of my life; of whom shall I be afraid?'"

He released Maire, who seemed as struck dumb with incredulity as her foster brother at Rowan's words, and returned to his horses. Although aware that the hot-tempered Declan might attack him from behind—or even Maire, for that matter—Rowan walked on without a backward glance, well able to imagine what they must be thinking.

Rowan had heard it all before. His words were those of madness. How had a man like him survived the battles his scarred body told of? Surely he'd taken some vicious blow to the head, which left him witless.

"He's fey as a swineherd!" Declan spat out.

The corners of Rowan's lips twitched. Aye, he'd heard that too.

SIX

Anger gave way to vexation as Maire watched him go. In the periphery of her vision, she saw Declan's dubious smirk. "Brude would not mislead us. There is more to this man than we can see. I feel it."

Or was *she* the drowning soul grasping at foam? Maire searched the dimly lit deck for the aged druid. She had to speak to him. She needed to know all there was to know about this man she was about to take as husband.

"I think what you feel, little sister, I could easily assuage."

Maire turned abruptly, struck dumb with disbelief. Recovering, she spat out, "If you had more brain than brawn, you'd know this is no time for jest."

Leaving Declan to his ridiculous notion, she strode across the deck to where she'd spied Brude. A small calf lay there, its head on the druid's lap, its round eyes wide with trust. It had no idea that it was to soon become a sacrifice. For a moment, Maire identified with the animal, both pitying and envying it for its blissful ignorance. Later, perhaps, its entrails would tell the druid what lay ahead for them all. For now, there was nothing to do but wait and hope that Brude would see it clearly.

A makeshift altar at the stern of the ship sufficed for the sacrifice of the calf. The blood was saved to sprinkle over the earth of the sacred grove in Gleannmara's hills, introducing the new to blend with the old. The meat was boiled for a hero's feast.

Coupled with the barrels of wine taken from the church stores, no banqueting lodge needed more.

When they did finally have a chance to speak, Brude answered Maire's concerns with that exasperating druid talk, his words filling the air with the ring of wisdom, yet saying nothing she understood. *Change was in the air and change was good.* What in the name of Crom Cruach did that mean? There was nothing left to do but to join her men in the victory celebration; to enjoy the day because not even the gods knew what the morrow promised.

Lifting cups of hollowed horn, Maire toasted with her fellow warriors till she could no longer ride the gentle roll of the deck beneath her kid-laced feet. Then the men hoisted her upon their shoulders, heaving her to each other in riotous joy as though she were a child's doll, until Brude intervened for fear her human steeds might charge recklessly over the rail of the tacking ship, taking her with them.

There were more colors than the rainbow among the collection of voluminous brats her men wore draped and pinned over bare shoulders, so their battle wounds showed like badges of honor. Gabran and Brandub of Clan Colmáin, Fergus and Conall of the MacCormac, Dathal and Cellach sons of Muirdach—all of Gleannmara's families were represented, all except the Cairthan, the highland tribe, who once had been masters of the tuath. That lot had yet to pay proper homage to Maeve or Morlach. What they couldn't produce in their lofty isolation, they stole from their neighbors in right Celtic style. They had to be given credit for that. *"Gnats,"* Morlach labeled them, worrisome but not worth the effort to eliminate them in their own element.

Neither their weapons nor their voices were missed. The day had been won and now the southern clans of the Uí Niall sang songs, so embellished with heart and wine that breath alone might carry them all the way to Erin's green shore. Like the breeze filling the sails, the drink fueled their appreciation of not only the day's blessings, but also those undoubtedly to come. For all the toasts and speeches, not one was repeated. It was their queen's first victory celebration and glorious. It was the warrior's way.

By the time the druid hailed the sun at the break of the following day, the boisterous company had expired of grandiose words and melody. The crew of the ship wrestled with the sails overhead to seize the advantage of the rare east wind while the adventurers sprawled about the deck as though slain by their excessive celebration. Maire slept on a pallet under a leather canopy, dead to the noise of the working ship and the cries of the gulls following it. The sunlight bearing down upon the cover cast an innocent glow over the sleeping queen.

But for the leather trappings of a warrior laced on her shins and wrists, one might have taken her for an angel. Still, Rowan knew it was just an illusion. Whatever Maire of Gleannmara was, she was no angel. And while she'd already proven her skill, neither was she just another Scotti warrior, no matter how valiantly she'd withstood the victory celebration.

Despite being invited to participate, Rowan had watched from his pallet near his prize horses. It wasn't his celebration, even if he believed this was God's plan for him. As the Scotti exalted in their triumph, good peace-loving families of the fishing village mourned their dead while those who remained of the clergy sought to comfort them. God forgive him, he was grateful Emrys had been spared, but he could not help the resentment he felt for those who were not...especially Justinian. Still, Declan had said Rowan's God did not protect his *church*—not his church*men*.

Rowan had heard that much clearly, even in the heat of his initial reaction at seeing the ring he'd given Justinian on Declan's finger. Knowing the priest, he'd have handed over the gift and asked God to forgive the thieves as he did so—and the

Celts would not slaughter such a man in those conditions. It was, at the least, ignoble.

Glad that, unlike the fishermen, the priest had grace enough to keep a cool head, Rowan devoted his attention to observation of the enemy who now held him hostage, their queen in particular. Surprisingly, he'd been entertained as well as intrigued. Maire had dumped noggin after noggin of wine into the drains cut in the side of the ship when she thought no one was looking. She'd won the approval of her men and did her level best to appear worthy. Yet, as she'd been tossed like a revered toy from one hulk of a warrior to another, Rowan had not missed the occasional insecure glances she cast in the direction of the overseeing druid.

Something about her reminded him of a child suddenly cast into a coveted adult role, one for which she was not fully prepared. Except Maire of Gleannmara was no child. Suddenly aware of staring, Rowan gave up his study of the long, slender limbs exposed by the disarray of her saffron leine or tunic. In the periphery of his vision, he caught a movement and looked back in time to see a floating swath of bright woven wool settle over the comely curves of Maire's body. Kneeling at her side, the warrior Declan glared back at him with open contempt, his fingers fastening a princely broach to the short kilt he wore about his waist, in place of the brat he'd used as a blanket for his queen.

Rowan met the young man's glare with a conjured smile. No matter how he came by it, the young cock would be dead had he flashed Justinian's ring in Rowan's face a few years ago. The sight of the gift he'd given his teacher and friend would have destroyed Rowan's ability to reason out what most likely had happened. The pagan owed his life to the very God he scorned, for Rowan knew he alone did not possess the strength to resist this old, too familiar thirst for vengeance.

Faith, but vengeance was a bitter potion to swallow. It lodged in his chest like a bone in a dog's throat, making it difficult to breathe, much less bellow. Better to consider the nature of the Scot's relationship with the queen before demon anger gained sway of thought and action.

Was the golden-maned warrior the queen's bodyguard? her lover? or both? The thought undermined his indifference, vexing Rowan even more. It made no difference to him. It wasn't as if the pagan marriage he was about to enter meant anything to him as a Christian, or to them in regard to eternity. The Scotti were a passionate people and did not consider wedlock binding for life. Sometimes no more than a year and a day were promised, or so he'd heard. Afterward, a couple might go their separate ways by mutual consent.

While Rowan had found that idea appealing at one time, he didn't now. If he ever really took a woman as wife, it would be with the blessing of the church for as long as he lived. Women, at least in wifely terms, had not fit into his plans. Until now. Aye, he'd stand with the Scotti queen and go through her heathen ceremony, for it was his means to Gleannmara and, with luck, an opportunity to find his blood clan. For reasons beyond human understanding, God used Maire's quandary with this Morlach as an instrument to make the way for Rowan to follow the calling he'd been given. He felt it deeply in his soul, this calling that had brought him back from death's door to see life in a totally different light than before. It was a precious gift of which he strove to be worthy.

"You bear a gift, Rowan of Emrys, but it isn't yours to give."

Rowan started from his reverie to see the elderly druid standing next to Shahar, stroking the stallion's velvet nose with gnarled fingers. In a single fluid effort, Rowan rose to his feet and brushed away the straw clinging to his robe. He possessed clothes fit for a prince, but the humble garment kept him centered on his purpose, God's purpose. The weave rubbed coarse against his skin, reminding him that his road would not be smooth as silk.

"I assure you, Brude, these animals are mine to give. Their

bloodlines will make Gleannmara's horses the envy of Erin."

Brude's smile was one of mild tolerance. It obviously wasn't the answer the druid was looking for. His gaze grew intense beneath the snowy thicket separating it from his high brow, which was shaven in the tonsure of his profession.

"We must talk, Emrys, but there is much to be done before we see landfall. Do you notice nothing amiss with the wind?"

"Only that it favors your ship, but then, I was a horse soldier not a seaman."

"And what are you now, good son?"

"A hostage."

The sun made Rowan squint as he studied the tall mast, strained to its very root in the hull by the unfurled sails. It groaned in occasional protest but held fast, a proud testimony to the craftsmen of the vessel.

"Your sacrifice must have appeased your spirits," Rowan said at length, preferring to divert the conversation from himself.

Again the bland smile. "The Great One's many faces have smiled upon us, true. But this does not fit the pattern." The old man sniffed, as though something in the air might solve the riddle plaguing him. It did not. He shook his head, eluded.

"I must awaken our queen. We shall need the blessing of the full sun to forge this union for the good of Gleannmara's future. Enough time has wasted away."

When Brude laid his hand upon Maire's shoulder, the joyous revelry in her dream disappeared in a flash. Gone were the familiar faces of her tribe gathered in Gleannmara's hero's hall, including those of her parents, who by some trick of obscurity, were not only present but proud of her success. Instead, it was the druid's face she now saw. In lieu of the smoke from the roasting fires, the smell of hay and livestock tinged with the incongruous freshness of salt air filled her nostrils. Where the solid ground of Gleannmara had stood beneath her feet, a ship's deck waltzed with the sea.

"The wedding must take place while the sun is at its strongest. Yesterday you became queen; today you become a bride."

Maire nodded. Her stomach breached a swell in concert with the motion of the ship. The wine that had delighted her mouth last night had turned sour and dry. Would that she could take out her tongue and wash it with spring water like the women laundering clothes along the brook. She refreshed her lungs with a deep breath and glanced about her.

Many of her men lay about the deck like corpses, contented by the volume of food and wine consumed the night before. But for the working seamen, the deck might well have been the straw-strewn floor of the hero's hall. Although a formal election needed to take place on their return, she really was their queen. They'd embraced her as one of them and lifted her above them. All those years of training had finally come to fruition. It was this for which she'd been groomed.

With the vigor of her youth, Maire rose to her feet and shook out the tangled mane of hair cascading down her back. The salt breeze tossed it with gentle fingers, teasing the shorter locks about her face. Queen Maire. For all that had come about in the last cycle of the sun, it was still hard to believe.

"Did you sleep well, Queen Maire?"

Still hampered by the clutches of sleep, Maire turned to see her youngest foster brother holding out a noggin of wine. By its color, she could see it had been diluted.

"Too well." She took the cup with a grateful grin.

"Your mother would have been proud."

Declan picked up his brat and threw it carelessly over a sun-bronzed shoulder. His long, golden hair was a brilliant contrast to the reds, blues, and greens the women of the tribe had crosswoven into the fabric's pattern. He resembled a proud, young sun god, Maire admitted, reluctantly agreeing with the opinion of many of Gleannmara's maids. But he knew it, and she never was a girl to feed a man's vanity. She kept her observation to herself.

"Thank you for covering me."

"Maire, please think this through."

Their words came out together. Both smiled, embarrassed.

"All you need do is marry," Declan said, recovering first. "We've grown up together, trained together. We know each other better than we know ourselves."

"Are you saying I should marry you?"

"That's the thrust of it, aye." The young man drew himself up to his full height, one that Maire almost met equally. "It will solve your problem with Morlach."

"And create others."

Maire jumped slightly at the words. Brude had a way of fading into the background when he chose, so that people forgot his presence. His hard gaze challenged Maire to think.

Eochan, the elder of the brothers, held much favor among her tribesmen. Should Maire be killed in battle, there would be no heirs of Maeve's direct lineage. Maire was the last. But her foster family was *ainfine*, kin descended from a common ancestor—a clan chief generations back. His male descendants were eligible to be elected. Morlach would likely become overlord, as the king's promise to Maeve had been fulfilled. Still, a chieftain would be elected from the clans of Gleannmara, and Eochan stood the better chance of such an honor than his younger, more impetuous brother. For all his roar, the bear had a keen wit, an even temper, and a gentle heart.

"It's unfair to ask me to choose you over Eochan, who knows me just as well as you, brother. I love you both. Such a decision would be impossible."

"But I asked first."

Brude spoke up, his tone mild yet firm. "The queen must be true to her word. The choice was pledged in a battle of honor. It follows the pattern."

"Patterns!" Declan spat in rebellion. "Sometimes I think you druids conjure patterns to suit your own purpose."

Maire gasped in horror. "Declan!" Surely the young man had lost his senses, challenging Brude. She'd heard of men driven to destroy themselves after crossing words with a druid. A satire, a toss of straw, and uncontrollable madness was unleashed within them.

"And what purpose might that be, my young cockerel?"

Declan did not back down from the older man's challenge. Nor could he come up with an answer. No one argued with a druid, save another of his kind.

"I have seen the sword that will save Gleannmara, and it is not yours."

"What do druids know of swords?"

"What do warriors know of the future?" Brude responded in a dismissing tone. "I have read the entrails of the sacrifice."

Aware that they had attracted the attention of those working the ship as well as those awakened by the rise of voices, Declan gave way. "Forgive me, sir. My devotion to our queen has made me reckless."

"Valor and humility are good mates."

With the same hand that might have cast a spell of death, Brude blessed the warrior, saving his face in the public eye. The tension coiling in Maire gave way to relief. There were times she could strangle Declan with her bare hands for his brashness, but never in truth would she wish him harm.

As the reckless warrior stomped toward the bow of the ship, Maire moved closer to Brude. "This vision of the sword, Brude. Was it Maeve's?"

"No. Now we must prepare for your marriage." The druid guided Maire with his hand toward the ancient chest containing all of his belongings, the subject of swords clearly at a discouraging finish.

So she was not to save Gleannmara with her mother's sword. That could only mean one thing.

Her gaze found Rowan ap Emrys as if by command. His—
the weapon of a stranger—was the champion sword of
Gleannmara. Even as their gazes met, Maire felt a disconcerting
charge of awareness sweep through her—strange, yet familiar;
chilling, yet warm; alarming, yet soothing. His face revealed no
more thought or emotion than hers, yet her senses reeled, one
against another.

Marriage? Maire fought a swell of panic as the ship beneath
her battled with that of the tide, barely mastering it. There had
been hardly enough time for her to accept that she was now a
queen. At least she'd been trained for the leadership of her
tuatha. There was no one to prepare her to become a
bride...no one but the druid.

"What must I do, Brude?" Her voice croaked like that of a
boy breaching manhood.

"You must trust the Spirit of all spirits. Our lives, like our
surroundings, are a series of patterns, and you, my queen, are
but a half-finished part of a great masterpiece."

Maire wanted to pull the druid away from the chest containing the white folded linen he thoughtfully fingered and
demand to know in plain terms what he meant, but she feared
his answer. Instead, she studied the curious marks of ogham
on the timeworn wood as she waited for whatever voice had
gained his attention to release him back to her. She'd always
thought there to be magic in the druid's chest. Brude had
allowed her to search for it when she was a child missing as
many teeth as he, but all she'd found were clothes and a few
meager personal items. It amazed her, considering the kingly
gifts the druid received in his position. He was always passing
them on to others, claiming his search for the truth of life
required few worldly goods. Such things impaired the spirit. A
druid's mind was as much a mystery as his magic.

As the old man straightened, a flash of gold and silver, fired
by the sun's rays, surprised her. It was a girdle, finely crafted,
like nothing she'd ever seen in the druid's trunk.

"This was made from Maeve's jewelry. Wear it with the gift from Emrys's mother. Both are fit for a queen."

"Won't it hang on my breastplate?"

"You will be a bride today, not a warrior. Save your armor for the days that follow."

Although there was no hint of humor on Brude's lips, it fairly danced with glee in his gaze. It was the same look he'd given her years ago when she'd announced in grand disappointment that there was no magic to be found in his chest.

Maire's heart took a grudging plunge. There was no way she would inquire now as to the secrets shared between man and wife, once she and Emrys were declared so. What if he changed his mind about their agreement regarding intimacy? From her observations of men with females, their word didn't mean a whole lot in the scheme of things. There would be no real defense against that—no legal one anyway.

And if that came to pass, Maire knew as well as Emrys what she was supposed to do. The tactics were not the question, but the execution. Would it be like her first battle, where the anticipation and flush of excitement would catch her up and carry her through? Once she'd started the fight on Emrys's soil, there'd been no time to think about what she was doing. She'd had to do and survive because if she dwelt upon it—

"Emrys will wear this."

One battle at a time. Maire retreated from her thoughts with an involuntary shudder. Brude held her father's torque in his hand; the same princely one he'd worn when taken hostage by his conquering queen. The gold with silver inlay of his native tribe's design had been polished to a sheen. She remembered tracing the small concentric circles with her fingers as he held her in his arms. Part of her protested as she nodded in agreement. It was only fitting.

"Brude." She placed a hand on the druid's leathery forearm. Despite the shrinkage of many winters, the muscle beneath was as strong and pliant as the wires on his harp. She lowered her voice. "What exactly did you see last night, in the entrails of the calf?" She had to know.

"Nothing but entrails."

Maire's heart sank. "But..."

"'Twas later, in my sleep, that I saw the triumph of light over darkness."

Relief flooded through her veins. She hated it when her mentor druid baited her with nibbles at the fruit of knowledge instead of biting through to its core. "Then the spirits are with us and against Morlach?"

"The spirits of light have many faces. That of the dark is only one. Anything else is shadowy illusion."

"Is it Emrys's sword you saw?"

"I saw light triumph. When there is more to tell, you shall be the first to hear, my queen."

He saw light, so they were going to triumph over Morlach. If only she knew how, Maire thought, resigned to Brude's final word. Trust did not come easily to her. Yet she had no choice. And so, with the beautifully wrought belt over her arm, she turned to face her destiny.

As his protégé walked away, head high, shoulders squared, grace in every step, the aging druid blinked his eyes. They filled with the mist of nostalgia. She looked like Maeve, he mused. The little princess had grown into a woman, and now the welfare of her people depended on her. Brude wished he could tell her more, but the fact was, he did not understand the signs himself. Light and darkness had swirled in his mind—a quagmire of energy, power against power.

As his spirit was drawn into the fray, he'd been blinded by the overwhelming brilliance of triumph. It consumed him so that he knew no fear when he could not see the enemy's black fist. Instead, he'd felt an unprecedented peace. It permeated his very essence as the sun warms the freshly turned earth of a field. There were no more patterns for him to decipher, for they were all blended into one. In that instant, while his human mind groped for understanding, he knew the spirit that survives the body from this world to the next had at last seen the truth his ancestors had sought from time's beginning. And the sun was but a small star in its glow.

Even the wind held its breath as the gathering of warriors stood solemnly around the altar at the stern of the ship. No part of the wooden deck was sheltered from the high sun burning unchallenged in a cloudless sky. The victory fire, renewed with faggots of oak and rowan, licked at them with hungry forked tongues. Brude waved his arms over it as he had many times, his skin unscathed, and turned toward the couple standing at the fore of the crowd.

Maire resisted the urge to wipe a bead of sweat from her brow, trying to recall any time in the past when she'd seen the tribe's chief druid perspire. She couldn't.

For all the water on her brow, her mouth was as dry as ground bone. She shifted from one foot to the other. The hem of the silken dress from Delwyn ap Emrys brushed against her calves and stuck. A proper wedding costume would skim her ankles, but this was hardly a planned affair. She'd pledge, he'd pledge, and it would be done. It could be undone just as quickly before a court of the Brehons after Morlach's threat was disposed of. It was the in-between that plagued her.

"Do you both understand the significance of this union?"

"I understand." Rowan ap Emrys's voice rang deep and clear as the thickest of harp strings beside her.

Maire stared at the altar, unable to bring herself to look at the man she was marrying. Having stolen a glance from behind the leather-curtained enclosure where she'd dressed, she knew exactly what he looked like: a cleric with a warrior's collar, except his hair had not been shaven at the crown but grew thick and raven black. 'Twould be a glorious mane were he disposed to let it grow past his shoulders in the Scotti fashion.

At least the gods had given his skull a comely shape that needed no particular cover. It was nobly proportioned, set upon a strong sinewy neck now adorned with her late father's torque. But then, all of him seemed well proportioned.

"My queen?"

It was to be in name only, she told herself. "I understand."

"May the guardian spirits bless you with communication of the heart, mind, and body from the east; warmth of heart and home from the south; the deep commitment, excitement, and cleansing of the waters of the west; and the fertility of the north; that you and your fields may multiply."

"May we so be blessed."

"Yes…blessed," Maire mumbled simultaneously with the man at her side, her voice a mere whisper above the thunderous pillage of inner panic. She was queen. She was the ruler. The marriage was in name only. Anxiety stirred the wine and bread she'd consumed on rising. Even her stomach resisted this course.

"Rowan, will you cause her pain, burden, or anger?"

"I may," she heard him answer shortly.

"Is that your purpose?"

"No."

"Maire, will you cause him pain, burden, or anger?"

"Aye, very likely." The thought became words before she could call them back. Her eyes widened in dismay beneath Brude's stern gaze.

"And will that be your intention?"

For the first time, Maire cast a sideways look at Rowan. By her mother's gods, he was all but laughing at her. One side of his mouth was pulled like that of a fish hooked good and proper. A flush of indignation steadied her voice. "Not unless he oversteps himself."

A tide of amusement rippled through the assembly. Chin

jutting in defiance, Maire slashed a satisfied smile at her groom and turned back to Brude expectantly. Her satisfaction withered under the druid's silent reproach.

"Nay, then," she conceded.

"Rowan, will you share Maire's laughter, her dreams, and honor her?"

"In as much as I am not required to offend or abandon the Lord, my God."

"Will you share our queen's laughter and dreams and honor her?" Brude's impatience was like an explosion of thunder on a clear summer's day.

"In as much as I am not required to offend or abandon the Lord, my God," the Welshman repeated. "'Tis no less than I agreed to when the bargain was struck, druid. I stand by my honor to keep it."

For an immeasurable length of time Brude studied the upstart, then offered, "As we stand by ours."

A collective sigh of relief, Maire's included, surrounded them. The spirits surely protected Rowan ap Emrys, or Brude would have reduced him to a blubbering idiot before all.

"And you, Queen Maire, will you share your laughter, your dreams, and honor Emrys?"

"I will," she replied, swallowing the stipulation she was about to blurt out about when he deserved them.

"I'll have your hands."

Maire put her right hand out, palm up beside Rowan's. Brude neatly sliced Rowan's dominant finger first. He then squeezed a single droplet of his blood into a silver cup of wine. A similar cut was made across her finger. It stung, but she refused to flinch. She stared as a scarlet drop of her blood fell into the cup.

"The marriage of your blood is like the marriage of your spirits," Brude announced in a louder voice. "Drink."

He offered Rowan the first sip, then Maire. She inadvertently licked away the mustache dealt by the druid's shaking hand. He turned and poured the remaining contents over the fire. With a hiss, the wine was quickly evaporated.

"I will have the symbols of your vows. Yours for protection," he said to the groom.

The sword Rowan surrendered at Emrys was handed to him hilt first. Bracing agilely as the ship veered to one side, Rowan placed the blade on the deck between them and the druid.

"And yours for hearth and home."

At Brude's prompt, Maire took up the sword she'd inherited from her mother and laid it across the other sword, forming an X.

"No broom for our queen," someone remarked behind them.

A hint of a smile tugged at the corner of Maire's lips. The bride usually contributed a broom, representing hearth and home.

"It seems we'll have a well-protected home."

These were not only the first words Rowan had spoken directly to Maire that day, but his first as her husband.

"So it appears." Maire offered her hand to him for the dance. A piper struck a note as Rowan clasped it with his own. The instrument filled the air like the lark's joyous welcome of new day.

This nonsense meant nothing to him or his God, but that didn't mean that Rowan could not appreciate the beauty and grace of the woman whose feet moved like graceful butterflies, lighting between the crossed blades just long enough to spring over the next. A wreath of mistletoe crowned her glorious titan hair; she was a vision of femininity, surely one of God's most exquisite creations.

It was hard to believe that the delicate hand he held as they danced a pattern around and over the swords had sliced his rib cage with a blade, much less that it could wield a sword that would tax some men's strength to lift. A flash of a smile revealed teeth that would shame the finest pearls, and the challenge tossed from the demure slant of her green eyes as she caught his gaze and as quickly let it go was enough to warm a statue to the core. Her Celtic blood fired every motion, every look, with the passion of the ages.

The piper gave out before either Maire or Rowan would admit fatigue. With a gallant bow, Rowan stepped back for Eochan to take over the pattern dance. Having pretended to sip from the wedding cup to avoid breaking the Lord's law against drinking blood, he eagerly accepted a noggin of drink. While draining it, he was surrounded by well-wishing warriors who'd been ready to take off his head the day before.

Scotti hospitality was instilled in them before they had memory. Such was the temperament of these people, as quick to embrace over a barrel of wine as to fight over it. At least it was the temperament of most of them. They made good allies and formidable foes.

Instinct drew Rowan's gaze to the ship's rail, where Declan wore a scowl as dark as his features were fair. Cup in hand, the Scot could not tear his gaze from Maire as she danced first with one of her clansmen and then another. Though it nagged at Rowan for reasons beyond his ken, he could not blame the man. There was something about Gleannmara's queen more dangerous to Rowan than her sword. It struck contrary sparks of fear and anticipation against the tinder of his senses, as though, were he not careful, even his heart was at risk.

SEVEN

"C onsummated!"

Maire looked at the wizened druid, certain she'd mis- understood. After all, the noise of the revelry had esca- lated with each barrel tapped and drained dry that day. In truth, her head felt as though it were light as the cherub white clouds of summer. Her dress, damp from the wild dancing, clung to her frame, though her throat was wrung dry and her voice hoarse from song. Her incredulous echo of the druid's word came out, tweaked by strain.

Brude, whose strong voice, even after the sun and moon's full cycle of song, never failed, repeated himself. "The union must be real. Morlach will not be bluffed. I've stayed his hand as long as I can, but even now the east wind picks up again."

Maire glanced uncertainly at the sails. They were puffed like a well-fed babe's cheeks, straining toward Erin. The seamen aloft scrambled like cats in a tree full of birds working the ropes and chains to make the most of the favorable weather.

"Are you saying Morlach has summoned the east wind?"

"It does go against the natural pattern."

"But who is to say that we still do not coast on the fair wind of our victory?"

"Are you willing to take that chance, Queen Maire? Erin was nigh on three days journey behind us with the natural pat- tern, yet she will be barely two on return, should the east con- tinue to fill our sails. By the new sun, our homeland will rise on the horizon."

That was good news to Maire. She had no love of the sea.

Thankfully, she had not given into the heaving sickness that had threatened her their first day out. Warriors bigger than she had been brought to their knees by it. Celt to the bone, even in their misery, they'd made it a competition, turning the sickest into a weak-kneed, grinning victor.

"By all the natural elements, we should not set foot on Erin's soil till the third daybreak. The ship's crew is wary and demands to know the meaning of this strange wind."

"I wasn't aware Clon's men noticed anything but their share of the booty." That was what Eochan had to promise the Dal Raidi captain. The closing of a tin mine had put the trader in dire need of goods, so he was amicable to a mutually beneficial adventure.

"Do you think Morlach will not know he is being tricked?"

"By my mother's gods, Brude, what would you have me do? Lay with Emrys before the eyes of all? We made the vows. We danced the dance."

She felt the fire of anger in her cheeks. Give her an enemy with weapons she could see and feel the bite of, not one who conjured spells and changed the patterns of the universe.

At Brude's answering silence, she gave in to exasperation. "Then cast a spell to blind Morlach!" Crom's toes, she'd worried about Rowan changing his mind but never dreamed Brude would be insistent on such a thing.

"If Morlach is indeed the reason for our speedy return, I cannot compete with such magic."

"A sacrifice then." How foolish she'd been! But there'd been so little time to consider all consequences when the deal was agreed to.

"The blood of your innocence, Maire. That is the only sacrifice that will stand." Brude reassured her with a knobby hand on her shoulder, but it did not help the panic running amok in her mind.

"I've no training—"

"To become what you already are requires no training. You were born a woman."

"But I told him this would be in name only. 'Twould be dishonorable to change now." Honoring the verbal agreement had stood Rowan well during the wedding rite, when he'd changed the wording to suit his purpose. Maire hoped against her last hope it would stand now.

"From the way his gaze mated with yours during the pattern dance, I don't think he'll mind a change of heart."

Maire wanted to pretend she didn't know what the druid was speaking of, but she couldn't. The unsettling awareness of each other, which charged across their arm's length as they'd moved in unison over and about the crossed symbols of their marriage, flared anew. She could hear the sudden rush of blood past her temples above the clamor of drink, dance, and song surrounding them. How could it rise so strong when she felt her pride sinking to the pit of dark defeat?

But she was queen first, warrior second, and woman last. She had no choice but to protect her people in whatever manner she could. Since hers was not the saving sword of Gleannmara's, she must seal the union with the man who possessed the key. Foolish hopes of love, even courtship, were a luxury not often afforded a queen.

"It isn't my heart I'm changing, Brude," she answered at last. "Only my mind. And that I'm doing for Gleannmara, nothing—"

"Man overboard!"

The warning from the loft above fell like a sobering blanket upon the celebration below, settling first upon a few, then upon all. Men scrambled to the sides of the ship, straining to peer at the rolling green water in search of the floundering soul.

"To the larboard!" came the direction from above, sending those who'd gathered to the right over to the left. Elbows and shoulders collided in the confusion exacting grunts and curses.

Eochan was the first to spy the unfortunate. "Cling to this, lad!"

With bearlike strength, the warrior lifted the empty wine

keg he'd been sitting on and heaved it over the side. Maire squeezed through the crowd to her foster brother's side and watched the cask splash into a deep rolling trough, where it bobbed as if on the tongue of a gaping watery mouth.

"I don't see—"

A golden head surfaced beside it, gasping for air and cutting her off in midsentence.

"Declan!" she shrieked, recognition and horror colliding.

She rose on tiptoe as if that might help her to see better as her foster brother clawed his way toward the floating barrel. Someone steadied her from behind. The voluminous folds of Declan's brat worked like an overblown monster against him, holding him in place. He might as well have tried to pull himself up a rope of air, for all the progress he made. Then his head disappeared beneath the foamy surface again, and Maire strangled as though she were with him.

"Throw him a rope!" someone shouted along the rail.

"Aye, hand it to me and I'll take it to him!" Eochan vaulted up on the ship's rail with amazing agility for his size and turned to catch the heavy line tossed his way. The whip of the rope past her face shattered her numbing fear. Reason rallied. Maire stayed his arm in protest.

"Ye can't swim any better than him."

"He's my brother!" the man bellowed back at her, as though that would give him the skill he needed.

He was her brother as well, but Maire had heard too many tales of well-meaning men drowning with the victim. She knew she was no match for the waves on her own, much less with the weight of another dragging her down. Eochan was no more at home in the water.

Declan broke the surface again, shoving against it as if to lift himself from it. He coughed up water, unable to cry for the help he needed. Where the swelling sea left off, his hair closed about his face to smother and blind him to the presence of the barrel, floating just a body's length away.

Eochan leaned forward, tearing out of Maire's grip, but instead of diving into the water, he sprawled backward as though an unseen ram had driven into his chest. Landing upon the deck amid the feet and legs of his clansmen, he shouted in outrage, but the man who'd thrown him aside was already in the water. It wasn't until his head broke the crest of a swell a few feet from the thrashing Declan, that Maire recognized him.

It was Emrys, his wet shoulders glistening in the setting of the sun. He moved as if he'd been born to the sea, with fins for feet and arms. With long powerful strokes, the Welshman closed the distance between him and the thrashing Scot, but Declan went down again, just before Rowan reached him.

It felt as if a team of oxen were pulling at her chest, Maire was so drawn to the drama unfolding below. Rowan rose like the sea god himself, his upper torso shooting above the water. With a mighty lung full of air, he dove into the deep again after her foster brother. Maire leaned further over the rail, her own breath corked in her chest.

Brude!

Not even her fervent plea for the druid to use his powers escaped, but she felt the responding cold of his hand upon her arm, drawing her back. She'd never known the old man to have warm hands.

The riggings clapped and billowed above with the crew's effort to slow the ship, but the scene between her and the spot where the two men had gone down was as still as the mosaic pictures on Emrys's villa walls. A whispering wave passed through it, distracting her gaze until Maire wondered if she was searching the wrong place for signs of movement.

Please! She pleaded in silent desperation, not really knowing which spirit, if any, would listen. *Please!*

"There they are! By the barrel."

The sea had played a sleight of hand with her eyes. Maire moved toward the stern and fixed her gaze to where Rowan struggled to shove his uncooperative comrade's upper torso over the slippery barrel. Declan's face was out of the water, but it appeared to do him no good. The water had bleached the color from his skin, leaving a ghastly pallor. The color was not unfamiliar—Maire had seen it too many times—that which had lived in the young Scot's carcass had fled to the other world.

"Toss me the line!"

Two lines went out simultaneously at Rowan's hoarse command, one landing short of its mark; the other struck his shoulder. In an instant, it was in his grasp. He wrapped it around one muscled arm, keeping Declan's head and shoulders over the barrel with the other. Once it was secure, he devoted both hands to stabilizing the barrel and shouted for the men at the rail to haul them in.

Time, in its fickle way, struck a leisurely course. It seemed to Maire an eternity before Declan's limp form was pulled over the side and dragged onto the deck. His lips were blue, his skin bloodless and cold. She wanted to cry, but that was a luxury not afforded a warrior, much less a queen. Even so, emotion welled up in her, demanding release.

Silly fool, how could he have fallen overboard? Only a while ago she'd warned him about perching on the rail, drunk as he'd been.

"Curse you, Declan! I told you to get down from the rail."

Crying was not allowed, but anger was. Maire fell upon him, striking his chest a sound blow with all her weight. It was her queenly right to admonish him for not heeding her word. By her mother's gods, she'd not have it. To her astonishment, the moment she landed on his cold, still form, his knees drew up in a spasmodic response. What little breath was left in his chest loosened, bullying seawater from his throat in a spurt.

Riding fierce on emotion's tide, Maire tugged at his shoulder. "Help me turn him! Give us room!"

Eochan rolled his brother on his side and held the young man's head as his body convulsed and purged the death-dealing brine. Maire felt no sympathetic nausea, but an exhilarating relief. He was coming back to her! Just as she thought he could cough no more, Declan fell weakly on his back and moaned. His eyes fluttered, reluctant to return to the waking world.

"So the wine wasn't enough for you, was it?"

Joy rather than admonishment flooded Maire's voice. She placed her hands on either side of Declan's face and shook him until his gaze widened enough to ensure her he was going to stay with them.

"First you fight the sea, and now you try to drink it."

The young man's mouth twitched with an attempt to smile, but it had clearly sapped all his strength to fight his way across the divide between life and death. He shivered uncontrollably, folding his arms across his chest.

"Let me get you out of them wet clothes and into a dry, warm bed, whelp," Eochan offered, recognizing the ensuing shock taking hold of his brother. Before Declan could protest, the bear hoisted him up like a babe. "A bit of rest, and you'll be ready to fight the wind."

"I'll help." Maire rose, taken aback to find her own legs were not so steady. She might well have been pulled from the water herself, for the way her strength foundered. Declan had not overstated himself in regard to their closeness; they had grown up as close as any blood kin. Her foster brother could make her laugh, even in the darkest of moods. She'd hurt him with her rejection, and guilt would never have let her be if he hadn't survived.

"A queen learns to delegate what she can, so that she might attend to what others cannot," Brude reminded her with gentle but firm words. "The cockerel is in good hands. You have a good husband to thank for that."

Emrys! Maire had forgotten him in her concern for Declan. Across the deck, a handful of clansmen clapped Rowan on the back as though he'd been kin all his life. If his blade had not earned their admiration, his valor had. Few mariners swam well enough to rescue fellows from the churning waters of the sea. Land dwellers such as Maire and her clan might be able to make their way about in a pool or lake, but their skills fell short in the rolling fists of water that could toss a ship about like a toy.

In the dying light of the horizon, his wet body glistened, its scars all but erased. Maire tried not to admire the virile interplay of sinew as he donned his meanly spun robe again, but she dared not glance away like a shy maid as she approached him. There were too many eyes upon her to humor her modesty. She'd seen nearly naked men before; Emrys should not demand exception. At least that's what her mind said. Her body seemed of another opinion.

"The blood of the Scotti may not run in your veins, Emrys, but you possess its spirit. Your valor has pleased us. Now you must please me."

At least her outward demeanor was regal and assured. Gripping her father's torque with one hand, she drew Rowan's face down to hers and pressed her lips to his with as much fervor as when she'd fought him. When he reacted, threatening to pull away, she caught the back of his head with her free arm, holding him fast. Her clenched teeth would surely grind against his own through the flesh, but she would leave no doubt to the witnesses that this was the beginning of their mating ritual, and that she was as in charge as any swaggering groom at Beltaine.

Apparently her adversary's shock thawed, for he surprised her by drawing her into his arms. About the two of them, various remarks and sounds of approval echoed, but Maire was too distracted to gain satisfaction or be embarrassed. Rowan's embrace was rib crushing. She had no choice but to lessen the force of her kiss in order to breathe. Suddenly, she was keenly aware that she was no longer the aggressor.

Like a moth that ventured too close to a flame, her emotions ignited, defying reason. The man's skin was cold from his saltwater bath. Her fingers, clenched about his bulging biceps told her so, but it made no difference. She'd stepped onto an unfamiliar battleground where senses could not be relied on. Retreat was the only solution. A thousand echoes of how bounced about in her head, dodging traitorous whispers to surrender.

But surrender was not acceptable to a warrior. She reached for her training, shining like a bright spear of hope in a confusing rain of arrows. Driving her heel down upon his instep, she ground it in a slow, deliberate fashion. It was an act of passion, true enough, but a passion to escape, to be free of the emotions roiling through her. Thankfully, those watching could not see her action stemmed from deliberation rather than desire. She felt Rowan's flinch of pain. Both tensed. Then, as if by mutual accord, a truce was declared.

Maire stepped away, resisting the urge to wipe her lips dry of his taste. "Since I've no women to prepare our bridal chamber, you can help."

Rowan bowed with a cryptic smirk. "At your service, my queen."

A fluttering rise of humor died with Maire's forbidding glance at her men. In matters of the conjugal bed, all men were allies, brother beasts in a common pen. She was still, however, queen of that pen.

"Our accommodations are not as luxurious as those you are accustomed to, sir, but I assure you, you'll find no complaint."

With a purposeful swagger, she led the way across the deck to her canopy. The curtains that had been dropped to afford her privacy in dressing earlier were still in place. Pulling one aside, she entered the makeshift room, leaving Rowan to follow. Bread, cheese, and a skin of wine lay at the head of the two pallets that had been placed side by side, arranged as one bed beneath a coverlet of white linen. The linen from Brude's trunk.

Maire stopped short, wondering how he'd known to bring

it, much less when he had found time to do this. Had the druid seen the need of a wedding bed before they'd left Erin? Somehow she'd imagined she and Emrys making the best of the single pallet. No, that was not true. She hadn't imagined anything, because she'd refused to think of this moment. Now that it had arrived, her mind had grown dull as an ox.

"We…" Her voice cracked as Emrys bumped into her. There was no room for anyone to stand in the cubicle. It had but one purpose tonight.

"We won't have to take off our clothes," she announced, stepping onto the bed. Her knees turned to water as she knelt down, bone jamming the deck, despite the mattress of straw between. She was not about to wallow naked, queenly duty or nay. "But we should finish this wine," she went on, sitting back on her folded legs. "Your God certainly blesses the church vineyards."

By the bones of her ancestors, everything she said sounded as though it came from the mouth of a fool! What did a woman say to a man as a prelude to their wedding night? There was certainly no love to inspire words of endearment or desire.

Rowan dropped down across from her in one fell movement, his legs crossed before him. No doubt he'd spent many a night before a campfire like so when he'd been a warrior. His mouth was curled up slightly on one side, whether in agreement or amusement, she couldn't discern.

Although this was a political marriage, politics hardly seemed appropriate, either. Certainly, speaking about Morlach would not put her at ease. He was at the root of this predicament. Maire yanked out the stopper of wineskin, as if it were the evil druid's neck, and took a vengeful drought. At last she wiped on her arm the remnant of their abrasive kiss from her mouth and handed the skin over to her companion, who was not helping this situation at all with his very loud silence.

Talk about him. That's it, Maire thought, recalling an

inkling of the wisdom passed amongst the women doing needlework in the *grianán* above the warriors' hall. She wished she'd paid more heed while up there in the sun loft, but Maire had intended to become a warrior and didn't consider that worth her mind's time. She gathered confidence from the one observation she knew to be true: Men liked to talk about themselves.

"So," she said, face brightening. "Tell me how you got that deep scar on your back."

EIGHT

T he surprise on Rowan's face at her question flustered her. "I...I saw it during our contest," she added hastily. "And you had no bard to sing of your victories," Maire explained further, disconcerted by her companion's silence.

"That is because my victories are of no great concern," he said at length.

Maire laughed nervously. "Don't be telling me that you let the men who inflicted those wounds go without their due. Such modesty does not become a warrior."

"I'm no longer a warrior, my queen, at least not one of the sword."

"Tell that to my flesh." Maire pointed to one of several nicks his skillful blade had dealt. "Besides, I'm counting on your sword, Emrys. You gave your word. We took a blood oath."

"I gave my word to support you and your people, so long as what you require does not conflict with my Lord's will. And since we are now on so intimate a field, my name is Rowan, not Emrys."

Although he'd not moved a hair's width toward her, Maire felt as though she were on the run on some other level of existence. "Rowan, then."

The name was soft to the tongue, warming as cider served round a fire in the late fall, but Maire refused to be taken in so easily.

"So, what manner of God would have you cast aside your honor and forsake your right to tell of your victories?"

Her curiosity was pricked by the converse humility in the

man. It matched neither his skill nor the wealed banners of his triumphs. She'd seen more than that one vicious scar as she locked swords with him. She looked at one now, where it skimmed the top of his left eyebrow, telling of yet another brush with death. This was not the body of a humble man, but one of a brash, valiant fighter.

"All triumph, glory, and honor belong to my God. Without Him, I am as useless as the dust of the earth."

What a strange concept. Intrigued, Maire leaned on one elbow, her hair falling over her shoulder like a silken mantle. Although there was a small lamp next to the wooden plate of bread and cheese, its light was not enough for her to make out more than Rowan's profile. The soul of his eyes was hidden to her, evasive as the real meat of his words. It was like listening to Brude.

"I think you seek to have me underestimate you, Rowan, though I'm confounded by your purpose. Tell me where you fought and with whom. Tell me why you wear the robe of a cleric, which fits neither form nor character. You needn't put it to rhyme," she added, knowing that gifts of verse and sword were rarely matched in one person.

It was her turn to be studied. Maire felt the measure of his gaze upon her face, as though he were reaching beyond to ascertain if she could be trusted with his secrets. She withstood it, waiting in queenly expectation. When at last he spoke, she realized she'd been holding her breath.

"My father is from a long line of soldiers. Both parents have Roman and Welsh blood. I was trained to follow in my father's footsteps."

As her companion began to unfold his story, his words flowed through her like heady wine, satiating, relaxing. Rowan of Emrys fought against the Picts and, sometimes the Scotti as well, on the northern frontier of Alba. He was a horse soldier, the youngest captain in that theater. But horse soldiers were of little value fighting against those who had no tactical training, save to find the closest foe and split his head open. Rowan became competent in both arenas, but most interesting of all, he made his horse his partner in combat. What glory he did not afford to his God, he gave to his horse, amazing Maire with stories of what a trained warhorse could do.

"And this pair you brought with us can do such things in battle?"

Maire found it hard to believe, magnificent beasts though they were, that horses were good for more than racing, pulling chariots, or delivering a man to the fray. That they could be trained to use their hooves as weapons and their bodies as both rams and shields was beyond her. She could ride Gleannmara's steeds like a second skin, but if Emrys could train the animals to this extent, then he was indeed gifted as a druid.

She reached again for the wineskin and was astounded to find it empty. Emrys's words had no bard's rhythm or rhyme, but she'd not noticed the eve slipping into the deep of the night. Once again fickle time vexed her, skittering fast through her fingers like dry sand. A few yards away, she could hear a group of her men singing. Well in their cups, their besotted mood had swung from jolly to the melancholy forerunner of slumber. She licked the rim of the spout and grinned, fortified by the spirits of the vine and relaxed by the camaraderie she'd shared, one warrior with another. It must be done.

Maire no more looked forward to the task ahead than when Brude convinced her of its necessity, but she was no longer afraid. Rowan was a reasonable man in manner, not some barbarous brute. He, a hostage among captors, had risked his own life to save Declan. She owed him for that.

Besides, the act itself didn't hurt all that much, or so she'd heard. 'Twould be like mastering mounting an unbroken horse, an intimidating task but not impossible.

"It must be done, I suppose," she sighed, unaware of the repugnance infecting her voice.

"And what's that?"

Maire narrowed her gaze at her companion's shadowed features. Either he was making fun of her or he was an idiot. Since she knew the latter not to be the case, there was only one alternative.

"I'll not be insulted, Emrys. You know as well as I what we are here for." With exasperated breath, Maire fell on her back against the pallet, stirring a cloud of dust from the straw in the dim light. "Do what you must." Curse her if she showed him the least interest.

"Why should I have all the burden?"

Burden? This was supposed to be a natural joy for men.

"Because I'm the queen and the service is yours to perform, not mine." An unladylike oath hissed through her clenched teeth. "Believe me, Emrys, I've no more heart for this than yourself. Nay, I've less, to be sure."

The mattress rustled under his weight as Rowan stretched out full length at Maire's side. Propelled by his elbow, he leaned toward her as though to kiss her.

She turned her face away. "And keep your kisses to yourself. I've no use for them."

Although his plight was far from humorous, it was all Rowan could do to contain the bellow of laughter welling in his chest at this unorthodox mode of seduction. When the young queen first sauntered up to him and assaulted his lips—for her tight-mouthed, clenched teeth kiss was nothing more—he'd been taken back. Then, in less than a gnat's breath, he'd recognized her bravado was as false as her passion and fell into the game, wondering how far it would carry her.

A thousand warnings rang in his brain as he'd followed her into the tent, knowing he walked into temptation. This woman was nothing but a means for him to return to Gleannmara, but God knew his human weaknesses. He'd asked fervently for the strength to ignore the carnal longings belonging to the man he once was. That man would have had his fill of her lithe and lovely body by now and been ready for more. Instead, he lost himself in talk of battle tactics and his horses, avoiding the specifics of the blood he'd spilled, particularly of his last day on the field.

Perhaps it was the wonder-filled way she'd clung to his every word, prodding his memory for more. At some point, she'd ceased to be a queen and a woman and became a comrade of the warrior heart. Her admiration was genuine, contrary to the shallow adoration of a camp wench or a general's wife. Maire appreciated the skill and training involved in the tactics he described. Her questions were of merit, not feminine whimsy. In truth, his vanity had swelled unchecked in the attentive glow of her gaze. From where he sat, he'd watched the lantern light dance amid her eyes' many shades of green.

Or had it been the wine that washed away the barriers between them? Regardless, Maire of Gleannmara made no pretense of wanting their union, but not to her desired effect. Instead, her words and actions worked their way with the man in him as if she were a practiced courtesan. Heaven help him, for he was on the verge of a dangerous fall! Desperate, Rowan seized at reason, humor deserting as fast as it had materialized.

"If this is so distasteful to you, why go through with it? You're the *queen.*"

She took a deep breath, her chest rising beneath the modest cloak of his mother's gown. Rowan watched her face as she stared at the canopy overhead, unaware of the conflict she fueled in him. She meant nothing to him, yet her troubled expression wrung at his soul. Her vulnerability should be to his favor, not contribute to his undoing.

"Our marriage must be real, or Morlach will use it against us. The king favors the druid marrying me sooner than make him an enemy. And Brude says there must be proof that we..." The girl seized her lip to stop its quiver. "Ah, just get it done, Emrys!"

Rowan was struck with an urge to assuage the quiver with his own lips. Although she'd stood toe to toe with a man half again her size in battle, Queen Maire was afraid—genuinely afraid—of this druid. The Scotti were a flighty lot when it came to spirits. Worse, she was just as afraid of him. That should please Rowan, but it didn't.

He knew the taste of fear, the icy crush of the monster, but that was before he'd met death face to face and been given another chance at life. Comforting Maire was as futile as convincing a wild animal in a trap that he meant no harm when he freed it. How could he share what he knew so she'd understand? Perhaps in time he'd find a way to win her trust, but, heaven help him, this was now.

"Give me your hand, Maire."

The dark lashes trembling against her cheeks in dismay flew open.

"My God is stronger than this druid, but for now, we will fight this Morlach's illusion of power with one of our own. Your hand, little queen."

She watched with uncertainty as Rowan clasped the finger of the hand the druid had cut for the wedding rite and squeezed it. The dried blood that sealed it gave way to fresh.

"Stain the bedding with it," he instructed gently.

"The druids will know." In spite of her protest, Maire did as he asked, wringing her finger and smearing her life's blood on the white weave of the bedding. "This is an old trick."

"It will be your blood." At least that much would be the truth. Hopefully he wouldn't have to explain further. "The only one who knows it's true source, besides you and me, is my God. The powers of others are just illusions."

"Your god let you become my hostage."

Despite her words, he could tell she wanted to believe him, but doubt would not let her. Nor could Rowan blame her. There was a time when he'd wanted to believe, but could not. And that was with his parents urging his trust in God, not a stranger, an enemy for all intent and purpose.

"He has a plan for me, just as He has for you."

"What kind of god plans for his people to be conquered?"

The contempt was familiar too, bringing back forgotten questions he'd had himself. What kind of God allowed good men to die? What good was a God who let His faithful suffer?

"The same God who let His own Son be sacrificed that all mankind might be saved; a God of love beyond all human understanding."

This clearly extended beyond the borders of Maire's comprehension. She shook her head, rallying in disdain. "Declan was right. You are a fool, Emrys! But fool or nay, I need your cooperation for this despicable deed. I can't do it alone."

She began to pull the hem of her dress up, angrily resolved to her dark destiny, but Rowan stopped her. The warm smoothness of her skin against his fingers made that of the silk hem seem lifeless and rough in comparison. Rowan willed away the urge to assuage the entire flat of his hand, which had starved for the softness of a woman without his realizing it until now. With a silent plea of *Father!*, he stepped off destiny's ledge.

"Maire, I'll take the sheet to Brude. If the druid knows it's a farce, then I'll do what you ask. I give you my word."

"Your word seems good."

There was no doubt that Maire wanted desperately to believe Rowan's scheme would work. Her words were brittle, as though a Dane's winter had settled in her chest. Her chin was palsied, trembling like an ancient one's hand. Finally she thawed enough to roll to one side, allowing Rowan to pull the stained coverlet out from under her.

"And I sacrificed my blood. Perhaps between that and your God's sway, you might convince Brude." She wrapped her arms about herself and rubbed them, as though becoming aware for the first time of the chilly fear entrapping her. "And you certainly have some power, Rowan of Emrys. Brude said so, but even I begin to sense it now. You've a way of...of making me feel safe."

Safe. It was the last thing Maire should feel with him, considering the effect of her sudden trust and that wide-eyed look of innocence she turned his way. Rowan cleared the raw huskiness from his throat, wishing he could rid himself as easily of the rest of the desire that suddenly overtook him. Faith, it had been years since he'd felt like this toward a woman—like a man in need. But he had no real right to the feelings. She was not his wife—not in God's eyes, nor in his own—and that was that. God would see him through; God was his strength.

"We'll wait an appropriate while in the darkness." With a renewed discipline, he turned his back to temptation and reached for the light.

NINE

Oddly content to let this curious man take charge, Maire watched as Rowan blew out the flame. With the scent of smoke in the wake of the vanquished light taunting her nostrils, she lay back against her pallet and stared up at the darkness. Next to her, Rowan's mattress rustled as he settled on it to wait. In little more than a sun's cycle, she'd battled him as her enemy and now she'd handed him her trust in lieu of Brude, who never failed her.

Unlike hers, Rowan's breathing eventually fell into a natural pattern. Maire tried to coordinate hers with it, to ignore the haunting plague of doubt that played cat and mouse with her mind. What if Morlach knew of their deceit and Brude did not?

True, Rowan of Emrys was a man of courage and honor. His namesake, the tree, was almost as sacred as the oak, a symbol of power and purity. It was his sword, Brude had said, that would triumph for Gleannmara, even though the warrior himself belittled his skill. She could still see his face just before he rushed to blow out the light. It was flooded with relief—relief that he had been spared sharing a bed with her.

Yet another emotion tore into Maire's fragile defenses, that of wounded vanity. It was new and not at all welcome. What a confounding man!

Maire tossed over on her side, placing a cold back to her companion. She would oust him with her foot, if his plan weren't so suited to her purpose. Her seesawing thoughts made her head ache. Dare she listen to her heart instead of her mind? In which should she place her faith? As a woman, she had the right to do this, but did that right extend to a queen?

Time hammered away the night in concert with the ache in her head until she became aware of a quiet, rhythmic sound. Soothing as a lullaby, Rowan's snoring stirred envy and resentment in her soul. At least a fool's God lets him sleep in peace.

When slumber finally claimed her, Maire didn't know. Suddenly it was morning, and Rowan was no longer at her side. She'd missed the sun song, welcoming the day. It was a *geis* to do so, forbidden for the elected leader of the tuath. Her pulse quickened, banishing the last of sleep fog from her mind. She was approved by Brude but not yet elected. Bones, but she was sinking deeper and deeper into trouble, breaking tradition like so many eggs.

The linen coverlet was gone. Rowan evidently had kept his promise. Everyone on deck either believed by now that they were man and wife in the most physical sense or Brude was waiting for her with a terrible penance in mind.

Drawing the curtain slightly aside, Maire peeked out, almost afraid of what she might see. Those of her men who were not curled here and sprawled there on the deck, still in the grip of last night's drink, were gathered about a kettle near the cook's shed. An outburst of hearty laughter rose from the group as the cook, a swarthy slave from the east with a stump for a foot, handed a steaming bowl to Rowan. Maire's cheeks burned like forge coals as he was teased about taking seconds and needing to rebuild his strength after his wedding night.

"'Haps Brude has a potion to revive ye, Emrys," one of the Muirdach shouted.

"Aye, if Maire is half the woman she is a fighter, he's in sore shape, to be sure."

Maire didn't hear the druid's reply to the merriment, if he even dignified the crudeness with one. Letting the curtain drop, she leaned back, hardly knowing whether to be relieved or indignant. She should have been the first one up and about. Now it looked as though Rowan had bested her. It was beyond

her ken why men always considered themselves the con-
querors in the bedchamber.

Except that she wasn't about to be the one to show Brude
the proof of their union. It was best this way, she admitted, sitting back on her folded legs. Still, she dreaded facing the druid.
Her face was always like a mirror of her mind to him.

Sunlight suddenly burst into the room preceding Rowan of
Emrys. In his hand was a bowl of porridge. His smile was
toothy as a donkey's and twice as grating.

"Good morning, Maire. I thought you might like something
to eat."

"What of Brude?" she asked, more urgent matters on her
mind than stung ego.

"He's well." Rowan dropped cross-legged on his side of the
bed.

"Did he believe you or not?" Maire demanded, her patience
tested beyond its limit. The buffoon was enjoying this!

"He showed the coverlet around to the guardian spirits. The
men couldn't possibly have missed it. Then he put it in his
trunk and welcomed me into the Uí Niall."

"So he believes."

"He gave no sign that he didn't."

If Brude did not see through their charade, the chances
were good that Morlach wouldn't either. Closing her eyes,
Maire heaved a sigh of relief. The gods were still with her.

"My sentiments exactly."

Rowan's remark snapped Maire to sharp attention. "For one
who finds the idea of our marriage bed so repulsive, you certainly seem to take a lion's share of credit! And if you keep that
ridiculous grin on your face, I'll be obliged to remove it with
my fist."

His features pulled into a model of innocence, her companion shrugged. "I am only trying to be convincing, my queen. A
man fresh from a night of conjugal bliss walks on air, lifted by
the wings of love."

"Lifted by the hot air of his conceit, more likely."

"You would do well to act as if you, too, were…well….er…satisfied," he decided, obviously charmed by his word choice.

Curse him, the man was right, but Maire didn't like it or the fact that he did! Yet, two could play the game. She pushed herself to her feet and shook out the hem of the dress from where it had cinched up about her hips. It clung of its own accord to the taper of her legs, where the short leine she wore in battle ended.

"Aye, I suppose you're right." She pushed aside the curtain, flooding the enclosure with sunlight.

"What about your breakfast?"

"You eat it," she shot back, aware of the undivided attention her emergence drew. "'Tis you who needs it, sir, for my appetite has just been appeased."

With a perfectly wicked grin, she ignored the poorly disguised snorts and sniggers echoing among those close by and gathered her unfurled hair off her neck in a long feline stretch.

"Good day, gentlemen!" she greeted them. "Glorious, don't you think?"

Upon unwinding a leather thong from her wrist, she tied her hair neatly at the nape of her neck. That done, she helped her face to a refreshing splash of water from a bucket hung on the sides of the ship for the purpose of bathing. A deep breath of salt air was equally renewing, ridding her body of sleep's stale remnant. With the sun at her back, Maire studied the horizon ahead, where the morning mist still clung to the sea green water.

Behind her, Rowan exited the makeshift bedchamber. "Nothing like a satisfied woman," he remarked, slapping her backside with the palm of his hand in passing.

Maire nearly choked on the affront. Spinning around, she returned the gesture, striking his hard buttocks with such force that it stung her hand. Having earned Rowan's abrupt attention, she lifted her chin in defiance.

"I always give as good as I get! You ought to know that well by now, Emrys."

"Rowan, love." He cupped her chin. "Faith, I've never heard my name whispered with such longing as from these lips."

Before Maire could react, he leaned down and sealed in her rush of fury with a kiss. It wasn't as hard as her first one had been, but it gave no less quarter. It was as though he were drinking her dry of strength and thought. No man had ever dared as much. None! When he let her go, she was grateful for the rail at her back. With a forced nonchalance, she rested her arms against it. Her lips curled, a convincing facade of mild amusement.

"You learn quickly for a Welshman, Rowan."

A loud whistle rose above the flutter of laughter the confrontation evoked in the ranks. Maire had held her own, but had no idea what to expect next from this bulliken. His tongue was as prickly and troublesome as that of the legendary Brichriu, who had turned a kingdom upon itself for the sake of pure entertainment.

A cry from the loft came to Maire's rescue. "Land ho!"

She turned toward the horizon where invisible fingers had pulled back the drape of mist. There, emerging from the sea, was the sun-kissed shore of Wicklow. The sparkling strip of sand was studded with moss-covered rock and flanked by the rise of time-gentled mountains and thick, game-rich forests. The most accomplished poet had no words that could do justice to the magnificent hues of green, gray, and blue.

Home! Maire's heart swelled with the sight, her sparring with Rowan forgotten. She longed to set foot on the land won by her mother, sword land taken from masters of another era when bronze gave way to iron. As her foster parents Erc and Maida had raised her upon Maeve's death, so this land had nurtured her and her people. Now that she was queen, Maire would be one with it, her life dedicated to its welfare, her love to its people. The gods had chosen her as its steward and ruler.

She mustn't let Morlach defile the earth and her people with his dark greed. As the gods had led her to victory, so they would continue to do so. Maire had left Gleannmara a girl in warrior's garb. She returned a queen with a husband, who, despite his annoying side, was an upright man with the skilled sword destined to protect their tuath—even from the evil intentions of the druid lord.

"Wait till you see Gleannmara," she told Rowan. Already her spirit was as renewed by the tuath's nearness as its meadows were by spring green. "It will be satisfied with nothing less than your soul, Rowan of Emrys, and that you'll willingly give once under its spell." She clasped his hand, capable yet gentle as it was strong.

"Feel her heartbeat," she said, pressing his palm in place that he might know the excitement beating from her heart, Gleannmara's heart. "Nine long years away from her have not weakened it. Together, we'll protect her and make her happy."

The ship plied toward the shore as though drawn by a magnet. The men gathered at the rail, lifting a victorious song to the sky until the vessel dared not go closer. There was neither bulkhead nor enough water to tie her up if there were. Anchors splashed at the bow and stern to stabilize her, while the crew furled the leather sails, which had served them so well. The pent up excitement broke with the scurry to put a boat over the side.

Even as Maire's men wrestled with the lines, there was a storm of activity taking place on the shore. Eager crews pushed off boats that would transport the plunder to dry land. Maire remained glued to the land side of the ship, wanting to miss nothing. She, Rowan, and her captains would be the first to disembark. And Brude, of course.

Maire turned to search the deck for the druid. Her exhilaration upon seeing her homeland had momentarily erased all thought of him. She found him sitting by the altar fire, where the ashes of the sacred fire that had blessed their return voyage still smoked. The stern rail at his back and his head bowed, he looked as though he slept through the chaos. Had he kept the flames going all through the night?

She loped across the deck, dodging men about their own purpose and stopped before the elderly man. There was a pile of bones spread on the deck, the remains of the pig the cook had roasted the day before for the wedding feast.

"Brude, we're home." She placed a gentle hand on his rounded shoulder.

Instead of answering, the druid held up his hand, as though to quiet her. Through half-lidded eyes, he stared at the bones, searching for an augury.

"Won't you sing our song of victory?"

Brude's fist came down amid the pile so suddenly that Maire jumped back. Weakness settled in her stomach as the druid's angry gaze lifted to her face. He knew she'd deceived him! The sickening thought barely registered before he spoke.

"The battle isn't over, my queen. Morlach still holds Gleannmara. You must be elected by the people."

Maire went cold at the grim implication in Brude's voice. "What did you see?"

Brude gathered up the bones and, with her help, rose to his feet. The stiffness of his limbs made Maire wince in empathy, but the man made no verbal complaint. He tossed the bones on the dying fire and watched as the moisture in them hissed and crackled.

"Was it bad?" Whatever Brude saw unleashed fingers of alarm along her spine.

"There was nothing." The druid wiped his hands on his robe in frustration. "Nothing! You have given Gleannmara all she would ask of you, and I have failed you."

"Perhaps there's nothing to see." Maire had never seen Brude so distraught.

"Oh, it's there, masked by darkness, but there, nonetheless."

"Morlach?"

"Who else?"

"Perhaps the Welshman."

Maire started at the unexpected suggestion coming from behind her. She turned to see her youngest foster brother.

"Declan! You're looking well for all of yesterday's misfortune. You gave us quite a scare."

It was true. The Scot's bronzed color had come back to him, but with it, his ill humor. Worse, it was infectious.

"How can you accuse any evil of the man who saved your life?"

"I never asked him to!"

"At least pretend it was worth his trouble!"

Declan closed a warning hand about her arm. "You've made a grave mistake. He isn't as he seems, Maire. I feel it in my bones. Beware that husband of yours."

"That I will do," she assured him. Her foster brother was given to melodrama, but this was neither the time nor place. She lifted one of the long braids the warrior wore to keep the hair from his face and flipped it over his shoulder in an effort to diffuse the tension. "Just as I've kept you out of trouble all these years...or tried, at least."

The Scot suddenly pulled her closer and pressed his lips against her forehead. "I'll be here for ye, *anmchara*. Never doubt it."

"Aye, soul friend," Maire replied lightly. So it had always been—she, Declan, and Eochan together. Raised together. Trained together. One was her right arm, the other her left. "The three of us make a good lot, tho' 'tis hard to say for what."

The intimacy of their pledge was no more sealed by the clasping of arms when Maire found herself being lifted into the air with a mighty roar. She seized the tousled head of her friendly assailant to keep from falling backward, laughing.

"Eochan, you've scared me out of a year's growth!"

"Time to stake your claim as queen," the burly Scot told her. "And I'm bound to present ye, sure as I'm livin'."

"She must take Emrys ashore."

"But he's needed to get them horses to land, Brude," Eochan objected.

"'Twould be a shame for them to drown in our hands," Declan chimed in. "Let the Scotti carry their queen and the hostage the plunder."

To Maire's astonishment, the druid pondered the suggestion for a moment. It wasn't like Brude to back away from one of his decisions.

"Perhaps it would be best to keep Rowan a secret until he's needed." She slid off Eochan's shoulder.

A strange glimmer in his gray gaze, Brude looked over to where Rowan soothed the snow-white horses. "I've been feeding them my special hay, but they are high-strung animals. The man has a gift."

"So do you." Maire placed an affectionate hand on the druid's shoulder. Few dared to touch Brude, but he'd carried her as a child on his shoulder as Eochan had just done. She never thought twice about the privilege. "I think the sea air is unkind to the bones of a landsman such as yourself, Brude. No doubt once you're back in your lodge, the augury will come back, painting pictures of the future in your mind as it always has."

Maire saw that Brude was lowered into the boat first by means of a leather sling before she and the others joined them. Her men took to the oars with eager hands, eyes fixed on the beach ahead. It wasn't likely their families awaited them, but the shore clans would give them royal welcome. Tomorrow, wagons would be hired to transport the booty to Gleannmara.

"Look, comin' down to the shore," a MacCormac shouted.

Maire looked in the direction her captain pointed, where a retinue made its way to the beach through the cluster of lodges at the crest of the rise. Fluttering from tall poles were the royal blue and gold of Gleannmara—and the red and black colors of Rathcoe, Morlach's domain.

"Brude?"

"Aye, like a painted picture," the druid answered her. "I thought 'twas Morlach's ink muddying my sight, just as he turned the wind to bring you more quickly to his clutches."

His words pebbled her arms with gooseflesh. A man with common weapons, she could fight. But one who wielded spirits...

"The confrontation comes sooner than I anticipated."

"I'll stand with you, Maire," Declan vowed from the seat across from her.

"And I!" said Eochan.

"And I!"

"And I!"

The chorus was unanimous. Gleannmara's men were not about to hand her over to the wizard of Rathcoe without a fight. Deeply touched, Maire steeled the glaze in her eyes and stood up in the boat, her feet braced to ride its rocky course to the sea-soaked sands.

"Gleannmara!" she shouted, raising her arm over her head.

"Gleannmara!" the men chimed with her.

"Queen Maire!" Declan shouted, starting a chant in sync with the beat of the oars in the foamy surf.

"Queen Maire...Queen Maire...Queen Maire..."

A wave caught the vessel. Eochan steadied Maire as they were swept toward the beach. The men vaulted out in the shallow water and used the momentum to push the craft well onto the sand. Eochan lifted Maire free and handed her over to her captains, who carried her on their shoulders out of the reach of the lapping surf to where the colorful retinue awaited.

Morlach was not among them. At the lead was his apprentice, Cromthal. Though his years were but half those of his master, Cromthal's black hair was shot with gray and his skin drawn like the bark of a tree on his gawky frame. Maire thought he resembled the black heron on Morlach's crest.

As the junior druid stepped down from his wicker chariot,

the men quieted. Head held high, Maire moved to the fore of her ready captains, Eochan and Declan flanking her on either side.

"I greet you a free man, Cromthal."

"And you a free woman, Queen of Gleannmara. I take it from the revel that you have indeed proved yourself worthy."

"Before many witnesses," Brude assured him, stepping up beside her.

Cromthal spared his elder no more than a glance. "Though your departure was a surprise to my master, your victorious return is not. Morlach awaits you at Gleannmara. Guests from all five provinces are gathered there to witness your homecoming and your marriage, including Diarhmott's own Finnaid, who has come to perform the ceremony. The master has been preparing for your birthday for many cycles of the moon."

"Then Morlach has overestimated himself," Maire said, glad that the panic running riot inside her was not betrayed by her strong voice. One of Diarhmott's own druids. By all the tides, they were done for! Surely he'd see through Rowan's charade. "I welcome the victory celebration, but there will be no marriage between us. You see, Cromthal, I've not only brought home prizes of great worth, but a husband as well."

Had thunder struck the apprentice, he couldn't have looked more staggered. Maire's tenuous advantage, however, was short lived, for Cromthal recouped his authoritative demeanor in a breath. His words fairly boiled over with incredulity. "What manner of trickery is this?"

"'Tis no trickery," Brude assured him. "I blessed the union myself and have the sacrificial bridal blanket in my trunk, bearing the proof of the consummation. We've more than good number of witnesses who will testify to this truth for the high king, should Diarhmott require it."

"Then show the man to me!" Cromthal grew white with anger, his eyes burning demon black. "Show him!" he demanded, the muscles of his neck taut as a bowstring.

"Here!"

Startled, Maire turned to see Rowan of Emrys emerging from the sand-lapping sea on the white stallion. The animal snorted, blowing saltwater and foam from its nostrils, and pranced up to them as though delighted to be on solid ground again.

Man and beast, they were a sight to behold. Shahar's back was as high as the head of the druid's chariot horse and his breadth half again wider. Rowan sat high on the magnificent steed, looking every inch a warrior king. His wet skin glistened in the sun; at his lean waist was his sword, its jeweled sheath flashing with fire of its own.

As though on cue, the stallion reared, pawing at air, its neck arched in perfection. The man on its back, no less perfect a specimen in his own right, maintained his seat with no more than his knees and one hand buried in Shahar's corn-silk mane. Everyone, Maire included, stood rooted to the earth as he introduced himself.

"I am Rowan ap Emrys, hostage, protector, and *husband* to the courageous and beautiful Queen Maire. What is the urgency of your business with Gleannmara's new lord, druid?"

TEN

Cromthal's skin blanched whiter than death's own banshee. He'd summoned his twelve years of training and focused the evil eye on Rowan ap Emrys, yet the impudent usurper sat proud upon the back of his horse and returned the stare, undaunted. Not even the legendary Balor, whose look was certain death, would phase this one. Instead of dropping dead, the new husband of Gleannmara's queen simply treated the whole thing as though it were a contest of wills.

Then the sun caught an amulet about the warrior's neck, casting a light into Cromthal's eye so that he had no choice but to look away or be blinded.

Was the man's power from the amulet or from the god it represented? Doubt and confusion swirled, unleashed, in Cromthal's mind. Perhaps the stranger paled because he had to look up at his intended victim. His chest ached, as though a cold stone were lodged there, trying to beat as a heart.

"I fear no man or god, druid, save the one God," the dark-haired stranger declared, his magnificent white steed pawing at the damp sand. "Tell Morlach that he and his kind are not welcome at Gleannmara from this day hence."

The queen's intake of breath was as sharp as Cromthal's at the insult. The druid's skin crawled at the thought of passing such a message to his master.

"Then banish Brude as well." It was a lame reply. The curl of Brude's lip only added to Cromthal's shame for not being capable of conjuring up a spell to knock the arrogant Emrys from the back of his horse. The old bard made him feel as foolish as the desperate remark had.

"Gleannmara's druid has a true heart that searches for the light, for truth, not the darkness spawned by a black lust for greed and power."

"You have no idea with whom you deal, Emrys. Do not be surprised when your skin blisters with sores and withers away from the bone until your body begs to give up its breath."

Cromthal dared not try his hand at the satire. He couldn't collect his thoughts enough, but was sure this was the least Morlach would do to this upstart.

The satire was not entirely wasted. Discomfiture washed over the crowd like the waters on the beach, on all save Emrys and the mysteriously smiling Brude. Turning from Gleannmara's bard, Cromthal felt the heat of the warrior's steel blue gaze boring into his back. He had to make himself walk, rather than run, to his waiting chariot.

From out of nowhere, he stumbled over a rock he'd have sworn had not been there upon his approach. The ripple of laughter at the spectacle he made sprawling to his knees destroyed the last shred of power the druid had over the audience. The sunlight was cool on the black wool of his robe compared to the heat of his humiliation. As he climbed into the waiting chariot, the druid was vexed by sweat and chill at the same time. He could not make his escape fast enough from the obvious power of Emrys's god.

Cromthal slowed his shaggy steed, pulling him closer and closer to Rathcoe and Morlach's assured rage. Perhaps this is what the fish felt when it leapt from the searing scorch of the pan into fire itself.

The tuath of Rothcoe was ruled from a *crannóg*. Surrounded by water, there was only one way to the man-made island, and that was only when the drawbridge was down as it was now. The crisp click of the pony's hooves upon the strong planks of oak was as rapid as the heartbeat now thundering in Cromthal's chest.

Over the gate, colorful banners waved, raised to welcome Morlach's bride. They were the only sign of brightness in the damp fortress. The master's best attempt to make the stone tower inside the stockade of stout logs inviting failed as miserably as Cromthal failed in bringing home Morlach's betrothed.

Inside the lake fortress, swine and chickens scurried out of the chariot's way. The snorting pony was anxious to return to its stall where fodder awaited. Cromthal descended with as much dignity as was entitled to Morlach's chief apprentice and walked toward the arched entrance to the stone keep, where the druid warrior himself awaited.

The air inside was rank with a combination of smoke, mold, and animal scents; it was more abusive to the nostrils than Cromthal had noticed in the past. It was like breathing the decay of death. The apprentice climbed the steep winding steps of the keep to the second floor where Morlach entertained his guests. That they were few was indicative of his popularity among the nobility. The *aire* respected him—if fear could be called respect—but did not like him.

Even as he entered the hall, where most of the crannóg's activity took place, Cromthal saw Morlach rise from the gaming table he shared with Finnaid of Tara. Likewise, the apprentice's hair rose with anticipation. Like the figures on the chessboard, the master manipulated people. This time, however, his queen had eluded him. The apprentice evaded the looks of both his master and Tara's druid.

"So she comes?"

Morlach was always intimidating, measuring a good half a head above the average man. The volumes of his fine linen robe made him appear even larger across the shoulders, where a woven yoke of golden thread adorned the garment. It swirled in homage about his ankles as he stepped down from the dais expectantly.

"I didn't hear the horn heralding her approach," he drawled, voice laden with suspicion.

"The trumpeters did not see her, master."

It never occurred to Cromthal to lie. It would do no good. He swallowed, his palate was so dry his tongue stuck to it. Morlach surely knew. He merely intended to play a game, like the cat with a cornered mouse.

"She is returned safely, is she not?"

"Aye, Maire has returned, and her men cheer of her valor and the success of her raid."

Morlach's dark thatched brow knit, his gaze boring down on the apprentice. "And…"

The torque at Cromthal's neck grew tight, as if to squeeze the answer from him.

"She has returned with a husband, master."

Better to die quickly than to be prodded to death with questions to which Morlach already knew the answers.

"Who is this man?"

Cromthal's fingers confirmed the torque had not shrunk as it felt, but they held no sway over Morlach's will.

"Emrys…Rowan ap Emrys…a Welsh lord and hostage."

Morlach inhaled, his chest swelling with the heat of the rage singeing his face.

"And you have something of his for me?"

Cromthal had nothing belonging to the lord on the prancing stallion. Nothing Morlach could use to do him harm. He'd dared not go near the horse's hooves for fear its master would run him down. He shook his head, his tongue paralyzed with icy fear.

The druid refused to let Cromthal tear away from his gaze. The apprentice stood as though chained to the spot. Not even when Morlach slung his fist toward him, did Cromthal move. He saw the carved stone chess piece coming at his face but was helpless to protect himself from its painful slam against his forehead. He heard the crack of bone amid the red riot of pain exploding in his consciousness. Then darkness as black as his master's mood smothered even that out.

—⚭—

Gleannmara.

Maire looked up at the run-down hill fort built by her parents in disbelief. Nine years she'd been away and it had come to this? Parts of the earthen works were washed away, allowing the coming and going of livestock, at least to the outer *fosse*. The ditch itself was overgrown with all manner of thorn and brush. One of the entrance gates lay against the fence surrounding the inner court, while its mate hung ineffectively on one hinge.

This couldn't possibly be the prosperous tuath she'd left nine years ago. Gleannmara's walls and buildings had glistened stately white, topped with golden thatch. Its earthen works were green, closely trimmed by fat cattle and shot gray with stone here and there. The livestock wandering aimless about the settlement now were gaunt and wiry, despite the green of Gleannmara's pasturelands. And where were the neatly tilled fields surrounding the keep? Granted, her people were more herdsmen than farmers, but there had been a few well-tended tracts of land, enough to supply the people of the hill fort and its surrounds sufficient corn throughout the winter months.

"This is your doing, Emrys. The evil eye is upon Gleannmara, while you go untouched."

Maire glared at the man who'd stood up to the druid and insulted his master.

"This is not my doing nor the work of an evil eye." Rowan studied the lay of the land and its habitats with an unfathomable expression.

"Brude," Maire called the druid, as if to confirm what her own eyes could not—would not—see. A druid could see past illusion. "Where are my people? What has happened here?"

Maire remembered Gleannmara's glory—the song and laughter, the abundance of field and forest to feed the many friends who frequented its tables, the remarkable precision with which the seasons came and went, each cherished in its own way. What lay before her now looked to be the result of nine years of winter, and this already spring.

"What do you see, child?"

"Abandonment."

"And…"

Maire glanced at the druid. Disappointment and disillusionment stung her eyes, but she refused to give them sway. Chin jutting, shoulders squared, she turned back to examine the disheartening landscape. Here and there a wisp of smoke curled gray against the blue of the sky. She sniffed the air where its familiar scent wafted on the breeze. Her assumption was too hasty.

"No, not abandonment."

She chewed her thumb, as though she were the legendary Finn, seeking wisdom. But Maire had not touched the Salmon of Knowledge as the Finian soldier had done more than a century before. If this were some horrible spell, however, perhaps this would break it, and she would see her home as it really was, proud and gleaming from its hilltop.

"My people are hiding," she said at last, not the least certain. She was neither Finn nor a druid, so the result was just the hapless measure of a disconcerted young woman, chewing at her thumbnail.

"What manner of cowards are you?" Declan shouted behind her. Her foster brother began to beat on his shield. "Queen Maire! Queen Maire!"

One by one, two by two, more and more of her people were delivered from their stunned silence by Declan's prompting until the hills roared her name. Maire hardly felt worthy. She was grateful for the spirited mare she rode alongside a silent Emrys, because had she been afoot, her legs might have betrayed her. She'd heard how Morlach had bled her people, but this was worse than she thought even *he* could do.

From behind, the warriors who'd mustered from the

fortress before the voyage rushed forward, carrying the blue and gold colors of Gleannmara. "Make way for Queen Maire! The scion of Maeve and Rhian rules Gleannmara again!" Unable to hold back from seeking out their loved ones, some of her men broke away to search the hedgerows and forest edge for sign of them.

"By the tides, Maire, 'tis worse than we thought." Eochan stepped up to her side. "No wonder Morlach sought to lure you to Rathcoe for the wedding."

"Morlach!" Maire spat the name out like risen bile, even as the trees and brush began to give up those hiding among them. Women and children mostly surged forward to meet the returning warriors. The only men who remained behind were those unable to fight due to age or infirmity. "By my mother's gods, Brude, he must pay for this."

Kneeing the mare forward, Maire sped toward the boisterous reunion of her clan. Hers. Not Eochan's nor Declan's but the blood of her blood. Would she know them after nine years, these cousins and cousin's cousins?

Raising her spear over her head, Maire whooped in triumph. They would know her. She would be the queen who restored Gleannmara to its former status. The booty of the raid would rebuild her home, making it a dwelling place fit for the queen the victory had made her.

"Look well, Rowan ap Emrys. 'Tis the last time your eyes will see this keep in such a sorry state."

Although he didn't believe in such things, Rowan could swear Maire was a shape-shifter. On the ship, her transformation from quarrelsome vixen to queen of passion for her tuatha robbed Rowan of his earlier mischief. When Maire looked up at him as she was now, he wanted nothing more than to please rather than tease her. Her excitement was infectious, jarring as the impact of her sword against his had been so many days ago. The effect flowed through his fingers to the very core of his senses.

She'd almost made him believe *she* was Gleannmara, shape-shifted into the comely form of a woman. Well he could accept that Gleannmara's spirit coursed through her veins like the running waters of its hills and vales. It was then that he knew for certain that it was the voice of this warrior queen that called him home rather than that of Glasdam, the trusted servant of his blood family whom Rowan thought he'd seen in the visions.

"The last time," Maire vowed again, shaking him from his reverie with the fervor of her emotion.

"God willing," he conceded, fighting a war of his own as he looked around the hills he'd roamed as a boy.

Little could the young woman know how much better it looked to him than the last time he'd seen it. There'd been no fosse or hill fort. Apparently, when Maire's parents captured the best land on Gleannmara for themselves, they'd erected the fortified enclosure. When Clan Cairthan had occupied it, the cattle ran as free as those who herded it. In truth, then, his home was more of an encampment, a gathering of friendly fires with makeshift huts, which could quickly be knocked down and moved to the next site where greener pastures awaited.

The Niall were clearly the stronger or at least more progressive of the two tribes. So where was his family? Driven into the hills to exist as they might? Or worse yet, was the Cairthan slaughtered defending their land? It had to be one or the other, for he saw no sign of his own.

He wasn't prepared for the mixed feelings that clashed within as he kept his stallion at a respectable distance behind Maire to watch her reception. One part of him seethed to think of his family members driven off their land; another saw his brother's fate at least as justice for what he'd done to Rowan.

But it wasn't up to Rowan to judge, he reminded himself sternly. He had not come home to gloat or to exact revenge. His, he prayed, was a higher purpose; although exactly what it was and how it was to be accomplished had yet to be revealed to him.

Desperately, he floundered in a storm-tossed sea of emotion, reaching for the Word. That was his mission, his reason for being here, he told himself sternly. His was not to champion Emrys, the Niall, or the Cairthan—not even Maire. His was to champion God's Word, the Way, for where it lived, so lived true happiness.

Safe at the church and seminary at Emrys, he'd studied and lived the Word without significant price. Now he was in another country, in a contrary role as hostage, husband, king, and man. The cost rose significantly with each passing moment he spent with the unpredictable pagan queen and the people who may have eradicated his own clan.

Lord, I cannot meet this challenge as servant and champion to any but You.

"It was the thievin' Cairthan!"

Declan's heated exclamation snatched Rowan from his earnest prayer to where the enraged Scot raced toward Maire with the news. Relief calmed the roaring sea of resentment and dismay in Rowan's mind. The Cairthan lived! God answered his prayer before he'd uttered it. Better his people were cattle thieves than dead.

"They waited until our men mustered away on the ship and then raided," Declan informed the group clustering about him.

"Cowards all, takin' a herd from the likes of women and children!" Eochan chimed in with his brother.

"Say the word, Maire, and we're after them."

Declan stepped up to Maire's horse, looking up expectantly. His youthful face was flushed at the prospect of another battle. He cut his teeth on stories of valor. He'd been born and trained to fight.

How well Rowan remembered that primal rush of excitement, before he came to equate the spilling of blood with the destruction of one of God's own children. Before, his enemies were nameless, soulless animals, and slaughtered as easily as a sacrificial offering. His gaze was drawn to Maire as she inadvertently moistened her lips to reply.

"Best we secure what we have before we go after that which we've lost."

Satisfaction tugged at the corner of his mouth. Again he thanked God—for one so young and naive, the queen had a good head on her shoulders. He credited Brude's influence, for it was obvious the druid had overseen Maire's education, while her foster father saw to her combat training.

Yet it was more than her tutelage Rowan admired. It was her use of what she'd learned. Few sons of kings, for all their counsel, would have held their disappointment and resulting rage in check as the warrior queen had just done. Its sting had struck its mark, but she hadn't flinched. Its scarlet colored her cheek, but she'd kept a level head, the head of a leader…such a beautiful one.

Rowan drew himself from the spell the warrior queen guilelessly cast before he lost his own wit. Beauty and brains were a dangerous combination in the hands of a woman—especially one so undeniably skilled with a sword as sharp as her wit.

ELEVEN

That the hall and chief's house stood unblemished by Morlach's greed was a credit to the craftsmen who built them. At least Maire could hold her head up when Emrys strode into the hall, which was some thirty meters in diameter, and took a seat opposite the door, beside her on the royal bench. Made of polished wood and intricately carved, it was as elegant, if not as luxurious, as the couch in his parents' home. Maire's hostage had little to say since their arrival, not that he'd not said enough for a score of men to Cromthal. 'Twas small wonder Gleannmara stood at all, for Morlach would not tolerate her refusal in good grace.

While this wasn't the grand homecoming she'd expected, her clansmen had pulled together a feast fit for a king. The Cairthan hadn't taken the remnants of the summer fare from last year, and a whole beef had been boiled in honor of Maire's coronation, after Brude made a ceremony of sacrificing it and sprinkling its blood in the sacred grove. Her new shoes, made of the softest leather for the official inauguration to come, felt strange to her feet, as strange as sitting on Gleannmara's royal seat. The shoes were a mite small and always would be. Rather than break them in to the shape of her foot, she would wear them just twice—now for the tribal druid's acknowledgment and later for the royal inauguration by the high king's man. Later the slippers would be sewn together and placed among Gleannmara's trophies. Still, it was all so strange.

Aye, she'd been here before in whimsy or a dream, but this time it was real. She was queen, responsible for her people's welfare and hardly off to a good beginning. Her muster of the rath's men had left it defenseless against its enemies. True, they'd come along readily and the damage could be repaired, but it bothered her as much as the threat posed by Morlach. They celebrated their new queen with such enthusiasm that Maire was hard put to believe she could live up to it.

Had Maeve smiled as Maire did now, while anxiety wreaked havoc behind her image of pleasure?

The weight of her new authority rested heavily on Maire's mind as she watched her men pass about horns of plundered mead and wine with one hand, while stuffing their mouths with the fresh-baked breads scattered on each table. Those women who weren't serving were gathered in the grianán. In a similar perch across from the sun loft, Brude's apprentices plied their harps and voices with tales of valor and love long past.

Gleannmara's bard secluded himself in the conical stone dwelling, which had been his home, when the hall and chief's residence belonged to Maeve and Rhian. After their deaths, according to his pledge, Brude accompanied young Maire to her foster home to see that she was prepared to become queen when she came of age. Now he composed a song to glorify the raid and her return as queen. It would be the crowning event of the return.

"You are still troubled by the druid."

Maire cast an annoyed look at her new husband, yet another worry to be reckoned with. "And you'd do well to do the same, if your brain was larger than a mouse's teat."

Rowan held out his arms, sturdy, well-muscled, bronzed by the sun—they were arms made for protection. "I see no sores nor withering flesh."

It was a shame such limbs were attached to a half-wit. Maire glanced away to where Declan sat, a pretty wench on each knee. One was her cousin, Lianna, a feminine creature with a mass of golden brown curls falling over her shoulders. The other girl was probably a distant relative, one Maire did not recognize. Both laughed as the warrior attempted to empty his horn by embracing the two of them at the same time. The wine spilled down his chin and splashed onto their dresses, evoking giggles and laughter among all.

"The night isn't over, Emrys."

Her gaze returned to the strong bare arms, now folded across a broad chest, swathed in the coarse cloth of a priest. What in the name of her mother's gods was wrong with her? While she certainly wanted no part of Declan's folly, Maire found herself wondering what it would be like to know the security of the Welshman's embrace. Security...she hadn't known such a feeling since she was a child upon Rhian's knee, right there on that very bench. Nothing could harm her then. Her only worry was that she'd be sent to bed before the revelry was over.

Today, when he'd ridden Shahar to shore, emerging from the sea like a god, Maire had never known such relief. The sheer power and majesty of his visage suggested that nothing born of this world or any other could daunt him. It only took the Welshman a few blustering words of bravado backed by his faith in that strange god of his to end her hope. If only *she* could be so sure of her beliefs.

Maire shook her head, refusing the loaf of bread he offered her. With a crook of a smile, he shrugged and broke it in half.

"Leave the Cairthan to me."

To her astonishment, Emrys was in earnest. The tilt of his lips dropped as he awaited her reply.

"Do I look as if my mother's crown has banished the last of my wits?"

Instead of taking offense, he leaned toward her. "Nay, Maire, you've all the wits a queen merits, but think a moment...the last thing you need is another enemy."

Her ear grew warm at the low rumble of his whisper against it.

"No thanks to you."

"Your enmity with Morlach was made the moment you

decided against marrying him. I'll not be blamed for that."

"Hah, no! And you just made him all the madder."

"Did I? Do you really think he'd kill you any more for my words than for your refusal?"

Maire snatched up the discarded half of the loaf, pulled off a pinch, and popped it into her mouth. With each chew, the truth became increasingly clear: She was taking out her anger, her fear, on Rowan.

"And what will you do with the Cairthan? March up to their hills and challenge their champion for the return of our livestock?"

"If necessary. Better for you to show good judgment and a cool head. As you once said, you could use all the swords you can muster to go against Morlach."

"Ally with that ragged lot of dung spreaders?" Maire laughed, totally without humor. "You're more fey than I thought. Maeve took their land, leastwise, the best of it. I sit on what they consider to be their throne. I'd never be able to turn my back on a one of them."

"Keep them to your side, Maire, not to your back."

"Aye, in chains, mayhap."

"Shoulder to shoulder, sword in hand, should it come to that with Morlach. I suspect it will."

"And how will you bring this about? You, a Welshman, who has never set foot on Scotti soil."

Something kindled in Rowan's gaze, something that smacked of self-assurance, and she had the oddest sense...as though he knew something she did not. He leaned back on the bench with a look that suggested he'd won their debate.

"The race is not to the swift nor the battle to the strong."

Maire frowned. "What is that supposed to mean?"

"Ecclesiastes."

"Who?"

"It doesn't matter. What matters is that even the greatest of man- or womankind can't always win solely on strength or speed."

"But with wit?" Maire ventured. Emrys might fight like a soldier, but he talked like a priest, with words that made little sense, more often than not.

"Wit enough to recognize there are times when we need help…and faith in God to supply it."

"I have faith in the strength and speed of the good warriors gathered here. And in my wit and Brude's council."

"Then why are you so troubled?"

"Because I've a wart the size of a full grown man sitting at my side, blatherin' on, witless as a pig in a mud wallow." Maire liked it better when the man was silent. He saw too much, this one, as though he could read her thoughts like letters in a book.

"I will ask God to show me the way to make friends of worthy opponents."

"Then do it somewhere else. I've no yearnin' to hear about god, nor any more of this nonesuch."

Maire gave an involuntary shudder at the thought of speaking one on one with this god. Still, if a god actually gave advice directly to the man…

"And let me know what this god has to say about the Cairthan. Like as not, if he's made their acquaintance, he'd see us run them clear to Connaught."

Emrys smiled, seemingly satisfied. And though Maire was bemused at what put the crook in his lips, at least he was quiet.

A commotion at the door opposite them drew her attention from the Welshman to where Brude entered followed by his servant Glas. Maire's pulse quickened as the druid acknowledged her with a bow of his half-shaven head. The gathered crowd parted like a sea to allow the white-robed Brude through, their revelry quieted in reverence to his presence. The song of triumph was done. Their victory would be commemorated to lyric and passed down from generation to generation until children whispered their names as though they were legend.

Brude took the seat of honor next to Maire, where he'd sat years before and sung to the glory of Maeve, Rhian, and their predecessors. He knew Maire's genealogy back to their Milesian forefathers. Her claim was blood royal, her role as queen her birthright.

Beside Maire, Rowan ap Emrys sat suddenly upright, but the new queen paid him little attention. She watched Glas hand over Macha, the druid's harp.

Suddenly Rowan was on his feet. With an oath, he took two strides toward the thin, bent Glas and turned the man toward him to study his face.

"It is you, Glasdam!"

The servant stared up at the warrior with wide, wary eyes.

Rowan shook him gently. "Do you not know me, friend?"

Glas raised a gnarled hand to his mouth, shaking his head slowly.

"He's a half-wit," Maire informed her husband. "Brude found him badly beaten, his tongue cut out and near death."

Brude nodded slowly. "I nursed my good friend back to health, such as was possible. He's been with me ever since." Brow arched, the druid looked from Glas to Rowan curiously. "You believe you know him?"

The Welshman hesitated. "I thought I did. Perhaps I was mistaken."

Brude turned to the servant. "Do you know this man, Glas?"

The man answered in a series of frantic gestures.

"We developed a simple method of communicating with hand signals," the druid explained. "He says he isn't certain, but that you were not the man who beat him and left him for dead. As Queen Maire's new husband, he is honored to know you. The men who did this to him were Cairthan."

"Is this true?"

Rowan's bellow gave Maire a start. Where insult failed, an injustice to an old man fired her husband's gaze hot as a smith's bellows. Anger knotted his facial muscles and flared at his nostrils. Indeed, she'd married a curious man, as curious as his god. Would she even know him long enough to understand him?

Not that she needed to, she reminded herself as Brude's man confirmed the answer with a nod. She was queen. It was her will and whim that counted. And in this case, she was right.

"And you'd seek an alliance with men who would do this to a helpless old man?"

The fire of her companion's gaze shifted to her. Whatever reply he had was trapped behind the steel of his clenched jaw. Instead of answering he sat back on the bench in brooding silence.

"And now, my queen," Brude spoke up. "As you have pleased the gods and honored your clan in battle and wisdom, it is only fitting that your song be sung for its first time on the night of your inauguration."

The druid took up a horned cup from one of the serving wenches and raised it.

"May he who lives in the sun and created both heaven and earth bless you with heirs as worthy of Maeve's bench as yourself."

The tension precipitated by Brude's arrival and increased by the Welshman's outburst gave way to cheers and huzzahs all around. Maire's name echoed from the high-pitched ceiling, where the smoke of two hearth fires curled in confusion before seeking escape through the vent hole left by the thatchers. Gradually the cheering gave way to demand for the song that would honor their new queen.

The clear ring of Macha's strings cut it off clean as a sharp blade did a tender vine. Anticipation waited on each face as Brude began to pluck a noble tune from the harp with fingers skilled from years of experience. Like magic, the music drew men and women alike to the edge of their seats, entranced, anxious to hear the words that would accompany it. Then came the words.

First, Maire's genealogy and the story of Maeve and Rhian flowed from the druid's lips, setting the stage for Maire's story. Maire heard of her birth and the grand celebration as her parents presented a squalling redhaired babe, already able to scream like a banshee, to their clansmen. Declan and Eochan sat taller when honor was given to Drumkilly and the foster family who raised the queen to fulfill her destiny. At the mention of each clan that accompanied her on her first foray across the sea, the so-named members cheered their recognition.

It was all there, the taking of the plunder from the monastery, as well as the battle of champions between the new queen and the man now at her side. Brude praised her wisdom in avoiding bloodshed by taking on the risk alone against the skilled blade of Rowan ap Emrys. Surely the mating of two such warriors would produce kings and queens to protect and carry Gleannmara's glory into eternity.

He heralded her courage in standing up to the man who had bled her people dry and put into lyric the noble vision of Rowan ap Emrys emerging from the sea on his white warhorse to send the apprentice of evil scampering back to his master with Gleannmara's rejection.

It was such a grand account, Maire hardly recognized the bold, fearless, decisive leader described in the poem. Memories of her uncertainty and anxiety told a different account, but they would have no place in Brude's history. Again, Maire wondered if her mother had such memories at odds with accounts of her deeds and her reign.

"And so it was that fair Gleannmara came to be ruled by Maire and Rowan, with the courage and skill of the Finians, the wisdom of the Sacred Salmon of the Boyne, and the justice of the Brehons. May the light of their love and deeds shine forever cherished in the minds of generations to come."

The massive framework of the hall literally shook with the applause of voice, weapon, hands, and feet when Brude strummed a final chord across Macha's strings. Yet the words thundering in Maire's mind were not as easily accepted. Produce kings and queens…light of their love…

Had her mother loved Rhian at first? Was Maire the product of love or of breeding? She lifted her cup of mead high in acknowledgment of her peoples' homage and smiled, her face a mask of royal satisfaction. Maire was drawn from her inner thoughts as Rowan stood up at her side and turned to honor her with lifted cup.

All signs of his earlier anger were gone. His eyes danced as he spoke in a raised voice.

"There is but one addition I would make to your song, Maire of Gleannmara."

Maire stiffened warily. What was Emrys about now?

"Your Brude records that I was conquered by your sword in a fair fight, but that is not exactly the case."

Declan was on his feet like a shot, his hand flying to the hilt of his weapon. "How dare you insult our queen!"

As hostage, Emrys had no weapon with which to defend himself. Maire inserted herself between the two men before her foster brother reached the royal bench.

Seemingly oblivious to his danger, Rowan turned her with one hand, his glass lifted in the other as he went on, bowing slightly. "Stay still, rooster, for I mean to compliment my wife."

Compliment? Now Maire was truly leery.

"A man's sword skill is of little use when his adversary is possessed of a far greater weapon."

So that's where he was going. "The use of my stinger was just as—"

"Let Maire's beauty and wit, not the bite of steel, be recorded as the weapons with which Rowan ap Emrys was smitten into surrender."

The man's silver tongue has delivered him again, Maire realized as her people's acceptance roared in her ears. What true-blooded Celt could possibly object?

Stepping up at Declan's side, the comely Lianna ran admiring fingers over his arm's muscled taper, but her eyes were for none other than Rowan ap Emrys.

"Gleannmara's king has not only the body of a god and the skill of a warrior but the heart and wit of a bard. Well chosen, good cousin," the young woman acknowledged without so much as a glance at the new queen.

TWELVE

I t was only fitting that the new queen and her husband be escorted to the chief's dwelling when the revelry reached its peak. The canopy of vines, which once connected the dwelling to the hall so that the royal family might traverse in inclement weather without becoming soaked, had collapsed. Maire fondly remembered the round, wattled dwelling from childhood with its two-foot thick double wall filled with moss and earth to preserve heat in the winter. Its massive wooden frame—two circles of poles that supported the shaggy thatched roof and into which the walls were tenoned—looked as tall as the trees in the sacred grove. Her father's carvings decorated those left exposed, for Rhian's talents extended from the sword to a set of intricate carving tools, which he'd kept rolled in a leather cloth.

Maire stepped inside, amazed to see the room had shrunk considerably. The fact that the Roman bed took up so much floor space, leaving scant room for a fire, tossed the folly of her choice in her face. Rowan's short laugh added force to it.

"Your desire for grandeur dwarfs your accommodations, Maire."

"Queen Maire to you, hostage."

As she spoke, she whirled round to slap him for his insolence, but thought better of it. Not that she was afraid of her husband, but in truth, there was merit to his humor. It was a ridiculous sight. A smile tweaked the corner of her mouth, giving way to amusement. Maire plopped down on the mattress. Freshly stuffed with rushes, it moved plump and soft beneath her weight as she looked around the room, taking it all in.

The walls and carved columns were dull with the soot of years, not white with lime or polished with oil. She could hardly make out the marvelous art her father had created on the poles. She recalled lying in bed and studying their symmetry on the oiled wood until she faded into sleep. The light of the fire made it glisten like a fairy's staff.

"I was just a child when I last saw this place. It was so much brighter and decidedly bigger then." Maire sobered from her whimsy. "Morlach has even blighted my home!"

"I don't think you can blame the druid for this, my queen. The structure hasn't shrunk from its original size, but you now look upon it with the eyes of a full grown woman, not a little girl."

It was true, Maire knew. She ran a nostalgic finger along the notches Rhian had made to mark his only child's growth near the door. They were scarcely higher than her breastplate now. So this was how it looked to her parents, at least from the perspective of size. Pulled from her musings by her companion's shadow moving on the wall hanging, she returned to the present.

Rowan shrugged off his cloak and tossed it on the foot of the bed. The mean robe he wore beneath starkly contrasted the luxurious weave of the dressings, yet it in no way diminished the nobility of his stature. In coarse wool or the finest of silk, Rowan ap Emrys would stand tall and commanding among men. And women, Maire mused, watching him walk around the bed to the table placed against the curved wall. There he poured water from a golden pitcher into a matching bowl. Inlaid with an intricate silver pattern of circles to signify everlasting life and love, it had been a wedding gift from Diarhmott to her mother and father.

"And where did you disappear to when Brude left the hall?" Her question was not spawned of jealousy; although its green fingers plucked at her the way some of the women flirted outright with Rowan. She couldn't say he'd encouraged it, but neither had it been discouraged.

"I left to speak to the druid's servant. I was certain that we've met somewhere in the past."

"Did he remember you?"

"He acted as though he did; though he could not tell me from when or where our last meeting was."

The Welshman was honest, if nothing else. While she was, at least on the surface, involved in the revel and games, Maire had not missed Rowan's discreet exit. With Declan beginning to slur speech over his cup, she'd sent Eochan after the man. Her foster brother reported that the hostage followed the druid back to his lodge and met briefly with Brude's servant. Glas had to be calmed, such was his joy to finally recognize Emrys.

"Perhaps Brude could discern the mystery for you."

Rowan shook his head. "I need no augury performed in my name. The facts will come out in time. So what do you think, lovely queen? Do we dare trust the fire not to leap to the bed or the wall?"

The fire had been moved from its central position in the round enclosure to the foot of the bed. It was too close to both in Maire's judgment. Still, winter had not quite let go of the air and a toasty fire would dissolve its chilly grasp, at least beneath her roof.

"Bank the fire. We'll make other arrangements tomorrow. For tonight, I am exhausted."

"Then by your leave..." Rowan knelt beside the bed and folded his hands against his chest.

"I'll have a larger lodge built and one for your temple altar. That way you needn't worship the bed or perform your augury in here."

The man looked up at Maire, his face a mirror of a father's patience with its child. Nonetheless, it rankled Maire to be at the disadvantage of ignorance.

"I'm not worshiping the bed, Maire. I'm kneeling in reverence to God. And even that isn't necessary, for I often speak to Him when I'm walking the fields or riding the hills. As for a temple or altar, my queen, it is here." He placed his hand over his amulet.

"In the Chi-Rho?"

"This is but an earthly symbol. My temple is in my heart, my soul. It's here that I speak with God."

Perhaps she should have taken the large gold cross he'd prayed to after all, since neither he nor, evidently, his God, were particularly attached to such things.

"Good, because we've much to do to rebuild our defenses before I can indulge in a larger dwelling place. We'll store away the bed till then and use the bed box my parents shared."

Except that they would not share it as her parents had.

Aware that her breath had sharpened, Maire unlaced the ceremonial shoes and removed them, focusing her attention on something less disconcerting. After the royal coronation, they would be sewn together and hung by the chieftain's door. When the time came, she would be buried with them and other trappings from her rule. When she entered the other world in the west, perhaps they would fit her spirit's feet better than hers.

Crom's toes, this Christian had her thinking about spirits now! She cut a sidewise glance at him. His eyes were closed, their lashes thick and dark upon the noble ridges of his cheeks, but it was his lips that caught her attention. They moved in silent earnest, and with each syllable, the furrows of his brow faded until just a trace of their presence remained. Whatever had deepened them earlier that evening and knotted up the muscles of his temples and jaws had left, at least for the present.

Would that she could whisper away her own burdens so easily. Rising, she unfastened her breastplate and hung it on the wall beside her shield and sword. She hardly knew which quandary to face first—the Cairthan, Morlach, restoring

Gleannmara, or making certain of her allies at Tara. Then there was this curious man she'd taken as her husband and his even stranger god.

Tomorrow she would find out more about it from Brude, so she wouldn't appear so ignorant as to be talked to like a child. Not that Rowan had spoken down to her. She'd simply felt inadequate. It wasn't a queenly feeling and she didn't care for it one jot. Maeve had left a huge legacy to her, a great shadow for her to fill. All her confidence was needed, if not for her own sake then for her people's.

"What?"

Maire blinked, realizing that Rowan had opened his eyes and caught her staring at him. "What what?"

"What are you staring at?"

Embarrassment flushed Maire's face. She'd need neither fire nor warmth the rest of the night given the burn of her skin.

"You, you kneeling nitwit. I'm waitin' for you to finish your quiet chant so that I can give rest to these weary bones." She pointed at the mattress. "I'll not be laying down like some poor goat on an altar with you kneeling there like that."

To her deepening distraction, Rowan chuckled outright. "Ah, Maire, I don't think I've ever known a woman such as yourself before. You're a walking canon of contradiction."

The man talked as if he'd swallowed every book ever written. Uncertain as to whether she'd been insulted or nay, Maire replied, "Now there's the cauldron chargin' the kettle o' blackness."

"*A walking canon of contradiction.*" Sure as the daylight emerged beyond the sea on the morrow, she'd have the meaning of that from Brude before the sun song was finished.

"We act like a couple too long married and it's only our second night as man and wife."

"What?"

Rowan tossed back the covers and got into the bed, as if he were in his own home. Thankfully, he wore the loose fitting robe. Maire had heard that many men slept in the clothes nature had given them. She daren't let her thoughts dwell on that, the way her heart just skipped a beat. Like as not, the sight of Rowan in nature's glory would stop it outright.

"I said—"

"I heard what you said, fool, but we agreed that this is strictly a marriage of convenience, so if you—"

"The way we speak to each other," the man explained. "I was only referring to our cross manner...or rather, your cross manner. If you've a mind to be a stubborn, barbed-tongued Mebhe to my Ailill, have at it. I for one am quite content with things as they are."

"And what would a Welshman know of Connaught lore? Mebhe indeed! She was a proud queen with a braying mule for a husband. The man deserved the trouble she gave him and then some."

Never mind the harm that came of it, or the bloodshed. Maire held that thought back, for it hardly served her, watching as Rowan folded his arms behind his head on the plump pillows, which had come with the bed. Grand arms, she admitted to herself, made to embrace a woman, to protect her—arms immune to the druid's satire.

None of the sores or blisters that Cromthal promised from Morlach marred Rowan's sun-ripened flesh. The black crisps of hair that lightly covered his skin spoke of virility...

Maire recovered quickly. *Content,* he'd said. "And well you should be content. Be thankful you're not in chains, Emrys, though the night is not yet out."

That a priest should turn her insides to a molten mass of confusion made her as irritable as she was disturbed. Lifting the blankets on her side of the massive pallet, she slipped beneath them and turned her back to her adversary. With a fling, she tossed her unbound hair behind her, away from her face.

"I have thanked God for many things this night, Maire, and that is one of them."

She snorted. "Humph! Better to thank *me* than your god."

Maire stiffened at the sense more than the actual feel of fingers winding in her hair. What folly had she committed? This man was making her fey as a swineherd. She'd turned her back on him—her hostage—and that with her stinger still lodged in her breastplate on the wall, a body's length away. He could strangle her with her own hair, and she'd not…

She spun over, fists drawn for a life's struggle and froze at the sight of Rowan ap Emrys lifting the lightest of her curls to his mouth.

"What are you doing?" Her voice was little more than a croak.

"Thanking you, Queen Maire."

The gaze he cast over the tresses he brushed ever so lightly with his lips reflected the lamplight she'd forgotten to put out; although something told her that even darkness would not smother what she saw burning there.

"And seeing if the fire in your hair was as warm to the touch as it was to the eyes," he added, his own tone, usually smooth as velvet, disrupted by strain. "Now, good night, little queen." He smiled, not with humor or with smugness as she rolled away, tugging from his grasp in order to pinch out the smoky tallow flame.

"Sleep well, hostage."

The reminder of his station was the most she could muster, given her inner state of turmoil. She slid back into the large bed, which suddenly felt as small as the wooden cradle her father had made for her. Perched on the farthest edge, she tried to relax, but her mind would not rest, nor would her senses. Every nerve seemed tender as a boil, ready to reel in response to a touch, no matter how innocent.

The events of her first day as Gleannmara's queen played across her mind: Cromthal's face, the visage of Rowan emerging from the sea on Shahar, the outright admiration of the women as the hostage revised Brude's rendition of Maire's victory song.

Scarcely four days a leader and already she was overwhelmed. When no sound stirred outside, save the occasional bay of a hound at the golden moon casting its glow through the vent in the thatched roof, Maire began to think a peaceful sleep was something she might never know again.

A faint rhythmic snore from the far side of the pallet pricked at her as much as her troubles. Her lips drew into a taut line, her exasperated sigh escaping from her nostrils. For all the foolraide he provoked in his followers, Emrys's god at least gave them peaceful sleep.

Neither her mother's gods nor nature itself would give Maire respite. No more had she relaxed when the effects of the numerous toasts to the success of her reign plagued her. Easing out of the comfortable bed, she padded across the rush-strewn floor. As she lifted the wooden latch, she froze at the sound of someone moving, running away from the other side. With an exclamation of surprise, Maire yanked open the door and hastened through it. She ran halfway around the lodge, stumbling blind, save for the cloud-filtered light of the moon, when she realized her sword was not at her waist. Even her stinger was left behind.

But the intruder's footfalls were light, like those of a female or perhaps a small man, and Maire's skill as a warrior was not limited to weapons alone. Swift as a deer at the bark of a hound, she sprang past the privy, her needs momentarily forgotten, and plunged through the breach in the earthen wall surrounding the royal enclosure. Ahead of her, a female raced toward the cluster of dwellings in the outer rath, her shift hiked above her knees as high as Maire's, which was shorter for battle.

Maire caught up with the woman just short of their cover and lunged, tackling her behind the knees. The female went down hard, her breath knocked from her body along with her cry of surprise. She was as wiry as Maire, yet didn't put up much of a fight. As Maire rolled her over, she crossed her arms over her face as though to protect herself.

"What mischief were you about at my door, woman?" Maire's shout drew the attention of the guards who'd been stationed at the entry of the outer fosse.

"None, my queen."

"Uncover your face then and keep your hands above your head, palms to the sky."

Maire's captive was as young as she, with dark hair and eyes that betrayed her feigned fear. Instinct bade the young queen be wary, even as the guards approached them, swords drawn.

Her captive's waist pinned by her weight, Maire quickly searched her for a hidden weapon.

"I am no threat to you, Queen Maire, I swear by my mother's gods."

"Then why did you run?"

"'Tis two wenches wrestling in the grass," the guard in the lead bellowed, yards away from being of use, had Maire needed him.

"Ah, the Sidhe take 'em for cuttin' me dream short!" the second swore.

"Why did you run?" Maire asked again, ignoring the bluster of the fast approaching men.

"I tend the fire for the king's lodge and was trying to decide if I should disturb you to bring in the rest of the wood I'd put aside."

"Your name, wench."

"Brona, my queen."

Maire climbed to her feet as the first guard reached them. "Do you know this woman?" she demanded, jerking a finger at the female still on the ground.

"I don't know either of ye, and 'twould serve justice if the fairy did take ye, wallerin' and squallin'…"

Maire drew to her full height, despite the hard grip of the guard on her arm. "I do not wallow or squall, O'Croinin."

"Queen Maire!"

The laggard slowed in shock. "Gleannmara herself?"

"I asked if you know this girl, either of you, or have you not yet run sleep's crust from your eyes?"

Maire had been busy with her captive, but her sharp ears hadn't missed the commentary between the approaching guards. How could anyone, save that Christian, sleep knowing that Morlach even now was planning his vengeance?

"A fine pair of watchmen Eochan has chosen for the night!"

The first guard hung his head, but the slower of the two afoot was not so in wit. "'Twas no less than them creepin' clouds what cast the sleep upon us. Morlach's at work already."

Ignoring the man, and the spontaneous chill that raked up her spine at his suggestion, Maire repeated her question louder. "Do either of you know this woman?" She motioned at the sprawled figure. "Go on, get up and turn your face toward the moonlight."

The woman did as she was told, slowly brushing her long unbound locks away from her face. It was the other girl with whom Declan had frolicked; the one Maire had not recognized. Her brows were dark and thick, etched against the uncommon white of her face. Yet her pallor was not one of fear. Her features were a mask of composure. Maire found it hard to believe her story of panic.

"Aye, that's Brona, daughter of Gwythan."

"The old herb woman?" Maire remembered from her childhood the frail, bent creature who collected herbs for Brude. It was a means for the widow to support herself. Maire would have remembered a daughter of this age, but Gwythan was childless. "How did Gwythan come by a daughter?"

"She found me abandoned in a meadow and took me to raise, my queen."

"Aye, that's the story we heard as well," one of the guards concurred.

"Well, regardless of where she came from, I caught her lurking outside the door of my lodge."

"I was leaving firewood, lest you needed it in the night. I didn't knock because I saw the light go out and…well, you and the Welshman are newly wed."

Brona's expression was guileless. The O'Croinin clansmen were not as adept at schooling their features. Not even their rough beards could hide their knowing smirks.

"And you ran from me because…?"

"The sound of the latch moving startled me, and I panicked. I didn't want you to think I had some perverse interest in your wedding bed."

If she had panicked, Brona was fully collected now. In fact, it was Maire who began to feel defensive and foolish. She wondered if Brona had told others how ridiculous the Roman bed looked in the lodge.

"Very well then. I'll take in the wood when I return," she announced, ending the affair. "And I thank you for your thought." She started away and then turned back. "And never run from me again. Running smacks of a guilty conscience."

"Yes, my queen."

After stopping at the privy, Maire returned to her new lodge in a fouler humor yet. Tomorrow she'd have the latrine cleaned and treated with a layer of the moss it had not seen in a good season, judging by the stench. Somehow, she had to restore Gleannmara's rath to a civilized state—after it was properly fortified.

As she wiped her feet free of the grass and dirt clinging to them from her barefoot chase, the mound of man, still sleeping like a babe at his mother's breast when she entered, turned over.

"Did you catch her?"

The clear ring of his question in the stillness startled her. "Who?"

"Brona."

"How did you—"

"I heard her soft approach and the rustle of the wood she

put down by the door, but you bolted out like a stone-footed bull before I could tell you of her." The mattress rustled as he shifted his weight. "I met her earlier."

A stone-footed bull!

"Well I *might* have heard her myself, were it not for your snorting like a pig in fresh mud. As it was, all I heard was someone running from my door at an unseemly hour. What with Morlach's mischief sure about, 'twas only natural to give chase."

"And you'd give a druid chase barehanded and barefooted, wearing nothing but a slip of linen for armor?"

"I knew I was equal or better to the figure I chased."

"Even if she knew magic?"

"You've more gall than a crazed boar, Emrys, to toy with me in my present humor." Maire hopped onto the bed and was astonished to collide with her companion. "Get you over to your side! I'm cold and tired and in no mood for your games."

"Most women would bid their man move closer to warm them."

For a moment, Maire thought certain she would feel the wrap of Emrys's strong arms about her, the press of his hard body, warmed by the haven of blankets, against her. Panic pebbled her flesh like a blast from Dane's winter, but it wasn't because she couldn't get away. It was because she might not want to.

"Well warm these first!"

She struck out with her feet and hands, planting them firmly against the flesh of his shoulders and legs, bared by his turn under the blankets.

Rowan skidded across the mattress away from her. "Mercy, woman! I've buried corpses in the dead of a Pict winter with feet warmer than yours."

"Get used to it, husband, for that's all the warmth you'll ever know in this bed."

Maire snatched back the woolen coverlet and bed robe of

wolf skin and snuggled down on the plump pallet, lightly warmed by Rowan's short occupation. On the other side of the large bed, her disgruntled companion jerked the bedclothes about him, mumbling something about ice. She was still wide awake, but at least now she had something to smile about.

THIRTEEN

I tell you, Brude, the man is crazed to think he can make the Cairthan our allies after all these years!"

Maire was up before the sun song and followed the elder druid back to his hut, trying not to step on his heels. He moved slower in the mornings, as though the stiffness that crept in during the night needed to be worked out in the sun. Beside them, his pet heron stood, its wings at its side as it mocked the rise in Maire's voice.

"Ho there, Nemh! Either find your own food or wait till I've had mine."

Brude brushed by the bird that was his shadow. It nipped at the swirling hem of the man's garment with its long beak, much like a playful pup. Some said the druid looked like his pet, long of limb and gawky with a curved neck and beaklike nose. Others said the man's spirit often traveled about in the bird, watching over the kingdom while his human form sat statue-still in meditation.

"Glas has ruined the fish eater with a taste for grain. It thinks to sleep in my lodge now instead of perched above the door."

"Brude, did you hear me? Emrys thinks I should let him handle the Cairthan, and him no more than a hostage himself."

Brude sighed heavily and dropped to a seat on the stone bench outside his lodge. Like Maire's, the entrance faced the east, so that the arms of the reborn sun might draw him into its invigorating embrace. To the west went the spirits of the dead, to sleep like the sun until their own rebirth. The lines on the druid's face told of the many such cycles he'd seen.

"Glas is Cairthan."

Maire did not hide her surprise. "I never knew that."

"Glas thinks that if anyone can unite Gleannmara's people, it is the new king."

"He told you that?"

"In so many gestures, aye."

Brude flexed his fingers, fisting them, then releasing. When he finished his morning ritual, every joint in his body had been worked until he was satisfied that his blood made a complete cycle through his veins. Maire never quite understood the why or the wherefore. It was druid training, most likely, not warrior, so she had no need of it.

"A wise ruler will seek counsel. A king who reins without counsel will be one without a kingdom."

"Aye, and the swiftest and strongest don't always win the race," Maire countered, recalling the Christian's words. Why, instead of talking in circles, couldn't either simply say she should call a counsel of chieftains?

Brude's bushy white brow shot up. "Well said, Maire. Few your age realize the merit of those words. Pride is their weakness, their downfall."

"I don't see how giving the Welshman a chance can hurt. I could get more done about here without him afoot to distract me. I don't need to tell you there's much to be done to fortify for Morlach's attack."

The other of the druid's eyebrows joined its mate, a white hedgerow dividing his face above the mercurial gray of his eyes. "He distracts you, does he?"

"Like a spur in the heel."

"Hah!" Brude's loud guffaw sent the heron scampering away. "Methinks our Maire has been equally met at last."

"You think him my equal?" Maire kept the indignation out of her voice, lest she be accused of the pride the druid had just disdained.

"I think you the heart of Gleannmara, and Emrys the soul."

The conversation ran like a Celtic pattern, in loops, covering space with eloquence, without a particular point.

"Then I'll send the tuath's soul out with Eochan and the most skilled in combat. The rest of us will remain behind to make repairs to the earth work and fosse."

"Go with him, Maire. Morlach will not come now. He is too devious to do the obvious."

"You did an augury?"

At the druid's short nod, Maire let out a sigh of relief. Would that she'd known that last night! Perhaps she might have done more than catnap between each movement of her bedmate.

"Emrys keeps a secret, one that promises glory for Gleannmara and its queen. Just what it is, the sacred stones did not say." With a frown, Brude stared at his upturned palms. "I even slept the night thus, and no more was revealed. Yet, soon as I accepted that Rowan ap Emrys and his God were with us, an uncommon peace bore down upon me as if I'd swallowed one of my own potions. Truth is like a light to the blind man and a balm to the wounded. To the naked eye, he still may not see and his wounds may yet seep, but the eyes of his spirit are sharp as a hawk's, and the seepage is no longer of consequence."

"If you feel Emrys is right for the task, that is all the truth I need. Perhaps I'd best accompany him with a force to the Cairthan's mountains before the lesser clans disburse to their own lands to make ready for the season."

Maire rose, the rest of the druid's words swimming in her mind like a fish just beyond her reach.

"You are certain we've the summer to prepare for Morlach?"

At Brude's nod, she turned and walked away.

Brude watched his protégé for a moment, knowing full well she felt like a dog chasing its tail. But unlike a hapless mongrel, Maire would eventually find her answers. Her heart was pure as her love for her people. She was denied a little girl's childhood to fulfill her destiny as their leader without complaint. The god who lived in the sun would bathe those of pure heart in light when the time was right to reveal the truth. For the same reason, those who sought to glorify themselves and their power, rather than truth, would never walk in the pure light. The more they sought for themselves, the more into darkness they retreated. Morlach walked in such darkness, his soul festering with greed for the powers of both worlds.

Before summoning Glas to prepare his chariot, Brude lifted his face to the sun's warmth and turned his right side to it in reverence to him who lived there. It would rouse no suspicion for him and his servant to go off into the rolling hills and glens of the tuath, perhaps even to the sacred grove of his peers. This time, Brude would seek the light elsewhere.

The ancient had heard of a Christian cleric near Glendalough, a pass to the western part of Erin through the Wicklow peaks. It was time to follow his own advice and seek the counsel of another prophet, one who followed the Christian god.

Brude was getting along in years. The time neared when he would pass through death's door to journey to the west and that incredible place of brightness where the sun retreated each night. But there were things to be done, questions yet to be asked, and answers he would need to prepare himself. He knew it, neither from the stones nor a conviction laid into his hands as he slept in wait. Instead, it was laid upon his heart.

"Methinks our Maire has been equally met at last."

Equally met indeed, Maire thought, buckling her breastplate in place. Emrys spent more time on his knees than he did on his feet. Hardly a kingly trait, she thought, watching her husband pray over his food.

"It isn't poisoned."

He looked up at her and smiled. "But I am thankful for it and wish it blessed to my use and God's service this day."

"Then I do, too, since I've decided to give you a chance with the Cairthan. I've given orders that we ride out after breaking the fast."

Maire dribbled a circle of honey over the thick oat porridge and topped it with a splash of cream. "And tell your god I'm thankful as well for the food, though I'm pressed to see what he has to do with it. 'Twas man's fingers that planted and harvested it and woman's fingers that ground and prepared it."

"And it was He who sent the sun and rain and made the earth rich that it might grow."

"Ach!" Maire interrupted, her mouth full. She swallowed. "It was cows what made the earth rich."

"God created the cows and the earth and the man and the woman."

"And gave you enough tongue for all." Exasperated, Maire pointed to Rowan's bowl. "Pray, put it to the food, and leave me eat in peace."

"I didn't think you approved of prayer, but I will gladly obey, little queen."

"I wasn't speakin' to your god, just his fool."

"He heard you."

"Your mother's honor!" Maire exclaimed in disbelief.

"I'm trying to obey, Maire, but you won't let me be."

Maire's jaw dropped open and then clamped back her retort as he reached over and wiped a smudge of honey from her chin. Her irritation deflated with a strange stirring as he popped his finger into his mouth and tasted it. His gaze held hers hostage for several heartbeats before she managed an undignified retreat to her porridge. She needed to gather her wits for her first official day as Gleannmara's queen, not dally with these strange feelings her new husband evoked in her.

When one of the servants took away her empty dish, Maire rose at the head table and struck it soundly with her empty cup until the amicable riot of the assembly quieted. She knew her orders would not be popular, but as Brude once told her, respect and popularity were not always one and the same.

To the ladies, she left the task of seeing the hall and her lodge swept, scoured, and limed afresh before the return of the retinue gathering in the outer ring of the hill fort. To the men who were not to accompany her and Rowan on the journey to deal with the Cairthan, she instructed the rebuilding of the earthen works, as well as clearing the fosse and latrines.

Riot ensued once more, but it was not amicable now. The men grumbled beneath their breath, but the ladies of upper rank clucked and squawked like a pen of angry hens. How could Maire ask them to give up their needlework in the gri-anán, where they were pampered by the sunlight and noble pursuit, to work shoulder to shoulder with their servants?

"Fine needlework requires soft hands, not those of a servant!"

"Aye, the roughness will pick at the delicate weave of the materials!"

"I'll not be doin' it and there's the end of it! That's servants' work, not that of a lady!"

"Tell me, ladies," Maire shouted above the cackling din. She waited until it died enough that she could be heard plainly. "Tell me, did your stitches fill your bellies or save them from the running ague this winter past? Or did you use the dainties to cover your noses so you wouldn't smell the stench of your own sties? Half your servants got away to the other world from starvation, and yet you still stitch and prattle as though those who remain can do the work of two."

"And you men—" Maire turned to those sulking about the fires, where they'd gathered to ward off the morning chill— "Have you lost your pride to let the land many of you bled for under my parent's reign waste away like this, ripe for the plunder of any vulture with senses keen enough to see its decay?"

"We didn't lose it, yer queenship. Morlach stole it! Swiped

the food from our mouths and the cattle from our fields whilst you played the tyke at war games in Drumkilly."

The knife twisted in Maire's belly whether she deserved it or not. She acknowledged the man with a somber nod and swept the room with a fierce gaze.

"Aye, and sadly I could not be born a full-grown warrior queen any more than I could stop Morlach's injustice as a child. But by my sword arm—"

Rage broke her voice; the vileness of what Morlach had done to her people rose in her throat.

Rowan shot up from the royal bench to stand at her side, giving her the chance to recover. "And by mine!"

"Gleannmara will be restored and Morlach's tyranny ended," Maire vowed in earnest.

"And by Drumkilly's!" Eochan roared, drawing his weapon and holding it high in salute to Maire.

"And the O'Croinin!"

"And the Colmáin!"

"And the MacCormac!"

"And the Muirdach!"

All those who'd followed Maire into battle were on their feet, weapons brandished, voices united. The noble women were slower to rally, but finally, Maire's maternal cousin Lianna leaped up upon a bench and raised her hand to Maire.

"Better to blister our hands now as Gleannmara's aires than later as Rathcoe's slaves. Long live Maire, queen of Gleannmara!"

The youngest of the women, caught up in the excitement of the moment, joined in before their elders, but soon all were of the same accord.

Maire wondered that the giant dome of thatch did not rise as she walked out with her men for the march to the highlands of the Cairthan.

Rowan surveyed the landscape as the entourage made its way up toward the mist-shrouded peaks of the Wicklow. It was sword land, won by the sword, preserved by the sword. There was no plough land to speak of, not enough at all, judging from the gaunt faces he'd seen along the way. But there was enough to feed many if put to proper use. Convert the tillable pastureland to the plough and move the cattle, which had grazed it to the dirt, to higher ground. He said as much to Maire.

"If we worked quickly, we could get in a late planting of grain."

"And I thought you were scanning the rock, looking for the Cairthan, cowards that they are."

"I was looking at your people. Their methods of scratching food from the earth for themselves and the cattle aren't enough."

"There's the tribute Emrys is to pay. If that's not enough, we'll take it elsewhere."

"Like the thieving Cairthan cowards?"

Maire looked away in silence.

"If the winter's been this harsh on the lowlands of Gleannmara, where food can be grown, you can be certain the Cairthan have suffered more."

"Crom's toes, Maire, he'll have you pitying the scoundrels." Declan snorted behind her. "Soon the smiths will be beating our swords into plough blades, and we'll be staring at an ox's hind half the day long."

"Better than being one, I'd say."

The glib remark was out before Rowan could squash it. The sound of Declan's outraged cry at the insult was underscored by the sound of his steel coming out of its bronze scabbard. Rowan had no intention of provoking a fight, much less engaging in one, but old ways were hard to leave behind. *Forgive me, Father.*

He kept his back to Declan as the latter raced up beside him on a shaggy steed.

"Now, Welshman, feel the bite of a man's blade."

Declan raised his sword, threatening, waiting for Rowan to respond in kind. Counting heavily on his knowledge of Celtic honor, he made no move toward his own weapon.

"Curse you, man, draw your sword." Declan nudged his wiry steed closer to the stallion and spat upon Rowan's leg.

Rowan pulled up Shahar and glanced down at the spittle glistening on laces of his boots. Another time, another place, and Declan of Drumkilly would be dead by now.

"I apologize. My remark was uncalled for. I provoked you into anger. On my account, you're willing to spill blood...possibly your own."

At this passive response, Declan glanced at Maire uncertainly. "He insults me again."

"I mean no insult, Declan, and I certainly will not fight you...not when it was I who provoked you."

"Declan spat on you," Maire pointed out. She sat stiff in her saddle, her gaze shifting from one to the other of them.

"Well," Declan added, "if that's all that stops you, take this!"

Rowan braced for the impact of the blade the young warrior swung at him, flat side out. But before it made contact, the clash of steel against steel cut through the air. Maire was off her horse and between them, holding her upstart captain at bay.

"His god will not allow him to fight over the foolishness of vanity, but my mother's gods don't care if I deflate *your* overblown pride with the prick of my sword."

Declan flinched as if he actually felt the angry strike of Maire's warning. His lip curling, he sneered with the bravado of a wounded dog. "And now he hides behind his god and a woman. He has no more fight in him than that Welsh priest when I took this ring."

Rowan prayed against the raging swell coursing through him, the clamor for revenge. It was bad enough Declan assaulted his honor, without reminding him of the injustice to his friend. The old Rowan would have already cut the ring from the braggart's finger and sent it back to Justinian, finger included. The tension in Rowan's voice was witness to the tug-of-war raging among his emotions.

"I stand by my apology. I was wrong." He took a deep, steadying breath and released it along with his will for retaliation. "I owe you some manner of retribution, some honor price."

"Such as?"

"For the rest of this day I shall serve you, save deeds contrary to my faith."

"The king of Gleannmara serves only the high king!" Maire objected. "Such as you are, you *are* king." The queen's expression was nothing less than incredulous.

"The King of all kings served His people."

Declan smiled. He had the look of cat ready to toy with its cornered prey. "See, little sister, his god condones it."

He'd rather take a whipping than serve this young fool, but such was the consequence of an unfettered tongue. Rowan could well imagine the advantage he'd just given the Scot. Of all his faults, this was the hardest to tame.

"What will you have me do, good sir?" He ignored the way Maire's incredulity turned to disillusionment. For a moment, he'd hoped she might understand, but it was clear that she thought him a coward as well.

"I'll have your stallion for one."

"Shahar is a spirited animal."

"There was never a horse born that Declan of Drumkilly couldn't master." He slid off his smaller mount and waited for Rowan to dismount. When Rowan took the other horse's reins in exchange for the stallion's, the young cock stopped him from swinging onto the gelding's back.

"Take him to the rear and lead him."

"You go too far, Declan," Maire warned, clearly perturbed

by the way events were unfolding, yet at a loss as to how to handle them.

"Once I am certain that Shahar will have you."

Rowan had raised and trained both the stallion and its mate, Tamar. He'd groomed Tamar so that his mother could ride over the fields of Emrys, for the Welsh in her was as fond of horseflesh as the Scot. While Rowan did not mind eating the dust of the entourage, he did object to the possibility that Shahar might bolt away with, or without, its strange rider. On this uneven ground, a runaway horse could easily stumble and break a limb, necessitating it be put to death.

His mouth a wide show of teeth, Declan vaulted up on Shahar's back. Before Rowan could say a word, the impetuous Scot shoved him aside with an unexpected kick to the chest and gigged Shahar with his heels. The stallion gave a mighty leap and bolted forward, nearly unseating its rider in the process. A round of mixed laughter and cheers followed them.

True to the equestrian reputation of his ancestry, Declan recovered, at least enough to hold on for what would have been the ride of his life, for there was no stopping the indignant Shahar. The stallion was trained to foot signals and commands, not the cursing and kicking of its current rider. It ran all the harder for the pull on its bit, as if to escape the maniac on its back.

The horse was about to plunge into a dense forest by the time Rowan recovered his footing and raised his fingers to his lips. His sharp whistle split the air, startling the laughing queen beside him. As though running into an invisible wall, Shahar stopped abruptly, feet jutted out, hooves digging up the turf beneath them. Declan continued forward only to be stopped by something of more substance. An oak.

"Care for your servants, Maire, and they will care for you. Mistreat them, even without the intention, and wind up like yon Declan, out of control and at their mercy."

"And huggin' a tree like his maithre's breast." Eochan came

up behind Rowan and clapped him on the back. "The lad's worrisome as a gnat sometimes, friend, but he's good-hearted, for all that."

Rowan stepped forward and caught the reins of the stallion that galloped back to him. He wasn't so sure of the latter assessment. "Does a man who steals a ring from a priest deserve such praise?"

"What need has a priest for such a bauble as that?" Eochan laughed. "Aye, me brother gave the man a scare, running up the stone tower and demandin' he fill the sack with anything of value, but no harm came from it, save the man near crossed himself to death."

"The priest was my friend. I *gave* Justinian that ring." Still, Rowan was grateful that his friend had been spared rough treatment, even if the bellowing tattooed warriors had frightened him. It wasn't a sight such a quiet soul was accustomed to.

"Ach, then. That's between you and him." Eochan nodded with new understanding.

"That animal is kin to the pooka!" Declan, his body barked and bleeding from his encounter with the tree, approached, sword raised over his head. "And by my father's gods, I'll have blood for blood!"

"Then you'll take mine first."

Sword still sheathed, Rowan stepped in the path of the enraged Scot.

"With pleasure." Declan let out a lusty war whoop and broke into a full run, straight at Rowan.

Maire moved to intervene, but Rowan quickly shoved her aside, into Eochan, and ran forward to meet his opponent in what appeared to be a suicidal charge. With timing the difference between life and death, he waited until he was a sword's length from Declan. As the latter launched a deadly swing, one that could cleave Rowan's head from his shoulders, Rowan dove straight for Declan's legs.

Declan twisted and went down, carried by the momentum

of his swing. The last of his outrage erupted in a loud grunt as he struck the ground. Rowan was on him in a flash, tossing away the sword, which fell from the man's hand, and twisting that same hand behind his back.

"Still, lad," he warned, as Declan recovered enough to struggle. "I've no desire to break your arm, but I will if you don't come to your God-given senses."

Declan growled through his clenched teeth and squirmed, helpless as a newborn calf. "I wouldn't have killed the beast. Crom's toes, I'm not that daft!"

"'Tis hard to judge by your actions."

"I vow, you'll regret this, Emrys."

"I already do," Rowan assured him. He'd added insult to injury where Declan's pride was concerned, but he truly didn't know what the hot-tempered warrior might do. He raised his voice so that the onlookers might hear. "And for that, I apologize, Drumkilly. But I'd not have you kill or maim my horse."

"I'd have you bash in Drumkilly's head, but there's no metal nor stone hard enough for the task," Maire remarked a few feet away in complete disgust. "That is, unless you use your own."

A ripple of laughter swept through the troop, relieving the taut grasp of tension infecting the men.

"Mayhap our queen is right." Rowan shoved to his feet.

Declan declined the hand offered, so Rowan took up Shahar's reins. "As I was going to say before you left us so quickly, Shahar is a highly trained warhorse and sensitive to signals of the hand and feet, so avoid irrational or untoward motions that might confuse and spook him. He expects his rider to be in control as well."

"White like that with moon eyes," Declan derided. "I still say he's kin to a pooka." He stared at the stallion, clearly in a muddle of second thought. "It isn't fit that our king should be seen walking behind like a mongrel, no matter how he deserves it," the warrior said at last. "I'll have my honor price in some other way."

Rowan clapped the man on the back. "You remained on his back longer than anyone else has, save myself."

His rage and humiliation unassuaged, Declan nodded and turned to his own mount. Once the Scot was astride the smaller beast, Rowan leapt to Shahar's back and took up the reins. The horse nickered and tossed its head, its white-gold mane shimmering like sunlight on rippled water.

"You should have made him apologize. You are king."

Rowan turned to Maire in surprise.

"A king serves justice. Declan suffered enough by his own hand without my adding to it. To inflict more would be injustice."

Maire stared, as if to see beyond the serene mask he wore, to the heart of him. For all her warriorlike appearance, she stared with the wonder of a child. To his surprise, she succeeded, for Rowan suddenly felt naked, exposed for all he was to this woman.

She saw, sure enough, but from the puzzlement in her gaze, she did not yet understand. For reasons deeper than his desire to spread God's Word and ways, Rowan wanted her to understand him—and that unnerved him more than any blade.

FOURTEEN

The night passed cool, with winter's memory still fresh on its mind.

Maire chose a protective niche in the increasingly rocky terrain of the higher Wicklows. An enemy would need wings to attack them from one side, or a suicidal wish to come head on through the only entrance. Although a watch was appointed, the night was uneventful, save Declan's vengeful retaliation in having Rowan serve him as a slave.

Maire watched the Welshman brush the last remnant of leaves from his body before mounting Shahar. He'd slept without cover last night, sheltered only by the clothes on his back and that which nature provided, while Declan enjoyed a soft bed of Emrys's blanket and cloak. Each time the fire died, Declan summoned Rowan to scavenge for more wood, to fetch him another noggin of beer, or to boil him some rabbit to go with the roast venison the rest of them ate.

It was so degrading, Maire stepped in twice to end the folly, but each time the Welshman ran her through with a warning look sharper than steel itself. For all its thrust, his words were humble. "I do service to my word, Maire. No man is exempt from the consequences of a wrong doing."

"But you were right. Declan is an ox's behind. And with each order he gives, he bellows the truth even louder."

"Then let him convict himself, for I will not be his judge."

From that point on, Declan, well within earshot, was at least less eager to humiliate this strange new king of theirs. Indeed, even the derisive snickers and comments about

Rowan's lack of backbone—about that which made him male—diminished. It was a show to watch, as one of the O'Croinin or the Muirdach returned from nature's call with another turn of wood for the fire. All the while Eochan swore he was hotter than his brother's boiled rabbit and tossed his blanket over to where Rowan made his bed.

For all his madness, Rowan ap Emrys was earning the respect and support of the men who'd taken him hostage, and their queen's respect as well. He'd done it, not by intimidation but by submission. It contradicted all logic Maire knew, but it was true, regardless. For the first time, in a muddled sort of way, she was beginning to see that Brude might be right. After all, there was more than one way to Tara's heart, besides that which she knew.

Her mind meandered back to the present, tuning into the conversation between Rowan and Declan. The younger warrior clapped Rowan on the back that morning and declared his honor price paid in full. Now he rode beside his former adversary and sought all he might learn of Shahar and Tamar's breed and training.

They came originally from the east and were bred as warhorses, not just to carry men into battle but also to participate by protecting their master with their hooves. They moved into defensive positions along with other warriors on like steeds, so that the rider was least likely to be attacked from a blind side.

"Aye, the training looks odd with a horse by itself, as if it were being taught to dance, but a force of them in motion is a formidable sight to behold. I suppose fighting on the border enabled me to see the best techniques of all sides save one."

"And what was that?" Declan leaned forward, over his steed's neck, curiosity whetted.

"The battle strategy for the soul."

Declan's bemused expression reflected Maire's reaction. There the man went again, talking in mystic riddles.

"Looking death in the face opens a man's eyes to what is most important, in this world and the next."

Maire snapped to attention. "You've been to the other side?" She'd never heard of anyone who'd passed through death's gate and come back as more than a spirit.

Rowan sighed, lost in thought. "They said I was dead."

"In a wounded sleep, no doubt," Declan ventured. "No one comes back same as he was before."

"That's true, very true, friend."

"Well, you've the same body, scars and all. I've seen them close up." Maire bit her lip and glanced at Rowan uneasily. "That is…"

"A wife's prerogative."

Condemned whether she agreed or not, Maire sat back in silence.

"So what part of you has changed?" Declan asked warily. "That is, if ye've really been to the other side."

"My heart."

"Cairthan!"

Eochan's roar ended the conversation, which pleased Maire more than it bothered her. Chances were the Welshman was spinning a tale to pass the time. He proved to be as much bard and priest as warrior, and all such men were given to embellishment of a good story. If she heard the women dreamily prattling on about how Maire had won his heart with her beauty rather than her blade once, she heard it a thousand times and one too many.

She looked ahead to a ridge where a disheveled line of men gathered. They were armed and watching her troops approach in charged silence. Their faces, unpainted for the most part, told her that they'd barely mustered, not expecting an attack so soon in the making. That they were not already screaming like banshees and advancing downhill with swords raised was evidence of her wise decision to take a show of considerable force.

Would that Morlach would be so intimidated…

Maire dismissed the thought. Better to fight one enemy at a time. She glanced aside at Rowan, who studied the men with the keen edge of his gaze. It was sword blue, the color of a blade as it tempers in the smith's water, cold and growing harder.

"And ye think they've gathered to welcome us?"

"No, lass, they've gathered to give their last life's blood for their honor...or what's left of it. Faith, they look like death's own henchmen, nothing but racks of bone swathed in ragged cloth; they are your people, Maire."

"They'd not kneel to Gleannmara," Maire exclaimed, indignant that Rowan should cast the shadow of blame on her.

"Glasdom said your mother let them live with their pride, I'll give her that. Gleannmara was fat enough to feed everyone, and a cattle raid now and then was good sport where none suffered starvation as a result. Morlach stripped them of even that."

To steal a cow from a man who had two was not nearly as severe a crime as to steal his only beast. The ancient law said as much. Maire couldn't recall the Cairthan being more than a nuisance in her mother's day, one that was only given chase when there was no more serious war to see after. Yet it was Rowan's reference to the mute servant that made Maire's thoughts stumble.

"They'd not kneel to Gleannmara," she repeated lamely. *The man speaks like a druid. He talks directly to his god. He says he's been to the other side. That now he claims to have carried on a conversation with a tongueless servant shouldn't baffle me so.*

"Let me ride up there and speak to them," Rowan said at her side.

"Aye, he's already been to the other world and back. A second trip might rid us of at least one menace."

Maire gave Declan a cutting look. Brude said Rowan would unite the tribes. And if he had been to the other side and back, perhaps there was merit in him, after all. She looked over her shoulder, scanning the brave men who'd followed her, ready to give their lives if necessary.

For all things, there was a season, or so Brude taught her, even for fighting. Not that it would be much of a fight, from the looks of the gaunt men on the hill. The memory of the fishing villagers so over mounted by Maire and her men still haunted her sleep and churned in her stomach.

"Aye, go on then," she said at last. "But I'll go with you."

"No!"

"No!"

"No!"

The word echoed so many times, almost all at once, that its force nearly unseated Maire from the back of the proud mare.

"We'd not send our queen to the slaughter. I'll go." Eochan rode forward.

"No, *I* shall," Declan argued.

"They are right," Rowan told her. "You should remain back, in case something should go wrong. No need to leave the clan without king and queen."

Maire was taken back by the gentleness, not in his voice, but his look. If she didn't know better, she'd suspect he really cared for her welfare. A strange warmth embraced her; one she'd not known since basking in the loving care of her parents. It almost made her want to stay behind as he wished.

She puzzled over it, reason warring with emotion. When had emotion moved to such prominence in her thoughts?

"He's right, Maire. So choose which of us is to go with him."

Maire looked at Declan then Eochan. If there was the slightest chance that Rowan could talk the Cairthan into an alliance, he would need a cool head at his side.

"Eochan will go," she said, cutting off Declan's protest. "Let them get a close look at the size of him, and they'll think twice about meeting his kin."

While he neither nodded nor commented, Rowan acknowledged approval of her choice with the slightest dip of his eyelids.

Again Maire flushed. As he urged Shahar forward, he called over his shoulder to Eochan.

"Keep your weapon sheathed."

Eochan shoved the half drawn weapon back into its etched scabbard and winked at Maire. "Like as not, they'll either think us daft as swineherds or be so bloomin' shocked they'll wait till second thought to kill us."

"Be careful, Welshman," Maire called after Rowan.

Rowan swung Shahar around and, to the astonishment of all watching, both horse and rider bowed low to the ground in homage.

"Did you ever see the like?" Maire whispered as he turned Shahar back to the task at hand. The horse trick was a feat in itself, but the Welshman's smile nearly tugged her off her own steed, heart first.

"He has his own style," Declan admitted at her side, his tone undecided as to whether he admired or reviled it. "Queer as a druid, that one."

Maire watched the enemy line for any sign of impending attack on the two lone riders. "Do you really think he went to the other side?"

Declan remained silent as he continued to stare after Rowan's broad, cloaked shoulders. "I don't know, little sister, but the way he looked when he spoke of it…" The man shuddered. "I'd as soon not know what he saw."

The shudder was contagious. Maire rubbed her arms up to the armbands of gold articulated knot work. "Nor I," she echoed, not completely honest. It wasn't for naught that Brude once accused her of having enough curiosity for a litter of cats.

It had been years, harsh ones, and a man's beard shot with premature gray covered Lorcan's face, yet Rowan recognized his brother standing slightly forward of the others. This was the last face Rowan had seen before he'd been bound, blindfolded, and carried aboard a merchant ship. What had his mother and father been told?

Tall as Rowan himself, Lorcan leaned on his sword, watching and waiting. A tattered shield on his arm told of many battles; although Rowan wondered if it had protected the winners or the losers. *Prosperous* was the last word that came to his mind.

A slew of others rose like bile, threatening to poison his intent. *Traitor, liar, usurper*—Lorcan was the senior of them, but Rowan had been the popular one. Lorcan was aiccid—had his people not been defeated by Maeve's forces, heir apparent to the kingship of Gleannmara—but such was his insecurity and desire for power that he'd sold his brother into slavery to make certain of his birthright, for birthright alone was naught without the favor that seemed heaped upon the younger of them. Rowan had plotted a thousand different deaths for Lorcan, all of which were too good for him.

The most recent, the cutting out of his tongue and feeding it to the dogs in front of him before taking his life, sprang to Rowan's mind, carried on the latent surge of rage spawned by what had been done to Glasdom. The faithful servant had done nothing more than serve their family well, but Lorcan took no chance that his lowly deed would be discovered.

Rowan willed his hand away from the hilt of his sword, where it tightened of its own accord. *Father, give me strength to yield to Your will and not mine, for mine is vile, and Yours is pure.*

"Half of them's no more than lads," Eochan exclaimed under his breath.

Rowan looked hard, as though the sight might evoke pity stronger than a lifetime of lust for revenge. It was true. Wild-haired youths whose faces had not yet known a full growth of whiskers stared at him and the giant Drumkilly warrior out of eyes blank and hollow. One, at Lorcan's right, bore a strong resemblance to his elder.

"Lorcan of Gleannmara, I bid you good day."

That Rowan used his name clearly put Lorcan off. "What's the good of it?"

"That God has given Gleannmara a new king and queen, who would be your ally, not your enemy."

"And that would be your god, no doubt?" A ripple of laughter filtered through the assembly, but it sadly lacked humor.

"The One God."

Lorcan snorted in disdain. "The one god indeed! 'Tis like sayin' the one pebble on the beach."

"This God has a message for you, Lorcan. One that can make you a noble chieftain if you choose to accept it."

"And if I don't?"

"A dead one, buried in disgrace with all your hidden secrets of treachery made known."

Lorcan put his hand up to his forehead to shade his eyes. "Step closer, man, that I might see who falsely accuses me of such things."

Rowan whispered to Eochan. "Stand ready to flee if this goes badly. And take Shahar with you."

"Ye don't trust the man!" Eochan's surprise was clear.

"Nay, which is why you must do as I say. Better one fool die than two, eh?"

"I'll not—"

"Maire will need you alive more than I will dead." Rowan handed Eochan the reins. "Not that I expect the worst to happen."

Leaving the bewildered, red-haired giant behind, Rowan strode, sword still sheathed, toward Lorcan. It was hard to make out his brother's shaded expression, but there were other signs that told him all he needed to know: the stiffening of his large frame, the sudden ebb of blood from his ruddy complexion, the way his jaw dropped...and the way his lips moved with the syllables of Rowan's name.

Rowan covered Lorcan's sword hand with his own and leaned forward, clapping him on the back.

"What will it be, brother?"

Lorcan stared at him, too stricken to speak.

"Will you do homage to Gleannmara as a kinsman or suffer as an enemy?"

"If you must kill me, I beg one favor."

His brother's low rush of words, the pleading grasp of his gaze, kindled something within Rowan's chest. Pity? Rowan hoped for forgiveness, but old grudges were not so easily dismissed. He still yearned to snap Lorcan's thick neck. *Help me, Father!*

"Do not slay me in front of my son."

Rowan gathered a deep breath. "Would I be asking you to be my ally if I intended on killing you, man?" He squeezed Lorcan's shoulder, resisting the urge to wince at the poor sharpness of it. "Kneel and hand me your sword."

"In surrender, before my kinsmen?"

"Nay, in exchange for mine."

"But—"

"Faith, Lorcan, do not try me more."

The wiry man dropped to his knees. Behind them a swell of murmurs and grumbles washed over the onlookers.

"Nay, father—"

"Back, boy!" Lorcan roared as the younger version of himself started forward, ax in hand. "I know this man. He is worthy of my sword and trust."

Disfavor turned to a tide of surprise. Rowan was aware of how the other Cairthan strained to see his face, but his gaze was only for the man kneeling before him. *Father, stay my blade. Temper my heart.*

Upon receiving Lorcan's sword, Rowan felt his knees give and he knelt in turn. He knew the sword. It had been their father's. "He's dead?"

"Slain by Morlach's henchmen just before his grandson was born."

Rowan glanced at the fiery-eyed youth, held barely in check by Lorcan's warning. "And Mother?"

"Alive and well."

Still kneeling, Rowan unsheathed his own sword and handed it to Lorcan. He heard Eochan swear behind him, something about a swineherd. No doubt everyone thought him daft. Indeed, he might think so himself were he to dwell upon his feelings and thoughts rather than the sheer power of the heavenly hand guiding him. This might not be what he wanted, but he knew it was right.

"It's Roman."

Nodding, Rowan indicated Lorcan should sheath the sword while he did the same.

"It's a long story," he told his brother, clasping his arms as they rose together. "I've had a good life, in spite of what you did."

"I've suffered the worse for it, for whatever that might mean to ye."

The cold hardness knotted in Rowan's chest dissolved a bit more.

"Make no mention of who I am to anyone, not even our maithre, till I say so."

Lorcan nodded solemnly. "None could know ye, lad. 'Twas only my guilt and shame that knew ye." His gruff voice cracked. "And I've done worse than that, something for which there can be no forgiveness."

"There is nothing God will not forgive, if the heart is truly repentant."

"He cannot know."

"He knows, Lorcan. But now is not the time."

What Rowan felt was the last thing he'd anticipated. Little did he expect to know the emotions swirling on Lorcan's tortured face, creating upheaval in his own. He dared not give into them, not now, when Gleannmara needed a leader of strength and conviction. God had chosen him to be that man. God would see he met the task.

"I will send my man with you as a token of good faith and take your son with me. Go prepare a feast fit for a queen with what you stole from her pastures. And do not worry about excess. Together our clans will replenish all that was lost."

"What of Morlach? He was to marry the young queen."

"God leads us but one step at a time. I married Queen Maire. Today we ally our clans. Tonight we will rejoice the mutual benefit of this peace."

"And tomorrow?"

"Is in God's hands."

"Then here's to his havin' mighty big ones!" Swinging around, Lorcan motioned to his son. "Go with the man, Garret."

The young man glanced at Rowan and back at his father with uncertainty.

"He's a Niall."

"I give my man in exchange for you, lad, and my word that you'll come to no harm." Rowan assured him.

Garret glared. "I'm not afraid of any Niall."

Rowan smiled. "I can see that you've got courage, but do you have the wisdom your good father gave you to go with it? There's the test."

"Are ye sure about this?" Eochan questioned to Rowan's right.

"Aye. Lorcan and the Cairthan will not risk the life of the aiccid, nor will Maire risk yours. This will keep both tribes in check until our good intent is proved."

Eochan hesitated. Rowan couldn't blame him. The man did not know if his new king was fey or nay. When the giant took off his sword belt and handed it to Lorcan, the breath in Rowan's chest gave way in relief. At Rowan's expectant look, the wild-haired youth reluctantly did the same.

"You do your clan and father honor, lad," Rowan told his nephew upon starting back down the hill to where Maire and her men awaited.

"I do not understand, but I will obey my father."

Rowan clapped him on the back. "Your father and I have agreed to ally our clans against a common enemy who would annihilate the lot of us. Eochan and your father go back to your village to prepare a feast for the visiting queen. His is the enviable task. You and I have a more difficult one, one which will require a leash on your tongue and temper."

"And that is?"

"Persuading Gleannmara's new queen that the people who just raided her clan and stole her cattle are willing to ally themselves with her. She has reason to doubt."

"As do we."

"Which is why we must do or say nothing to set off a spark in this dry brush."

"I make no promises."

Rowan resisted ruffling the boy's hair. That he felt the urge to do so surprised him. Had he missed the blood of his blood and flesh of his flesh that much? He hadn't thought so. He'd lived a good full life with his foster family, more likely faring better than he would have had he remained at Gleannmara.

His thoughts screeched to a halt at the conclusion that smacked him in the face. This was too much to attribute to coincidence. God had caused him to be sent as a slave to Wales for one purpose: to unite Gleannmara. How could Rowan hold anything against Lorcan, when his brother had been but an instrument in a plan bigger than the human eye could see? As in the Scripture regarding Joseph, the weakness of man had been used for a heavenly purpose.

"Rowan!"

Looking up from his motionless daze, Rowan saw Maire running toward him. Her unbound tresses flew like copper banners from her face—a beautiful face creased with concern.

"What happened, man? Are ye sick?"

A tide of emotion welled up inside him, fit to sweep him away. Although Maire stopped just short of him in wariness, he engulfed her in his arms and swung her around with a loud whoop.

"No, sweet queen, I'm *healed!*"

FIFTEEN

W ell, it's clearly not your brain that's improved."
Maire stared at Rowan. He'd had no boils, no visible
ailment. But she had more than her new husband's
vast number of peculiarities to consider, so she shrugged her
curiosity away for a more immediate problem.

It had been all Maire could do to hold Declan and the others back when they saw Eochan leaving with the Cairthan. But
for the big man's assuring wave, it would have been impossible.
So much trust she'd put in the man who now set her down,
grinning like a calf eating brambles.

Rowan looked as boyish as the sullen lad he brought back
with him, except that Maire knew from the strength of the
arms that released her that the Welshman was as manly as any
she'd known.

He made her feel so peculiar inside, as if there were another
woman in there, eager to be released. This stranger within
pulled rebelliously at the restraints Maire enforced upon herself. Maire was a warrior queen first, a woman second. Besides,
she didn't know this woman within—nor did she trust her.

"This is Garret, son of the chief of the Cairthan."

Maire ignored the boy. She nearly had a rebellion on her
hands.

"Ye gave the man your sword and Eochan? By my mother's
gods, did your god tell ye to do such a thing?"

"Aye, for I had no idea of exactly what I would do or say
when I climbed that hill."

"He speaks directly to his god," Maire explained, taking

some satisfaction at the sudden widening of the Cairthan lad's eyes.

"He's a druid warrior?" Garret whispered. "Then that explains how he bewitched me father."

"It was your father's heart and mind that made his decision, nothing to do with spells of any sort."

"I've never seen Lorcan with water wellin' in his eyes. 'Twas surely some kind of magic."

Maire felt as though she were walking blind across a brook, with no foreknowledge of whether a rock or water would support her next step. She stared at Rowan, as full of doubt and wonder as the newest hostage, but he gave in to neither of them.

"No magic, just common sense and fairness." He raised his voice so that all could hear. "We will go to the Cairthan village where Lorcan has gone to prepare a feast to welcome Queen Maire and his new allies."

"Allies!"

"Allies!" Declan echoed Maire's gasp.

"They agreed?" Maire could hardly believe it. Brude said Rowan could do such a thing, but she was hard put to see how. So was he, if he was to be believed.

"Like as not, they've gone to prepare an ambush!"

Garret turned on Declan, his hand flying to the hilt of his dagger. "My father gave his word, dung mouth, and the word of the Cairthan is as good as gold!"

"If it is gold, then ye can be sure, 'twas stolen."

Rowan placed a restraining hand on the boy's shoulder, holding him to the spot.

"And I gave my word, which is just as good," he said to Declan.

"And you trust them?"

All eyes were upon the Welshman now. What respect Brude's blessing hadn't earned him, he'd earned for himself. But to trust a lifelong enemy went against every instinct. Garret stared at him with equal expectation.

"I must. The only way to build trust is to lay the first building block."

"Well, my blade will be ready, I can tell ye that!" Declan swore.

"And mine!" Garret rallied back in defiance.

"Stand with me on this, Maire," Rowan whispered aside before shouting, "And I will cut off the first hand to draw a blade or land a blow on either side, and you know me to be a man of my word."

"And if he doesn't, then I will!"

Maire heard her affirmation with a strange mix of conviction and warmth. The conviction came from believing this man and his queer god could do anything. The warmth was spawned from his request for her support. Often she'd listened while her parents lay abed, talking about decisions to be made for the best of their people. They might have differed in opinion, but before their eyes were shut, they were of one accord.

A divided rule was no rule at all, so Rhian told her once, after he yielded to her mother's decision, not totally convinced she was right. But then, he wasn't certain of his own stance, either. Only hold to that which is total certainty, he advised Maire, and never close the ear to an alternative, which might accomplish the same end.

Maire shook her head, as if to clear the confounding meeting of yesterday with today. Crom's toes, she was starting to think like a bard as well.

Later, when she rode into the Cairthan village, she wondered if she and Rowan could take on both clans should a fight ensue. It was clear that neither side trusted the other. As for the man Lorcan, who also pledged his blade against an instigator, Maire was intrigued. There was something about him that struck a familiar chord, yet she'd never laid eyes upon him before now.

While Lorcan was the host and bade them welcome at his

table, such as it was, it was Rowan who appeared the most at ease. Lorcan acted like one who walked barefoot on a hot rock. Several times she caught him looking at Rowan, almost as though in fear of the man. Had the Welshman's god worked magic? Given his scars and wiry frame, Lorcan was no stranger to courage. No matter what Rowan said, it had to be his god's magic.

"We've no bard to entertain us," the Cairthan chief apologized after a filling meal of roasted and boiled beef. "But we sing the songs of our ancestors as well as any. Garret, fetch the harp from Maithre."

The clan chief's mother was unable to come from the ramshackle dwelling of twig and mud, claiming weakness of heart and ague of the limb. Her grandson dutifully carried her portion of the meal to the mean shelter. And that was one of the better ones, Maire noted. The level of poverty to which these proud people were reduced shocked her. They lived like vagabonds, weathering the winters in huts as cold within as without. Sadly, they could not live on the grass upon which their cattle thrived. The stony Wicklow slopes wouldn't allow it.

Rowan said as much to the men gathered around the cook fire where the remains of the slain beef dripped their juices into the fire.

"I know you believe this land to be sword land. It was for your fathers and mothers before. But there are more of you now. Plough land is necessary to feed both man and beast."

"And who's to tend it, even if a patch of ground could be cleared in these hills?" Lorcan challenged. "The men we have need to stay sharp with weapons, not ploughs!"

"Aye, he's right," Maire agreed. "Look at your own people, Welshman."

"It's true that peace dulled their battle skills and sharpened the plough blades. I can't say if they will ever know such a period again."

Rowan's gaze wandered to the hut into which Garret disappeared. For a moment, he seemed distracted.

"And like as not, neither of these two clans will know it either, at least for long. So we must mend our ways to survive the famine the strength of the sword leaves us to…"

"Unless we plunder."

Lorcan and Declan were caught off-guard by their simultaneous agreement.

"Or unless we develop skill with the sword *and* the plough. The people of Israel built their temple walls with swords in hand after the enemy had destroyed it."

"Who in Crom's name are they?" Declan demanded suspiciously.

"They are the people in the book of Rowan's god, the god's chosen ones."

Maire couldn't help but smile at her husband's look of utter surprise. She'd learned all she could from Brude before they left Gleannmara. The more she found out, the more questions she had.

"Aye, the Jews," Lorcan chimed in. He eyed Rowan's amulet. "I see you're a Christian too."

The Welshman's brow arched even higher. "Too?"

"Some o' the women 'ave been seein' that priest in the glen since he settled there."

"Tomás, I think his name is," Garret said, handing over the harp to his father. "I seen 'im, meself. He talks a lot like you, Emrys. Should have known ye were two of the same kind."

Lorcan locked gazes with Rowan and then passed the instrument. "Play us a tune, Rowan of Emrys…one fit for a king."

Was there no end to her husband's surprises? "You play the harp?"

"I've plucked the strings before."

She looked sharp to Lorcan. "And how did ye know he played?"

"The fingers, Queen Maire. They're long and nimble with calluses on the tips."

"I would tell a story, if it please our queen," Rowan said, drawing her attention back to him. "It won't be poetry, but like those told by bards, 'tis true and a lesson lies within."

Even the crossest of Celts could not resist a good tale over a warm fire, especially with his belly full and his cup brimming with beer. Each man gravitated toward his own clan, so that a line could be drawn to separate the two factions, and they still gathered closer. The Welshman began to pluck at the strings, his voice an octave or so deeper than the instrument, but just as clear.

"This is a story of brothers' treachery..."

Maire started when Lorcan lunged suddenly at Rowan.

"By the gods, you promised!"

Rowan never flinched as the Cairthan chief's blade flashed toward his throat, but Maire was already drawing her sword, as were many on both sides of the campfire.

With warning for all in his tone, the Welshman finished explosively: "And their love!"

The deadly blade stopped short of its intended mark. Maire's sword froze, just clear of its sheath. Like two wolves assessing each other, she and Lorcan slowly backed away—he from Rowan, she from him. Likewise about the campsite, the clan members fell to their respective sides. Weapons, which had appeared almost out of thin air, disappeared. The silence was such that the only sound cutting through the air was that of the harp strings, a rhythmic progression of a plucked chord. With each note, the tension unraveled strand by strand.

Maire's heart drummed double-time to it. Gradually, each successive breath restored it to normalcy. She'd been so taken with Rowan that she'd given the Cairthan the advantage. What she'd have stopped with her blade, her husband stopped with the command in his voice alone. Unless that god of his was walking amongst them with an invisible cloak. She glanced about uneasily for any sign of something moving, which she couldn't see. A kick of dust, an unnatural movement in the grass.

She saw nothing amiss, save that two hostile clans sat little more than a weapon's length apart, and instead of watching each other, they watched the Welshman. 'Twas as if the harp had put a spell on them.

"Joseph, being the son born to Israel in his old age, was the godly man's favorite."

"This Israel is an old man? I thought he was a country of Jews."

"Israel was a father of the nation later named for him."

"Crom's toes, how many wives did he have?"

"Just listen to the story of the brothers, Maire."

Maire bit back the legion of questions that sprang to her mind. Again she scanned the faces, wondering if they found this as farfetched as she.

"Joseph's brothers couldn't bear to kill him, so they sold him into slavery instead and told their father that his favorite had been killed by a wild beast. They gave the old man Joseph's coat of many colors—"

"How many?" Maire squirmed beneath Rowan's sharp glance. "Well, if he had many colors in his brat, like as not he was a prince."

Everyone knew the number of colors in a person's cloak was a sign of nobility and wealth.

"And so he was carried away to the land of Egypt."

Egypt, now she'd heard of that place.

"But even being forced to live among strangers in a strange land, he never blamed God for his misfortune. He never stopped worshiping the Lord of hosts."

"Your god?"

"The One God, my queen."

"So you say."

Maire thought better of further questioning, at least aloud. Feeling like a chastised child, she settled back, her hand resting on her sword, lest the Cairthan offer further threat.

Gradually, sheer wonder overtook her and she listened as attentively as those around her. This Joseph, despite all the horrible things that happened to him, still clung to a god who, for all sight and purpose, seemed to have abandoned the lad. In fact, he had more troubles than Crom had toes, what with his master's wife chasing after him and him being put in prison falsely charged. It looked like nothing was ever going to go right for this lad again.

Were it her, Maire would have found another god. She repressed her thought though, for the story was flowing over them like a soothing brook on a warm day—and the Welshman made it clear he didn't take kindly to interruption. He talked like a bard, played like a bard, and acted like one, to be sure. He also mesmerized like one.

She had no idea of how much time passed as the story of how Joseph's faith in this invisible god delivered him from slavery and treachery to the highest esteem in the king's court. His god spoke to him with his dreams and gave him counsel, which saved an entire nation from starvation. The Egyptians had put enough away because of the warning in the dreams, then they shared their stores with people who suffered in neighboring lands when the seven years of blight struck.

"It was then that Joseph's brothers came to him, not knowing who he was, and asked for help."

"And he gave it?"

Rowan smiled at her and strummed across the strings. "Aye, he gave it."

"He should have cut them up and sewed the barren fields with their blood and flesh!"

To hear the indignant huzzahs in agreement with Declan's fervent opinion, one would think the men here were Joseph himself!

"He could have, but he didn't because his God is one of forgiveness. There had been enough trouble and heartache without bringing more about by taking revenge."

"Aye, one act of vengeance will beget another."

"Which is why we're sitting here now, thanks to the wisdom

of Maire and Lorcan rather than drawing each other's blood."

The Welshman blessed both the Cairthan chief and her with his approving gaze. Maire wondered if Lorcan felt half as good as she did at that moment.

"So when did Joseph tell them who he was?" Garret prompted. The lad leaned forward eagerly waiting.

Maire was at least glad the man put his brothers through a scare before revealing the truth of his identity and that he intended to forgive them. It was only fitting. That they'd not killed youngest Benjamin, now the old chief's favorite, and that they'd been so distraught when Joseph held the lad hostage were good signs the lot had changed for the better.

It was a shame Brude was not here to hear this tale, not that the bard could tell it better. The only noise, save the harp and Rowan's voice, was the occasional dollop of drink being poured into the listeners' cups. The bard, however, could make a fine rhyme of it, so that it could be passed down, word for word, without the slightest change or embellishment in the way the Celtic past was preserved. And this story should be preserved, she thought, blinking away the emotion that blurred her vision as Rowan stood, signifying the approaching end of his song.

"And he fell upon Benjamin's neck and wept, and Benjamin wept upon his neck. Moreover, he kissed all his brethren and wept upon them. And after that, his brethren talked with him."

"Ah, preserve us, 'twas a damp time," Eochan exclaimed. "Here, little flower. Let me get that."

The burly warrior took up the hem of his brat and leaned forward to wipe a tear from the cheek of a brown-haired young maid, who'd been giving him special attention since they'd arrived. He'd introduced her earlier as Blath. Maire smiled. At least that was one pair of Cairthan and Niall that wouldn't be warring tonight. And a strange mix they were. One was as small and delicate as the other was large and hearty.

"So, Rowan ap Emrys…" Lorcan cleared this throat before going on. "Is it time now?"

"Aye, son, it's time."

"Maithre!"

Maire rose, uncertain which shock to react to first. An older woman stood at the edge of the circle, her salt-and-pepper hair braided and wrapped in a crown about her head. It was her only adornment, save the silver broach holding her cloak around thin shoulders. She smiled through tears, and with the smile seemed to grow younger before Maire's eyes. Furrows plowed by age and worry faded, revealing what once must have been a youthful beauty. The woman stepped forward, extending her hand to Rowan.

"I knew 'twas you the moment you began to play."

"'Twas you who taught me, Maithre."

Maithre? But Delwyn ap Emrys was Rowan's mother, not this woman. Maire compared the woman's face and coloring to that of the Welshman. It was the same, as was the Cairthan chief.

"By my father's blood...Maire, ye've married a Cairthan!"

Declan moved up beside her. Although he was as taken aback as she, Maire was glad to have him at her back because she wasn't so sure of her knees at the moment.

Rowan had deceived her and her clan. No wonder he wanted peace between their peoples!

"And will you be speaking with me, brother, like in the story?" Lorcan asked.

Maire wondered at the odd note of hope in Lorcan's voice.

"Aye, but I'll not be weeping on your thick neck!" Rowan released his mother from his arms and turned to his brother to embrace him. The two clapped each other on the back soundly. Around them, emotions as mixed as those Maire felt were reflected in murmurs and oaths of surprise.

"He's my uncle?"

"Aye, lad," Lorcan assured his son. "And king of Gleannmara."

"But under false pretenses." Maire moved forward. "I agreed

to marry no Cairthan."

"You married *me*, Maire," Rowan reminded her sternly, "and I am Cairthan by blood."

"You said the Roman and his Welsh wife were your parents."

"They were. They bought me and then raised me as their son rather than a slave. But my real mother is Ciara of the Cairthan, wife of Bearach."

Garret looked at his father in disbelief. "You sold your own brother as a slave?"

"I'm not proud of it, lad. I'm just grateful to the stars that I've had the chance to right things."

"Not the stars, Lorcan," Ciara said gently. "Thank God. The same God who saved Joseph and his family."

"This story was real then?" Maire asked. "Not some farce ye spun to pass the night?"

At that moment, if someone told her Declan were a ghost and his brother a faery, she'd not dispute them. All the faith she'd built in Rowan crumbled in confusion. Maire wished she'd insisted on Brude accompanying them, but the trip across the sea had worn the old druid out. She had to consider his age.

"Maire, by following God's will, Joseph saved not only his people but his captors as well."

Rowan took her by the shoulders, his fingers tightening as though he could force her to believe in him.

"Maire, I believe God sent you to me so that I could help the people of Gleannmara…not just Cairthan or Niall, but all those who depend on this land as home."

"We have a common enemy," he shouted above the growing din of disbelief and doubt. "This enemy has bled Gleannmara! He has robbed all her people of food and of dignity. He is the blight we must unite to extinguish."

"Extinguish a druid?" Even Lorcan was hard pressed to believe what he heard, though it benefited him to do so.

"The God of Israel gave Joseph the meaning of dreams the pharaoh's magicians and soothsayers could not discern. He is greater than any druid, for it was He who created them, as well as us. Who knows better how to deal with them than the Creator of all?"

"So he talks to you in your dreams?"

Rowan shook his head at his brother. "Nay, but..."

"The Lord God answers prayer," his mother finished. "And if you do not believe the story of Joseph, then believe this." She laid her hand on Rowan's arm. "I never thought you dead. And when Father Tomás told me of this God, I prayed that somehow you would return to Gleannmara someday and set things right."

"You suspected me, Maithre?"

Ciara smiled sadly. "Nay, Lorcan. I thought you had been fooled as well. I did not think you had a hand in Rowan's disappearance. Looking back, I should have. I have seen you brood in the still of the night, tortured by a deed or memory you kept to yourself. Now I can praise God that I may someday lay my head to rest without the pain of knowing one son exacted deadly vengeance on the other."

"Maithre!"

Rowan and Lorcan reached for Ciara as she swayed unsteadily. The latter stepped aside so that his younger brother might assist the woman.

"Sit, Maithre." He eased her onto a skin-covered rock, which served as a bench for the chief and his guests. "You've overdone yourself."

The temper that tried to muster over Rowan's trickery would not form. Instead, compassion forced it aside. Maire knelt at the woman's knee.

"Here, take my horn and sip. 'Twill give you strength."

Instead of taking the drink, Ciara brushed Maire's cheek with the back of her fingers. "Do you know God, daughter?"

It shamed Maire to shake her head in denial. The more she

heard of him, the more she desired to know him. Yet there was something frightening about it that held her back.

"I welcome his help, though," she answered lamely. "What Rowan says is true. We have a common enemy, more than one, by the look of things. Morlach and the deprivation he's wrought upon us."

Maire shoved up to her feet, accepting Rowan's helping hand.

"Emrys may have misled me, but his reason is sound. The Niall have a druid and he says that our king is the one who will lead Gleannmara back to peace and prosperity. Emrys's god will show him how."

"If he really did create the druids," Eochan murmured, not fully convinced.

"But He did, you red-headed oaf!" The girl Blath thumped the warrior's thick biceps with her fist. "He created the world and all its creatures, man included, in six days, no less."

"Ach, a man can't build a house in six days, much less a world," Declan sneered. "'Tis a faery tale, I'm thinking."

"An almighty, all-powerful God can do anything," Rowan reminded him patiently.

Declan pulled his cloak tighter about his shoulder. "Then have him rush in the summer a bit quicker! 'Tis no night to sleep outside."

"Our old women sleep out in nights worse that this, Drumkilly," Garret boasted. "My grandmother only uses the lodge because she's mother of the chief. It's station, not fragility, that puts her there."

Eochan hooted with laughter and called out to his brother. "Come on, little miss! We've chased the moon from one side of the sky to the other, with all this talk of gods and brothers. Time we tucked ye in, lest ye take a chill!"

Laughter cut loose on both sides of the camp. Some men started to take Eochan's advice to heart and wandered off.

"Queen Maire, will you and Rowan share my humble

lodge?" Ciara asked. "It's the largest and warmest we have to offer."

"Nay, Maithre." Rowan placed his arm around Maire's shoulders. "We're newlyweds. We need no lodge to keep us warm yet."

Maire colored as the direction of the amusement turned toward her. "Aye, he has more hot air than one of those furnaces his folks use to heat their baths."

"Heated baths?" Garret echoed, the idea clearly a novelty.

"Aye, he left a near palace to come back and play this Joseph." She elbowed Rowan playfully. "My guess is, he's either daft or there is some merit to this god he rambles on about. I've yet to decide."

Rowan bent down and rumbled against her ear. "But we've just begun to get acquainted, right, *muirnait?*"

Beloved? He called her beloved? Oh, that a word should wreak such havoc with her mind! She felt as bubbly inside as shaken beer, and near drunk from it! Since there was no hope of coherent reply, Maire suffered this sweet torture in silence.

SIXTEEN

Wait now. You mean to say ye want them what has a knack for working the land to move to lower lands and them that is cattle folk to tend to the livestock in the high pastures?"

The Cairthan chief expressed the same doubt Maire kept to herself. Rowan had worked miracles thus far, but when would he overstep the patience and cooperation of the two rival tribes? How far would his god allow the man to go? Lorcan's reaction was the exact one she expected of her own people when they heard the plan.

"What have they got to lose here?" Rowan swept his arm across the landscape of tumbledown lodgings. "Certainly not their homes. And at least they'll have decent ground to work. Pasture grass will grow wherever there's a patch of earth in the rock, but not so corn, at least to any useful quantity. And cattle can be moved much easier than crops to better land, once they've chewed down their current place."

"To the innocent ear, this plan has merit." Lorcan's thick brow knitted, foretelling his objection. "But this ear isn't innocent, brother. Ye'd have my people grow corn for hers."

"And hers tend cattle for you, the combination of both our herds. While closer to the rath, we grow enough grain to last both clans and livestock through the barren winter months."

"And what do you think of this, Queen Maire? Will your people come up here to live with mine and keep track of the herds?"

Maire wasn't certain, but Rowan had not misled her yet in

195

the welfare of Gleannmara's people. "Perhaps as hostages of goodwill at first. We'll exchange our cattle tenders for your farmers and builders."

Rowan's approving gaze took the early morning chill away from her bones. Maire gave him a hint of a smile in return, but he'd already turned back to his brother.

"You see, Lorcan, we've more than one enemy between us. Aye, we have Morlach to contend with, but we have the survival of our peoples to consider as well. I want more than survival for them. I want prosperity. So long as you keep to the highlands, you'll never be able to support yourselves with any success except by digging out scraps from the wilds or stealing the fruits of another's labor."

"It has kept the Cairthan alive and well for years—"

"Alive, aye," Rowan cut in, "but hardly well. How many did you lose this last winter?"

Garret, who stood behind his father, spoke up. "Some twenty, not countin' the babes."

The lad had been listening all the while the men spoke, as had Declan and Eochan. In fact, it astonished Maire that her foster brothers hadn't objected from the moment the ideas formed on Rowan's lips.

Rowan nodded. "The boy makes my point. What have you to lose?"

"Our pride."

Declan broke his silence at last. "By our mother's gods, man! The Welshman—" He broke off, realizing that was no longer the case. "Our king is offering you an alliance, not charity. I'd wager there'll be those at the rath who'll not take to coming up here and staring at the backside of cows all day as something to be proud of either. But I'll tell ye this." The fair-haired warrior leaned forward. "By the looks of things, we've less reason to come up here than you have to come down to us."

"Aye, think, man," Eochan agreed. "Our peoples will share the best of both worlds."

Lorcan was not as optimistic. "If Morlach lets us live long enough."

"Your brother stood up to Morlach's apprentice without so much as a blink when the druid put the curse of boils and plague upon him. See ye any blemish, Cairthan?"

Maire ran her hand over the muscled plain of Rowan's bare arm. All that her tactile senses registered was smooth skin, bristled with a manly scatter of hair. Suddenly, as if the warmth of his arm were as hot as the coals smoldering in the cook fire nearby, she snatched her hand away.

She was not the only one disconcerted, however. Rowan glanced at her and their eyes locked for what seemed the balance of the day. Yet the sun still held its spot in the morning sky, still as Maire's breath.

"Is this true?" Lorcan asked skeptically. Garret stepped closer to look at his uncle's arms, which were bared by the short sleeve of his sackcloth robe.

"I saw it with me own eyes," Eochan averred.

"And I." Declan's echo seemed to repeat itself among those of the Niall who'd been with them the day of the beach landing.

Maire found her voice. "He told Cromthal to tell Morlach that neither he nor any of his kind was welcome at Gleannmara and ordered the man away."

Odd that she'd once thought the man fey, crazy as a swineherd, yet now she spoke of the incident with pride. She'd chosen well. But then, there hadn't been many other choices, had there?

She watched her husband's face as he continued to present his case to the assembly of men. Its strong, masculine features were those of a leader, well placed, chiseled by a masterful hand. His god? If this god was truly the creator of man and woman, he'd done a fine job with Rowan ap Emrys...or should she say O'Cairthan?

"I think Rowan has a sound idea." Ciara stepped into the

circle with a large pot of porridge hanging from her arm. "And I've see more years than either of you."

The men took bowls and cups from Blath so that Ciara might dish them out their share of the meal. Chunks of meat left over from the night before had been put in the mix for additional flavor.

"Things are not always as good as they look, Maithre," Lorcan reminded her.

Ciara handed over the serving pot to Blath, but Eochan leapt to his feet and intercepted it.

"Here, let me carry this for you."

Blath turned pink, a shy smile showing her acceptance and appreciation of the big man's gesture. Behind him, Declan snorted and elbowed Maire. Her foster brother didn't need to elaborate. It was clear as day that Eochan of Drumkilly was smitten by the Cairthan lass and that his affection was returned. Maire had seen the two of them wander off into the darkness for a while the night before, longer than it took to fetch a turn of wood for the fire.

"As I see it," Ciara said, taking a seat next to Lorcan, "it's no different than deciding which bolt of cloth to use for which garment. The heavier cloth is more suited to a cloak, while the lighter is ideal for a robe."

"Or choosing a weapon that's best suited for combat," Garret suggested eagerly. "At close quarters a sword or axe is too awkward. Only a dagger will do."

"Or this!" Eochan boasted, holding out his fist.

Maire chuckled along with everyone else in earshot. It was so unlike her eldest foster brother to brag. Declan did enough for the two of them. But then this attraction between a man and a woman made even the most predictable of man unpredictable.

Or woman, for that matter.

That very morning, she'd awakened before the sun's first light to find herself curled against her husband, tight enough to cramp a flea between them. Their blankets had been doubled over them rather than wrapped separately about each as they'd started out the night before. There was enough land about the camp to graze dozens of cattle, yet she'd wound up next to Rowan, in his arms, no less! When she opened her eyes, his grin was the first sight to greet her. Rightly, she rolled away in an instant, but by the bite of the frost on the ground, she missed the warmth of their cozy nest.

The conversation at hand gave way to other topics as the clans took their meal. No small amount of admiration and speculation was centered on the two warhorses grazing nearby. Other men and women ventured to say who was best suited to the land and who to the sword or the livestock.

Rowan's idea had germinated at least, Maire observed. Whether it would take root remained to be seen. It did sound good, but how long could this testy camaraderie last before someone came to blows?

The only way to build trust is to give one the chance to provide the building block for it.

Rowan's words of the previous day rang true in her heart. Brude told her to follow her heart. Maire scooped up some of porridge with the scone one of the Cairthan women handed out and popped it into her mouth, chewing thoughtfully. Her decision was made. There was no doubt in her mind the decision was good for Gleannmara. The problem lay in getting two peoples to accept it. As queen, however, she would stand by Rowan's idea and personally run through the first rebel who tried to disrupt it!

"Look, a rider approaches, there, at the bottom of the slope!"

Maire and the others stood, staring in the direction young Garret pointed. Indeed, there was someone coming. His coming on horseback suggested the news he brought was urgent. One word, one name came to Maire's mind, wiping out everything except the cold dread that seeped through her veins.

Morlach!

The messenger was from Erc of Drumkilly, Maire's foster father. Morlach and Finnaid had passed through Declan and Eochan's home tuath with an entourage headed for Tara. It was Morlach's intent to appeal to the high king for justice regarding Maire's keeping Gleannmara from his clutches by marrying Rowan instead of him. His honor had been insulted. The good faith with which he'd invested his time and money in running Gleannmara while Maire came of age deserved more than being forbidden to set foot on its land by some hostage, a stranger taken and married by the queen to keep Morlach from his just reward. The druid expected to extract an honor price at the least, if not have Maire's marriage dissolved. She had married someone else while under royal contract to him.

"But there was no contract. I pledged nothing!" Fury consumed Maire's voice. "If I owe the blackguard anything, it's my sword through his heart for what he's done here!"

"If he has a heart," Garret remarked dourly. "The druid has done us both much harm."

Lorcan was even less optimistic. "Aye, but who will petition the high king against him?" He turned to Rowan. "Boils and satire is one thing, but if Morlach wins Diarhmott's support, the Uí Niall and the Cairthan can marry to the last couple, for all the good it will do when they die to last couple as well."

Rowan closed his eyes for a moment, as if steeling himself. Or was he talking to his god? Maire shivered, wondering if the god came as spirit or man in an invisible cloak.

"I don't believe Diarhmott will take up arms against us, if we can convince him that there is more to this matter than politics, that it's a spiritual matter as well. He has a Christian wife and the support of Armagh."

Declan sneered. "Think ye a wife and a cluster of priests will sway the king against a druid as powerful as Morlach?"

Rowan smiled. "But Diarhmott will not be going against a

woman or an old priest. He'll be going against their God, the one God. And that, good people, he will not do."

"He's no Christian!" Lorcan declared. "And Morlach helped him to power."

"Along with Maeve and the Niall," Maire pointed out, not about to let the druid take all the glory. She wished she had the same self-assurance Rowan conveyed. She wished Brude were here. He'd know what to do. Perhaps she should send for the druid.

"But 'twas an Armagh bishop, I think, that presided with the druid over his coronation," Ciara put in.

Garret backed her up, grinning. "Aye, the old man nearly put his staff through the king's foot, so I hear."

Rowan stepped up on one of the stone benches situated around the campfire.

"Enough!" he shouted, silencing the individual discussions of speculation that ensued. "I will go to the high king myself to present Gleannmara's case." He glanced down at Maire and held out his hand. "Will you go with me, little queen?"

Maire pulled herself up on the flat rock with it. "Aye, I'll go with my king. And I'll tell Diarhmott of how well Morlach cared for my land and its people!" She turned to Lorcan. "And will you go to speak for the Cairthan?"

Garret jumped up in his father's place before the older man could make up his mind. "I will! I am the aiccid."

Lorcan was not as eager, nor as convinced as the others who volunteered to follow Rowan to Tara. He stared at his brother as though looking through the man, but his answer was nowhere to be found. Ciara put a hand on his arm.

"Let me go with him, son."

"Nay, Maithre, your legs—" Rowan started.

"I'll ride," the lady answered, cutting him off. "Aching bones is the least of my worries."

"Aye, like as not, Morlach told Drumkilly of his plans so that Rowan and his queen would hasten to Tara as well to rebuke him."

Lorcan shoved himself to his feet, the slowness of his rising telling that the same cold, which bothered his mother, had begun to plague him too.

"But no soul from Gleannmara will ever see Tara," he predicted eerily. "I'd wager my sword hand he plans an attack."

"And I'll wager mine that we will be expecting it," Rowan countered. "But we will reach Tara, and I will win Diarhmott's neutrality, if not his support."

"Then you go, but neither our mother nor my son will go with you."

"Father!"

The rebellious fire in Ciara's gaze took Lorcan back.

"I'll not be told by the son I bore into this world and reared from a squallin' pup what to do."

"Do what ye will then, but that squallin' pup—" he pointed to Garret—"will not be goin'."

"I'm just gone sixteen! I've a right to make my own decisions, Da!" Garret stepped next to Rowan. "And I'm goin' with the king, if he'll have me."

"Ye'd risk my only child on this god of yours?" Lorcan challenged his brother.

"I'd say the risk is up to him to take. He carries himself with reason beyond his years, from what I've seen."

"Then I'll go!"

Broad, thin shoulders dropping in resignation, Lorcan turned from his son's defiant pose and extended his right hand to Rowan. "I lost his mother to Morlach's greed, and I robbed my mother of one of her own born. Crom Cruach's shadow has blighted my days ever since."

A handshake not quite enough, Lorcan embraced his younger brother fully. "Have a care with them, Rowan of Gleannmara, and go in the light of this god of yours. Succeed, and the Cairthan will do whatever you think is best for Gleannmara." He cleared his throat and backed away, but the blur in his eyes was not one of tenderness but threat.

"Fail and, should you survive, I will kill you with my bare hands…and we'll have nothin' more to do with a clan destined for sure destruction. We'll not stand against Morlach's black art, not even with that old Uí Niall druid behind ye."

"Brude has forgotten more than Morlach has ever learned!"

"Aye, lass, that's the point. Your Brude has forgotten!"

"The one God forgets nothing and knows all." That said, Rowan stepped down from the rock and turned to help Maire. She needed no assistance, but at the moment, she needed the reassurance of his touch, of his conviction. She wanted to believe this god was as strong as Rowan claimed. It appeared that Rowan did have the god's ear. Brude said as much. But years of fear in which the power of the druids was drummed into her head were hard to dismiss as lightly as her husband did.

"If we return with Diarhmott's promise of neutrality, will the Cairthan not only swear allegiance to me and Maire, but to the one God?"

"If your god brings you back alive and in one piece *with* the high king's word to keep out o' this muck of a squabble, I'll kiss the bottoms of this god's boots!"

Rowan laughed. Despite Lorcan's hostility, he embraced his elder sibling in a bear hug. "Good enough, brother. I'll hold you to that."

Ciara placed an arm at Maire's back. Without looking at her, the men's mother sighed.

"I prayed long for that sight, my queen. Now God has answered my prayers beyond my wildest dreams."

"So you believe all will be well then?"

Ciara's face was aglow when she looked at Maire. It looked as though the sun erased the lines of age and replaced them with joy. "Aye, I do, so long as we walk in God's will and give Him the glory for all our blessings."

Maire scowled. "So this god doesn't take well to failure, I suppose."

"He never fails," the woman answered patiently. "*We* do, but He doesn't."

"But if he's with us and we fail…"

"Then we fail because of something amiss with us, not Him. But He'll give us the strength and courage to try again."

For all he was claimed to be, this god was a confounding one!

"This is making my head hurt, woman! First your god will see it done, but if it isn't, it's not his fault, but he'll help pick up the pieces and try again. Why doesn't he just make us do it right to start with and be done with it?"

Maire's exasperation drew Rowan's attention. He glanced in concern from his mother to Maire.

"Is something wrong?"

Ciara smiled. "Only that God gives us the will to choose right or wrong, and that if we choose wrong…"

"He lets a fool fall right on his face!" Maire finished with an enlightened look. "Now that makes sense."

Satisfied, at least for the moment, she turned to Declan.

"We've a trip ahead of us, brother. Best see what can be put together to see us to Tara."

Declan bowed shortly in acknowledgment. Then, spinning on his heels, he slapped Eochan, who was leaning over Blath in a conversation totally apart from that which occupied the rest of them, across the back of the head. "Come, lover boy, we've work to do."

Maire chuckled when Eochan came up swinging, but the younger, more agile Declan avoided the halfhearted blow and was away. At the touch of a hand at her back, she turned, expecting to see Ciara again, but it was not Rowan's mother whose arm slipped about her waist. It was her husband himself.

"You make me proud to serve you, Maire." The earnestness of his gaze was enough to melt the heart of a stone statue, much less that of a mere woman. And at that moment, that was what Maire felt like, not warrior nor queen but all woman.

She wished for some equally moving reply, but all that came to her rattled mind was out before she could stop it.

"So this god of yours, he wears boots, does he?"

The travelers from Gleannmara spent that night in Drumkilly's hall. Erc and Maida, Maire's foster parents, put on a sumptuous feast in the tall thatch-domed hall. Garret and Ciara enjoyed places of honor along with Maire, Rowan, and Declan. Eochan elected to remain with the Cairthan, allegedly to help Lorcan decide which of his people were best suited for the planting and building and which would remain behind to tend the cattle. Declan put it most likely when he remarked that the man had fallen in love with being a hostage. Eochan managed a show of indignation at the jibe, but it was his cheeky grin that gave him away as he rode away from them to deliver the message to Brude to meet them at Tara.

Servants kept food and drink in plenty until Maire had to say no or let out her belt. The latter being a sign of overindulgence, she covered her cup with her hand each time one passed with a flagon of wine or pitcher of beer. Rowan, too, kept a clear head and satisfied belly, no more, no less. He played the part of king to her queen as if he'd been born to the role.

In truth, Maire supposed he had. He was a lord in his own right in Wales and by birth at Gleannmara. If she was to follow the man's line of reason, his God had delivered his crown, or in his case, Rhian's torque, through her. Whether this same God would bless her remained to be seen. So as not to offend him, however, she did bow her head when Rowan asked blessing on the meal. So, she noticed, did the others. It was out of respect and hospitality. She supposed this god deserved at least that much for allying the Cairthan with them. Blood ties were strong. As Erc pointed out, half in heart and half in jest, she'd done well by Gleannmara despite that red-headed temper of hers.

After hearing the tales of their adventures in Wales, with Rowan and Declan playing the bards, games were suggested, but Maire declined. Between the ale, the food, and the good company, sleep called louder than her hosts.

"We'll make up the celebration at the May games, I promise," Maire told the older couple.

Erc and Maida held hands throughout most of the evening, and the smiles they exchanged when no one was looking embraced Maire's heart. That was what she wanted, that kind of love. Were Maeve and Rhian still holding hands on the other side? As she lay on a plump pallet of straw on the floor of the hall, where servants and visitors alike had settled for the night, she sighed dreamily.

"What was that about?" Rowan's low whisper startled her. "What thoughts make our queen sigh like a lovestruck maid?"

"Hold my hand, Rowan."

This time, it was his turn to be taken back. "What?"

"Are you deaf? I said hold my hand!"

Impatient, she reached across the short space between their pallets. In a moment, her hand was enveloped in the strength and warmth of the man lying at her side.

"Are you certain you don't want me to hold all of you?"

Her heart tripped. He spoke so low, to avoid the ears of those resting about them, that she didn't quite make out his words. Or perhaps she simply didn't believe what she heard.

"What?"

A low rumble of response escaped his chest. He propped himself up on his elbow, still clinging to the hand she instinctively threatened to pull away. The glow of the dying firelight highlighted his handsome features. His was the kind of face the stonecutters fashioned effigies from. Clean lines, chiseled to the right proportion. Handsome. A girlish sigh built in her chest, but his wry reply killed it.

"Are you deaf, woman?" He moved closer. "Or is this some feminine wile of yours trying to get me to move closer?"

Maire arched one skeptical brow. To her astonishment, Rowan leaned over and brushed it with his lips.

"What game are you about now, Emrys?"

"Every morning I wake up with you fitted against me as if we were two nestled cups. If you wish to come into my arms, then come outright rather than sneak up on me while I sleep."

Blood ran hot to Maire's cheeks. "Of all the—"

Rowan silenced her indignation, devastating it with a kiss. Her lips moved, not with words but in concert with his. And when he pulled her to him, her body obeyed eagerly, as if it craved the warmth it had secretly sought out in her sleep.

Except that she was not asleep. How could one sleep when a ferocious tide catapulted through her veins and sweet thunder clapped in her brain? She wanted to reach for her head to secure it, but it was Rowan's hair her hands clasped. On a mission of their own, her fingers entwined in the dark, thick locks secured by a leather thong at his neck. In a moment they were freed.

Then, with no warning, Rowan stiffened and rolled away, leaving naught but the strip of leather in her hand. His chest rose and fell, as if though took all his breath to keep up with it. He closed his eyes and swallowed.

Maire watched the bob of his Adam's apple, alarm invading the rhapsody his ardor still played on the strings of her heart.

"What is it?"

A few feet away, someone rolled over and raised his head. Realizing she'd raised her voice, she crawled closer and whispered again.

"Rowan, are you sick?" Maire remembered his declaring how he'd been healed upon coming down the hill from meeting with the Cairthan.

"Nay, I'm just tired."

"Then what were you healed of the other day?" So much

had come about so quickly she'd never had the chance to satisfy her curiosity.

"I was wronged by my brother, and hatred festered in me like a green-headed boil, no matter how I meant to please God. And the moment I forgave Lorcan, it was gone. It was as if a weight had been removed from my heart." He laughed to himself. "How many times I've told others that forgiveness is oft the first step in healing a scarred heart, and never took my own advice."

With a heavy sigh, he pulled up his blanket and jerked over on his side, his back turned to her.

"Best get some sleep, little queen. We've a long day ahead tomorrow."

Sleep?

Never had any idea seemed so outlandish. Her pulse stumbled over itself, pushing blood through her veins as though she'd been pulled from the midst of a heated race; and he babbles on about forgiveness and sleep.

Well, she certainly wasn't about to forgive *him*, workin' a body up with his absurd ideas of married intimacy and then philosophizing about forgiveness and sleep.

Maire threw her blanket aside and climbed to her feet.

Gathering up her sword, she started for the door of the lodge, picking her way around those sleeping in her path. The night was star cast, a veritable blanket of diamonds glittering against a blue velvet sky. She knew the layout of the rath, so she could have found the training posts with or without the help of nature's light.

Sleep indeed.

The thick post took the full force of her blow.

It was fitting that it was hewed from a rowan, for its ability to endure. Yet it was another Rowan she pictured as she struck again.

The commotion drew the attention of Drumkilly's guards, but she continued. The muscles in her arms trembled with the bone-jarring vibration of her last blow. Still, she delivered another, hacking at the hard wood again and again. Let them watch, she thought, drawing back the heavy metal blade, its tip starting to drag on the retreat. But woe to the one who tried to stop her before this wild binge of energy had run its course.

SEVENTEEN

The open sky of the following night spared the travelers a blanket of frost for their early morning bed. Rowan and his mother arose to pray, while the others sang the sun song as the eastern light feasted on a covering of dew instead. It glistened everywhere, from treetops to meadow blades, giving the land a faerylike appearance. No hint of the imminent danger that had kept posted guards awake all night made itself known.

Maire rolled up her blanket and skins and kicked into the campfire the piece of wood she'd placed between her and Rowan the night before. Indeed, the air was warmer, but not enough to replace what he had to offer her. It stung that he'd not protested her precaution to keep them apart. In fact, he'd looked relieved as he'd settled down and turned his back to her. So she'd spent another troubled night, while he snored, maddeningly at peace.

Tonight, she'd give this prayer a try, she decided after a breakfast of cold scones and cheese from Drumkilly's kitchen added to leftover goose, which the men killed and roasted for supper the night before. The truth was, now that her belly was full Maire wanted a nice warm bed, not another day astride Tamar. Her head bobbed in time with the mare's soft *clip-clop*. With each step her chin fell closer and closer to her chest.

The queen didn't know when it finally struck. All she knew was suddenly she was face down in the horse's shining mane and keeling off to the side. In a panicked state of mind, she released the reins and outstretched her arms to break her headlong fall to the well-worn road. Her lungs full of a startled gasp, she waited for the earth to knock it from her, but instead, it was cinched out by the band of living muscle, which caught her full weight at her waist.

"Ho, sleepyhead. One night away from me and look what you've come to!"

The men about them snickered as Rowan hauled a befuddled Maire over to Shahar's back in front of him. She shook the sleep from her head—what would leave it, that is.

"'Tis the nights *with* you that's led me to this."

Her sharp retort cut loose the poor restraint of the eavesdroppers. Outright laughter erupted round them, blowing scarlet into Maire's neck and face.

"That's *not* what I meant, you giggling bunch of nitwits!"

"That you enjoy my son's company of a night is your right as his wife," Ciara assured her with matronly approval. "It's one of God's gifts to be shared."

Maire started to deny any such gift had been shared, much less enjoyed, but the tightening of Rowan's arm about her and the gruff clearing of his throat warned her against it. They were *supposed* to be married and enjoying the conjugal rights. With little choice but to acquiesce in silence, Maire sat stiffly.

"Well, there's nothing this god has to say about sharin' a horse, is there?"

Rowan laughed at her peevish utterance, and Maire's face grew even hotter.

"No, *I'm* having the say on this. I'll not have our queen falling off her horse and breaking her lovely neck before things are right with Gleannmara. It simply wouldn't be a kingly thing to do."

"Ho, Maire, if you're as well met in private as ye are in this mischief, 'tis no wonder you can't keep your eyes open," Declan teased.

"Look, brother!" Maire pointed to a tall, stately oak shading a curve in the road ahead. "Why don't ye save that tongue for kissin' another tree?"

With some semblance of satisfaction from the guffaws her remark spawned, Maire turned her gaze toward the rise ahead. At least she was not the only one with a red face now. And it *was* her prerogative, if she chose, to lean against the stalwart chest to her back. Besides, she'd need a clear, well rested head for the confrontation that surely awaited at Tara.

Off and on, Maire catnapped. The forested roadside was the perfect place for ambush, but she could not hold her head up. Instinct told her that she was safe from any human danger, cradled as she was in her husband's arms. There was no such refuge from that of a spiritual kind. For that, she was forced to rely on Rowan's god.

If only Brude traveled with them, she thought sleepily. But there'd been no time to lose in heading Morlach off before he gained too much sway with the high king, so they'd sent for Gleannmara's druid with a message for Brude to meet them with all haste at Tara. Until then, they were on their own.

"Hold, who goes there?"

At the distant shout of one of the rear guards, Maire stiffened in front of Rowan. Suddenly she was lifted from her perch and dropped unceremoniously to the ground. Her knees, unprepared for the impact, nearly buckled beneath her.

"Stay here while I find out what's amiss," Rowan told her, turning the horse in its own space with a jerk of the reins.

Dazed, Maire watched him ride through the men on foot toward where the O'Croinin guarded their flank. Gathering her wits, Maire launched up into Tamar's saddle and started after her husband. She was a warrior queen, not some wide-eyed ninny afraid of tearin' the hem of her skirt!

By now she and her men had drawn their weapons, but no enemy was in sight. The forest dared to be as still as it had been the night before, despite the feeling in every bone that something wasn't quite right.

As the mare raced ahead, closing the distance between Maire and Rowan, the carpet of damp leaves and debris muffled the impact of hoofs on the ground. Maire shouted over the muted thunder of their approach.

"Where are they, O'Croinin?"

"I…" The burly watchman glanced over his shoulder at the approaching king and back again at the voluminous tree-shrouded road behind them.

"Well?" Maire's heart beat furiously against her chest, as if she'd run, rather than rode to the rear of the troop.

"It wasn't what I saw exactly."

The guard's slow remark raised the hair on Maire's neck and arms. *Spirits?* She turned wide eyes upon her husband.

Oblivious to her alarm, Rowan took the man's befuddlement in patient stride. "Then what made you issue your challenge?"

"I heard voices. They was arguin'—and I felt like I was bein' watched."

"What kind of voices?" The possible answer unnerved her.

"Men's voices. They argued and then they was gone."

"Ye ain't been swillin' that Cairthan mead in yer pouch, have ye, Dub?" one of the men teased.

The others laughed, releasing the anxiety that had held every muscle and tongue in check.

"Ach, how far do ye think we'd 'a been if ye hadn't let your imagination run away with ye, man?" Gilly O'Croinan teased his red-faced brother.

"Three lengths of a fool, Gilly, and if ye don't believe me, lay down yourself and measure it!"

The men roared and slapped Dublach on the back before forming into a haphazard column to march again. Even Gilly acknowledged his brother's quick wit, laughing as loud as any.

"What do you think?" Maire asked Rowan, scanning the trees to either side of the road as intently as he.

"I think we need a song. Not even a demon will strike stouthearted men in voice."

Without further adieu, Rowan began a familiar marching song in the old tongue. His voice was as clear and melodic as a thick harp string plucked by a master's hand. One by one, the men joined in with him—voices high and low, some carrying the melody and others blending in harmony. It was a lively Finnian tune about the carefree life of living in the wild with the sky as a blanket and a map. Maire knew it well. Adding her harmony, she had to admit 'twould have to be a sorely tortured spirit that interrupted this intrepid chorus.

Five roads from the five provinces of Erin converged on the hill of Tara. From that hill a clear day permitted a view of all. The circular stone rath of Temair rose stately, the high king of fortifications, built and expanded over the ages to some three hundred or so meters across. Its stones were held in place by the skill of its craftsmen, rather than mortar.

Surrounding it, other buildings paid homage. There was the Rath of the Synods, where druid and priest collaborated to amend the law. The banqueting hall, a giant among the structures, was reported to house a thousand soldiers. With fourteen doors, seven to the east and seven to the west, visitors could foretell their intentions by the door they chose to enter.

A traffic of females, many richly adorned with gold and embroidery, identified the House of Women. Maire had heard of the place. It was some eastern notion, providing a lodging exclusively for females of Tara's court. Maire, raised in a man's world, found the idea curious, if not demeaning. A fainter, more doll-like lot she'd never seen.

Like as not, they'd swoon at the sights she'd seen. Her attempt to assuage her wounded pride that Rowan was not immune to the admiration such beauties generated among the visiting Niall warriors fell short of its mark. The man stared as if he'd not seen a feminine figure before. She bit back a peeved lower lip. But then, these females wore jewels and finery enough to draw even her eye. Perhaps that was what her husband admired.

Near Temair was a cluster of tents lodging excess visitors to the place of kings and lawmakers. Among the tents, familiar banners fluttered in the westerly breeze. The red and black colors of Rathcoe banished Maire's curiosity and peeve at a glance, replacing it with wariness and dread. She'd been so taken with the sights she'd nearly forgotten her purpose.

"'Twould seem Morlach already has an audience," Rowan remarked to no one in particular.

At least he wasn't *totally* befuddled by the sight of the comely women.

"See to the camp here," he decided at length. "I'll speak with the guards about seeing the high king."

Maire nodded, heeding his order without thought or reservation. There'd been ample opportunity for a lowly ambush by Morlach's henchmen, but, despite Dub O'Croinin's false alarm, it never came. Like her men, more and more, she was gaining respect for both her husband and his god. There appeared no odds that did not sway to Gleannmara's favor, although defeating Morlach by the merit of her sword certainly would be a more glorious triumph.

And more unlikely. Steel was no match for druid magic.

Declan dismounted his shaggy steed beside Maire. "I thought your husband first a fool and coward. Now, I am not so certain." Her foster brother's words gave voice to Maire's thought.

Declan followed Rowan with his gaze, all the while fidgeting with the crested ring on his finger. "A finer horse than Rowan's can't be found, but would that he wore more kingly attire than sackcloth. Emrys, wait!" he called out suddenly, as the new king rode up to the guards standing at the banqueting hall.

Maire observed with interest as Declan ran after Rowan and slipped the ring from his finger onto Rowan's. So Eochan *had* told his younger brother why Gleannmara's new king had such an interest in the ring—and in the priest from whom it was stolen.

"Do ye think that will earn him more respect or attention?" she asked her foster brother upon his return.

Declan grinned sheepishly. "Nay, like as not, it wouldn't...but it makes *me* feel better."

"Besides, who ever saw a king in a priest's robe, wearing a gold torque, Gleannmara's blue and gold brat, and a Roman ring?" Her laugh stemmed from awe and admiration, rather than in jest. "He does have a way of drawing attention, that one."

"By my sword, I don't believe my eyes."

Maire looked to where Declan pointed in time to see a heron flap its wings near the door to the House of the Synod.

"Isn't that Brude's bird?"

"Aye." She nodded uncertainly. "It looks it. But how could Brude make it to Tara before us?"

Even if Eochan had ridden straight to him, the elderly druid was a day farther from Tara than Maire's company.

Declan came to the same conclusion. "Nay, he couldn't have made the journey so hastily. And all the druids have their queer pets."

As if to back Declan up, one of the learned scholars passed them, headed for the Hall, with a small, black, speckled pig at his heels.

"At least a dog can be trained to do more than eat and—"

Maire cut her companion short. "Trail its owner like a shadow?"

"That wasn't what I was goin' to say." Declan grinned impishly.

"And well I know it." Maire returned his look with equal mischief.

After a lull of silence, Declan spoke again.

"Does he treat ye fairly, Maire? I mean, is he a decent husband?" The youngest Drumkilly was suddenly sober as the druid who'd just passed them.

It took Maire a moment to catch up with him and another

to recover from the shock of his question. "Decent enough. We've a strong alliance that is...good for Gleannmara. Of that, I've no doubt." She dismounted Tamar and gave the mare an affectionate pet. "What of it?"

Declan stumbled for speech, like a dog that had suddenly caught a retreating bear and now knew not what to do with it. "Well, I—"

"Sure your brat's not still in a tangle because I took Rowan to husband?"

The warrior's ruddy complexion grew a deep shade of red. "Ach, I'd have married ye just to help ye out. I'd give my life for you and Gleannmara, Maire, but it isn't *that.*" He glanced away from the slim, red brow Maire arched at him. "I was just wonderin' how ye found married life."

"Why?"

Maire didn't think it possible, but Declan actually grew darker still. With luck, whatever distracted him so would keep him from noticing her own discomfiture. No one must know that she and Rowan were married by law alone and not by nature.

"Ach, never mind." He swore impatiently. "I'll not have ye thinkin' I'm unnaturally interested in such. 'Tis clear enough, a wife's not worth it."

Before Maire could question him further, the captain turned and involved himself in the making of the camp. *A wife!* Declan was thinking of a wife? She shook her head in disbelief. But when? Who? She had misheard him to be sure.

Maire stripped the halter from Tamar's tapered head, her fingers brushing the velvet of the mare's nose. Perhaps her foster brother was referring to her lacking of wifely qualities.

Maire closed her eyes in exasperation. These women's matters would make her witless as a crazed cow. 'Twas burden enough to worry about Morlach and Gleannmara, without having to learn how to be a suitable wife as well! Her skills were those of a warrior, not a coquettish maid raised to serve a man and keep his household.

And yet, in spite of herself, Maire was plagued by wondering just how much weight being such a maid carried in the eyes of a man like Rowan ap Emrys.

"The Uí Niall King and Queen of Gleannmara!"

Maire entered at Rowan's side through the door set aside for petitions, and the grandeur that met her eye nearly stole her breath. The banqueting hall at Tara was indeed as grand as the poets declared. Along oaken walls several warriors high were hung trophies and weapons of late and of old. Some thirty spits turned all at once over a cook fire by a marvelous contraption. The roasting meat and fowl filled the air with its sumptuous invitation.

"Look at all the cooks! There must be three times fifty."

When Rowan didn't answer, she recalled herself. After all, she was Queen Maire of Gleannmara, not some wide-eyed child. Standing taller, she marched forward and followed Rowan's lead, bowing before Diarhmott, high king of Ireland.

She'd made the right decision in keeping on her armor and leine rather than changing into the dress Delwynn ap Emrys had given her. This was a place for warriors, not women. The dark-haired *bruns* and fairer descendants of the Milesian fathers presented a fearsome sight. Tall and well-proportioned, surely no force ever assembled was more impressive. Men with red manes and beards—as well as yellow, black, and brown—with eyes from the palest blue to the darkest ebony turned toward her. She was tempted to stare back at them, the way they looked at her, but the high king addressed the Gleannmara contingent.

"Queen Maire, I have heard the song of your victory over the Cymry."

How on earth had he heard about the Welsh raid?

As though reading her mind, Diarhmott pointed over to a table of honor occupied by robed druids. "Yon Brude entertained us well, and I now see that he did not exaggerate your beauty. 'Tis no wonder the Welshman surrendered."

So the bird *was* Nemh! The druid must have come straight away to Tara as soon as the Niall left to deal with the Cairthan threat. And she'd thought some pilgrimage to the Sacred Grove preoccupied him. She schooled her features to hide her surprise...and her annoyance.

"He fought a gallant fight, my lord."

It grated Maire to lend credence to Rowan's adaptation of the fight, but she was no novice to politics. Brude saw to that. If she wanted respect afforded her husband, it would not do to have his name bandied about as an inferior combatant. The romantic Celtic pride might suffer defeat of beauty over steel, but never would it ignore ineptitude.

Granted, he *had* gotten the upperhand momentarily...

"Gleannmara's tribute is impressive."

Tribute? Maire dared not give away her ignorance by glancing at Brude.

"It is well placed, sir," the druid replied. "Gleannmara is pleased to pay the high king his due."

"And this is your *husband?*"

The intonation Diarhmott used in reference to Rowan did not bode well. Maire nodded, the hair lifting on her neck upon glimpsing the rest of the court assembly.

Morlach and Finead, the druid Diarhmott had sent to perform Maire's and Morlach's wedding, sat among the honored on the other side of Diarhmott, while Brude was relegated to the scholar's company.

"I am, sir. Rowan of Gleannmara, equally at the service of the high king."

Diarhmott leaned forward on the carved, stone throne. The tassels on the plush cushions beneath him quivered, drawing the attention of the two great wolfhounds lazing about his feet. Maire was grateful for the hand Rowan placed at her back. The high king was an imposing specimen of a man, for no Celt lacking in any physical way could serve such a post. She hoped his wisdom was as sound as his body.

"Tell me of this wedding, Queen Maire."

Although she trembled within like a dog in a wet sack, Maire drew to her full height, composed as her station demanded. She rested her hand on the hilt of her blade—not in a threatening manner, but one of ease.

"My husband chose wisely to champion his land to spare bloodshed. I won the match, but I was so well met that I considered him a good prospect as both hostage and husband. Emrys is a prosperous tuath which will pay a handsome ransom and more to Gleannmara with Rowan as my king."

"You were aware that I favored your marriage to my good and faithful Morlach?"

Maire lifted her chin proudly. "Aye, I was, but—"

Morlach stood, an accusing finger pointed at her. "There! She admits defying you, my lord!"

"May I finish?" Maire said crisply.

It wasn't a question for the druid, but aimed directly at the king. So help her, Morlach might strike her down with the evil eye for ignoring him thus, but even death was better than marriage to him. Rowan's fist tightened behind her, but a darting sideways glance revealed he smiled at her. With what? Pride?

"By all means, *dear.*"

The term of affection tripped her thoughts, but Maire gathered her wit and courage, turning back to Diarhmott. "I did what I thought best for Gleannmara, for, while your majesty has not seen the devastation Morlach's rule has wrought over my homeland, I have. She has been bled dry, my lord. My people starve, the best of the livestock is now at Rathcoe. Even the Cairthan, our former enemy, will swear to Morlach's greed."

"I took only my due as overlord," Morlach protested. "And the Cairthan are a thorn in the side of justice, brigands all."

Maire was grateful that Garret and Ciara were outside in their camp, yet she felt compelled to come to their defense. "To take what the people did not have to give is enough to make them resort to raids. Ask Brude. He has seen Gleannmara's suffering."

Brude started to stand, but the high king waved him to stay down. "This hearing is not to condemn my servant for following the law, but to decide if this marriage of yours is lawful."

"Again, ask Brude. 'Twas he who performed the rite. And I've witnesses a plenty." Maire waved behind her to where Declan and the others stood.

"'Tis true," her foster brother testified. "We heard the vows well enough, *and* we saw the bridal linen stained with a maid's blood."

"Oh, I've no doubt that a wedding took place," Diarhmott said, "But that is not enough."

Maire felt the color drain from her face. They *knew* she and Rowan had not consummated the marriage.

"Then why do you question us?" Rowan asked boldly. "Have we not met our obligation to the law?"

"But *whose* law, Gleannmara?" Morlach spoke up. "Will you vow before your Christian god that you are wed in his eye?"

Rowan's jaw clenched, tight as an angry fist.

Diarhmott pounced on Rowan's hesitation. "Are you wed in the eyes of the church, Rowan of Gleannmara?"

Maire looked up at her husband expectantly. Where was his god?

Rowan met Diarhmott's challenge with defiance. "No, I am not, but the law of my church means nothing to the likes of Morlach except when it serves his greed."

It was over. Maire wanted to strike Rowan *and* his god, for now she was at Morlach's mercy.

"If it please the high king, I would speak." Brude rose at Diarhmott's nod. "There was no time for a Christian ceremony on Cymry soil. Hence, I married the queen to this man according to her law."

"But you have heard it from his own lips, your majesty," Morlach railed. "He does not feel honor bound by this marriage. He mocks our law, binding one of us, but not himself."

"Your majesty!" Brude had to shout over the uproar caused by Morlach's accusation. "*That* is why we have come here—so that you may *personally* witness at least the second ceremony. Father Tomás awaits at this moment to make this marriage sound in the eyes of both Brehon *and* Christian, according to the Synod of Patrick."

The high king and Morlach shared a disconcerted look. Clearly they were not expecting this. Bless Brude and all his wisdom!

"You see, your majesty," Gleannmara's druid went on, "the wedding had to wait until we were able to mend the long rift between the Uí Niall and the Cairthan. The tuath was in chaos when Maire came to its high seat."

Maire saw where Brude was going and picked up the baton. "And because I chose my new king well, the Cairthan and Niall are one people, united by our marriage."

Morlach sputtered. "What trickery is this?"

"No trickery, sire. The Cairthan aiccid and the chief's mother travel with us. Shall I bring them forward to vouch for my king's word?" Maire asked Diarhmott.

"They travel with you as hostages, I'd wager," Morlach contested, "but—"

Diarhmott silenced the flustered druid with a raised, jeweled hand. "Are they hostages or friends to Gleannmara?" he asked Rowan.

"Neither. They are my kin."

A deafening silence enveloped the room, servant and lord alike.

The first to recover was Morlach. "He *lies!*"

Brude smiled, triumphant. "He does not lie, your majesty, for that is a geis imposed by his God."

Morlach could say little in argument, for to break a geis issued by a god was unthinkable to the Celtic mind. Hero, king, and druid alike had perished for such a crime.

"His word is as solid as the walls of Temair," Brude claimed with all his authority.

"Garret and Ciara of the Cairthan are my nephew and mother," Rowan explained. "I was carried away by slavers from my clan when I was a boy and adopted by a Welsh-Roman family. While I am lord of Emrys, I am also brother to Lorcan, chief of the Cairthan."

Diarhmott retreated to silence, mulling over this new revelation. His furtive glance toward Morlach told Maire he was backed against the wall, but it was with a flicker of admiration that the high king addressed the Welshman-turned-Scot.

"You weave a sound net, Rowan of Gleannmara. You have done what not even Maeve could do. Well, Finead, what say you of this?"

The druid nodded, lamplight shining on the shaven half of his head.

Maire held her breath, her knuckles white about the handle of her sword—Maeve's sword.

"These circumstances are quite remarkable." Finead pulled his long beard thoughtfully, most likely to gain time. "Given what has been revealed here, there is little choice, if justice is to be served, but to celebrate a wedding."

Clearly caught by surprise by the changing tide of support, Morlach exploded. "And what of *my* justice? You promised the lass to me, Diarhmott. You owe me your kingdom!"

Face coloring to equal the druid's, Diarhmott rose from the royal seat and pointed a warning finger. *"And* to the queen's parents, whose untimely and sinister death is *still* a mystery!"

At the high king's insinuation, Maire turned her head so quickly it was a wonder her neck failed to snap. "But they were killed gloriously in battle!"

Diarhmott regained himself. "Aye, that they were. But 'twas still untimely and sinister for all who knew and loved them."

Her gaze shifted to Morlach. "Not even *you* dare such a travesty against Gleannmara."

"It isn't for me to interfere with one's destiny. It is obvious that since Maeve and Rhian were united in battle, they should pass to the other side in the same manner." The druid nodded, obviously pleased with his reply. "Aye, there's the ring of true love destined for an eternity's remembrance."

Maire took no pleasure in Morlach's observation, nor did she find it in the least romantic to her Celtic soul. More likely, it was responsible for the icy curdle in her stomach. Was that to be her and Rowan's fate as well? She shot a furtive glance at Brude. To her relief, the elder druid assured her otherwise with the slightest shake of his head and the kindest, most fatherly of looks.

"So let us make plans for the celebration of their daughter's destiny with love." Diarhmott picked up a golden goblet, encrusted with a jeweled crest. "To Gleannmara, one of Tara's most beloved kingdoms."

The high king's toast broke the tension that had seized the room at Morlach's outburst. True to their enthusiastic and romantic nature, the people around them broke into huzzahs of good cheer. In a burst of wild relief, Maire threw herself into Rowan's arms and kissed him soundly on the cheek. When his return embrace was markedly belated, she stepped back.

"You *do* wish to marry me?" she whispered for his ear only.

His answer cooled her elation like the icy cascade of Gleannmara's own waterfalls. "Ah, little queen, is there any other choice?"

Maire didn't know which unnerved her more—the underlying discontent of Rowan's answer or the sinister calculation in Morlach's hostile glare. This wasn't the way a woman about to be married should feel—as though the future of the union promised misery, death—or both. But Maire was no ordinary woman with ordinary expectations where love was concerned. She was queen of Gleannmara.

EIGHTEEN

Father Tomás was a slightly built man, who looked as if he eked out a living in the rock-studded earth of the Wicklows. Unlike Brude's tonsure, which was shaven from middle of the head forward to demonstrate the high brow of intelligence, this man wore a crown of brown hair, shaven clean in the center and trimmed, it appeared, with a bowl. He had a warm quality of character that put Maire at ease—until he began to question her regarding her acceptance of Rowan's god.

"Well, of course I accept him. If I didn't, do ye think I'd be here now?"

The cleric was patient. "I mean, you must accept God as the one and only God, forsaking all other deities."

"Even the gods of my mother?" Maire was incredulous. She looked at Brude, whom she'd insisted remain with her.

"There is only one God, Maire. It is the Christian God."

"But how can ye say that, Brude? Sure, I've seen you preside over sacrifices to more gods than him."

The elder druid leaned forward. Beneath the white hedge of his eyebrows, a fire burned in his gaze, the likes of which Maire had not seen before. "The priest and I have talked long on our hasty journey to Tara."

"Speaking of which, how did you know to come and bring a tribute?"

The sharpness of Brude's tone showed he was perturbed by her interruption. "Given our years and a spiritual hand, we knew. Accept it!"

We? The priest as well? Maire didn't ask the question, but she couldn't resist glancing at the unimposing cleric with a new respect. She supposed if Rowan could speak to his god, a priest of this god certainly would also have a good communication.

"But listen well, Maire. I say this for the first time, but it will not be the last—"

The skin on Maire's arms prickled at the ominous tone her friend and mentor used. He'd taught her many things beginning with those words, but none had ever been imbued with such intensity.

"Many of us magi believe in the one God, who lives in the sun. He is not God of the sun alone, but God and Creator of all things. For centuries we have sought the truth of Him, of how He uses the five elements and the moon and stars to govern nature and the world around us. But His spiritual essence is one that we believed the common man incapable of understanding. Man too often needs something he can detect with his five senses and not his sixth."

"Which is why we have you, druid." Maire didn't like the direction this was taking her, but then, she was beginning to get used to that feeling.

"Aye, we've done the spiritual searching while allowing man his worship of nature and the elements, when they were only creations of the one God. But the time has come to give this God *all* the glory, not His creations. To do otherwise would be no different than worshiping each other, for we, too, are of His making."

Maire digested the words. It made sense enough. Why revere the oak if man was made by the same hand? Maybe one creation was no better than the other—though the oak seemed to her a sight more reliable than many men. She started to say so, but Father Tomás cut her off.

"The King of all kings came to give us that message, Queen Maire. God's Son gave His life that no more sacrifices need be made to the Father and so man did not have to go through a priest to speak to Him."

"This god has a son?" Ach, the oak was still on her mind. Here she was worried about marrying a man who had no choice in the matter, or so he said, while another had the intention of destroying them both—or at least her prospective husband. And yet these two holy men, instead of seeing this prickly matter done, were lecturing her on things that battered her sore head with confusion and contradictions of all she'd been taught was true. Her exasperation gained the better part of politeness. "*Must* we talk about this now?"

"Maire, you must confess to God of your sins, pledge your allegiance to Him alone, and accept Jesus Christ as your Savior or this marriage will not hold in His eye."

So now the priest was accusing her? It was too much.

"What sins?" Maire challenged. "I've done nothing I'm ashamed of, much less something I need to account for to my husband's god."

"Her heart is good, Tomás, and Maire has a sharp mind, but this is much to digest at once," Brude said to the priest. "She's not had the benefit of a druid's life devoted solely to finding truth. She's not heard the ancient accounts of the birth and death of Jesus."

By *all* gods, real or nay, now Brude was on the Christian priest's side, making her sound like ninny pup!

"And who is this Jesus whose going to save me?" The edge of her voice betrayed her frayed nerves. She was near done with this nonsense. "Seems to me he's a bit late to help me out, so unless he's got to be here for the wedding, can we just get on with it?"

"Do you wish this wedding to be real, recognized by all, including your Christian husband?" Tomás was as stubborn as he was gentle.

"Aye, but—"

"Then you must spend this night hearing a story, Maire," Brude's interruption was not nearly so gentle. "Would you enter into battle without knowing who was with you?"

Maire scowled. "What has battle got to do with this? First it's foolraide about one god and confessing sins, then this Jesus man, and now we speak of battle? Crom's toes, are ye tellin' me the marriage will be a battle?"

"Life is full of battles, Queen Maire," Tomás pointed out, "not all of them fought with the sword, but with faith and prayer."

"And Rowan's faith and prayer to this one God has brought us safe thus far, Maire," Brude chimed in. "You can't deny it."

Maire sighed heavily. Collapsing against the wall behind her bench, she folded her arms across her chest. Her lower lip protruded, displaying her displeasure. In truth, she'd wanted to know more about this god, but not with so much else plying her brain and emotions.

"This isn't convenient..." She felt like the drowning person going under for the final time.

A hint of smile toyed with the priest's thin lips. "Little in life is convenient, Maire, especially the important things."

Such a druidlike thing to say. Maire searched desperately for one last path of escape. "All right then, if Brude accepts this god as the only one, so do I. As for sins, I've none to admit to."

"You would swear by all that's dear and sacred to you that there is nothing you've ever done that left you troubled?"

Maire bolted upright with indignation at being called a liar—or as much so—but the Welsh fisherman's face appeared in her memory, stilling the objection forming on her lips. The contorted facial features of his head severed from his body by her bloody sword would haunt Maire forever.

"I killed a man, but if I hadn't, he'd have killed me. That's nothing to be ashamed of. It was war."

It wasn't, she told herself, squirming under Father Tomás's gaze. The man wasn't accusing her. His gaze was full of compassion. It was a voice inside that accosted her conscience.

"But it bothers you, child. You see his face at night, and it keeps you from sleep."

"What doesn't keep a queen from sleep?" How could a man she'd never laid eyes upon till this day know such a thing? "And I'd not kill Rowan, so what has it to do with this?"

The stubborn pose her chin struck made the priest chuckle. "I think we've got a long night ahead, Brude."

Maire's mentor put his hand on her shoulder. "'Twill not be the first we've spent on lessons to make you a wise ruler, will it?"

Maire shook her head in resignation. At least she and priest agreed on one thing: it *was* going to be a long night. Between Morlach's calculating glare, Rowan's insinuation that he'd just as soon not have her as his wife, and this Christian god—not to mention the man Jesus—sure, she'd never sleep again.

Yet, Brude's unfolding story of the ancient royal druids of the east, who'd seen a great star and followed it to a small village called Bethlehem, banished her need for sleep before she knew it. The sign in the heavens meant, so the legend said, that a King of all kings had been born. *This* was the Jesus they talked about.

"And how did the man save me when I never knew him? Why, if he were alive, he'd be old as a Sidhe elder." It was said some faeries were older than the earth itself.

"But *He* knew you, Maire, as He does to this day. He is God's son."

"And for all we know, the faeries may be his servants. Tomás calls them angels or messengers." Brude seemed to be thinking aloud. Mayhap he, too, still worked this revelation out in his brain. "At least the good faeries. But hold your questions, child, till the story is done."

If it challenged the druid's head so, what chance did she have of grasping all this?

Thankfully, priests were teachers and their stories made it at least interesting, she thought as Brude and Father Tomás began the telling of an old legend. Maire had many times before heard the story of the great king Conn's death, for this was one of Erin's most beloved rulers.

Conn had been inadvertently wounded in a friendly contest when his opponent threw a trophy at the king. The stone-hard, lime-preserved, shriveled brain of a worthy enemy, which was considered the essence of the man, lodged in the back of Conn's head. The best of healers could not heal the wound completely. Because Conn was such a good ruler, the Celtic law that a king be in perfect physical condition was overlooked. However, the healers warned the king, who was still possessed of all his faculties, that he must not exert himself overmuch lest the incurable wound kill him.

One day, a few years after when Conn saw how the sun turned dark in the sky, he summoned his magi to explain it. The druids who studied the heaven and stars told him that the King of all kings had been executed on a tree by his own people, and the one true God in the sun turned off its light in His grief. The kindhearted Conn was so moved and outraged that he took vengeance on the sacred grove of oaks, smiting the mighty and ancient trees until he collapsed in death and despair.

So this Jesus was the King of all kings! Now she saw the significance, although it was beyond her ken how this one god forgave the traitors for killing his son, much less that this Jesus asked that they be forgiven as he died. Despite Brude's earlier warning, she couldn't hold her tongue.

"I'd have knocked them down with thunder and burned them in their boots with lightning!"

"But *you* didn't create them and love them as God did." Father Tomás's eyes were kind. "We are His children. God loved us so much, that He gave His life on that cross as payment for every sin that was ever committed by man and every sin that ever would be committed."

Maire reflected on the man's words. "But I thought you said it was his son, Jesus, that died, not him."

"Is not the son a part of the father?" Brude reminded her.

Maire liked it better when the druids pondered such deep things. "Aye, I suppose."

"The Christian God exists in three forms," Tomás explained. "He is the Father in the heavens. He is the Son, who came to earth as man for a while, and He is the Holy Spirit, which comes to dwell in those who accept Him as their Lord and Savior."

"A shape-shifter?" Why didn't the man just say so?

"Of a sort, except that all three are one. God is like water," Brude elaborated, as much for himself as his student. "Water is water, whether it's frozen as ice, running in a stream, or steaming the air wet over a boiling pot."

There was some reason in that, Maire mused, trying hard to grasp it. And if Brude believed this, then so would she.

"This god is greater than Morlach?" She wanted to make certain she understood on her own terms.

"Morlach manipulates God's creations, but God created them. The powers of the druid come from this masterful order of things created by the Master of all. It is a dangerous and evil knowledge when used for one's own glory instead of God's," Brude explained.

"Which," Tomás added, "is why we discourage Christians in dabbling in such knowledge, for we humans cannot know for certain whether it comes from light or darkness. You see, we *all* have that sixth spiritual sense to some degree, Maire, but it is like fire—a good servant and a poor master."

"We lack God's discernment to know which spirits are good and which are bad, because one can parade as the other and easily fool us." Brude gave her a moment to mull this over, his keen gaze searching her own, apparently watching to see if the seedlings of knowledge that he and Tomás had sowed were taking root. "So, what do you think, Maire?"

Maire shifted uncomfortably, loathe to disappoint her mentor. "I want no part of this mystical knowledge," she began reluctantly, "and while I accept this Christian god…or all three of him, I just don't think much of this spirit living in me."

"But it is your friend," Tomás assured her, "the one who tells God what troubles you when you hardly know yourself or can't make sense of it with words."

Maire nodded. This was much to digest. To ask more questions would only make the night longer. In truth, her head ached now.

As though the priest sensed her desperation, he paused, then asked, "So you will confess your sins to God, all those boils that plague your memory with regret?"

She would gladly if this god would take away that dying fisherman's face from her mind. "Aye, I'll confess what I know."

Tomás smiled. "It's all God expects. He expects us to do our best, not to be perfect. Only His Son was perfect."

"Well, he sounds a reasonable enough God." Maire hesitated. Old fears instilled since youth, especially about spirits, died hard. "But will you two stay with me when I talk to him, at least till this spirit has settled in?"

To her surprise, Father Tomás rose and gave her a huge hug. "We will pray with you, Maire, for when you invite God into your heart, He is there in an instant."

Maire followed their lead and knelt on the floor, folding her hands as she'd seen Rowan do. She was tired and confused, not to mention uneasy, but this was something that had to be done. It was best for Gleannmara and not just because Brude said so. Her conviction came from somewhere else, from deep within, rather than without.

Suddenly, the casement burst open, banging forcefully against the wall. All that saved the precious glass from shattering was the tapestry hanging next to it, which bore the brunt of the impact. Were she not so frozen with fear, Maire would have bolted to her feet. Instead she clasped her hands even tighter.

"Please tell me that's this holy spirit comin' in," she asked Brude in a voice too tiny for a whisper.

"Or perhaps just the wind," Tomás suggested as he closed it and ran the bolt through its keeper.

"When light enters in, Maire, darkness must flee. It is nothing to fear."

When you invite God into your heart, He is there in an instant.

Her eyes flew open with wonder. Wind or spirits, Maire knew with more conviction than she'd ever felt, that Brude spoke the truth! Slowly, fearfully, she began to pray what was in heart and mind at that very moment.

Father God, wherever and whatever Ye are, I feel Your presence. I don't understand it, mind Ye, but by my mother's eyes, I know this spirit of Yours is here. It's as though You're both inside me and wrapped around me at the same time!

The wonder of it gave Maire cause to stop. It was as close as she'd ever come to recapturing the warmth and protection of her own father's arms. Tears spilled down her cheeks, but when she went to wipe them away, Brude stopped her.

"Do not wipe away the tribute of your love and sincerity before God. 'Twas He that gave them to you."

Maire glanced askew at Brude. How could he know what she was feeling, why she cried, when she couldn't explain it herself? She might have asked, but it seemed impolite to speak to someone else while talking to the One who created druid and queen alike.

Not that she knew what she intended to say—only that she was afraid of what lay ahead and needed all the help God could offer that she might see it through as a good queen to her people. And as a good wife to the husband she would acknowledge before Him on the morrow…

When she had laid all her concerns before her God's invisible throne, Maire found that it had not been a frightening experience at all, but a blessing beyond her mortal ability to express.

Later, for the first night in many, she slept sound as a babe in its mother's arms—but the arms were not Maeve's, they were those of Rowan's God, of Brude's God—of Gleannmara's God.

Rowan tossed the blankets off his bed and, not for the first time that night, knelt beside the gilded carved box with its overstuffed pallet. Princely trappings would give him no more rest than a pauper's this night. His knees ached, despite the thick rug of eastern design that cushioned his weight on the floor.

"Father, this *marriage...*"

Rowan wanted to do God's will, but knew his tone belied it. He'd yet to be convicted that this unholy union *was* God's will. What if he considered it for selfish reasons, like taking Maire with her beguiling combination of innocence and bravado as a wife in every sense? Now that was hardly a priestly pursuit.

Again the list of nobler reasons began to unfold in the troubled man's mind: the true union of Gleannmara with an heir of both clans of her soil, the only way at present to continue to keep his word to protect the queen and her land from Morlach's greed and ambition, a chance to make the tuath and its people—his people—prosper in peace.

Rowan beat his brow against his fist, trapped by his own web of deceit. He'd let Maire and her people think he was their king according to their law when he knew in his heart that he was not so in the only law that mattered: God's law.

Still, he rebelled, seeking to follow the light *his* way. All his learning came to naught when put to the test of this fire. The heat of it made his forehead ooze with perspiration. He wanted to spread the Word as one of God's priests. That was how he saw himself, not as king to a pagan queen—even if she was the most desirable woman he'd ever known.

"See, God? This is hardly a saintly reaction."

Jumping to his feet, Rowan went to the window and pulled it open. A brisk night wind washed over him, yet the baser heat that claimed him each time he thought of Maire would not yield to it. Somehow, the little queen had gotten under his skin, into his blood. And he would spill it to save her, he vowed to the stars glittering in the clear night sky.

But was he prepared to marry her, to take her as a Christian wife in *all* the scriptural senses? Hanging his head, Rowan closed the door, as if the heavenly reminders of the sun's ever-present light scorched his conscience. Jaw jutting, he padded back to the bed and flopped back onto the mattress.

No, he was not so prepared. He would have the marriage annulled when Morlach was no longer a threat. Death was the eminent path Morlach chose for himself. It was just a matter of time. As for Gleannmara, time too would prove to Niall and Cairthan alike that working together was to their best interest. When the tuath prospered, then he could pursue his godly studies with a mind uncluttered by husbandly or lordly concerns.

Relieved, he closed his eyes. No consummation, no valid marriage. There was still a way to meet his obligations *and* pursue his calling. Of that he was certain now, at least in his mind. His heart, though, not as easily swayed by reason, held out for further debate.

NINETEEN

The ceremony was performed the next day after the nunday repast. Unlike that of the Celts, the Christian marriage favored no particular season, such as Tailtain's spring fair, where contracts were made, or Imbolc, when the ceremonies took place.

Rowan's Cairthan mother attended Maire, helping her dress and preparing her to become a bride.

"You're a beautiful bride," Maire's mother-in-law-to-be told her. "What a glorious mane of hair you have." She crowned Maire with a wreath of early blossoms and bowed her head for the happiness of the newlyweds.

Maire peeped through half-lidded eyes at her reflection in the mirror. *Mane* was an appropriate choice of words, for she felt like a horse with four legs struggling in a full hobble of skirts. She'd far rather don the short leine she usually wore. As for glorious, there was a sure bounty of hair when it was freed from the leather-wrapped braid she wore daily for training and battle. It was as close to the unbound tresses of an unmarried maid as her calling customarily allowed.

It wasn't until she saw her intended groom that Maire gave any credit to Ciara's admiration of her appearance. Rowan's grim gaze took on new light when she entered the queen's chapel where the wedding was to take place. Suddenly, seeing the look in his eyes, for the first time she could remember, she *felt* beautiful. It was a new and pleasing experience. Now if she could just be a good wife, given her lack of training for it.

When Maire heard Rowan vow to love her no matter what

happened until she went to the other side, something heart jarring came over her. She watched his face—the way his jaw
squared, the added depth of his gaze, which was fairly churning with a fierceness of emotion she'd never seen before, the
movement of his bloodless lips as his rich and deep "I do so
solemnly swear" passed through them.

She'd not yet said a word of commitment, still she was
already one with him. She knew his anxiety, his frustration, the
way the vows were strained pure through his heart and soul
before they were fit for God's ear. And then it was her turn.
Rowan's gaze enveloped her so that she hardly saw the priest.

For the first time in her life, Maire feared she might
swoon—or worse, lose her stomach like a sniveling weakling
before Diarhmott and the court of Tara.

"Do you so swear, Maire of Gleannmara?" Father Tomás's
words echoed inside her skull, bouncing about to the pound-
ing of her blood. Invisible hands wrung her throat so that her
words scarcely made it out.

"Aye, I swear, same as him."

The corner of Rowan's mouth curled ever so slightly, but it
was enough to snap the fingers binding her throat so that she
could breath—even smile back. His hands, folded over her
own, tightened, and the warmth was a balm to every screaming
nerve in Maire's body. Once again she had the sensation of
being enveloped, but this time it was by the same power that
heard her prayer the night before. She wondered if Rowan felt
the hug of the Holy Spirit too.

Of course, scores of questions continued to arise regarding
this Christian God she had accepted above all others, but she
dared not voice them lest she spend another ordeal of hours
with Brude and the cleric. Her mind was full enough for now
with this God's spell.

Later, at the wedding feast, the spell was broken by the
abundance of distractions. A swirling quandary of emotions
heaved within Maire's stomach, threatening what little she con-

sumed from the bread plate she shared with her groom. Soon they would share more than the meal.

When it came time for music and dancing, Rowan led his bride to the center of the hall where they were joined by others. One anxiety gave way to another, as once again her legs struggled within the skirts of her wedding dress, each one tripping upon the other. It required her full attention to keep from sprawling like a drunken cow among the lovelier and surely more graceful maids that surrounded them. Yet an occasional surreptitious glance at her husband reassured her that Rowan had eyes only for her.

Even after they were separated by the merriment to take other partners, she caught his smile meeting the curious glances she cast over her shoulder. That smile took out her knees with its warmth. Tripping over a second set of invisible feet, she sprawled headlong into Declan's arms.

"Ach, look at me," she cried out in dismay. "I dance like a clumsy nag. The footwork of swordplay comes natural, but this confounded dress is nothing less than a hobble in disguise!"

"You let your heart free, Maire, and it will guide your feet."

"But what if my heart isn't sure?"

"Then ye dance like a clumsy nag." Declan couldn't keep his face straight for long. With a laugh, he eased her back into step. When he saw Maire was really disturbed, his tone grew helpful. "I would wager the lasses at Gleannmara might help you more there than I, lass. Though by the way your husband looks at you, I don't think it's your dancin' he's thinkin' about."

Her foster brother didn't need to elaborate. Maire wouldn't even think about what could happen when they were alone, finally blessed by the Christian God. Would the bargain they'd made be forgotten?

"Lianna is a sunny-hearted lass, but that Brona is grace itself." Declan's wistful words drifted into her thoughts. "Reminds me of the moon, giving less of herself than the sun, yet her secrets call out to man, beggin' to be discovered."

Maire stumbled from her contemplation. "Brona? Gwythan's foster daughter? Ach, cupid's arrow has already run Eochan through. Tell me there won't be two weddings at Drumkilly instead of one."

"Now don't be gettin' *those* ideas. I'm not about to ask her to live in my heart and pay no rent, although the blanket doubled is warmer." Declan grinned, devilment aplenty in the pale blue of his eyes. "Ye know well enough what I'm talkin' about. No doubt ye took a chill this mornin' without Rowan and his blanket to warm ye."

"'Tis none of your concern how many blankets I like, much less whose. It's no one's business for that matter."

"It is when you're a queen, Maire."

"I'm thinking bein' a queen is a worrisome task."

Did it plague her mother as much as it dogged her? Husbands, druids, and now this God threesome…the Trinity, her tutor called it.

The music ended momentarily, giving the multitude of conversations going on at the same time the entire share of the company's hearing. As Maire and Declan walked out of the center of dancers, bits and pieces of this subject and that snagged her attention. Some women discussed the Welsh embroidery on her dress. A couple of servants fretted over keeping the platters on the guests' tables filled. But it was a loud disclaimer near the high king's table that abruptly shushed them all.

"*I tell you, druid, I cast no spell!*" Brude's strong voice rose in annoyance from the cluster of scholars next to the head table. "I came apart from the queen and her company, traveling with Father Tomás from his sanctuary at Glenloch."

From the table of the high king, Morlach conjured a look of innocence. His voice carried past two of the fires lit to take the night's heralding chill out of the banqueting hall. "Good Brude, I only said that Gleannmara's company, who arrived at almost the same time as my guards from Rathcoe, had to have passed the captain and his men on the road under the invisible cloak of a spell, or they'd been shape-shifted into a herd of deer."

"Faith, we traveled neither invisible, nor silent...and certainly not as deer." Rowan laughed. "This close to Tara, our carcasses would be hanging over these fires, were that the case."

"Are you sure you saw a herd of deer, Culhain?" Diarhmott questioned, turning to a nearby table where Rathcoes' guards sank deep into the cups with merriment.

"Aye, thirty or more in number," the man at the head assured the ruler. "The same number as Gleannmara's company."

"And were they by chance singing, man?" Rowan asked, tongue in cheek.

Culhain scowled and scratched his head thoughtfully. "Now that you mention it, they was makin' some kind of fuss, unnatural-like." He soothed his ending shudder with a big gulp of beer and belched loudly.

"But I heard Diarhmott's best hunters report that there are no deer within two days travel of Tara," Morlach pointed out. The nobles gathered closer to the king's table. All issued remarks or nods of assent, showing the druid was not the only one aware of the anomaly.

The lead musician counted off a beat, but stopped at Rowan's challenge. "Besides, why were your men looking for Gleannmara's company? I was not aware that Gleannmara and Rathcoe were given to sharing a hearth or campfire willingly."

Morlach, clad ever in black, narrowed his eyes, which were colder and darker than the charred wood of last night's fire. Yet his answer was guileless as a babe's cackle. "It's just that Culhain traveled along the same route and arrived shortly after you, but not once did anyone catch a glimpse of Gleannmara's colors, much less of you and your company. It appears the work of magic."

"Aye." Cromthal, who until now had cowered behind Morlach, spoke up. "All we saw was a herd of deer passing, nigh the same number as your party."

"Ye sure they wasn't goats or sheep?" one of the king's royal hunters teased from the next fire over.

"No, they were deer, I say!"

"Perhaps they sang the Song of Patrick."

The new voice joining the conversation belonged to Diarhmott's wife. She walked up to the high king's table, and Maire took in the turkey-leg-sized gold and jeweled cross hanging about her neck. Diarhmott stood and motioned for her take the empty seat next to his.

"My apologies, dearest king," she said, "but I fear the ladies lulled me away from you longer than I intended." Once seated, the queen snapped her fingers at the harpist, who in turn struck a chord. "Indulge me, Diarhmott, and hear the Song of the Deer."

"As you wish." He nodded to the musician to proceed.

With dancing ended for the moment, the dancers wandered to their respective tables in quiet deference to the clear voice of the bard. Declan and Maire joined Rowan's small group, standing between the royal and academic tables, rather than cause further disturbance by crossing to their own seats.

The time was that of High King Logaire; the place, the road to Tara. The king's prophets warned Logaire that the approaching Patrick, the late bishop of Armagh, and his clergy meant an end to pagan Ireland, to the druids themselves. Thus, men were sent to attack the robed saints before they reached Tara's high hill, to thwart the prophecy.

The ambushers waited in the thick wood by the road day and night, but never once saw Patrick and his followers until they heard the news that the priest had already arrived at Tara and gained audience with Logaire. At Patrick's encouragement, his men chanted the song of the deer, giving voice and praise to God as they'd passed their unseen enemies. In return, God made them appear as a herd of passing deer.

At the pluck of the last chord, only the crackling of the

cook fires and the creaking of benches beneath the shifting weight of the seated guests filled the air. Maire started at the lilting words from Gleannmara's druid.

"Perhaps if the one God saw men waiting in ambush for Gleannmara's party," Brude theorized aloud, "He gave them the same cover as His clerics."

"Utter foolraide," Morlach grumbled. "'Twas not the work of any god, but druid magic." He rose to his feet and shook his fist at Brude. "Fool all the people you will, Brude, I know what I know."

"As do I, druid. As do I."

"Then you know well that this is not the end of Gleannmara's story." Morlach turned a seething look on Rowan, so sinister that Maire, standing at his side, felt her skin crawling with dread.

"Cromthal!" Morlach shouted without looking at his servant.

Maire followed the master druid and his shadow with her gaze. Even after they left the room, an unsettling darkness, invisible to the naked eye, lingered in their wake, freezing tongue and limb alike.

Diarhmott waved his hand at the musicians. They struck their strings again with a lively tune that would not leave the feet of any Celt still. Here and there conversations ensued. Those inclined to dance skipped their way to the spot set aside for it. Soon, music, the stomp of the dancers, and words blended in resumed merriment.

Rowan caught Maire's arm, and her pulse stumbled, then doubled its rate. It was early yet, but not for a newlywed couple. Tonight they would share the carved box bed in the guest room in Temair. It wasn't nearly as large as the Roman one. She and her husband would surely touch and, if that were to happen, Maire wasn't certain what she'd do. Part of her longed for it; another dreaded it. Ach, there were too many voices she didn't know living in her head these days. It was a wonder she was sound of mind enough to present herself.

"If it please Diarhmott, I would like to retire with my bride for the evening."

"You're not feeling well?" Finnead inquired.

Maire looked at the king's druid curiously. Now why was he concerned with Rowan's health, unless the cur had reason to expect something amiss. He and Morlach were thick as fleas on the same dog. Alarm put her thoughts to a race—but Rowan had prayed over their food, asking his God to bless it. If it were poisoned—

"Are you ill?" she asked suddenly.

Rowan glanced down at her and smiled. "Only if wishing to retire early with my lovely bride is considered a sickness."

He pulled her into his arms and kissed her full on the mouth. Now it was *she* who felt sick. Except she couldn't exactly call this sickness. It wasn't unpleasant, but rather agreeably unsettling, rendering her senses all atwitter.

The paradoxical malady only worsened as they bid their host and company good night and retreated to the room in the stone tower. A fire burned on a small hearth vented diagonally through the wall. It made the confine cozy, as well as smaller. After the feast and dancing, not to mention her husband's toe-curling kiss, Maire hardly needed heat or confinement.

Rowan took some of the wood left by Diarhmott's servants and tossed it on the fiery coals, sending an explosion of sparks toward the hole in the wall above. Pretending to be caught in a preoccupation of her own, Maire spotted a flagon of wine on a small table near the bed. She removed her cup from the belt at her waist and helped herself. It was sweet, and, like that she'd consumed earlier, soothed her rawly hewn nerves no better than spring water.

Still wearing his robe, her husband knelt down beside the bed for his nightly prayer.

"Wait. I'll pray with you. It works wonderfully well for sleep, don't you think?"

A lifted eyebrow was her only answer as Maire hurriedly took her place beside him.

"If you say the words aloud, like Father Tomás, I can just vouch for them until I can do them on my own." Maire blushed beneath his measuring stare. Folding her hands, she bowed her head, as unsettled as sparks flying every which way up the fire vent.

In the flickering firelight, gowned in her embroidered dress and kneeling prayerfully, Rowan thought Maire looked like an angel. A serenity and innocence pervaded her face. Her features were as perfect as the imported statue of Mary in the chapel at Emrys, except that his bride had a smaller, more delicate nose, slightly turned up at the end as if to betray a mischievous nature. Her dark lashes lay like feathered fans upon the rosiness of her cheeks. Her lips were pursed in reverence.

Yet, the Italian marble statue never stirred Rowan like this. Maire's pagan beauty in her garb of warrior queen was hard enough to resist, but this saintly apparition was impossible for the man in him to ignore.

Father, help me stay on the path of righteousness!

The annulment of their unconsummated marriage was the only way for him to continue his priestly studies. Rowan had to resist, not just for himself, but for Maire. He recalled her fear when she thought they would have to consummate their marriage on the ship. He had every intention of keeping his promise that theirs was to be a marriage in name only.

Next to him his companion opened one eye and slanted it toward him. A more beguiling look he'd never seen.

"Crom's toes, it isn't polite to keep the God waitin', man. Startin's a third of the work."

Now both eyes stared at him. Till now, Rowan never thought of the color green as a warm one. It was fresh and wholesome, appealing to the eye, but not bone-warming as it was now in her eyes. Was it the firelight playing in them?

"Heavenly Father…"

Rowan's mind went blank, as if the bat of Maire's closing lashes blew all lucid thought away. He wanted to kiss her, but knew the desire building in him would only be whetted by it. Better he save his kisses for when they were in public and an audience would keep his baser nature in check. In public, he'd have no choice but to restrain himself. Of its own mind, his gaze dropped from her face down to where her breath swelled beneath the embroidered yoke of her gown, moving the daintily folded hands against it. He focused on the intricate gold pattern of the ring his father had given Ciara, the one he'd exchanged for that of Maire's father, Rhian.

"Bless this marriage and the hands that prepared it…I mean, the mouth…the priest who married us and all those who participated—"

Rowan closed his eyes tightly, before temptation reduced him to total foolery. Voice raised as thought to halt his thoughts from skipping the way his heart was, he stumbled on.

"Give us the wisdom to rebuild Gleannmara, that we may give You the glory and…" Blankness. Nothing but utter blankness loomed for him to draw upon. Desperation spurred his thoughts.

Father, I know she looks at me as though I've taken leave of my senses. Faith, You must look at me in the same way, but lead me not into the valley of the shadow of temptation.

Rowan groaned inwardly. He couldn't even *think* straight. Maire was his for the taking. He knew an attraction sparked between them, one he might use to seduce her body, if not her mind. But that was not his purpose here. The reassuring feel of the Chi-Rho amulet beneath his tightly clasped hands helped him concentrate on higher goals, reminding him of the true source of his strength.

"Father, let this union be Your instrument of peace for Gleannmara, that Cairthan and Niall may work together as one people. Protect us from Morlach and his dark practices, for Father, I know his powers come from the prince of darkness and not the Lord of light."

Maire stirred beside him. "Who's this prince of darkness?"

"Don't interrupt." Rowan needed no more distraction. If her body were not enough, that childlike faith blossoming within her was nearly irresistible. He wanted to love her all the way to salvation.

"And don't forget sleep. He's good at givin' that."

Her logic was as impeccable as her ability to distract him. Rowan squeezed his eyes tightly, pulling his heart back onto the road his head traveled with an angry jerk. "And Father, teach Maire when to hold that wagging tongue of hers."

Rowan glared at her. He couldn't help himself. Faith, she tested him mind, body, and soul. "And forgive her, for she knows not what she says."

"In a pig's eye, I don't! It's you blessin' our weddin' food, ye flea wit. Sure, this Holy Spirit is laughing His head off straightening that out, and the heavenly Father is rolling on His throne."

Instead of shaking the fiery little twit, Rowan rose to his feet. "I can't do this. I can't pray with you interrupting and confusing me. You're supposed to be reverent, not chattering like a magpie with two mouths."

"And where do you think you're going?"

"For a walk and to pray in peace and quiet as the good Lord intended."

Rowan was halted in his tracks, not by word, but by a sudden fearful look that overtook Maire's face. For all her bravado, she was truly afraid of something.

He frowned. "You've nothing to fear here at Tara. No one would dare harm you."

She bit the quiver of her lower lip and leapt to her feet, but he saw through the paltry attempt to maintain her dignity. "No body of flesh and blood frightens me."

"Then what does, Maire?"

The sight of her struggling for words calmed the last of whatever angry wind had filled his sails. Humiliation tingeing her features, she folded her arms as though chilled and turned to the fire. She stared at it a long while before speaking.

"I've never talked with this Spirit or God alone." Her voice was as small as Rowan felt for his outburst. "And I can't think that if I have a few questions about Him, that He'd think any less of me. He might move in *here* in an instant, but that doesn't mean I know all about Him." She held her fist against her chest, as if to stop the sob that escaped anyway. "And I've not heard Him say one how do ye do or pleased to be here. I think He's left already. I don't think He wants me any more than you do."

Maire's pain and confusion struck Rowan's soul with the power of a blacksmith's hammer. She didn't understand. In truth, neither did he, at least not completely. That kind of knowledge started as a trickle and grew steadily till the soul was filled, and this side of heaven, they would never know *all* there was to understand.

He'd been where she was, a fledgling still wet from the egg. Remembering how his Christian family accepted him with open arms and patience when he'd deserved none, Rowan went to her. He hugged Maire close and brushed the top of her head with his lips. The scent of the bridal wreath filled his nostrils, as sweet and fragile as the feel of her in his arms.

"It isn't always *feeling*, Maire, as much as it's *knowing*. It's a conviction that grows with our knowledge of God and His Word."

He turned her to face him. Her eyes swam with unshed tears.

"And it's the obligation of those who know to share it with others, not dismiss their questions or answer them in anger. I'm sorry for my impatience."

He looked at the ceiling of rough, whitewashed plank in

frustration. "Sometimes, when I'm with you, my tongue is tied in knots my teeth can't undo. *My* weakness is what annoyed me, not you, little queen."

Lifting her chin, he delved deeply into the pool of her eyes with his own. No longer did they speak man to woman, but as soul mate to soul mate. Here were new waters for Rowan. He prayed he wouldn't drown.

"The night is young, *anmchara*. So ask away."

TWENTY

lood boiling like a witch's brew with anger, Morlach
watched the entourage from Gleannmara leave. The
blue and the gold should belong to him, along with the
pretty queen. For years he'd waited for her and her property,
while Drumkilly brought her up and trained her instead of
him. That task should have been his as well. It had been his
intent when he'd set the plan into motion to orphan the child.
But even that had failed when Diarhmott's wife thought the
family situation would be best, and put Maire into her foster
family's care.

The elder druid swore and swung away abruptly, nearly colliding with Cromthal. "The high king is becoming more and
more like wind every day, powerful, but given to blow this way
and that." Shoving Cromthal aside, Morlach ducked into his
tent. Nearby, an owl hooted from its roost in the House of
Synod. Morlach needed no such pets as those his peers
favored. He had humans to toy with and observe.

"Cromthal!"

At his angry bark, the servant scrambled inside. "Aye, my
lord?"

"Rowan of Emrys was looking mightily well this morning,
was he not?"

Cromthal shifted guiltily. "Aye, he did."

And well he should. Morlach lowered his head, but his gaze
burned from beneath his brow, intentionally intimidating. "He
did not have the look to me of a man who ingested the poison
you concocted and sprinkled on his food."

The younger man's composure crumbled. "I swear, 'twas mixed by your own recipe and dropped unnoticed into his cup while the table awaited the wedding company."

"You took care to be certain it was his cup?"

"I asked the steward which was the groom's seat, so that I might leave a message by his chair. As I feigned putting a fold of paper beneath his goblet, I stood so the steward could not see the goblet and sprinkled the poison in it. I tell you, I made no mistake. Perhaps the chant Emrys said over it before drinking—"

"Bah, meaningless words, nothing more! Emrys is no fool. He'd take no wine he hadn't seen poured from the same bottle as the others."

"So you think he poured it out?"

"Have I trained you since you were weaned from your mother's breast for nothing?" Morlach glared at his apprentice in utter disgust. "One of the king's hounds died last night, of some sort of gut-wrenching fit."

The alarm on his apprentice's face faded. "Aye, that's it. Emrys poured it out."

"Pity the whole of the dung-sniffing lot didn't lap it up. I've no more use for dogs, than for incompetent students." Morlach's gaze narrowed as he turned the force of his rage on the apprentice. "You failed me."

"I could not force the man to drink!" Cromthal protested.

"Perhaps you should have poisoned the entire flagon."

"But others—"

"Emrys would be dead." Morlach smiled and gave a humorless snarl that turned the rest of his words into a hiss. "And I would not be disappointed in you."

"I have done all you asked!"

"And yet Emrys lives."

Cromthal tried to shrink away from the accusation. "But if the Christian's god was powerful enough to make Gleannmara's company appear as deer—"

"Bah!" Morlach exploded. "'Twas druid magic, not the work of a god, you witless gnat. Or maybe the priest possesses magic."

"Well—"

"No, the priest is too humble to seize secrets of illusion and put them to work. But Brude…Gleannmara would be helpless with-out…." Morlach's words trailed off into a dark contemplation.

"But there was the prophecy," Cromthal reminded him. "Our ancestors, Logaire's seers, foretold of the coming of the priests who would drive the serpents from Ireland."

The master druid tore himself from the seductive thought tantalizing him. "What?"

"The prophesy of Logaire's magi foretelling—"

"We serpents of knowledge will not be driven from our own home by these charlatans! First Diarhmott gives them heed and now you, one of our own does the same." He slammed one fist into the other. Spinning abruptly, Morlach held his hand over the flame of the candle lamp. It seared the flesh of his palm, yet he smiled as though it were a maid's caress. "Look you trembling whelp, for as I snuff out this flame, so I will destroy all who cross me, be they druid, priest, or upstart usurper. *I command the power of life and death!*"

With a vengeance, Morlach slammed his hand downward, crushing fire and wax, grinding it into the rough grain of the table until it, too, gave way.

Dodging a lamp as Morlach kicked it toward him, Cromthal was grateful he was not within the druid's reach. The knot over his eye had barely healed. All that remained was yellowish dis-coloration about a red scar. Once he'd nearly worshiped Morlach and his words, yet now he was no longer certain of the man's power or principles. And it wasn't the abuse alone that placed doubt in the apprentice's mind.

He'd heard talk in the House of Synods regarding this

Christian faith, and Morlach was right to some extent. Many druids would not be driven from the green island. They spoke of turning their life and study of truth to this faith. The ancient accounts of the star of the east and the blackening of the sun on the day of Conn's death had been recalled from distant memory and shaken out for all to consider in this new light. A Christian priest even tutored the royal daughters.

"Brude and this priest will pay for their work in destroying my plan—" Morlach closed his eyes, and Cromthal had the uneasy impression the druid was envisioning some terrible retribution—"as will Emrys and his queen."

Cromthal's stomach felt as though it were suddenly filled with cold stones. "Think not rashly, master. Remember it is forbidden to spill the blood of another serpent, unless per his wish." The blood of a druid was his life, and if his life forsook him, so knowledge forsook the brotherhood, at least for this lifetime.

The anger that emerged from Morlach's opening eyes was hot enough to force the apprentice back a full step. Ebony glowed bright only when it was afire.

"A serpent does not think rashly, fool. It lies in wait for the right time and opportunity. Then, and only then, does it strike."

The s of the last word came out like a hiss and raised the hairs on Cromthal's body with its foreboding.

"Take two of our best bowmen and follow Gleannmara. When the time is right, rid us of Emrys and his priest."

"But the priest is a serpent of knowledge too! Not a druid, perhaps, but he has studied many years—" Cromthal thought twice about mentioning the shape-shifting deer again and changed his tack. "And he has the ear of the Christian god."

"He studied myths and lies, for what has he to show for his labor—that wooden cross hanging about his neck?" Morlach waved one hand over his fist, and when he opened it, a nugget of gold glistened in the sunlight shafting in the window. "I prefer gold to wood, don't you?"

Cromthal nodded, but he did not agree with what his master suggested. Morlach would have to kill Father Tomás himself. He stared at his companion as he would look death itself in the face, with both fear and revulsion, and wondered how he once could have felt love and respect for the man. Rathcoe no longer belonged to the fraternity of knowledge, but festered like a cankerous sore in their midst.

"Then I'd best be on my way," Cromthal said aloud, breaking his traitorous train of thought before his master detected it. "Nightfall will give us our best opportunity. No one will know from whence the arrows came."

Turning without appearing too eager, he ducked through the opening of the tent, his master's words following him, raking at his spine like fingers of ice: "To fail is to wish for death, Cromthal. Remember this well."

Maire stared into the campfire, listening to Brude and Father Tomás speak about the Synod of Patrick. Nearby Ciara, Garret, and the others who were not standing guard already slept. Grasping battle tactics came easier to the queen than these political and spiritual issues that the Christian priests, druids, and kings changed in the old Brehon Laws, to bring them in line with the teachings of Christ. Try as she might, she was hard pressed to listen as to why paying the price of an *eric* for a transgression was better than simply killing the offender.

Humane and God-worthy as such a law seemed, Maire considered it futile as long as there were those who had no respect for either life or God. The image of Morlach's face, laughing in contempt, took shape in the crackling blaze. Maire blinked and stared again, but this time only the lapping tongues of the fire were there. She let out her frozen breath of relief.

"I think the old bishop of Armagh was wise indeed to invite the input of all," Brude said, looking across the same fire at Maire. "It serves neither man nor the one God to obliterate all trace of that which is familiar to the common man."

"God asks only for His rightful recognition as the only God and Creator of all," Father Tomás agreed. "How He is honored is not nearly as important as the fact that He is given *all* honor. Scripture bids us make a joyful noise unto the Lord."

"So when we light the fires at Beltaine, we no longer honor Bel, the sun god?" Maire asked, drawn in by confusion.

"The *taine* is a symbolic cleansing element of God, Maire," Rowan explained patiently. "Fire purifies gold and makes steel stronger."

"Like the eating of communion bread is to remind us of Christ's sacrifice of flesh—and the drinking of the wine represents the blood He spilled for us. As food nourishes our body, our remembrance of Christ's sacrifice nourishes our spirit. Understand?" Father Tomás looked at Maire expectantly.

She nodded, trying to gather it all in. "So it's still all right to light the fires at Beltaine and run the cattle through them—"

"Except the fires now represent God's cleansing and strengthening power, not Bel's," Rowan reiterated.

"And Bel's been takin' all the glory for it." She scowled, looking at Rowan. "Then why—" Maire stopped, overwhelmed. "I don't know as I'll ever understand it all!" She swore, shoving to her feet.

Brude laughed, and Maire felt a frustrated heat seep into her face in response.

"Ach, Maire, you want to learn everything all at once. You walked and crawled within the same day. But this is different. It's like learning to be a queen or a warrior; it will take a lifetime of effort, trying earnestly each day to make it better than the last."

"And if we make a mistake," Rowan added, "then we just admit it and try again. God knows we are human and as such, imperfect."

"Well, if He loved us so much, why didn't He make us perfect to start with? Seems like there'd be a lot less confusion and trouble all around." She kicked a log into the campfire and stretched.

"We *are* made perfect, Maire," Rowan insisted. "It's our God-given ability to choose whether to listen to Him or not. And that ability to choose is what is imperfect."

"So we're *not* perfect."

Clearly thrown off by her logic, Rowan glanced at Tomás and Brude for help. Brude picked up the gauntlet. "Would you have the people of Gleannmara follow you because they want to or because you gave them no choice?"

"Well, I'd have them want to follow me, sure, but if they've not got the good sense to, I'm better off without 'em," she declared in a huff of indignation.

"I hope you will visit Gleannmara *frequently*, Father," Rowan said. He sucked in his cheeks as if to stay his combined humor and exasperation.

With a hard glare at her husband, Maire turned and walked to where she'd made up a bed of leaves close by. She'd learn the gist of this faith, if for no other reason than to squelch her husband's overblown opinion of himself.

As she reached down for the blankets, something whooshed overhead and landed straight in the midst of the fire. "What was *th*—?"

Before she finished, a second followed it, straight into the fiery abyss.

One of the watchmen's shouts echoed in the forest beyond. "Halt in the name of Gleannmara!"

The group about the fire instinctively broke for the cover of the trees, taking those rudely awakened from slumber with them. Whoever fired the bolts at them had obviously never held a bow before. For that much, Maire was grateful.

"Stay where ye are!" she shouted as Rowan risked leaving the cover to join her.

The unseen enemy was entirely too close. Only magic could have gotten them past the double guard Rowan posted—

Morlach's black-hearted magic. A third bolt released. Maire heard it before she saw it. To her horror it streaked straight toward Rowan.

Father God, save him!

Her fists clenched. She was more aware of the nails biting into the flesh of her palms than the fact that she just uttered her first uncoached prayer to the one God for the safety of the man she loved. Unable to close her eyes, to shut out the unthinkable, she watched. From her vantage, the bolt looked as though it went right through him and thudded into the fire just beyond.

"Have ye lost what little wit your mother gave ye?" she fumed, pulling aside his cloak to hold it in the light cast from the fire. Surely the arrow had passed straight through it. That, or it had swerved around it. But there was no sign that harm had come anywhere near him, save the memory of what she saw. Swallowing nothing but air, she latched on to angry relief, which was far more comfortable than the other chilling emotions clamoring for control of the moment.

She pinned her husband with a glare. "I'm in no need of coddling like a wet babe!"

"No, you're not, but I'd feel better if we remained together." Tugging his brat away, he pulled her under its wing, like a mother hen tucking in its chick. "Maithre and Garret are safe with Tomás and Brude in the cover of the rock."

"And how would ye feel with a bolt in yer spleen?"

Loathe as she was to admit it, the warmth of his nearness, the scent of the woolen material—man, wood smoke, and the fresh forest air—was welcome. They waited for further sign of the enemy so close to them, but all they heard was the confusing exchanges of the guards.

"Over there!"

"No, I see them. This way!"

"The bolt came from there. I heard the blackguard fire it!"

A rivulet of ice shivered up Maire's spine, setting every

nerve in her body on edge. But a queen could not afford the luxury of either panic or comfort.

"Split in four directions—" Maire's order came out simultaneously with Rowan's, word for word. Smiling, he nodded to her to proceed. Crom's toes, like as not they were about to be slaughtered and here, in the midst of her alarm, she was feeling giddy as a lovestruck cow because they'd share the same thought.

"And work your way out," she finished, steeling herself against all the confounding feelings. "We'll go this way."

Still, Maire didn't object when Rowan shoved her behind him and took the lead. If a bolt passed seemingly right through him—or *around* him—then clearly something was protecting him. That Holy Spirit perhaps? That had to be it! She caught herself looking at the ground, but it was too dark to see her own feet, much less the footprints of a ghost.

Ach, Holy Ghost, I'm scared. Please don't let the dark spirits harm us.

Her second prayer was as spontaneous and unwitting as the first. Maire's focus was on taking care to stay with Rowan in the cover of tree to tree, her gaze sweeping the forest around them.

It wasn't until the guards gave up their chase and made their way back that she breathed normally and straightened from her crouched position.

"Well?" she asked Cellach of the Muirdach.

"'Twas like chasin' a black fairy, all shadows and smoke."

"Aye," his brother Dathal chimed in. "First they was here, then they was there…" He shook his head.

"They just split up," Rowan said with the voice of authority. Apparently, like Maire, he sensed the fragile thread of reason about to snap among the men. "I'll wager my sword arm that the bolts we find in the fire came from no spirit's bow. But come see for yourselves. Then get back to your posts."

The bolts were real enough, though the fire had done its best to consume them. Brude held the remnants of one. Then as if it had spoken to him, he stiffened, then turned and headed away from the campsite. Rowan and Maire joined him, as well as the guards. A hundred or so good strides into the thick of the shrouded forest, he came to a stop, knelt, and picked up a discarded crossbow.

"This is its mother. Morlach's men were here."

In the torchlight, the red and black paint of the crossbow gleamed.

"Rathcoe." Rowan's comment was accepted without surprise. He looked around, but the trees would tell no more, at least not in the dead of night. "Resume your positions," he said to the guards.

"Shouldn't we kill the fire?" Maire suggested grimly.

"No. They're gone, in good speed, it appears," Brude answered, his lips hinting at amusement. "I imagine they've seen enough tonight."

"Seen enough?" Maire scowled. "Then they've seen more than I have."

"No doubt, child, no doubt."

Maire waited for Brude to go on, but he turned back toward the campsite.

"Did you see anything?" she asked Rowan as they fell in step behind the druid.

No less bewildered than Maire, he shook his head. "No, but know this one thing, little queen, and rest in it tonight: God is protecting us and He never sleeps."

"How can He do that?"

"Because He was, He is, and He will always be."

Maire met his answer with a flat stare. "Now *that's* a druid answer, if there ever was one."

Still, she tried giving thanks to the one God for sparing them harm thus far and asking Him for rest, uncertain that anyone or anything really heard her. It didn't matter, she supposed, whether this God was there for Rowan or Father Tomás or any one of them—just so He was there.

The following morning, however, when she awakened, having dropped off into sleep almost the moment she tugged her blankets about her shoulder, she knew Rowan was right. God had watched them while they slept.

TWENTY-ONE

Gleannmara was a welcome sight as it rose on the horizon ahead of the travelers. Unlike the last time Maire approached her home, she was met at the gate by a cheer from the guards. Inside the outer rath, some of the inhabitants raced up to greet them. The reception was enough to make Maire's heart dance like the blue and gold banners overhead.

The reason for the eager welcome was obvious. The rath and its buildings already showed the benefit of the work she'd assigned before leaving. Men—those who weren't already in the fields—were busy whitewashing and repairing. Unlike the first time she set eyes on the place upon her return from Emrys, it looked alive.

Two men opened the newly hung doors at the entrance, swinging them back and forth, as if daring the greased hinges to squeak before the queen. As the entourage dismounted and the horses were given over to the stable hands, Lianna emerged from the hall, a bright smile on her face. Behind her came more of the women, both noble and servant, sleeves rolled and skirts hiked to free the feet for work.

"They look none the worse for their work." She half expected a rebellion on her hands after the initial reaction with which her orders had been received.

Rowan leaned over, agreeing. "You gave them work to do, aye, but you also gave them back their hope and pride."

"Welcome home, Queen Maire! We hope you find things more to your liking this time," Lianna called out to her.

"I vow, we'd not realized how the soot had darkened the walls, even in the grianán, until we took brushes to it!" the younger woman's companion said.

Maire didn't recognize the latter, but she was no peasant, judging from the bright green and pink of her dress. Her complexion was as white as the soot that smudged her face was black, as opposed to the ruddier skin of the serving women. When one of the O'Croinin, who'd accompanied them to Tara, picked the lady up and spun her around, the queen's assessment was confirmed. The lady was of the aires.

Maire would know them all by name, and soon, she vowed.

"I'd wager from the soot on the lot of ye, that not a smudge is left on the walls. The hall must be as bright and polished as it was the day Maeve's craftsmen finished it."

"Well, the last of the summer food's set out and waitin'. Ye men look as if ye've worked up a fine appetite." Lianna swayed like a willow branch in a soft breeze as she walked up to Declan and linked her arm with his. "And there's ale to whet your thirst."

"That's almost as temptin' as that pretty smile of yours," Declan said, bowing and sweeping his arm for her to lead the way. Looking past her, he asked, "And where's Brona?"

"Stop your teasin', Declan." Lianna slapped his shoulder playfully. "Since when have I been nursemaid to Gwythan's daughter?"

Maire glanced over at Dathal of Muirdach. He watched with the eyes of a father as his daughter sauntered off with the warrior on her arm. Like as not, he had good reason for a sharp eye, given Declan's reputation with the maids. The way Lianna smiled and walked was enough to invite the Drumkilly's attention, but not enough to hold it. He still glanced toward the royal lodge for a glimpse of its dark-haired keeper.

Maire too stared in that direction, but for another reason. She wanted to see if the lodge had improved as much as the hall reportedly had, but the women, noble and servant alike, stood by anxiously waiting her approval. She put a hand on the O'Croinin woman's shoulder.

"Well, O'Croinin, shall we see what havoc your wife has wreacked upon the soot?"

"Elsbeth, my lady," the woman suggested eagerly. "You will call me Elsbeth, I hope."

"Elsbeth, it is."

Maire walked with the couple into the banquet hall. Recalling Declan's suggestion that she look to Gleannmara's ladies to learn more genteel ways, she purposely imitated Lianna's sway. Her swinging sword was checked by the tight fist on its hilt, lest it become caught up on something or someone in its path. She was tempted to look behind her to see if Rowan watched her retreat as the men had watched Lianna's, but instead, took in the improvement in the hall with a grin of appreciation.

Elsbeth had not exaggerated. The room not only looked brighter, but bigger as well. Even the carved posts had been brushed and oiled so that their artwork gleamed in the sunlight from the empty grianán.

"It is most wonderful, ladies," Maire complimented them. She spied one of the elderly noblewomen with her hair tied up in a scarf, leveling out fresh rush with a rake. "But I didn't mean for you *all* to abandon your stitchery. Your name, milady."

"Medwyn of Muirdach, the Muirdach's mother," the woman replied.

"Surely we've enough servants to spare ladies of your disposition—"

Medwyn cut her off with a playful swish of the rake. "All that stitchery has tightened up my fingers. Pamperin' often makes regret. Besides, what with the calving and dairy work started, the servants were more needed elsewhere. I can still swing a rake, good as any."

"Indeed you can, Medwyn. 'Tis an honor to have such a stouthearted soul as yours among us."

"Stout hearts make stout walls. This work has done my old heart good, it has. This is what Gleannmara *should* look like, thanks to you."

Maire flushed at the praise. "Nay, Medwyn, thanks to all of *you*. I'm so proud of ye, I could burst. And this is just the beginning for our home. The king has this Joseph story to tell ye and 'twill make you even prouder for what you've accomplished when it's done."

"I do love a good story." Lianna poured Declan a cup of ale and handed it to him. Her lips were pursed as though she too could taste it when he took a hearty drink. Knowing her foster brother preferred Brona made Maire sorry for her cousin.

"Then you'll be happy as a pig in lavender with all the stories my Rowan can tell." Maire turned to leave, and came face to face with the subject of conversation.

"This hall is so bright, like as not, our voices will carry better with no soot to hold and slow them down. As an appreciative lord, I'll have to kiss every hand that was put to the task."

The ladies in attendance giggled.

"Leastwise wait till we're bathed and fit, Lord Rowan," Lianna protested with a coquettish smile.

Maire did not miss the agreeable wink that answered the girl. "Upon your wish, milady Lianna."

Why the woman couldn't keep her flirtation for one man at a time, Maire was vexed to understand. Worse, Rowan knew her by name. Was his memory sharp or was interest what kept it there? Crom's toes, she was starting to feel like a cat over a bowl of warm milk. Perhaps if he'd paid Maire the attention of more than tutor to her student on their wedding night, it wouldn't annoy her as much.

"Did two days on horse ail your back?"

Maire's peevish green musings screeched to a halt. "What?" The question registered. "Why do ye ask?"

"It's just that you were walking strangely when you entered the hall. I thought—"

"Though your concern is touchin', dear husband, I'll have ye know—" Maire's voice rose with her growing irritation— "That I can ride night and day with the rest of you and there's nothing wrong with my back." Without so much as a fare-thee-well, she spun on her heels and stalked out, parting the men who'd come in after Rowan with her glare. Better to lose her temper than to cry.

The door of her lodge slammed against the wall as Maire stormed in. Leaning over a freshly kindled fire, Brona bolted upright with a start.

"Queen Maire. I haven't had time to prepare the lodge for you. There's still a bit of spring's dampness in here."

"Do I look cold to you?"

The young woman shook her head, clearly at a loss for a reply.

Maire tore at the buckles of her breastplate, but they too tried her patience. Her thumbnail caught and pulled back. With an oath against mankind in general, she sucked on her anguished thumb to ease the pain.

"A hasty marriage leaves plenty of time for lengthy regret."

Brona had gall, Maire had to give her that. How dare she question their marriage? "What?"

"I said—"

"I heard ye. I just didn't believe what I heard. What right have you to go judgin' my marriage?"

"None, my queen. I only meant to sympathize with you, as one woman to another. Men are a trying lot at times. They do not understand us."

"I don't understand us and I'm a woman," Maire averred in exasperation. "It's like I'm two people inside. The warrior queen I know, but this other female…"

"The one who wishes to be loved and admired?"

"Aye, that's the one. And I'm not sure I like her."

"That is because she treats her need as a weakness, rather than a strength."

This Brona was more mature than her years. She knew exactly what Maire was feeling…and she spoke as if she had a solution. "And how would a woman use this need as a strength?"

Perhaps this was part of Brona's charm for Declan. Maire had never seen the woman flirt with the men outright, yet they watched her. Hers was a dignified attraction.

"A man likes to feel needed. It feeds his pride. A woman can use this to win his attentions."

"I *need* no man."

"Or," Brona suggested, "she can get him by other means."

"Such as?"

"You can make him want you." The woman fingered a small, silver-encased vial hanging from a cord about her neck. "I put this scent on the places where I can feel my blood pulse. A man can not resist it."

"Magic?"

"The oldest secret of women. It would make the heart pound in a statue."

"I'll think on it—" Maire eyed the vial uncertainly—"I'm not certain I want to be intimate with the king."

A light kindled in the servant's eyes, making Maire instantly regret her slip. But Brona slipped the vial out of the ornate casement and laid it on the table beside the wooden bed, which had been installed to replace the oversized Roman one.

"Use this only if you want a man to desire intimacy with you, Queen Maire, for it's too potent to toy with."

"Maire?" Ciara stood at the open door, peeking in hesitantly. "May I enter?"

"Of course. Ciara, mother of Rowan, King of Gleannmara, this is my servant, Brona."

Brona dipped solemnly. "How wonderful you crossed the sea to be with your son."

"Ciara is Rowan's real mother and mother to Lorcan of the Cairthan. Our peoples are one now, Brona."

It took a moment for this to digest. "I am pleased to hear it and to meet you, milady. If it please, Queen Maire, may I be excused?" Maire had an odd sense that Brona was masking her real feelings, but since she couldn't prove anything…

"Aye. And the lodge is much improved, Brona. Your efforts are appreciated."

The servant afforded Maire a nod of acknowledgment and slipped away in silence.

Ciara walked over to the table and picked up the vial. "You do not need this, Maire. My son loves you. I can tell by the way he speaks of you and looks at you."

Embarrassment robbed Maire of a ready reply.

"I apologize for my presumption, but as I approached, I couldn't help but overhear, what with the door open."

"My husband, to all eyes but my own, is in love with me," Maire said with disbelief. "But when we are alone, it is different."

The woman walked over to Maire and embraced her warmly. "Dear daughter, Rowan is a man of his word. He agreed to a marriage in name only and will hold to that until you tell him that contract is no longer valid. You need no magic scents for my son. He would have you for who you are, not because of some mix of herbs in a vial."

Ciara tossed the vial out the door. "What smacks of magic, smacks of deceit. Deceit has no place in marriage. Believe in yourself, daughter." She gave Maire an affectionate peck on the cheek.

Maire liked the hug better. She liked the idea that she gained not only a husband, but a mother as well. Her foster mother Maida did her best, but there was never any show of affection. Perhaps that was forbidden a girl destined to be queen, but how Maire missed this.

"Thank you, Maithre. I think our God has given me a mother when I needed one most." Maire's words shocked her. This Christian God was starting to feel like a person to her, an entity with compassion and feelings rather than stone or the strength in iron or a tree.

"God has blessed us all, Maire. Never think otherwise." With a wink, Ciara turned to leave.

"Oh, have you been given lodging?" Where *were* her manners? An inhospitable queen was a shame to her people.

"Rowan has seen to it. Garret and I will share Glasdam's lodge." Her face brightened. "It was so good to see our old friend. We'd thought him dead or carried off along with Rowan." She laughed softly. "Indeed, God is making me giddy with his goodness. The only thing that would complete my life would be a grandchild to ensure the peace and prosperity of Gleannmara, and for me to spoil horribly."

"Well, they say there's nothing this God can't do." Maire was beginning to believe it, even if she wasn't quite ready for motherhood. A squalling babe in her arms wasn't nearly as appealing as her being embraced in Rowan's. She sighed wistfully. Becoming a wife was the first battle ahead, but it had to be a role both Rowan and she could live with.

Never one to back down once her mind was made up, Maire decided on the course she would take. She was no coquette. Imitating one only made her look an idiot. She'd have no potion making her irresistible either. If she won Rowan of Emrys, it would be as herself.

No, this time Maire intended to approach her task as she'd been trained to: head on.

TWENTY-TWO

E mrys, I absolve you of all promises we've made to each other, save our marriage vows!"

Rowan choked. The ale he'd just sipped found its way up his nose and down his windpipe simultaneously. Around him, the after-dinner revelry in the hall continued, but it was silent compared to the roar of Maire's words. They echoed in his mind again and again, each time more loudly than before. There was no doubt he'd heard her right.

She slapped him on the back soundly. "Crom's toes, don't tell me I've killed ye."

He shook his head, his eyes blurring the sight of her concerned face. Just when he thought he knew the Niall queen and what to expect from her, she astonished him. When she'd stormed out of the hall that afternoon for reasons yet unknown to him, he hadn't been certain he'd be welcome in their lodge, much less in their bed. Certainly not their *marriage* bed. Surely she didn't know what she suggested.

The spasm subsided. Rowan managed to settle his confounded throat with a bit of bread chased by ale. Still, his voice told of the strain. "This is hardly the time for such unexpected news, Maire. Faith, we're surrounded by…"

She put a finger to his lips, silencing him. "I agree. Let's leave our people to their merriment and settle this in private."

"But we've yet to tell them of our plans."

"Look at them, Rowan. They're so happy to hear the news that the high king does not sanction Morlach, you could tell them to jump off Wicklow's highest falls and they'd do it."

Rowan could almost believe her. Garret, son of the Cairthan chief, sat at home next to Declan and the other Niall warriors, mesmerized by their embellished tales of valor. His grandmother Ciara joyfully shared whatever it was women spoke of when they were clustered together like a flock of hens. Servants and aires alike toasted him as king of Gleannmara to Maire's queen. Asking some of them to take their cattle and move to higher ground, however, was another proposition.

"Which makes this the perfect opportunity, while their bellies are full and their blood warm with ale." Upon seeing his words land a blow on Maire's face, he reached over and cupped her chin. "Make no mistake, Maire, your suggestion calls louder than that of our responsibilities as rulers, but we must put Gleannmara ahead of ourselves. The time for planting is nearly lost. The dairy and calving have begun."

Maire drew away, drawing on her admirable queenly strength and lifted her chin. "Aye, Gleannmara. Then let's do what we must." She laughed and gave him a devilish glance. "'Twas nothing but a jest anyway. The look on your face was worth it and well deserved after making fun of my walk."

Aye, the walk again. He'd thought her back unbalanced from the ride and, on his expressing concern, she'd flown out of the hall as if he'd plucked her tail feathers.

"I wasn't making fun—"

Maire stood up before Rowan finished and banged her cup on the table. "Listen, good friends, for our new king has a story to tell you. There is much to be learned from it, isn't there, Brude?"

The druid glanced up from his quiet contemplation and nodded. His was almost a constant state of meditation of late. It was hard to tell if the man was sleeping or pondering.

The story of Joseph becoming a savior of Egypt was new to most ears and proved no less entertaining than one of Brude's songs. Rowan spun it like rich tapestry, bringing it to life in the heart of all those who listened. When he'd finished, young Garret stood up.

"Ye might as well say my uncle, the king, is this Joseph, or well like him, for it was my own father who sold our king into slavery. And it was our king who forgave my father for it and offered the same opportunity to the Cairthan as Joseph to the Hebrews...a chance to prosper with the people of Egypt."

"Aye, his plan is a sound one, though strange at the first hearin' of it," Declan chimed in. "We've heard it, and it bodes well for us and the lad's people to do as he says. Give it a good listen, before ye toss it out with grumbles."

Rowan gave God a darting thanks for the support and the opportunity offered by the two least likely of his allies. But all things were possible where God was concerned. All things.

He glanced sideways at Maire and was nearly undone by the look of admiration in her gaze. Gleannmara's bride was an enigma he could easily spend a lifetime trying to fathom.

Maire smiled back at her husband. His honor and courage had won the respect of her people as well as her heart. When exactly it had happened she didn't know. It suddenly just *was*. He proceeded to explain the potential for the tuath and what was necessary to make it a reality. Like the Cairthan, many did not take a liking to it right away, but those who'd had time to think about the plan's merit and had seen the success of this stranger and his God swayed opinion favorably.

"Decide among yourselves where you are best suited, for you know it best and report it to your chiefs. They in turn will report to Declan, my captain at arms."

The look on Declan's face told Maire he could be felled by a feather. Gradually, he regained himself, beaming like a candle through glass.

"Those who go with the cattle will be hostages of good will at first, as will the Cairthan who come to our fields to work. Your lodges will be poorer, for the other clan has suffered far worse under Morlach's hand than you."

"They still stole from us!" one of the women protested. She was one of the *boaires,* the cattle lords. "They frightened us like—"

"The *old* ways are done on Gleannmara, woman. Didn't ye hear how this Joseph man forgave for the good of all?" Declan challenged. "And if our king can find forgiveness in his heart for a brother who sold him into slavery, then by his God, we can certainly forgive the Cairthan. That is, if we've a care for Gleannmara and the future of it for our children."

Maire's jaw slackened in amazement. Surely this wasn't the hothead she'd known all her life. What had come over her foster brother? It was one thing to stand by and brood, but that Declan would take up Rowan's cause was beyond her ken.

"Aye," Rowan agreed, lifting his cup. "To Gleannmara, home to the just and the compassionate; enemy to the greedy and ambitious."

"Brude, mayhap you can word that in a motto for our banners," Maire said, rising to lift her glass with Rowan's. "Brude?"

The old man shook himself from whatever possessed his thoughts. "What was that, you say?"

"Can you make up a motto for Gleannmara's banners that says *home to the just; enemy to the greedy and ambitious?*"

The old man thought a moment and nodded. "Aye, I will think on it. 'Tis a noble thought indeed."

"What do you think of this plan of the king's, Brude?" the woman who had protested earlier asked. "Have you seen any reason why some should pick up and leave for enemy land? I don't warm to the idea of turning our pastures to grass and takin' to the hills with them that just stole six head from us."

"I have *seen* no reason, woman, but I have *heard.*" The druid waited until the murmuring about him died down. Now all eyes were on him, those of servant and aire alike.

"King Rowan's God has a chosen people—His favorites, if you like. Many of us are descended from the ones who fled here when their nation fell because they refused to follow Him."

"The blood of the Milesian princes runs in these veins, druid," Declan boasted. "As for the bruns, I can't say." He poked one of the dark-haired Muirdach men and got as good as he gave.

"Many Milesians took Hebrew brides, but that is neither here nor there, in this story, metalhead."

The assembly roared at Brude's admonishment. Declan took it in good humor and sat down.

"The Christian God led the Hebrews from slavery and oppression to a land of milk and honey. There isn't a one of you who doesn't know that we have lived under Morlach's oppression."

A ripple of oaths and agreement testified to the old man's word.

"And there isn't a one among you who doesn't fear the man's power."

The agreement grew louder. What Morlach didn't take by force, he took by his magic.

"Well, I have seen firsthand the one God's power." The druid's tone heralded a sharing of the unknown, which hushed the assembly.

"Rowan and Maire's company walked without harm through Morlach's ambush to Tara. I was accused of making them appear as a herd of deer, for that was all the blackguards saw along the way, but it was not *my* power. I wasn't with them."

No murmur, nothing stirred in the hall, save the snapping and crackling of the fires. Even the cooks stopped stirring their pots, lest the rattle of the ladles against the sides interrupt.

"And the boils," Maire said as she grabbed Rowan's arm and held it. "I have yet to see a blemish from Cromthal's curse."

"Perhaps Rathcoe awaited on the wrong road," someone ventured uneasily.

"Perhaps," Brude conceded, "but once again we passed his ambush on the way home to Gleannmara. Two bowmen and his apprentice, Cromthal, waited for the chance to kill our king and the priest as well, but they dared not."

Maire was transfixed along with the rest of the gathering, Rowan included, by Brude's last words.

"Eight warriors garbed in white surrounded our king and the priest. Neither Rowan nor Tomás made a move but what these fierce men moved with them. They were armed with ready weapons and protected by armor that shined bright as the morning sun, even in the darkness."

So *that* was what Brude saw last night! The flesh pebbled on her arms and every hair on her scalp tingled. This was the stuff only the Sidhe and the druids could see.

"Father Tomás saw them, as did I, and, of course, Morlach's henchmen. They ran like scalded hounds through the brush, alerting the guards."

"Aye, that they did, and in every direction at the same time," one of the O'Croinin said to his wife Elsbeth. "Me and Dub never closed an eye after that."

"Nor Dath 'n' me," Cellach of the Muirdach vowed.

"And who were these warriors in white?" Maire demanded, peeved that her druid had waited until now to tell her. Druids! Always keeping secrets. And priests as well, she thought, eyeing the meanly clothed cleric crossing himself beside Brude.

"Angels!" Rowan's comment reflected the wonder on his face. He nodded slowly, accepting it. "Now our coming through unchallenged makes sense."

"What are these *angels* that walk among us like spirits?" Declan asked.

"God's Sidhe," Maire answered with an air of authority. She hadn't spent half a night trying to get the understanding of these beings for naught. "They are seen only when He wants them to be seen and they do what He wishes them to do."

"And you've *seen* them, Brude?" the warrior asked skeptically.

The old man nodded, the light from the lamps shining on

his wrinkled brow. "Aye, I've seen them. They are more beautiful and fierce than all the heroes of Erin. But enough of them." Brude reached down and picked up his walking stick. "'Twould take more than this lifetime to know all there is to know about this God and His warriors. Sadly, I do not have long to learn as much as I'd wish."

"You're ill, Brude?" Distracted from her annoyance by Brude's comment, Maire hurried around the head table to where the old man hobbled toward the door. Had he seen the banshee of death among the angels?

"Nay, Maire. I'm old." He looked over his shoulder at Rowan. "Tomorrow, I go to live with Father Tomás, to become the student."

Maire felt the blood drain from her face with such force, she half expected to see it pooling on the floor. "But Brude, what will the Niall do without you?" What would *she* do?

Where Brude once towered over her, he now looked her in the eye. When had he grown so bent?

"I have found the Creator of truth and light. So has your husband. Follow his lead, for he knows more of God than I."

For the first time in her life, the druid kissed her on the cheek. Heretofore, his affection had come only in the form of a nod or a smile of approval. "Gleannmara will know greatness so long as her fires burn for the Christian God alone."

"For darkness is destroyed by light." Another truth she'd learned the night before her wedding.

"You are the best student this old man ever taught."

"And you the best teacher." Whether it befitted a queen or not, Maire embraced the druid. Her eyes were wet as she drew away. Brude had been there always, but his mind was made up. To make more protest was to invite admonition and disgrace. Surely a part of her would go with him. How could she be whole without her Brude?

"Now I must rest these weary bones for the trip tomorrow."

Turning back to the head table, Maire saw Rowan seated,

his head bowed as if he slept, and the answer came. Now she understood. Brude was leaving so that Rowan might take his rightful place as her husband. In awe at the way this master plan seemed to be unfolding, she took her place beside Rowan. As she did, he enveloped her hand in his own and, lifting it, rose.

"We are not done with Morlach. Even as we celebrate God's blessings upon us, he conjures yet another blackness with which to strike us. But God is ever present, ever watchful, and ever protective of those who will accept Him."

"I'd hear more about him first," someone said.

"I'd *see* more of his work first," another agreed.

Those who did not fall in with one of the skeptics, sided with the other, save Declan and Garret. Drawing their swords, they made their way to the dais and knelt before Rowan and Maire.

"Drumkilly accepts this God."

"And the Cairthan," Garret echoed his new chosen mentor.

"So tell us more of Him," Dub O'Croinin suggested, garnering more encouragement from the listeners.

Rowan shook his head. "The hour is late, my friend. But I promise I will share what I know of Him, for it is my duty and honor." He took up Maire's hand unexpectedly. "But tonight, my *wife* is my honor and duty."

The hoots of approval would have scorched Maire's cheek with embarrassment before now. But as she walked out of the banqueting hall on Rowan's arm, past a smiling Ciara, she felt as though she would burst with pride. Or was it anxiety that threatened to overwhelm her?

In the privacy of their lodge, Rowan closed the door and slid the wooden bolt into place. Maire half expected him to turn on her and take her, then and there, as she'd heard happened when the baser nature of man consumed him. After all, she'd invited it more bluntly than a practiced coquette.

When he turned, though, his face was as solemn as a

druid's, not one of a prospective groom. He was Rowan, self-possessed and in control. She wondered which was worse.

"I want to be certain you understand what you say, Maire, before I take you to this bed."

"Not another night of these Jesus stories." Her nerves would not stand it.

Rowan chuckled quietly. "No, not a Jesus story. Just a few words of what you mean to me."

Ach, he was going to pledge his love. Perhaps that would give her heart time to settle back in her chest. She sat stiffly on the small bench at the foot of the bed, a smooth, oiled width of wood designed just for such a purpose and for dressing.

"Remember the story Father Tomás told of the creation and how Adam and Eve disregarded God's warning about the apple?"

"Aye, though I still think it was much ado over a piece of fruit."

Rowan looked about to take up an argument, but thought better of it. "I believe Adam ate the apple for one reason, Maire. Because he feared God would kill Eve for her disobedience and Adam could not bear to live without her. Better that God kill him, too."

She hadn't thought of this tale as a love story when Father Tomás told it to pass the time on the journey home, much less that this Adam was gallant. "And you'd give your life for me?"

"Aye, little queen. I was prepared to do that when we first met, sooner than take your life, but God showed us each an alternative to our problems."

Maire thought about this, wonderstruck, as he went on.

"God tells man to love his wife more than himself."

"And what does He tell a woman to do?"

"To submit to and respect her husband."

"If he's respectable and not without reason."

Rowan ran his fingers along the taper of her cheek. "We are to put no one ahead of the other, save God himself. We are to become one, Maire, in more ways than the obvious. In spirit and accord. Gleannmara has wedded us already in that sense."

"Aye, but…" The word *submit* was a stumbling stone she could not get past.

"Will it be so hard to submit to someone who puts you ahead of himself, who would die for you? To someone who is one with you in more ways than the physical? 'Tis what you've been doing all along, for the good of Gleannmara."

Submit. There had been times when Rhian and Maeve disagreed, but in the end, one submitted to the other for the good of the tuath. They were of one accord and one spirit, and they had ruled as one. They'd fought as heartily as they loved—as *one.*

Maire's eyes widened. He was offering her what she'd always wanted, a love like that of her parents.

"No, Rowan ap Emrys or O'Cairthan. It will not be hard." She took his hand and folded her own into it, pressing both against her heart, that he might hear its earnest testimony. "Like my father and mother before us, we *are* one in spirit and rule."

Maire went into Rowan's arms willingly, no longer fearful of where the commitment might lead. Before the night was out, to refuse to submit to this man would be to refuse to submit to herself. When he kissed her, she kissed him back with equal fervor. Desire flared, burning like incense to not only her senses, but his. It was not her passion that fanned the flames, nor his. It was *theirs.* It was not his touch, nor hers that exacted immeasurable pleasure, but *theirs.* It was not his nor her heart that beat with primitive madness, but *theirs,* playing a rhapsody as one.

As Maire fell back with Rowan against the soft bedding, frantically shedding all that was earthly between them, one thought rose to the surface of her mind. It was only fitting that they become one as man and wife in her parents' bed, which had known nothing but an enduring and sustaining love.

TWENTY-THREE

Daylight. It came as surely as God's judgment.

And where will I stand in either? Rowan wondered, riddled with self-recrimination as he paced the outer rath at the break of dawn. His weakness of the flesh barely spent, he'd torn himself from the bed, leaving the woman of his dreams—the love of his life—sleeping like an angel. Not that Maire had been the least angelic, once introduced to the throes of passion. She loved as fiercely as she fought.

Faith, the memory still stirred him in the midst of his humble meditation. "Father, how can I separate the physical from the spiritual where my wife is concerned?" he cried, falling to his knees in his exasperation.

"Why would you wish to?"

Rowan pivoted, astonished that he'd voiced his anguish and even more so, that he'd been heard. Father Tomás rose from a nearby rock, where apparently he too had sought to meditate in the stillness before sunrise.

Rowan made a frustrated grimace. "I intended to have the wedding annulled."

"For what purpose?"

"To pursue my studies in the priesthood...without the distraction of a wife. I thought I had it all worked out in my mind, exactly how to keep my promises to myself and to Maire, how to serve both God and Gleannmara, but..."

"But God's plan was different?"

Rowan looked up at the sky where the sun's first rays threatened to illuminate the horizon. "I don't know what is God's plan and what is mine. I wanted to become a priest, a teacher."

Tomás smiled. "You already are those things, Rowan of Gleannmara. It doesn't take a clerical robe to do that." At Rowan's bewildered look, the priest went on. "I have seen your example sway the queen and her people toward God in ways I could not possibly imitate. God has given you a passion for Him that is infectious."

"Then think of what I could do if—"

"To isolate it somewhere in a glen or on a mountaintop would be a disservice to Him and to yourself. You would not be content."

"I would *master* contentment!"

"As you master your desire for Maire?"

Rowan could not answer. The priest's point was well made. Rowan could master nothing without God's support.

"Do you love her?"

"Aye, that must be it, for she consumes my thoughts, both night and day, both in and out of my presence." Rowan chuckled in wonder. "For one so worldly, she is such an innocent…a treasure like no other woman I've ever met."

"The queen is indeed a collection of contrary qualities, much like her king."

Rowan glanced askew at the priest, uncertain if his words carried compliment or criticism. "'Tis an effect she has on a man. She can make me so angry that I nearly forget my faith in one moment, and then surrender my annoyance in the next."

"I would think marriage to her would truly test and refine a man's spiritual nature."

Marriage as a test of God? The idea had never occurred to Rowan. He'd seen the hardship and denial of the priesthood as the real test of a man's devotion to his God. And while he knew marriage required dedication and compromise, there were the more desirable aspects to sweeten the dish. They were what Rowan feared was seducing him from his chosen path to serve God, rather than himself.

"We are all chosen to serve God in our own special way, my son," Tomás told him patiently. "While I do not pretend to know God's plan, I can share what I have observed. Gleannmara needs a strong king and Maire needs a good husband. You have been both thus far and in doing so, you have served God well. You have reached beyond the glens and isolation of our priesthood and into many lives in a way that men like myself may never touch."

"But I thought as a priest I might serve God better."

"So did Zechariah. He cleaned the temple, all the while thinking the priesthood a more godly and worthy pursuit. Yet it was to the lowlier servant that God gave one of the greatest tasks, to father and raise John the Baptist, that the coming of the Messiah might be announced. So who was greater in God's eye, the man who honored Him by cleaning the temple or the priest?"

Rowan nodded, digesting the example. As in the army, there were no unimportant tasks. The messengers were as important as the front line soldiers or the generals. The difference lay in amount of recognition given. So were his reasons for wanting the priesthood self-serving? The idea struck Rowan a jolting blow.

God had been with him on all his pursuits save one: avoiding his attraction to the queen of Gleannmara. What he'd seen as test to overcome in order to join the priesthood—the forced marriage and his uncommon longing where Maire was concerned—was God's way of showing *His* will, rather than Rowan's.

How could he have been so blind? Rowan jumped to his feet and gave the priest a bear hug in his enthusiasm. The terrible weight was gone.

"Father Tomás, bless you and thank you."

Feeling as though he could fly, Rowan left the priest, speeding back toward the royal lodge and Maire—his queen, his lover, his friend, his *wife*.

Maire positively glowed, he thought later as they rode Shahar and Tamar across Gleannmara's fields and pastures. Envious, Rowan watched the sunlight and westerly breeze toy with the little wisps of hair that had escaped her braid. Like a little girl with a cherished doll, he'd helped her wrap its silken length in a leather casing after rising entirely too late for decency.

And the shy blush that overtook her face when she caught him watching her was a contrary mix of innocence and seduction at the same time. The discipline of life in the army and his godly studies were of no avail to him against this woman. He'd had to show his love and desire for her once more before they left the intimacy of their lodge for the day.

"I don't think the oxen are takin' kindly to that new blade of yours," Maire said, pointing to where six men wrestled with a team to work up the freshly cleared ground.

"It digs deeper, that's for certain."

And who'd have ever thought leather and armor could be so fetching? Not that a piece of sackcloth wouldn't look queenly on Maire. From now on, he'd see her clothed in the finest, and he'd fill the void of love and feminine attention that being raised as a warrior queen had denied her. Rowan tried to focus on the men struggling ahead of them.

"Let the oxen pull the blade," he shouted to the cursing men. "All you need do is hold it down. Work with them, not against them."

"Talk to the beasties, not us," Dathal Muirdach answered.

Dathal's brother swore. "We'll count it well to get this field worked and planted before the summer fair at Drumkilly!"

"Faith, good friend," Rowan called back to the man. "Do you fell a tree with one blow or many little ones?" He slid off Shahar's back and started toward them. "Let me see what I can do. Just remember, we need to cut it away a little at a time, not all at once."

A little at a time. Just as he'd fallen in love with Maire, without ever realizing it. Just like the Cairthan and Niall were growing accustomed to each other. Just like God revealed His plan for Gleannmara.

The days grew warmer and the nights sweeter. Spring settled in the air and the sun coaxed the seedlings to peek out of the warmed worked earth. Everywhere Maire looked, the reward for their hard work began to show—a little at a time. For most of Gleannmara's keep, each day began with prayer and a hymn dedicated to the one God, although some still sang the sun song. Each night ended with thanksgiving. There was so much work to do, so much love to share.

And when the fair opened at Drumkilly with the lighting of the fires, it was Father Tomás who performed the rite with Brude at his side. Each in turn lit the two giant piles of wood with a prayer.

"Praise the one God who created the sun and lives in the Heavens. May He in all His limitless grace and mercy bless these fires and all who pass through them, as a symbol of the cleansing power of the blood shed for us by His only Son, Jesus Christ. May all evil, all sickness, and all iniquity perish in these flames, so that only that which is pure and worthy of His holy name remain."

Maire was not the only one at the gathering who thought it strange to suddenly abandon the dedication of the fires to Bel, the sun god. The Celts believed change was good, but it didn't mean they were always at ease with it. She couldn't help but think Bel's name was being echoed here and there, particularly among the other clans. But tolerance would be the order of the day. The laws regarding the fairs forbade anything less.

An entire set of laws was set aside specifically for the hosts of the fair, the attendees, as well as the performers and merchants—which was another reason why the queen of

Gleannmara was pleased not to be the host. She hated being tied to rules. Besides, the tuath was not quite prepared for such a venture. It took all the combined effort of her people to get in the late clearing and planting. For all his skill as a warrior, Rowan was as equal to the tasks of farming too.

And of being a husband. It was a joy to submit to him, especially when she knew she'd pushed too far and he turned red with restraint, rather than give way to his temper. She learned so much from him about life—and more about love.

"Just look at the sea of goods!" Ciara remarked at her side as they wandered in and out of the stalls on the hill set aside for the markets.

Maire reluctantly withdrew her attention from another rise, where the men, stripped to the waist, practiced to represent Gleannmara in the games. In their midst, Rowan coached Garret on how to get the most distance with a javelin, while Declan and the Muirdach limbered up their throwing arms swinging heavy hammers.

"You know, you'd look lovely in that deep saffron."

"Aye, it's lovely enough, I suppose."

"We could make it for you, milady," Elsbeth joined in. "Now that you're a queen, 'tis only fitting you have a wardrobe worthy of your title. After all, it's the king's orders."

With one last longing look at the men's boisterous company, Maire fingered the material her mother-in-law held up. "Aye, it is pretty enough."

Of course Rowan would want a feminine looking wife, and Maire wanted to be one—some of the time. But the men's competitions were so much more interesting than this tedious shopping or those games set aside for the womenfolk. Footraces, chases, or tapping a ball around with a club were hardly pulse-pounding pursuits. At least she'd kept her hand in the spear and riding competition with a few of the other females who'd trained to fight rather than run a keep.

"Oh, this burnt umber velvet is exquisite!" Elsbeth picked

up a bolt and held it up against Maire's chest.

The sharp knock of her knuckles against the hard form of Maire's breastplate, hidden beneath the dress Delwyn of Emrys had given her, startled her. Maire blushed as the ladies surrounding her broke into laughter, lead by Rowan's own mother.

"Just because there's a law against fighting, doesn't mean a woman shouldn't be prepared," Maire said hotly.

And it *was* hot. Her leine, her breastplate, full armor, *and* the heavy linen gown with its braid and embroidery were about to render her like a fire did fat, but there was no way she could ride in her wedding dress and launch a spear with any hope of accuracy.

"And just the feel of that heavy velvet is enough make me drop from heat."

"But 'twill feel good this winter, Maire," Ciara reminded her gently. "We're to purchase enough material for your wardrobe and it must consist of both heavy and light fabric—"

"And all royal," Elsbeth chimed in. "Our queen will be the prettiest and best dressed in all of Erin, or I don't know which end of a needle is sharp."

Sure, she'd rather prepare for battle than set up a household. The dry goods and utensils of Gleannmara's hall and kitchens had been poorly kept. The list Ciara and Elsbeth compiled would take the whole three days of the fair to fill at this rate. Wishing she'd listened more to her foster mother Maida, Maire squared her chin and braced for action.

"All right then, let's get this done. I've a mind to practice on Tamar before the afternoon games," she said, cutting off any protest in the making amid the cluster of women. "Ciara, I'm giving you command of my wardrobe. Take Lianna with you and purchase as you please."

"But don't you want to see—"

"I trust in your judgment. And Elsbeth…" Maire turned toward the plump matron. "Fill the list of things needed for the hall and take care to pay a fair price." She handed the woman a coin pouch. "Get only what we *must* have. We'll have more to spend after the harvest."

Elsbeth sputtered. "B...but shouldn't you approve everything?"

"I'm a queen, not a steward. Brona?"

The dark-haired girl stepped out of the entourage expectantly. "Aye, milady."

"Replenish what herbs and roots we need for the sick. Medwyn, supervise the cooks' purchases."

"I'll let them buy nothing that can be grown in our own soil."

Maire nodded in approval at her captains. Perhaps running a household wasn't so different than planning a battle after all. "If any of you have a problem, I'll be with the horses." A wistful smile settle on her lips. "Or with my king."

Riding Tamar was like riding the wind, Maire thought later as she raced the magnificent warhorse toward the target. If one was in concert with it, it contributed to the speed and ease of the journey. Out of sync, it became a fight that slowed and exhausted the rider.

With nimble fingers, Maire turned the smooth lance in her hand and tightened her grip as the mare approached the bale of hay with its painted canvas cover. One, two, three!

Maire launched the spear, sending it straight to the center. As the audience erupted in huzzahs and whistles, she raised both fists over her head in triumph. Guiding the horse out of the small roped off arena with her knees, she beamed at the tall, dark-haired king of Gleannmara.

Time was, it was Brude's approval she sought, or Erc's, but no more. Maire wanted to please Rowan and his God.

"She rides as if on air, rather than earth," Maire called to him. She'd shed her dress for the competition, and the shock on his face alone had been worth suffering in the heat of the excess clothing. Although, if Rowan's look was any more stirring, she'd swoon like a sun-sick maid.

"So do you." He reached up to help Maire down from the mare, teasing, "I'm hard pressed to decide which of you is more magnificent."

"I'll keep that in mind tonight, when ye come snugglin' up to me, whisperin' sweetlings in my ear."

The chief of the Murragh rode into the arena on a shaggy steed, his brat beneath him for a blanket and his hairy chest damp with dust and sweat. Earlier, he and his clan had competed heartily in a game of football that left members of both teams bleeding and bandaged. The Murragh's knee was wrapped tight from a fray of kicking and tumbling just before the end of the game, but the clan emerged victorious.

Balancing the spear in his right arm, the clan chief kneed the wiry horse forward. It responded with a lunge that might have unseated a lesser skilled rider, but the Murragh leaned into ride, poised and ready. When the time was right, he threw the weapon. The crack of Maire's spear announced the dead-on hit, and the crowd went wild. With a wide grin belaying his nod of deference to the queen of Gleannmara, he trotted out of the arena.

"Looks like Gleannmara will have to ride again," Rowan observed, tongue in cheek.

Her eyes dancing, Maire met his mischief with her own. "And ride I will!"

She broke into a short run and vaulted up on Tamar's back, light as a feather. "Declan," she shouted playfully, "do ye think ye might tear yourself away from Lianna and the lasses long enough to hand me another spear?"

With a sweeping bow, her foster brother complied. "At my queen's command, though ye've met your match in Murragh. He rides as though he was fathered by a horse."

"Then I'll have to ride better, won't I?"

"Show this dolt what a woman can do when she puts her mind to it, milady," Lianna called out to her.

Maire wondered where Brona had gotten to, for it was the

darker lass she thought had won Declan's fancy, not Lianna. After a quick visual search of the crowd, Maire spied the other girl watching not far from where they stood. Like a shadow, not in the forefront, but always there…and always watching.

Was she jealous? Maire wondered. It was as easy to read druid Ogham marks as it was Brona's face. Try as she might, Maire could no more warm to the girl than she could a cromlech.

Oblivious to all but the adoring attention of Lianna, Declan leaned, whispering wickedly into the young woman's ear. Suddenly she slapped at him halfheartedly, drawing Maire's full attention.

"That's *not* the kind of ridin' I was referrin' to, ye randy cur!"

What could Maire say? It was spring. For the first time in her life, she understood the wry humor behind the excuse men and women gave for their foolraide. With a bold wink at Rowan, she rode Tamar back into the arena. To accustom the mare to the boundaries, she made a circle, well aware that Tamar paraded her mane and tail like banners of pride.

And well she had a right too, for back at the makeshift stable her four-week-old foal slept in a pile of fresh straw. Rowan had been offered a king's ransom for it, but little Sidhe was not for sale. Shahar's services, however, promised to more than replenish the coin in Gleannmara's coffers.

"One more ride, darlin', and it's back to your baby," Maire promised, bringing the horse up at the opposite end of the arena from the new target some men had just put in place.

At the slightest pressure of her knees, Tamar leapt forward with the grace of a deer. Two strides later, Maire vaulted to her feet, standing on the horse's back. A spontaneous mix of shouts and applause rose around the arena, but neither horse nor rider flinched. Two more contacts with the whispering earth and she posed, spear raised, and counted off the number of lopes until its release. Four, three, two, one, hurl!

Straight into the center of the target it went. The roar of

approval shook the banners flying from the various clan camp-
sites. There wouldn't be a bird left within a day's riding distance, Maire thought, deafened and delighted at the same time.
As Tamar trotted out of the arena, she leapt into Rowan's waiting arms.

"Don't drop me!" she laughed, as his knees buckled with
the impact of her weight.

"Have I ever let you down yet, muirnait?" He kissed her
lightly.

Maire returned the affection as fiercely as she'd competed,
drawing it out till need of breath would permit no more. She
scarcely noted the Murragh Chief take off his hat and swing it
in her direction, conceding the contest, nor did she pay heed
to the horns announcing her triumph. Her eyes and ears were
for the man who made her feel as though there was no higher
purpose in life than love.

"Nay, beloved, never."

That night, when couples wandered from the music and
stories abounding at the campfires of the gathered clans, Maire
and Rowan were among them. It was spring and the sky was a
star-studded blanket of midnight blue over a bed of new grass.
No longer were they king and queen of Gleannmara, but God's
children, laughing and playing, free of inhibition and sharing
as one their passion and love, their dreams and plans.

"By the stars, Emrys, if that thing chills me one more time,
I'll strangle ye with it!" Maire took Rowan's amulet and slinging
it over his back once more. "'Tis like trying to warm up to
body with a cold stone between us!"

"Then by all means, little queen, I'll take it off." In one
sweep, he removed the amulet and tossed it over his shoulder,
then pulled Maire against his chest.

Heartbeat to heartbeat, Maire caught her breath and struggled in the sweet, warm mire of his embrace. "But isn't that like
throwin' away your God?"

"Ah, Maire, how I love telling you of God's ways and sharing in His love." Rowan buried his face in the curve of her neck, nuzzling like a hungry colt.

Concentration on whatever wisdom he was about to impart was all but impossible.

"God is not in that metal disc or in things of this earth, muirnait. He lives within our souls." He pulled away suddenly. "Do you understand?"

This God made the metal, but He wasn't in it. He made man and woman, but He *was* in them. What chance did a mere queen ever have of knowing all about Him, when even Brude, a learned druid, was now a student? Maire would never understand it all, but she was in no humor for a lecture. She chose her words carefully.

"Understanding or nay, I believe what ye say."

"If I didn't know your heart, Maire of Gleannmara, I'd think you a wicked woman."

The light of the moon played upon the toe-curling look Rowan gave her. He knew she was evading the issue, but he was no more in the notion for a sermon than she. His longing gaze betrayed him.

Maire ventured a coy smile. "If it's wicked to love my husband, then, aye, I'm as wicked as they come."

The rakish tilt of her companion's mouth faded, and Maire's pulse skipped and sank. Had she said something wrong? Sure, it was in keeping with the very vows of her Christian marriage, wasn't it?

Rowan seized her by the arms, gentle, but no less firm. His voice cracked with the fierceness of his emotion. "Then believe this, muirnait. I will let nothing of this earth come between us."

With that, he took her into his arms and kissed her, sealing his vow with an urgency that was as delightful as it was infectious.

In the distance a night bird sang a lullaby to its young, but Maire paid it no heed. She was listening, instead, to the singing of her heart.

TWENTY-FOUR

Maire guided Tamar around the bountiful fields spreading out from the rath. Nearby Tamar's colt frolicked, kicking up its heels, running ahead and then back at the mare's sharp whinny. Little yellow ducklings scrambled after their mother in the pond where the framework of a mill had been started.

Rowan met a miller at the fair, who'd lost his place to fire. With no funds or manpower to rebuild, the man gladly agreed to move to Gleannmara, where all pitched in toward the building of the structure to serve the tuath.

Now that more land had been cleared with tillable soil to provide a good harvest for Cairthan and Niall, a mill nearby would be needed. The hard work made the blending of the two clans go more smoothly, for at the day's end, the men and women were too tired to quarrel. If only Rowan were there to warm her nights, life would be perfect.

Instead, at the onset of lambing season, he'd returned to the tuath's highlands to mediate peace after Eochan had come with the news of trouble. Since watching the cattle did not require as much energy as the fieldwork and building, the king had work in mind that would take the quarrel out of the two peoples. She imagined by now the men were putting up makeshift fences across natural enclosures. to keep the beasts from wandering, as well as from being easy prey for wolves of animal and human nature. It would also take some time to improve on the lodgings or lack of them.

Maire had no doubt that it was duty alone that took him

from her, for he demonstrated his reluctance to leave over and over in the most agreeable of ways. Indeed, marriage agreed with her. Had she known how well, she'd have been more eager for it. Speaking to God, however, was more difficult.

It wasn't voicing her thoughts that plagued Maire, but the fact that this God didn't talk back like a person. He revealed His presence and will through all manner of things, which left Maire at wit's end to figure what was normal and what wasn't. Overhead the trees at the edge of the Sacred Grove rustled with the breeze, calming as a lullaby. Was that God singing to her? She wished Rowan or Brude were here to ask.

"G'day, milady."

Maire had been so caught up in her musings, she hadn't seen Lianna emerge from the grove with sticks and kindling for the fires.

"May the sun shine on you for all of it, lass."

Lianna managed a hint of a smile, no more.

"You're not feeling well these days, are ye, Lianna?"

Not only was Lianna's ever-present smile missing, but so was the rose in her cheeks. Indeed, circles darkened beneath her eyes, which were lacking in their usual luster.

"Sure, I've felt better. My feet grow heavier with each passing day, it seems."

Maire slid off Tamar to spare Lianna the long walk back to the rath. "Then climb up on Tamar and give your feet *and* my buttocks a rest."

"Oh no, my queen. I couldn't!"

"I'm queen in ruling Gleannmara, but as a friend, I'm just Maire. This title is starting to wear on my nerves." Maire took the bundle from Lianna. "Now up with ye."

In truth, being a queen was lonely without her king. Not that *any* king would do.

"Now, tell me cousin, how is it that we're related?" She held her hands so that the weary lass might vault up on Tamar's wide back. Actually Maire knew their family connection, but she wanted to get the young woman to relax.

"Your grandfather and my grandmother were brother and sister."

Maire handed the bundle up to Lianna and took the mare's reins. The young woman weighed no more than a sprite. Her clothes hung loose about her waist. She'd lost weight for certain.

"So have ye been sick in the mornin', not keeping food on your stomach?" If Brude were here, he'd know what to do. But he *had* taught Maire her people were her responsibility. So she would give the servant her best thoughts on the matter.

"Or noon or evenin' for that matter. I've lost my want for food."

"You're not with child, are ye?"

"No. I bleed as regular as the moon comes full."

"Then we'll ask Ciara and the other women what they think, for it's clear you're not yerself."

A good queen sought counsel when she was uncertain. God's favorite king David often did. And he prayed.

"Would ye like to pray with me? Maybe this God'll show us what's makin' ye so pale and wan."

Maire still didn't like to pray alone. Often she sought out Ciara to share her evening vespers, now that Rowan was gone.

"I know nothin' of prayin'."

"Just listen to me and nod your head. The Ghost will tell God what's on your heart."

"Ghost?"

"Never ye mind, 'tis a good one." Maire took a deep breath and started. "Father God, this girl is sick and we're askin' Ye to show us what's wrong or fix it Yourself. Whatever is Your will. Amen."

"What did he say?"

"Most times He doesn't answer in words. He just does things in His own time." At least that's how Rowan had explained it to her. She hoped her dear Brude was understanding more of this Christian God than she. Thankfully, one didn't have to understand everything to enjoy God's blessings. They surrounded Maire, increasing by the day.

"And thank Ye kindly for all You've given us, amen," she added hastily. "If you agree, you can say—" Maire turned to Lianna just in time to see the young woman keel forward. "Ho, lass, hang on!" She righted her companion, shaking her from her lethargy. "Now hold on to Tamar's mane. I'm coming up behind ye."

It took two tries, but with a running start and Tamar's trained cooperation, Maire vaulted onto the horse's flank behind the sick girl. Taking up the reins, she urged the mare forward toward the rath.

The mare made the journey a short one. The spindly colt was winded when it caught up with its mother. Their hooves clicked on the log-planked road leading into the large enclosure. Coming out at the same time was Declan, leading a group of men who participated in the afternoon of combat training.

"Give us a hand, brother. The girl's sick, and I'd have Ciara see her. Take her to my lodge."

"No, Maire—"

"Hush, Lianna. Remember I *am* the queen."

Maire gave the protesting girl a mischievous wink, but it was lost upon her. Her eyes rolled as though she were in a swoon, and Declan gathered her into his strong arms. He gave orders for the men to proceed to the outer rath for training and carried Lianna to Maire's lodge.

"What's wrong with her?" His voice betrayed his concern.

"She fainted. I thought maybe she was with child but she says no."

The stricken expression on her foster brother's face told Maire that possibility could not be ruled out. He laid the girl on the bed with a tenderness she'd rarely seen him display. Lianna stirred, her eyes blinking in confusion.

"Thank ye, brother. Now best ye go for Ciara."

"Aye, I will." He took up Lianna's hand and kissed her

knuckles. "We'll have ye up and dancin' with me in no time, lass."

Lianna was clammy with perspiration, yet the day was fresh and pleasantly cool. While waiting for Rowan's mother, Maire poured water from a pitcher on the table onto a cloth and mopped her patient's brow.

"For weeks I've tried to get his attention and it takes the likes o' this to do it."

"Declan?"

"I owe even this much to a potion—a scent a man could not refuse."

Lianna reached into her apron and drew out a small vial. It looked like the one Brona had offered Maire.

"I'd have a man love me for myself and not because of what comes from a bottle, for when the bottle is empty, he'll be gone." Maire smelled the perfume. It had a bittersweet scent. "Where did you get this?"

"I found it tossed out among the wind-strewn leaves nearby and recognized it." Lianna looked away guiltily. "I should have given it back to Brona, but she has powers and I thought—"

"You'd use them to win Declan of Drumkilly," Maire finished flatly.

"Aye, and it's workin'. Did ye see the way he looked at me? It's young Garret who now pines after Brona."

Ciara entered, her sleeves rolled up to her elbows and her apron stained from working with the dairy maids. Their jobs would last out the season, making up the stores of summer food to see Gleannmara through winter. She smelled like fresh cream and butter. "What is that? I thought we'd thrown that away."

Maire looked at the bottle more closely. Men and women were known to try all manner of concoctions to win the attention of the opposite sex, and many, like Lianna, were the worse for it. If this was the same vial Brona had offered her, then it might well be her lying on the bed now, instead of her distant cousin.

"Lianna found it. I was just takin' a sniff." Maire held the open vial under Ciara's nose. "I see nothin' so irresistible about it."

"That because it's to affect a man, not you," their patient remarked.

Ciara sniffed it and started. Her expression grim, she took it from Maire, corked it, and slipped it into her apron. "Let's have a look at you, lass. Ye look sucked as dry as if ye'd laid in a bed of leeches."

After a number of questions and examining the patient's nails and breath, Ciara stood up. "Maire, I'd have a word with you outside." Her tone was now as grim as her expression.

Once beyond Lianna's hearing, her mother-in-law glanced around, as though to make sure no one else was within earshot. "Maire, the girl's been poisoned."

"You mean *intentionally?*" Maire was incredulous. Her surprise was soon pushed aside by something far stronger: anger. Brona had given the vial to *her,* not to Lianna. Was it possible the girl had dared try poisoning her queen?

"I'm not as expert on herbs as the druid, but I'd wager my beating heart that this vial has some manner of poison in it that seeps through the skin and into the blood. I know it has mandrake in it."

Gradually the full blow of Ciara's implication registered. But why would Brona do such a thing? What had Maire done to her? "Mandrake...like to keep a woman from conceivin'?"

"And something else, what I can't say."

"Will Lianna die?"

"I'll do what I can for her. Perhaps, if she'll drink a tea with charcoal ground fine in it, it may absorb the poison and carry it out. It depends on how much is in her system."

Maire had heard of applying charcoal poultices, but ingesting it was new. Nonetheless, she didn't question Ciara. Her questions were for the dark-haired girl who slipped like a spirit in and out of the royal lodge, her face always a mask. Touching the stinger strapped to her waist, Maire started for the door.

She intended to find out exactly what was hiding behind those piercing dark eyes of Brona's, even if she had to cut them out to see for herself.

Morlach is too devious to do the obvious.

Who'd said that? Maire stopped at the door. Was it Rowan or Brude? She started forward again. It didn't matter. She was certain the dark druid was behind this. All she needed was to find out the truth from Brona.

A horn from the gate froze Maire in midstep so suddenly that Ciara, who was on her heels, nearly collided with her.

"I'm off to fetch some things for Lianna."

Maire nodded. She'd have to deal with Brona later. Breaking into a trot, she headed toward the singular opening to the inner rath. Other people milling within and without approached as well, for the signal told of someone approaching. She prayed it was Rowan, returning from the higher grounds of Gleannmara.

Dub Muirdach pointed to a rise in the distance, which could easily be seen above the earthworks of the outer ring. A considerable contingent of armed riders approached, but it was the red and black colors flying above them that ran an icicle of fear through Maire's chest.

Morlach.

Declan saw them, too. Immediately he ordered the watchmen to herald in those still working the fields beyond. Those inside, armed and ready, were sent to stand atop the earthworks, shoulder to shoulder.

But if Morlach of Rathcoe intended to attack Gleannmara, despite what Brude or Rowan said, his force would have to be larger than that which Maire saw approaching. Even an untrained eye could see that. She ran up on the earthenworks and took a place next to her captain.

"It's the high king himself," Declan exclaimed, as surprised as Maire when a slight change in the approaching party's direction revealed the royal banners of Tara as well as those of Rathcoe.

"How can I send Morlach away when he travels with Diarhmott?" Maire fretted, adding an unladylike oath of exasperation.

"How could ye send him away, if the high king *wasn't* with him? 'Tis against the law to deny hospitality—"

"Not to an enemy."

"Whether it's here or there, it doesn't really matter, does it?" Her foster brother closed his hand on the hilt of his sword, forcing the blood from his knuckles. "I'm just hoping Diarhmott intends to keep the word he gave regarding his neutrality in this feud." He spat to the side. "And us with no more than a lot o' farmers. By my ancestors' bones, we'll have to plough 'em under, instead of kill them with sword and ax."

"If Diarhmott backs Morlach, all is lost anyway."

There was no way Gleannmara could defend itself against the high king and all the lords of Erin pledged to his service. They'd be needing a host of warrior angels.

Father God, help us!

Maire was shocked as the prayer sped heavenward of its own accord. The Ghost again, speaking her mind, when she was too dumbfounded to do so? Her hand flew to the small wooden cross, which Rowan had carved from his namesake tree, that hung on a cord about her neck—a paltry comparison to Maeve's gold torque, but just as treasured. It was all her armor.

She hoped it was enough.

The riders approached with a minimum stir of dust, for the summer had been soft, at least in the evenings. The rain and sun worked together like the two clans to bring up what promised to be a fine harvest. As green and encouraging as the fields were, the red and black of Rathcoe's banner cast a blight over those watching the entourage ride to the outer gate.

As they stopped, Maire recognized the white stallion among them. On Shahar sat Rowan of Emrys! He made no effort to come forward to meet her, but remained ensconced between

Diarhmott and Morlach. Relief flooded through her.

"Rowan!" She started to run down the embankment, when she realized her husband was not nearly as happy to see her as she was him. He neither waved, nor spoke. Chains bound his hands in front of him.

The sweat on Maire's brow turned to ice. Rowan, King of Gleannmara, in chains? Just as quickly, her shock melted with anger. "What is this?" she demanded, glaring at Diarhmott. High king or nay, she could not hold back her outrage.

"This," Morlach spoke up, jerking his head toward Rowan, "is a murderer."

How Maire's legs held her upright, she'd never know. "Says who?"

"Aye, who did our king slay?" Declan challenged.

From behind Diarhmott, the druid Finead rode forward, another horse in tow. On it was a body, wrapped in blankets. But Maire didn't need anyone to identify it. Flapping its wings and pecking at the ropes dangling loose from the ends of the wrappings was a familiar heron.

"Nemh!" she whispered, suddenly sick herself.

"This man and his priest have killed one of our own," Finead charged, pointing a gnarled finger at Rowan. "The priest got away, but we were able to capture at least *one* of the murderers."

Brude dead. With his death, so died Maire's childhood. He was her father and mother. He was her tutor and adviser. He was her truest friend. Disbelief and horror battled on her face as she looked from the body to Rowan.

"I didn't kill him, Maire."

"We found him at the scene, Brude's blood staining his hands," Morlach told her with a vicious smile.

"I received a summons from Brude that he and Father Tomás wished to see me." Rowan's explanation was not to the others, but to Maire. "There were witnesses."

His eyes pled with her to believe, but it wasn't necessary.

Maire knew in her heart Rowan of Emyrs was no murderer. Murder was a geis of God.

Finead turned on the prisoner. "The amulet with which Brude was strangled still hangs about his neck, when once it hung about yours. Its brand is burned into his forehead, and you'd have us believe you?"

Maire stared through stinging eyes at Rowan. He was blurred to her sight, but not to her mind. His nobility, his goodness, his light were unimpeachable. Yet darkness surrounded him. Where were his angels?

"I misplaced my amulet the night of the fair. Anyone could have found it, I suppose, and used it to such a loathsome task."

"He speaks the truth. We haven't seen it since we—" Maire broke off, a strange ache tearing at her at the memory of their nocturnal trip to the pool near the fairground. How they'd carried on…like two children, laughing one moment, loving the next. Rowan had tossed the amulet aside when Maire complained how cold it was between them. Like a stone, she'd said. Like the one in her chest at the moment…

They hadn't missed the amulet until the next morning when Rowan rose to dress. "We haven't seen it since we were at the fair, a good three moons ago."

This was Brona's work. It *had* to be. Maire should have trusted her instinctive suspicion of the woman the first night they'd met, rather than give her the benefit of the doubt for lurking about like a second shadow.

"Are we to accept the word of a lovestruck female, Diarhmott?" Morlach sneered. "Come now, Maire, do not insult our high king."

"*Insult?* I'll show you insult, Morlach."

"No, Maire," Rowan shouted.

"Hold, little sister."

The warning did not deter her, but Declan's quick hand did. He tightened his fingers about her arm until surely no blood passed. But he could not stop her words.

"Garret knows the amulet was missing! He rode with me the following day to look for it." Maire scanned the gathering for sign of Rowan's nephew. The young Cairthan's face was not among them. "Where is Garret?"

Declan lowered his voice. "I saw him ride out with Brona early this morning."

"Where were they going?"

"I didn't think it my business to ask, the way the pup's been taggin' after the girl."

Maire slandered Brona's birth mother beneath her breath. Frantic, she pointed to one of Gleannmara's guards. "Muirdach! Go find them! We'll settle this and quick!" As the man loped off toward the inner rath's stables, she addressed the high king.

"Just where is your impartiality, Diarhmott? The most common offender deserves a chance to speak for himself."

Diarhmott shifted on his horse, seemingly unsettled by Maire's accusation on one side and Morlach's silent daggers of warning on the other. "He has had a hearing before me and my druid."

So the high king had made up his mind. Maire rebelled at the very idea. "But I have witnesses—"

"Whom I will hear willingly if they come forward before the sentence is carried out."

"You risk war, man!" she charged blindly. "Neither Cairthan nor Niall will give over our king without a fight."

Rowan's voice thundered, stilling Maire with its blast. "There will be no talk of war. I have been heard, Maire; it is up to me to prove my innocence."

"But how?" She willed strength into her voice, where hope fell through. Her head shot up as Diarhmott's last words registered. *Before the sentence is carried out.* "What sentence?"

The high king spoke with all authority due him. "Trial by fire, Queen Maire. Let the fire decide the innocence or guilt of Rowan of Gleannmara."

Morlach leaned forward on his steed. His dark eyes glittered like those of a hungry cat about to pounce on its meal. "As the

Christian priest said at Beltaine, in the name of the one god, let the fire destroy all that is false and evil so than only purity and innocence remain." The druid laughed at the color Maire felt draining from her face. "If your *husband* is innocent, Queen Maire, he'll walk through untouched. His god will protect him." Cocking his head sideways, he drawled, "You do believe in the Christian god, don't you?"

TWENTY-FIVE

Gleannmara's hall was subdued. All who were per-
ceived as a threat to Diarhmott's justice had been
gathered and stripped of their weapons. Though they
were still allowed to sup in the hall, guards watched them with
hawk eyes. Maire was assigned a guard of her own, while
Rowan was locked in one of the storehouses that had been
emptied during the winter.

Declan acted the host to their uninvited guests in her stead.
Rather than take her evening meal with Morlach, Maire took
her supper with Ciara and Lianna, who was neither better, nor
worse. Hospitality be damned; she'd not feed with swine. If the
druid satirized her to the other side, so be it, for what would
life be in this world without Rowan?

Before their marriage, she'd been a shell of a female, struc-
tured by Brude's teachings and Erc's training. But Rowan had
given her life. She was more than a warrior now, more than a
queen—she was a woman. Where she once disdained being
treated like one, she now reveled in it. To take Rowan from her
would be to take away her heart and soul.

Her hopes of getting Garret's testimony were dashed when
Muirdach returned empty-handed. There was no sign of the
Cairthan heir apparent or of Brona. When Maire wasn't fretting
over her husband's fate, it was Garret that occupied her
thoughts. As far as she was concerned, the lad was in the company of a murderess, even if Lianna was not yet gone. The
women's best efforts to treat her illness seemed useless, for the
lass grew weaker by the moment.

When Maire and Ciara weren't trying to make her comfortable, they prayed for some sort of deliverance from the black fate awaiting not just Rowan but Gleannmara. The ache in Maire's heart was such that not even prayer gave her rest. It felt as though all three forms of the Christian God turned a deaf ear to her pleas.

Was ever there a night so long or a day so dark? Maire wondered as she walked toward the storehouse, a strapping guard on her heel like a dog. With Rowan's death and his own triumph imminent, Morlach was feeling generous and allowed the queen her second request to see her husband. How she'd love to have spent the night in Rowan's arms, at least one last time. Those Scriptures of his were right. She *was* created for him, to be loved and cherished as a part of him. The few months they'd shared together proved that again and again.

The guards admitted Maire inside the dark chamber. It smelled of mold and last year's fodder. After a moment to adjust her eyes to the lack of light, she spied Rowan sitting on the earthen floor, his wrists and ankles chained. Not caring who watched, she ran to him and threw her arms about him tightly.

"I have missed you sorely these last weeks, husband."

"And I never knew nights to be so cold, muirnait."

Beloved. That and more, Maire kissed him and he gave back as good he got, for not even iron could keep their souls apart, nor could onlookers dampen the love that flowed one to another. Still on her knees, Maire had yet to release him from her embrace. His warmth was like a balm to this terrible anguish knotting in her chest. Her voice broke to spite her brave facade as she raised her face to his.

"Oh, Rowan, what will we do?"

He kissed her wet cheeks, one, then the other. "We must pray and trust God to do what is best for us and for Gleannmara."

"I *have* prayed! My knees are so sore, I can hardly walk, but nothin's changed. I've heard no voice, nor seen any sign that God is with us."

"Ach, Maire, how can I help you understand?" He rolled back his head and looked at the darkness of the domed thatch overhead. "Just because you believe in God doesn't mean that evil will leave you alone. Satan is always ready to strike, to test just how much you do believe."

"The prince of darkness?"

Maire wondered if Morlach were not this Satan in human form. Tentatively, she caressed Rowan's brow where an ugly gash of congealed blood told of his harsh treatment.

"The very one," he answered, wincing.

"I hope you gave them that did this a taste of your sword and muscle."

"Actually," he chuckled, more in wonder than humor, "I didn't fight at all. I could see the cromlech was built to fall on my shoulders when they ignored Eochan and Lorcan's oath that I'd been with them since I left Gleannmara."

"Don't even speak of a stack of gravestones." She put her finger to his lips, unable to bear the thought. "Husband, there is a time to be peaceful and a time to fight. Crom's toes, this smacks of fightin' time to be sure."

Even as she voiced her angry words, Maire knew that a fight was futile. Morlach had manipulated things so as to make it treason to do so.

"I don't think I can stand to watch you burn for somethin' ye didn't do."

"I don't want you to, Maire, and there is always the chance that I won't."

Maire drew back, wanting to believe. If ever there was a time for God to send His angels or spirits, this was it! She'd fight with them and not even flinch at what they were. Spirit or flesh, she'd take anything or anyone to save the man she loved. *Father God, I beg You, do something.*

Rowan interrupted her prayer. "God has protected His

faithful from fire before. Three Christian men were tossed into a fiery furnace for refusing to bow to gods other than the one God. They emerged without so much as singed hair."

"He'd do this for you?" Maire couldn't see Rowan's gaze well in the darkness of the enclosure, but she knew he embraced her with it. It took away the damp morning chill.

"Aye, if that is His will."

"But—"

"Time's up, milady. They're lighting the fires already."

Maire ignored the guard. "But why wouldn't it be His will? What manner of God is it that would allow one of His own to suffer?"

"The same who gave up His only son to the cross so that you and I might be saved."

"But—"

"'Tis time, milady."

"Has Garret been found?" Rowan asked quickly as the guard eased Maire away by the arm. "And Lianna...how does she fare? And mother?"

There was so much more they needed to talk about, needed to say. Distressed beyond measure, Maire shook her head. "Muirdach took the men of his clan but could find nothing of Garret or that evil-hearted Brona. The scent that has Lianna lyin' abed near death was intended for me! Brona offered it to me to tempt you into my bed—" She broke off at the surprised lift of Rowan's brow. A sheepish color flowed to her cheeks, but Maire didn't mind admitting her desire for her husband's attention.

"You have been nothing but temptation since first I saw you in my dreams," he assured her. "Before we even met."

"*Before* we met?" Maire was taken back. He'd *dreamed* her? Surely that meant something.

"I should have known when I first recognized you that you were the one God chose for me, but, fool that I was, I fought it because I thought it would be too good for this servant. Ah, to think of the time I wasted."

His dark hair fell forward on his brow as he lapsed into a moment of regret. Maire wanted to brush it back with her fingers, but the guards held her more tightly. Then, as if snapping out of his thoughts, he raised his gaze to hers. Their souls embraced.

"But we were destined to be together, Maire, here at Gleannmara...even on to the other side."

Destined? Maire closed her eyes, wondering if some unseen plan of God was afoot. But she wasn't a druid. She sensed no spirits. She was a woman about to watch her love die a horrible death. All she felt was abandonment, and it tore at her with unmerciful claws.

"The other side?" She spat her pent up frustration with the words. "'Tis *now* that worries me, Rowan. What will I do without you *now*? What will Gleannmara do if I am forced to enter some unholy alliance with Rathcoe? *What about now?*"

"Enough, milady, you must leave," the guard insisted, his hand tightening on Maire's arm. Sympathy affected his voice and his grasp upon her arm, but it was only the slackening of his grasp that registered.

She tore away from him in anger, but it was with desperation that she threw herself at Rowan and clung to him as though to life itself. Words failed her, lost in this stew of anguish and fury seasoned with hopelessness.

Rowan kissed the top of her head gently, his voice betraying his own pain. "Ah, muirnait, I wish I could make you understand that the eternal life on the other side is more important than this temporary one."

Noble words, to be sure, but they made no sense to Maire—not now, not when facing life without her beloved. She couldn't accept it. She *wouldn't*. "No, it *isn't*," Maire shouted rebelliously as the guards combined their efforts to restrain her. "I swear, I'll kill Morlach on *both* sides of this green earth, if I have to."

As she was dragged to the door, a flurry of activity in the

yard gave her captors cause to hesitate. Beyond them, Tara and Rathcoe's occupying soldiers spilled from the hall toward the gate of the outer rath.

"What's the fuss?" one of her guard shouted.

"It's the Cairthan formin' up on the hill," one of the running soldiers called back. "They line the horizon thick as wild geese at Samhain."

Excitement sent Maire's heart soaring. Between the Niall *and* the Cairthan, they far outnumbered the small force Morlach and the high king brought with them. She tore out of the grasp of her guards. She'd waited for the right moment, for a sign to take matters into her own hands. In a flash, her stinger flashed free of its hidden sheath in her breastplate. It was at the guard's throat before he could recover.

A ferocious "Noooo!" from her husband checked its edge just shy of breaking flesh.

"One move, one excuse and I'll lay open your neck like a slaughtered pig," Maire growled at her victim. "Now you, unlock those chains."

"Best do as she says, man," the startled guard said to his partner. "There's no quarter in this one's eyes."

"Put away the knife, Maire."

Surely Rowan jested. He was a blade's length from freedom. "We can take them, Rowan!"

"And commit high treason."

"But—"

"The blood shed today would mean more tomorrow, and more the next, Maire—and the end of Gleannmara. Many are pledged to Diarhmott. Would you fight them all?" Rowan shook his head adamantly. "I will have no blood shed on my account. It's madness to take on the high king. You must tell Lorcan the same."

Certain Rowan had taken leave of his senses, Maire's gaze shot toward him. Before she could express her incredulity, much less challenge him, a terrible blow exploded on the back of her head. She saw red and white pictures of it competing for her vision, but in the end, darkness prevailed.

As she regained consciousness, her head swam in a black sea of pain, exceeded only by that in her heart. Slowly, Maire dragged herself up from the bed where she'd been placed next to Lianna. Disoriented at first, she shook the young woman to no avail. Lianna's eyes stared sightlessly at the ceiling, her white face cold as snow to the queen's touch.

Sickness churned in Maire's belly as she reeled away from the dead maid. First Brude, now her cousin. Through the fog of faces in her aching head, the image of Rowan arose to replace them all.

Rowan.

Panic seized Maire as she stumbled outside and saw how dark it was. Not even the sun wished to dignify the day, for the sky was overcast with clouds. Gradually it came back to her, the attack from behind when she'd tried to free Rowan. It was hard to tell how long she'd been unconscious.

Nothing stirred within in the inner rath, save some hens and a few mongrels. It was the outer one that had drawn the people. With neither dagger nor sword in sight, Maire raced toward the gate, her heart leaping with each footfall on the hard, packed earth. The smell of wood smoke and oil in the air moved her faster still.

Please, Father God, I mustn't be too late!

The prayer echoed over and over in her mind, for she could not think beyond that. She elbowed her way through those in the crowd, who did not see her coming.

"Let me through!"

Above their heads, Maire could see the black smoke of the wet wood used with the dry to prolong the spectacle. It rose above the fires like a demon in its own right. The eerie silence of the onlookers told her that her husband had not yet faced the trial. At the inner edge of the circle, a guard held up his shield, as though to block her way. Plowing into him with her training and an astonishing strength for one her size, Maire knocked him flat on his back and stumbled past to where the high king held his ignoble court.

The twin fires roared half again as high as a warrior's head and embraced each other like lovers that would not be parted, not by rain, nor wind, and certainly not by the man standing on the opposite side of them. Maire could barely make out Rowan's figure, so thick was the blaze.

"Ah, Queen Maire." Morlach gave her a mocking bow. "Have you come to see whose god is real and whose is false?"

"This is no trial," Maire shouted at Diarhmott, ignoring the druid. "This is murder of the commonest kind."

"Trial by fire is accepted by the law," Finead reminded her smugly. "If Rowan of Gleannmara is truly innocent of Brude's death, he has nothing to fear."

The druids were two of a kind, so blackhearted and evil that Maire shivered, despite the enveloping heat cast by the fires. Frantic, she glanced around for some hope, some help. No white-clad warriors stood armed and ready. Behind Rowan, the faces of Gleannmara stared back at her, as fraught with desperation as her own must be—Eochan and Declan, Lorcan, and Ciara. Rathcoe's guards held the disarmed company at bay.

"How could you let them take you?" she cried out at them. "We outnumber these fiendish devils better than two to one."

No man answered, but they avoided facing the piercing accusation of her gaze.

"I ordered them not to fight, Maire," Rowan told her.

Maire turned to him, torn between strangling him and begging for his life. "You *wish* to die?"

"Greater love hath no man than this, that a man lay down his life for his friends."

Words eluded her. There was a time she'd have labeled this cowardice, but she knew better now. Rowan was no coward.

Armed with his faith, he was as courageous a man as she'd ever known. But this was foolraide.

She stared at the two-headed fire beast, with its tongues lapping in all directions. If there were angels in there, she saw no sign of them. If only Brude were here, instead of lying lifeless in his lodge awaiting burial. All the people she relied upon were either gone or useless. Never had Maire felt so alone. Numbed by pain and confusion, she saw Diarhmott motion for the trial to begin.

"Rowan of Gleannmara, you stand charged with the murder of Brude, a druid and brother serpent of the highest order," Finead announced, commencing the proceeding. "Your amulet was used to strangle an old man, who accepted you and your god with the tolerance of our way. Yet you burned the symbol of your god into his forehead, marking him even unto death. What say you, sir?"

"I killed no one." Rowan's answer came strong and clear. One would think he had a legion at his beck and call.

Where are the angels?

The words screamed in her mind. Held at swordpoint, Maire appealed to the only source of help left to her; the God who made her husband the brave and noble man that he was. *Father God, I've said some harsh things about You and for that I'm truly sorry, but Ye must know how frightened I am. I asked before and now I'm beggin'. Help us.*

"Then how do you account for your amulet being found on the druid's body?"

At Morlach's challenge, Maire's head swam with the pain emanating from the knot on the back of her head. Her eyes became unfocused. She couldn't lose consciousness now. When her vision cleared, she caught sight of the slim, dark-haired female next to Morlach: *Brona.*

"You!" She pressed against the steel of the guard's restraining blade until it threatened to split her leather-clad breastplate. "Where is Garret? He can testify that the amulet has been missing

since the fair. Or have you killed him, like you killed Lianna?"

Diarhmott spoke up. "This is not Brona's trial, Queen Maire. It is your husband's. But I will hear your accusations, when this is done."

"I only gave the queen a love potion to win her husband's affection. I have no knowledge of how the maid Lianna came by it."

"It killed her, you peat-hearted she-dog, and it was intended for me!"

Brona shrugged, guileless as a newborn. "Some potions needs be used anon, lest they spoil. It's unfortunate that after it was tossed aside, Lianna found it and sought its use without consulting anyone. I have an antidote for such accidents."

"Lianna is as dead as Brude, and the stench is that of Rathcoe."

"Enough of this, Queen Maire," Diarhmott intervened. "I gave you my word that you will be heard regarding your charge."

"Then ask her what she did to the witness who can swear that amulet has been missing since—"

"My lord, I cannot say what became of that wild Cairthan lad Garret. We left yesterday to collect herbs near the Sacred Grove, and there we lost each other. I thought perhaps he'd left me to come back early, but he was not here either."

"Whether the amulet was missing or nay, does not erase the fact that Rowan of Gleannmara was caught with his hand still dripping with Brude's warm blood!"

"As might yours, Diarhmott, if you picked up the bloodied corpse of a friend in your grief on finding him so," Rowan suggested.

"And your friend, the priest, sir," Finead said skeptically. "Where was he when this travesty took place? Perhaps if you might give us *his* whereabouts, your word would smack more of truth?"

Rowan dropped his eyes. "I don't know. Father Tomás wasn't there when I arrived, only Brude. But I will swear on my life that Tomás did not kill the druid. Perhaps whoever killed Brude killed the priest too and disposed of the body."

"And *perhaps* bullfrogs fly." Morlach's facetious remark raised humor among the guards, but no one else. "Come, your majesty, the man was found covered in the blood with the emblem of *his* amulet burned into the victim's forehead! The amulet itself was wrapped about Brude's neck."

"A blind man can see Gleannmara is guilty of the murder of one of our brotherhood," Finead agreed.

"Only if that man *chose* to see," Maire countered.

"We have heard enough. We cannot base our judgment on testimonies of people not present, but only on what we have already seen and heard. It's best we finish this before the fires wither."

The high king hid safely behind his law, content to watch an innocent man die, rather than stand up to Morlach of Rathcoe. He was a coward of the worst sort. But Maire was not. Like Adam, she didn't want to live if that life was without the one she loved.

"Ach, we wouldn't want to put these murderers to too much trouble, now, would we?" Her chin trembled with rage. "And you fancy yourself a just king."

"Woman, you will hold your tongue, or be silenced and removed," Finead warned. "You try the benevolence of the high king."

Two guards came up on either side of Maire to reinforce their comrade's words with the sword. They seized her arms with viselike grips. It was decided. Rowan was to burn—no matter what his God had shown him in his dreams, no matter what Brude had seen, no matter that her heart was being torn in two.

"Where are the angels?" she cried aloud at the gray heaven as she was dragged aside.

"Let the prisoner walk through the fire, that it may tell the truth."

———~~~———

At the high king's command, Rowan peered through the leaping, hungry flames. Tears of helpless rage and agony filled
Maire's eyes as she struggled with the guards, but like the fire,
the men were unable to prevent his look from reaching her. He
longed to tell her their love knew no barrier, not in this world
or the next. They were one, made one in the eyes of the one
God.

*God, be merciful to her. I do not understand Your plan. I know
Maire cannot. But I know You hold my future in the palm of Your
hand. You are the truth and the light. As You had reason to witness
Your own Son's death, so You may have good reason for mine.*

"I do not walk into darkness, beloved, but into the light."
Rowan's shout rose above the roar and deadly crackle of the
flames between them.

Unable to speak, Maire strained against the hold of the
guards, leaning into the sword and toward the fire as though
she too were ready to walk into its deadly mouth, even if it
meant perishing with him. Behind him, Rowan heard Ciara
wail. Turning he gave her and Lorcan a smile.

"This is just the beginning," he told them, his voice dry
from breathing the smoke-filled air. Taking a deep breath, he
offered one last prayer with closed eyes. *Father, have mercy on
us all.* Seeking Maire out through the inferno one last time, he
mouthed, "I love you, Maire."

Rowan stepped to the fire's edge where the heat slapped
him and reached into his lungs with invisible hands, clutching
his breath. The perspiration on his forehead evaporated. *Lord,
use my example to Your glory.* He lifted his foot, ready to take the
final plunge from which there would be no return, when a
voice of protest cut through the bonds of tension holding all in
check, save the beasts of flame.

"Hold, in the name of God Almighty!"

TWENTY-SIX

The agonized quiet broke into chaos as the onlookers turned toward the outer rath gate, from whence the interruption came. No less confounded than the others, Rowan fell back a step from the blistering heat as the crowd opened up to admit someone. Whether human or spirit, he had no clue. All things were possible.

Instead of crusading angels, Morlach's apprentice Cromthal led a shaggy pony bearing a bandaged and bruised Father Tomás into the clearing. The priest looked as though he'd fallen off a cliff and struck every rock on the way to its bottom. With them was Garret, who was not in much better condition, given the bandages on his neck and face. His shredded shirt hung in strips from his shoulders, exposing blood-encrusted gashes on his back and chest.

"What trickery is *this?*" Morlach's beady eyes grew large, glittering black against the waning color of his usual swarthy complexion. He pointed an accusing finger at Rowan. "These be ghosts, summoned by *his* god."

"I am no ghost, druid, nor is this the work of trickery or illusion." Father Tomás's rebuff was stronger and larger than he looked capable of offering.

"Faith," Garret agreed, turning for all to see the marks cut into his flesh. "Sure no spirits ever hurt the likes of this!"

"My God!" Ciara broke free from the bonds of her surprise and ran with Lorcan to where her bedraggled grandson stood. "What happened to you?"

"But—" Morlach checked himself with an uneasy glance at

Diarhmott, recovering quickly. "Your majesty, my apprentice has done well. He's captured Gleannmara's accomplices."

"Seize them!" Finead commanded, following Morlach's lead. "Druid blood stains them. Good man, Cromthal." In an instant, two burly guards pulled Father Tomás off his steed's back and ushered him before the high king's company for his retribution. With the end of his journey at hand, Garret collapsed in his father's arms, half-conscious from exhaustion and weakness before he could be taken as well.

"Indeed," Morlach vowed. "You have saved the high king the inconvenience of *two* such trials, Cromthal. Well done."

Cromthal sneered, clearly unappeased by the compliment. "We all know the price of spilling druid blood is death, isn't it, Morlach?"

The insubordination of his inferior seemed to snap the druid's composure. "You sniveling, pockmarked dimwit, how *dare* you mock me? Was the satire I put upon you for failure not enough to teach you the dangers of trying to deceive your master?"

"Pockmarked?" Cromthal laid the pony's reins on its neck. Walking into the light so that all might see, he adjusted his robe, exposing his arms and legs to the view of the audience. "I purged your evil along with mine, Morlach. Look well, for I am clean of *your* darkness."

Morlach satirized Cromthal...and the latter went untouched? Maire was as stunned as the others who saw Cromthal's smooth, unmarked flesh. That the apprentice's earlier satire against Rowan was in vain was nothing compared to the master druid's failure. There were those who feared that a look from Morlach meant a terrible death.

Finead examined Cromthal. The man's face usually looked as pliable as a stone mask, but incredulity shattered it. "You spoke against this man and he goes free of harm?" he asked of his fellow magi.

"I *meant* no real harm to him, Finead." Morlach's explanation was as weak as it was hasty. "But his disobedience demanded a good scare at the least."

"May I speak, King Diarhmott?"

All gazes shifted to Father Tomás.

"Aye. Perhaps you can lend some sense to this murky cloud which has befallen us."

"But your majesty—"

Diarhmott cut Morlach off. "Even a condemned man is allowed his say. Speak, priest."

Tomás straightened his bent shoulders and smiled benevolently at Cromthal. "This man came to me covered with festering sores. Under my care, and with God's grace, they vanished without trace."

"You'd believe a *murderer* above one of your chief druids?" Morlach challenged.

"This priest has more the look of an intended victim than a murderer, your majesty," Rowan offered. "As does my nephew."

Garret looked as though a wild cat had torn into him with all four sets of claws.

Although it was evident it did not set well with him, Diarhmott could not help but agree. "Will you swear in the name of your god that you speak the truth, priest?"

"I so swear, for it was only by God's providence that I am here to do so—I was there when Brude was slain."

"Morlach's men slayed Brude." Cromthal nodded sharply at Brona. "She was there as well, with the Christian's amulet. It was Morlach himself who branded Gleannmara's druid with it. I saw it with my own eyes. I'd been gathering wood in the forest and had no choice, outnumbered as I was, but to watch Rathcoe's brigands work their evil on Brude and the priest."

Father Tomás took up the story. "They beat me senseless and when they thought me dead, they dropped my body into the lake, but Cromthal pulled me out in time. As we came to Gleannmara, we found another victim of Morlach's evil on the side of the road near the Sacred Grove."

The last thread of Morlach's composure broke. "You swore he was dead, daughter!"

"'Twas *your* concoction I gave him, master. I believed it would work, even though he got away," Brona countered in defiance. "Do not blame me for *your* failure."

Daughter? Rowan looked at Brona in disbelief. He'd heard rumor of children being abandoned by women who'd unwillingly born the druid's offspring from a dark seduction. What better watchman could there be than one's own kin?

"'Twas her intent to kill me, to be sure." Garret struggled to his feet. "She invited me for a picnic and then drugged the wine. In midst of her seduction, she turned into a wild hag, tryin' to slash my throat with her knife." The young man swayed against his father. "And when I knocked it from her hand, she came at me with her teeth and claws. 'Twas God's mercy and nothin' less that gave me the strength and wit to escape before I lost consciousness."

Enraged, Morlach turned on the girl at his side. "I *never* fail, wench!" Before the stunned listeners or Brona herself knew what he was about, the druid plunged a dagger into her heart. Her eyes grew round and kindled with a curse that died on her lips.

"And are ye blind to *that* as well, your majesty?" Lorcan challenged, holding the bulk of Garret's weight on his arm.

Rumbles of discontent and doubt swept over the crowd. Diarhmott had at last heard and seen enough. "Guards, seize Rathcoe."

It was only natural for the guards and warriors to hesitate. The master druid's reputation was formidable. Seizing the advantage, Morlach moved like lightning to where Rowan stood, still bound by chains. In the druid's raised hand was the dagger, with Brona's blood still dripping from it. No one moved to stop the man—all watched as though immobilized by some wretched spell.

His hasty prayer of thanksgiving for his deliverance cut

short by the sudden vicious attack, Rowan managed to dodge the knife on the first pass, but the chains hobbling his ankles tripped him. Dirt ground into his face as he struck the earth. Rolling over, he spat grit from his teeth as Morlach turned on him again. Weapon raised, the druid lunged forward, only to be stopped dead in his tracks by something in the fire, just beyond Rowan's head.

"Come, druid, taste the metal of my spear!"

Maire? Against all his instincts, Rowan took his gaze off Morlach, craning his neck to see the warrior queen leap through the fire like an avenging angel. Somehow shielded from the hungry tongues of flame, she landed clear of the blaze, lighting on the ground as though winged, the spear of one of her guards brandished in her hands. A snarl on her lips, Maire was as impervious to Rowan as he was to his former assailant. Fearing he might distract the queen, Rowan lay still, shifting his gaze back to their enemy. What he saw sent rivulets of ice up his spine, despite the singeing heat of the fire.

With a sinister smile, Morlach began to wave his arms in swirls, as if he drew art on thin air. From the ball of one foot to the other, he pranced, turning his back to Maire, his dark robe swirling playfully about his sandaled feet. The crowd closest to them, backed away from the druid's strange dance, but it was the only movement allowed by the spell he cast in a singsong voice. Then he pivoted.

The movement was so fast, Rowan scarcely had time to speak. "Maire, the dagger—!"

But the warrior queen had been trained in a dance of her own, and that training came to the fore with equal speed. Maire deflected the crooked blade flying at her with the stem of the spear, as though batting a shuttlecock, and growled with the feral delight settling in her eyes. Or was it the reflection of flames leaping in them?

"I'll skewer your heart, druid, and roast it over yon fire."

"Wait, Maire! Let him face the justice he deserves."

Her eyes still on Morlach, she argued with Rowan. "I want to see his black, brackish blood run!"

As Rowan struggled to his feet, Declan broke through the rattled line of guards to help him. "Best listen to the man, Maire. His God has certainly worked beyond all circumstance to see justice done. Ye've seen and heard the accounts."

"Thou shalt not kill, Queen Maire," Morlach taunted, a diabolical undertone infecting his voice. With his back to the fire, he swirled his hard cloak, spreading it so that he looked twice his size. "'Tis the law of the god you accepted... or haven't you *really* accepted him?"

"It's true, Maire," Rowan said softly, stepping up to her side. "Give me the spear and leave justice to God's law."

"Did you ever wonder who betrayed your parents, Maire...whose soldiers failed to back up Gleannmara's forces on the battlefield?"

Maire flinched. Rowan could almost see the anger and anguish racing to her mind to stomp out reason. If either won the race, there would be no stopping her. *Father God, help her.*

"No! Brude would have told me," she said, clearly unconvinced of her words.

"Unless he feared you would try to avenge them against me. Even your old druid knew you were no match for my power," Morlach taunted. "Nor, it seems, was he."

"Y...*you* caused Maeve and Rhian's death?" Diarhmott sputtered. "We knew there was a traitor among us but—I not only lost two of my bravest warriors, but nearly the battle as well because of your greed. By all the gods, men, I order you to seize him!"

The discomfited solders surrounded the druid, closing in with wary reluctance. To escape, Morlach would have to go through them, Maire, or the fire breathing at his back. Each was as dangerous and deadly as the other.

Father, help us. I can't stop her without hurting her. Rowan's prayer filled the eternity that froze the scene before Maire shattered it.

"Don't filthy your hands," she countered. "He admits to murdering all I hold dear save one and he nearly succeeded in that." Her fingers tightened, knuckles bloodless, refusing to let the weapon go.

"Leave it to justice, Maire. He *wants* you to kill him," Rowan warned her, trying to be still while Declan tried a key in the lock on the chains.

Conflicting emotions tore at her face, telling of the two wills battling for control of the woman: blood thirst versus submission.

The chains fell to the ground from Rowan's hands with a loud chink. "Maire…" He spoke softly, firmly, stepping toward her. "I know the feeling of betrayal, I know the hunger for revenge, for blood, but what good is law, if you change it to suit your own needs. That smacks of Morlach's reason, not yours."

"The *law* was nearly your death," she argued, teeth gritted, wavering still.

"The law may be wrong sometimes, little queen, but God's judgment awaits eternal and true for all, saint and sinner alike."

Finead joined the drama, well aware that the tide was no longer under his sway. "His fellow druids will deal with Morlach, Queen Maire. The druid who spills the blood of another will have no mercy, for he has slain knowledge. To willfully destroy knowledge is forbidden above all things."

Morlach cocked his head and stuck out his lower lip. "But oh, the damage I can do with my powers until justice is met." Without warning, he threw up both of his hands and the fire behind him danced higher and higher, as though in response. "First, I will curse the unborn child you carry."

Child? The surprising word with all its implications battered Rowan's conviction with the surge of an angry, protective tide. *Heavenly Father, she is with child?* He fought the urge to snatch away Maire's spear and finish the man on the spot. *God has brought us safe thus far, He will not fail us now.*

But he knew that Maire's communication with the Almighty was impeded by her newness to the faith. She'd had a lifetime of hearing of druid's power and only a few months of God's love. The darting look of panic she gave Rowan ran him through—and echoed his own panic that he'd not be able to stop her.

"God has let no harm come to us yet, muirnait. Why doubt His power now?" Rowan insisted gently. "Hand me the spear."

"But he threatened our—your—my—"

Morlach began to chant again with strange words, part Latin, part the native tongue, but it was his tone, rather than the little Rowan could make out, that carried the sharpest threat.

"He can do nothing, Maire." Rowan put his hand on her arm, ready to fight her again if he had to, to save her and their baby. "Morlach is a helpless charlatan. Don't sink to his level. Let Finead and the Brehon decided his fate. He taunts you to make you a murderer too, to make the mother of Gleannmara's heir a murderer."

The meat of his words were enough to turn his knees to water, yet Rowan stood strong. Mother of Gleannmara's heir—a son, perhaps? "Kill him, and he wins. You will have broken God's law."

Maire lifted her glittering gaze to meet his. Emotions warred; confusion reigned; her voice shook. "And our baby?"

"Is safe in God's hands, Maire. He can protect it better than we can."

Her grip slackened on the weapon. Carefully Rowan eased it from her hands. Once they'd given it up, they began to tremble.

"The light shows him for what he is, muirnait, a frightened, desperate soul drowning in his own darkness."

After a moment, Maire nodded and went willingly into Rowan's arms. Relieved, he drew her out of the way.

"Take the man and be done with it," he ordered curtly.

"Gleannmara need not fear his like."

Declan, who was now armed courtesy of a nearby guard, summoned the men of Gleannmara to take the unarmed druid. "Come men. Gleannmara is under the one God's protection. This serpent of darkness can no longer harm us."

The Drumkilly, the Cairthan, the Muirdach and their septs and subsepts moved as one to follow their king's order. They had seen Rowan's God at work and no longer feared the druid's magic.

It was Morlach's turn to know fear.

His battle experience had acquainted Rowan with the sight of fear. It had a way of drying up perspiration and turning the skin cold on the most scorching of days. Its stench was unmistakable, particularly when amplified by the hot breath of the fire nipping at the druid's back. Morlach had backed away from the circling men until one step more and his clothing would be consumed. The druid's snarl, his darting eyes…all were those of a cornered, desperate beast.

And desperation provoked insane reaction.

"Maire, Queen of Gleannmara!"

Maire stiffened in Rowan's embrace, unable to tear her attention from the fiend who called her name.

"I waited a lifetime for you to grow up. I can wait another."

"Seize him!" Rowan commanded, tightening his arms to quell the tremor that ran through the woman in his arms. "He babbles—"

Morlach threw up his cloak like a bird about to take flight. With a heinous laugh, he suddenly fell back into the roaring fire. "Remember me, queen!"

The same fire consuming the man's clothing added volume to his shrill taunt. It seemed to echo from Sheol's darkest depths. Maire clung to Rowan as though she might be drawn into the consuming, rasping abyss. The smell of burning hair surrounded them, its billowing breath driving all back. Grasping her belly, Maire leaned over and retched to no avail.

Behind them, the fragile framework of logs that had been laid to take Rowan's life collapsed under the weight of the one who masterminded the treachery. A shower of sparks rose, filling the air, the hot *whoosh* driving the sparks up, breaking the trance that held all spellbound. Confusion ensued as everyone scattered beyond harm's way.

Fearing for the safety of his wife and the child she carried, Rowan swept Maire up in his arms and ran from the macabre aftermath, toward the gate to the inner rath. Once inside the compound, he stopped to catch his breath, not so certain his own stomach was not about to rebel. Unless his knees betrayed him first.

But he was safe. Maire was safe. Their unborn child was safe. Gleannmara's earthen-work inner wall, with its newly restored stockade, stood like a fortress of security against the chaos on the other side, the chaos that was behind them, at least for now. God had given him the strength and courage he needed to face the enemy and his death, but not one heartbeat more. Rowan leaned against the stockade.

Maire seemed to sense he was nearly spent and squirmed out of his grasp to her feet. His legs buckled, then caught his weight with renewed strength. His loved ones were safe, his *beloved* now held his face between her hands and was showering him with frantic little kisses.

"Crom's toes, man, don't faint on me now. *I'm* the one with child, not you!" She stared up at him unashamed through the tears that ran down her cheeks. "You *are* all right, aren't you?"

"I'm weak with thanksgiving, lass, nothing more."

"'Tis the stench of Morlach's evil hide cookin' on that fire, I'm thinkin'. It gave my own stomach a turn." Maire looked to be fully recovered, standing squarely before him as if daring him to collapse. "And the thing of it is, I thought I'd enjoy it, both sight and smell of evil burnin', but in the end he was only a man. What made him evil didn't perish in the fire."

Rowan smiled in wonder, then drew this incredible creature

into his arms. He bussed the top of her head as he cradled it under his chin. "Faith, woman, you're starting to talk like a druid!"

Serious, she backed away. "But it's true, isn't it? That fella Satan will just find some other poor soul to court with that black magic. And then we'll face it again, sure as the sun rises on the same side of Erin every mornin'.""

How Rowan loved her. What he felt for her welled inside him until he could hold it back no more, even if he wished it. He gently traced the regal taper of her chin and ran his finger across the lips that spoke a wisdom far beyond their years. "Aye, muirnait, we'll not be done with sin until Christ comes again."

Maire pulled a look of dismay. "Ach, like as not He's so busy with the blackguards surely stirrin' trouble on the other side, He'll never get to us!"

"God has a plan all worked out to take care of that," Rowan assured her, brushing away the furrows of concern from her brow. "Trust me."

"By the sun, look at her shift! Not so much as soot on its hem." Elsbeth tugged on Maire's garment, making the two of them aware for the first time that most of Gleannmara's people had followed their king and queen into the rath.

Declan worked his way through the crowd, gently moving the plump noblewoman aside. "Diarhmott awaits outside," he reported to Rowan. "I'm thinkin' he's a bit concerned that he's no longer welcome at Gleannmara's table."

"But her dress!" Elsbeth insisted, shoving her way back to fondle the material of the queen's short leine. "Ye ran through the fire to defend your man, and not a flame dared touch ye! Sure, I thought Gleannmara would lose all that's dear to us." With a sob, Elsbeth tried to engulf Maire and Rowan in her short arms.

Rowan reached down and fingered the material as the woman's words registered. He'd seen Maire come through the fire untouched, but in the frenzy of the moment…

"But I don't remember…I just—" Maire glanced at Rowan, putting her fingers to her temples as if to retrieve the memory. "I just wanted to save you from Morlach. I don't even know how I escaped the guards. I just heard myself sayin', *Father God, help me* and…"

"And He did," Declan finished.

Maire's expression turned to wonder. "Aye, I remember now. 'Twas like a puff of wind blew away the guards and carried me straight through the fire! And I didn't really know I was praying, I was just hopin' against all hope, so that must'a been the Ghost talkin' for me." Her words came out in such a rush, Rowan could hardly understand them, much less what really happened. "And then there I was, with someone's spear, ready to run it through Morlach if he so much as breathed on ye!"

She pressed against Rowan, her lips quivering. "Was it angels?"

Rowan wanted nothing more than to assuage the tremble of his wife's lips. He wanted to be alone with her, to share his heart, body, and soul with her. He wanted to treat her as the treasured gift from heaven that she was. But another duty called, one that could not be ignored, not after all God had done for him that day.

He turned to those gathered about them. "People of Gleannmara, there is much to do ahead of us. We must welcome the high king. We must see to our dead and face our grief over their loss. We must take strength and comfort from each other in the hours and days ahead. But first, there is something I as your king and as God's servant must do."

The rumblings over the miracle of the queen's running through the burning pyres without so much as a thread of her garment or a pinch of her flesh being scorched stilled at Rowan's last words. Heads cocked, ears eager, they waited for him to go on.

Rowan swallowed the humble blade of emotion cutting at his throat. "I must give thanks to the one God, the *only* God, for sparing Gleannmara from Morlach's treachery. If any of you care to join me in honoring Him, you are welcome. Including you, your majesty," Rowan called out as Diarhmott and his company paused at the gate. "For I now kneel before the King of all kings."

"We need a chapel," Maire whispered, dropping down beside him as he knelt on the ground.

"Not to worship the God who created all this," Rowan answered. He pointed to where the sun was sinking low in a now cloud-banished sky and then to where the moon came up almost simultaneously on the opposite horizon.

With Cromthal's aide, Father Tomás took a place on his knees on Rowan's other side and was joined by his companion. Declan, Elsbeth, her husband, the Cairthan, with Lorcan and Ciara supporting Garret, and the remaining septs of the Niall—all went down in ones and twos, a group at a time.

If he had felt humbled before, Rowan was more so at the sight of them all. Even the high king knelt, ready, at least on the surface, to pay homage to their Creator and Savior. Beside Diarhmott, Finead bowed his half-shaven head in respect, if not reverence. Perhaps, given all that he'd witnessed this day, the druid would join the ranks of priests as Brude had. Only God knew. Rowan braced himself with a deep breath, but emotion welled in his voice.

"Father Tomás, will you...?" he managed, bowing to the priest to lead them.

Rowan and Cromthal helped the older saint back to his feet. In clear notes that gave no hint of the severity of his recent injuries, Father Tomás began to sing praises and glory to God. Over and over he repeated the lines in the native tongue. They sounded odd in the translation, but soon the congregation was of one voice, filling the air with heartfelt joy and thanksgiving.

Rowan had never heard a more beautiful sound.

TWENTY-SEVEN

T he hard work and conflict of the summer gave way to a peaceful winter and plentiful stores. Gleannmara's livestock grew fat with thickened coats. While sword land had rapidly acceded to plough land, military exercises were held regularly at the rath, weather permitting. Those who excelled at and preferred the discipline of the guard rather than the fields and pastures, served the just rule of the tuath's king and queen. And when it was Gleannmara's time to provide support for the high king, they represented their rulers at Tara.

Peace. Maire had once thought it a boring concept. Now she cherished it. Brude's prediction of a hostage's sword ensuring Gleannmara's glory was a reality, although it had been won more by a sword of faith than one of steel. Never in all Maire's training had she dreamed that love would prove stronger than might. Taking care not to lose balance in her awkward state of pregnancy, Maire knelt at the cromlach marking where her dear tutor and friend had been laid to rest.

With tenderness, she arranged the wildflowers of early spring she'd just picked around a stone cross that Rowan and Father Tomás had fashioned in Brude's honor.

"Dearest Brude, Rowan says that you can see how our beloved tuath prospers with love and peace from the other side. And if that's true, then you can hear me, like as not." Maire wiped the sentimental mist from one eye. "I just wanted to say how much you are missed, even though your memory lives on in us. And I want to thank you for being there when I needed you. I will love you always."

Maire kissed her fingers and then planted the gesture on the cross. Then slowly, clumsily, she leaned on it to climb to her feet. The women swore there was only one babe in her belly, but it felt like a full litter to her. Going from carrying not one ounce of spare flesh to bearing the weight of two was as tiring as it was awkward. But the naps Rowan insisted she take helped restore the sparkle to her eyes and blush to her cheeks, or so he claimed.

"I thought this was where I might find you."

Maire turned with a start to see the man of her thoughts in the flesh. Decidedly so, she mused, taking the muscled expanse of Rowan's upper torso, bared and glistening in the sun. She reached out to brush away some of the fresh dirt that clung to his damp skin.

"And did ye leave any on the ground for the planting?" There was no point in reminding him that he was the king and, as such, not required to get out in the fields with the farmers and livestock.

"There's plenty where it came from, believe me, woman." Leaning over, Rowan kissed the swell of her abdomen. "And how is our little one?"

"Kickin' like the ox you smell of." Maire ruffed her husband's dark hair. "I came lookin' for ye, to remind ye that the guests will be arrivin' this afternoon and 'twould be hospitable for the king to be there with me to welcome them."

Eochan was taking a Cairthan wife. With the hall not yet built for the highland sept, Maire and Rowan had offered to have the wedding at Gleannmara. Rowan's family and that of the bride had been in residence for over a week, but with the wedding date only a few days away, the Drumkilly Niall would soon be arriving. Maire especially looked forward to seeing Declan, who'd captained Gleannmara's guard at Tara for the last few weeks. No doubt he'd have stories to fill the nights of celebration.

A loud whinny from a nearby pasture drew their attention

momentarily to where Shahar, Tamar, and their colt frolicked. At Rowan's sharp whistle, the stallion stopped still and then bolted in their direction, the mare and colt in his wake. On reaching the edge of the stacked fence, the horse whickered in expectation. But as Rowan walked toward him, he veered away and kicked up his heels playfully.

"See," Maire laughed. "Even *he* doesn't recognize your scent!"

With a wry grimace, Rowan wiped ineffectively at the sweat and dirt on his chest. "Well, I suppose 'twould be easier to take a dip in the pond than put the servants to all the trouble of a bath, what with all the preparations they're busy with. That is, if I could persuade a certain well-rounded wench to join me."

"Bite your tongue, man, or this round wench will drown ye!" Maire knew the sharpness in her tone was belied by the mischievous twinkle in her eye. "I'll fetch the cart."

"No, *I'll* get it for you."

Before Maire could move, Rowan loped off to where Brude's shaggy pony had dragged what used to be the druid's chariot. With its wicker wrap restored and a seat installed, it had been converted into a cart for Maire's convenience. Once it had been established that she was with child, Rowan would not hear of her riding. Faith, he barely wanted her to walk!

"Just let me lead him down to the pond," she said, taking the pony by the bridle.

"When he's ready to give you a ride?"

At that moment, Nemh arrived with a loud flapping of wings and its forlorn squawk of greeting. Landing squarely in its master's old cart, the heron settled with authority.

"Well, that settles it," Marie announced with a laugh. "Looks like Glas, Cromthal, and Father Tomás are here."

The heron, as lost without Brude as the mute servant, had accompanied Glasdom to Father Tomás's abode, at first to help the priest recover from his wounds and then to serve him and his student Cromthal as he had once served the druid.

Rowan slipped his arm around Maire as she led the smaller horse down the slope toward the pond, where she and her husband frequently retreated for privacy, as well as a refreshing swim. Secreted by a cluster of oak and subordinate trees, it was a heavenly haven of clear water warmed slightly from an underground hot spring.

On reaching the quiet spot, Rowan unlaced his boots and put them aside. Maire sat on a nearby rock, her hand resting on a spot their unborn child had singled out for a kicking spree. When Rowan shed the multicolored wrap of cloth from his trim waist, she almost envied him.

Almost. Even though she felt big as a horse, there was something truly wonderful in knowing that the seed of their love grew inside her. It was the birth itself that gave her cause for concern. She'd heard enough women screaming in labor to wish there was another way.

"So, are you going to sit there scowling all day or join me?" Rowan extended his hand to her. "Though I'd suggest you shed that gown or Elsbeth will have both of us skewered on her needles."

Maire pushed up from her seat. "Aye, but I'll need some help with these fastens."

Elsbeth was matron of the queen's wardrobe, and if there was any doubt in Erin who was the master and who was the servant, all they had to do was witness one of Maire's fittings. Maire felt like a doll that would be stuck with a pin, if she didn't turn just right or make the appropriate responses to the dear's ceaseless prattle. The Muirdach's wife was just one of the matrons who'd taken the warrior queen under their wing to make a lady of her. Where Maire once had no mother, she now had a grianán full. And truth be known, she cherished the attention.

The lovely gown, embroidered by the talented seamstresses of Gleannmara, fell away from Maire's shoulders, skimming over her belly to gather at her feet. She would have picked it up, but for the man who drew her into his arms. She wrinkled her nose in protest as Rowan proceeded to kiss her, all the while coaxing her toward the pond's edge.

"Faith, man, 'tis like kissin' an ox," she complained half-heartedly.

Rowan nibbled at her neck, his retort vibrating against the increasingly rapid pulse there. "Ach, motherhood hasn't dulled your tongue, that's sure. What happened to the respect you owe me as your husband?"

Her thin undershift soaked up the cool water as they waded in deeper and deeper, but Maire hardly noticed the chill. "Respect? Why, not a thing. I respect the man, 'tis the dirt and stench I've no use for."

Even as the water reached her shoulders and lapped between them, disturbed by Rowan's increasing attentions, Maire was impervious to it.

"Nor has the babe dulled your wit."

Before Maire could retort, her husband ducked under the water and kissed the very spot where his child kicked in protest. His whisker-roughened cheek pricked through her shift, tickling as he lay his ear against her, as though trying to hear the babe.

After a moment, Maire grabbed him by the ears and pulled him up. "Well, fatherhood has certainly worn away what little you had! What are ye tryin' to do, drown yourself?"

Rowan took her face in his hands and shook his head. "Nay, muirnait, not fatherhood. 'Tis love."

With that, he kissed her, sweetly, tenderly. Then, as though worship alone were no longer enough, he embraced her, giving way to a passion that would be satisfied with nothing less than total possession.

'Tis love.

The words echoed again and again with each hungry beat of Maire's heart. It was a wonderful thing, this love. Without it, two hearts were incomplete. With it, they were truly one, not just with each other, but with God. If Maire never understood another thing about her new faith, she knew this to be true: God is love—and all things are possible in the name of love.

EPILOGUE

Now this isn't THE END, dear friends, but THE BEGINNING...

For so was lit the Pentecostal fire in me own heart and soul, turning sword land to saint land. 'Tis an eternal flame that spread like a wildfire and burns in the heart of my children to this very day. Mind ye, it isn't always understood, nor is it always tended faithfully. But there it shines, like a faithful candle in the darkest winds of time and turmoil, lighting the way for me dear sweet Maire, as will all the future daughters of Gleannmara.

GLOSSARY

Below is a wee list of words and phrases, legends and facts compiled for the sake of gettin' to know me and my children—where we come from and what made us say and do the things ye've witnessed in these pages. From oaths to ogham and faeries to Hebrews, 'tis a rich mix of me heart and soul, me past and present, put in me own words, just for you and yer likes to share over a noggin o' punch or cider by a friendly fire. So have at it—ponder, chuckle, and believe what ye will. May God bless, for only the good Lord Himself can truly separate me history from legend.

(A word in *italics* is one to look up for more o' the story.)

aiccid: heir apparent to kingship or clan chief
aire: a noble, most often in literary reference, but can refer to a free man
ainfine: kin descended from a common ancestor
anmchara: soul friend, confessor, a soul mate
ard rí (righ): high king
bard: poet or historian of the druidic order; these good fellows recorded Erin's history in verse and song. Their *literary license* is what makes the separation of history and legend so difficult for today's scholars to discern.

Interestin'ly enough, the Hebrews had no recorded history either, save in song or verse, until the Holy Scriptures. Not till the arrival of Christianity and the White Martyrs were Erin's stories recorded for posterity. No doubt about it, the Irish of today are nearly as Hebrew as Celtic.

Bethlehem, Star of: see Star of the East for the druid legend regarding Christ's birth

bóaire: self-sufficient farmer/cattleman

brat: outer cloak or wrap; the more colors, the higher the station of its wearer

Brichriu's tongue, by: Brichriu of the Poison Tongue was a satirist and cynic who hosted a grand feast of national importance, during which he deviously played upon the vanity of the wives of the heroes of the province. After readin' this, ye'll see plainly why the womenfolk often were *not* included in revelry.

With poet's persuasion, he insinuated privately to each lady, just prior to a stroll about his beautiful yard and gardens, that not only was she the most beautiful and her husband the greatest hero of Ulster's province, but that were she to arrive first at the hall of the festivities after the outing, she would become queen of the entire province. The result, according to a translation of the *Manuscript Materials of Irish History,* was a chaotic, full-fledged foot race, "like the rush of fifty chariots" which shook the entire hall. The champions, on hearing this mad approach, "started up for their arms, each striking his face against the other throughout the house."

Brehon Law: original Irish Celtic law as interpreted by the judges/lawyers, usually druids; was later altered to reflect Christian values and renamed the *Seanchus Mor* at the *Synod of Patrick* in the fifth century

Take a peek at this further along, because that in itself is one of the key reasons why my children embraced the Light so quickly.

brain ball: This grisly keepsake and/or weapon was a dried human brain, which was considered by the prehistoric Celts to be the essence of a man or of his knowledge. The brain usually came from exceptional heroes and men of knowledge, or as a battle trophy, having formerly belonged to a worthy foe. I'm thinkin' it lends a whole new meanin' to keeping your wits.

bride price: the price paid by the groom to the bride's family for the privilege and duration of his marriage to the lady.

Quite the opposite of the dowry, wouldn't ye say? And 'twas a custom mainly Irish and connected to Erin's *Hebrew* roots. Ye see, when the *Milesians* from Iberia settled in Erin, there was a shortage of women. So the Milesians asked the Hebrews, who'd been in Ireland since Japeth and Shem's children landed there after the Flood, if they might marry the Hebrew daughters. Yes, says the Hebrew elders, but only if a bride price is paid to the bride's family for the duration of the marriage. The rest was up to the groom.

Bear in mind, before Patrick, marriage was bindin' only as long as both parties agreed to it.

by my mother's gods (father's gods, ancestor's gods): A comprehensive oath to cover all possible gods (which were ever changing in importance) that a person might swear by without insulting one by leaving him/her out. Me children believed better safe than sorry and took no chances with this one.

cloidem: sword

Conor MacNessa: High king and poet associated with the Knights of the Red Branch at time of Christ in Erin's heroic period of chivalry; see *death of King of Kings,* also *Mebh crannóg,* an artificial, fortified lake dwelling

Crom; Crom Cruach; Crom Cruin: Crom is thought to mean great—Cruach or Cruin, as thunderer. This god is most often symbolized as the golden center in a circle of twelve stones, it's thought he is the great god in the sun, surrounded by the twelve signs of the Zodiac.

Now join me in takin' this one step further, given the druidic belief of the one God who lived in the sun, it is not too farfetched to consider this an early name of God. In other cultures, however, Crom was simply a sun god and human sacrifices were made to him, just as the prescriptural Hebrews once sacrificed their firstborns to Yahweh.

Crom's toes!: an oath reflecting the importance of the least part of the great god in the Celtic mind.

So I'm thinkin'…here's this Crom, big in me children's mind as all get out, his altars made of stone, not to mention all the following words associating him with stone, something hard and enduring. Does that make his *toes* the pebbles at the foot of such reverent places?

cromleac: altar of the Great God

cromlech: a cap stone resting on two upright pillar stones, sometimes forming a passage; usually marks the grave of a giant, a hero, or a saint

cumal: female slave; a monetary unit equal to one female slave

Death of King of kings: The druid/magi legend passed down about Conor MacNessa, a high king of early Ireland at the time of Christ. He summoned his druid astrologers for explanation upon seeing darkness in the middle of the day. His magi interpreted the sign, telling him that the King of all kings, the Son of the one God, had been killed by His own people on a tree. Outraged and in terrible grief that such a horrible thing could happen, the beloved king took an ax and began chopping down the sacred grove of oaks. Having been gravely wounded in a battle by a brain ball lodged in his head, he was warned by his physician Faith Liag that any exertion might kill him. But the distraught Conor continued hacking at the trees, demanding to know who the wretches were that killed such a noble, loving man, until he collapsed in death.

His legend, and that of the star of the East marking the birth of the King of kings, made druids who sought truth eager to accept the rest of the story of Christ. It was said that a representative of every race of mankind was on the hill of Calvary to witness Christ's death, and that Conal Cearnah represented the Gael. (See Ethna Carbery's book, *From the Celtic Past,* for the poignant story of Conal at the Crucifixion.)

druid: a term covering a number of an elevated Celtic learned class—spiritual leaders, teachers, lawyers, poets, bards, historians, magicians; often called *magi;* see *Star of the East*

(*Bethlehem*), *Death of King of kings*. St. Columba wrote, "My druid is Christ." Substitute *teacher* or *spiritual leader* for *druid* to catch the drift of his meaning.

Here I must add that these people were not just the black-robed sacrificers reported by Julius Caesar and other foreign observers of this secretive order. In fact, there's not a shred of evidence that human sacrifice was ever done on Erin's green shores, as was done in Gaul and Briton. Erin's druids sought the truth, the light. They believed in an afterlife and a form of regeneration or rebirth, with each rebirth resulting in a soul more highly evolved than the last. This soul was helped in its refinement throughout its lives by spiritual beings—like our angels, perhaps. They worshiped the one God, who lived in the sun, the Creator of Stars and the Five Elements—but they kept the secret of this supreme spiritual being among themselves, fearing the common man incapable of spiritual pursuits and understanding. They let the common man worship whatever earthly symbol he might understand, such as the sun for the farmer, the sea god for the fisherman, or the forest god for the hunter. They knew that man worshiped the creation, rather than the Creator, and saw no harm since the common man, in their learned opinion, could do no better.

All that changed with the coming of Christianity and the teaching of a one-on-one relationship with the one God for all men. Those who truly sought truth and light embraced it, giving up their preferential and revered status as druids to become humble servants of God as priests. So did many Irish kings and princes. Why? See *Star of the East* (Bethlehem) and *Death of King of kings*.

dun: a round tower fortification

Fianna: the legendary warrior-band associated with Finn MacCool, a prehistoric Leinsterman

Now these men were known for their stamina, their fighting abilities, and their love of the outdoors: they were much like mercenaries, often for hire, dashing with the ladies, and the subject of many a song and verse in Irish folklore.

fine: a kindred group, a basic social unit of early Irish society

Finn MacCool (Finn mac Cumaill): a prehistoric Leinster leader of the Fianna

Finn is oft referred to at Gleannmara. 'Twas him who first sucked his thumb after touchin' the Salmon of Knowledge, and wisdom was revealed to him as a result to see him through a puzzlin' situation. Sucking the thumb was thought to clear one's thinking and perception, allowing one to see through illusion conjured by magic.

foolraide: foolishness; insanity

fosse: a ditch or embankment

fosterage: custom of placing children of noble families into the care of others in order to form political alliances. Like my Maire was fostered out to Erc and Maida of Drumkilly, allying the tuaths of Drumkilly and Gleannmara. Many times, these children were closer to their foster families than their own blood.

geis: taboo, something forbidden; to break a geis was to invite certain death

grianán: solarium, sun room; 'twas here the ladies liked to do their stitchery while the men swapped tall tales in the hall

hall: the largest room or building in a fortification; used for dining, entertainment, administration, and often, sleeping quarters, at least for servants

Harp of Tara: Pictures of this harp, the likes of which were used in Tara's legendary halls, resemble Hebrew harps, like the one used by King David himself. 'Tis no small wonder, and that you'll see plainly, if ye read about the Lia Fal and Hebrews in Ireland.

Hebrews in Ireland: After the flood, descendants of Noah's sons, Japheth and Shem, settled in Ireland. Japheth's people were a reasonable lot, blendin' in with all them that came, conquered, and ruled for a while, but Shem's were a worrisome lot of pirates and brigands and became known later as the

Fomorians. See *Lia Faille (Fal)*, *Harp of Tara, bride price,
Milesians.*

hostage cimbid: a person taken from a clan or tuath to guarantee a tribute or loyalty to his captors; some were treated as
guests; others were treated as prisoners, depending on the disposition of the captors

leine: tunic

Lia Falle [Fal]: the sacred coronation stone of Ireland; Conn
of a Hundred Battles discovered it when he stepped upon it
and it shrieked. His druids explained after fifty-three days of
consideration that the stone's name was Fal, from the Island of
Fal. It shrieks in recognition of the true high king and cries out
each of his successors. Some claim it was taken to Scotland by
the Dal Raidi kings where it became their coronation stone.
Later, the English thought they stole it and put it in
Westminster Abbey for safe keeping. That's the official story.

But there's more to the Lia Faille than all that. Some say the
original stone was smuggled into Ireland after the first destruction of Solomon's temple and it's no ordinary stone from the
Holy Land, but the very one called Jacob's Pillow! For it was
this stone pillow upon which Jacob slept and from which he
ascended into heaven. The prophet Jeremiah brought it along
with other temple treasures, including, it's said, the ark of the
covenant. And all these treasures, them what haven't been
taken to Scotland, are still buried deep in the hill of Tara. See
Hebrews in Ireland and *Harp of Tara.*

Logaire, King and druidic prophesy: Logaire was the high king
of Tara at the time of St. Patrick.

It was his druids who foretold of the coming of Christianity
and the end of the druidic as they knew it. Despite Patrick's
effort to give him the salvation message, Logaire died a pagan,
struck by lightning. Makes a soul think, doesn't it?

Maire: a feminine Gaelic name, pronounced "MOY-ruh"
(the first syllable sounds like the word *soy,* and the last a soft-
sounding *uh*). At least that's as close as a non-Gaelic soul can

get to the root name, which means Mary, as in the mother of our Christ. And steppin' back even more, ye'll find the Hebrew name Miriam.

maithre: mother

Mebhe, Queen and King of Ulster: According to the *Tain Bo Cuailgne* or "Cattle Raid of Cuailgne," Mebhe (Maeve), daughter of High King of early Ireland Eochaid Feidlech, married thrice: first to Conor MacNessa of Ulster; second, to the king of Connaught; and lastly, to Ailill of Ulster. She became involved with the latter in a match of counting worldly possessions.

The gist is that Ailill had one prize bull, the brown bull of Cuailgne, the likes of which none in Mebhe's herds could match. What started out as a loan of said bull, evolved into a full-blown war with four-fifths of Ireland at Mebhe's call to arms. Aside from the senseless bloodshed over such a foolish thing, another marvelous legend was born—Cuchullain, foster son of Conor MacNessa, stood at the gap of Ulster and defended the fifth province of Ireland single-handed against Mebhe's four. Mebhe was not often remembered or referred to with fondness, but Cuchullain's victory has helped many a cold Celtic night pass more easily.

Milesians: the last conquering race of Ireland and the ancestors of Irish nobility. The journey of these Celts from Iberia to Ireland was a feat in itself, but there's even more to it than the original record in the Song of Amergin, which tells of the incredible voyage for that time period and the battle in which these brave people take Ireland as their own.

Of Christian interest, however, is the origin of these people. In the time of the Exodus, the Hebrews stopped at a village on the sea. The people of this village gave them supplies for their journey and incurred pharaoh's wrath as a result. The pharaoh sent his legions to destroy every man, woman, and child. These frantic people escaped by boats into the Mediterranean, whereupon God blessed them with a rare east wind, which carried them to the Iberian shores. Because they helped God's chosen, the sea would always be a friend to their descendants, who later became not only the Milesians, but the Phoenicians, one of the greatest early sea-faring races.

muirnait: beloved, little love

ogham: early Irish runic-alphabet; pronounced OM, which oddly enough is a *Hebrew* syllable pronounced the very same way.

One God in the sun: The early magi of the druidry believed that there was only one God, one Creator, and that He lived in the sun, which was their equivalent to the heavens. Now, He was not to be confused with a sun god. Howsomeever, because these magi felt the common man could not comprehend such an omniscient being, they allowed him to associate the Creator with the sun.

Early scholars, basing opinion on Celtic art, which features the sun frequently, assumed the druidry itself worshiped the sun, but that is now challenged by academics of equal knowledge and standing.

In truth, them druids were a lot like the high priests of Jesus' day, who kept the common man a priest's length from our God, 'cause they didn't think him worthy of direct contact with the Almighty. Then along comes the Son—in every sense and sound o' the word—and enlightens the world to the fact that our Father in heaven *wants* His children to speak to Him directly, not through a priest, who, for all his good intentions is still human and given to the temptations of this earthly life. What a glorious God He was, is, and will ever be!

pooka: a precocious spirit, usually in the form of a horse, that can lead a person to faeries or misfortune, depending on its whim

rath: a circular fortification surrounded by earthen walls; home of a warrior chief

Salmon of Knowledge: A legendary fish from the River Boyne, that if eaten by a human, gave said human all knowledge. A famous druid caught it and was about to sup, when it was said that Finn MacCool accidentally touched the fish and acquired a portion of its gift in his thumb, making said druid furious.

satire: much like a curse or a spell; to be satirized by a druid could lead to affliction or death

scían: dagger

serpent: symbol of knowledge; a druid

serpents driven into the sea: Some scholars feel that the legend that St. Patrick drove the serpents into the sea was symbolic of Christianity separating the old druid order—those who sought truth and light became priests, while those who preferred to use their knowledge to further their own greed and ambition took to the sea for Gaul or Britain.

Sidhe: the magical faerie people who lived underground and in caves, possibly the remaining members of the *Tuatha De Dananns.*

Star of the East; Star of Bethlehem (druidic legend of the magi): In Scriptures, three magi traveled to Bethlehem to find out the significance of the star that commemorated the birth of the King of kings. This knowledge was handed down from magi to magi—druid to druid—and when Christianity came to Ireland, the druids who sought truth and light in earnest remembered the star and its legend, as well as that of the darkness at Christ's death. These learned teachers then became students again to become priests and spread the Word of God and the rest of the story of the King of kings.

Seanchus Mor: The *Brehon Laws* rewritten and edited to reflect Christian values; wisely Patrick gathered three high druids, three kings, and three priests to do this revision of Irish law, in order to permit the people to retain all their treasured heritage that was not contrary to the Word of God. Allowing them to keep the pagan holiday celebrations by rededicating the glory to God and His saints was another secret to the acceptance of Christianity in Ireland.

Tara: Essentially the capital of early Ireland in its Golden Age, beginning as the burial place of Tea-Mur, first queen of the

Milesian's ruler Eremon and daughter of one of the kings of Spain. It was said that from Tara's hill, all five provinces of Erin could be seen on a clear day, and it was at Tara that the Five Roads of Erin converged. Not only was it the seat of the High Kings of Erin, but boasted seven *duns,* each with multiple buildings of wood and stone.

Here kings, druids of all manner—from doctors to lawmakers to poets and historians—heroes, and Erin's loveliest ladies gathered in a glory not seen since. Most well known was its banqueting hall, attached to the high king's dun. The hall housed a thousand warriors. Each of Erin's province kings had their own lodges and buildings for various purposes of administration and hospitality. Today's archeology testifies that the songs and legends of its splendor were not exaggerated.

torque: a neck band, often made of gold or silver; many times took the place of a crown for a king or queen; its degree of elegance often indicated rank in society

tuath: a kingdom; a land

tuatha: a people

Tuatha De Dana: These were a learned race who were thought to come from the north. Because of their extensive knowledge of astrology, medicine, and the science of the time, they were thought by the common man to be gods. They reigned supreme in Ireland until the coming of the Milesians and the Iron Age. Upon their defeat in a battle where their druids matched wits and magic with the Milesian druids, it was thought that they shape-changed into spirits or faeries and went to live in the hills. More likely, they lived in caves in the hills and continued to study nature, the stars, and the elements. However, folklore has them becoming the *Sidhe*—faerie people.

Uí Niall: formal for *of the clan Niall,* as opposed to the familiar *Niall,* meaning the same thing

vallum: area within a *rath* or circular fortification, usually an inner and outer vallums divided by an inner *fosse,* or ditch, and enclosed by an outer one

White Martyrs (White Saints): Peculiar to Ireland were the saints who did not have to shed their blood or die the horrible death of a martyr for their faith. These were a Pentecostal, fire-hearted lot, who sought to spread the Word with love and humility, rather than with force.

Their willin'ness to allow me children to keep all familiar and precious customs and laws which did not conflict with Scripture added to the druidic legends and prophesies regarding Christ. And the end of the druidic order as it was known, paved the way for the fervent embrace of Christianity. Taking pagan holidays and rededicating all the glory and honor to God, rather than its former god or purpose, was yet another way in which they won the heart and souls of Erin's children.

These were a feisty lot, a combination of saint and warrior for Christ. They made mistakes in their zeal, just like ordinary folks, but their love for the truth in the gospel always brought them back in line with Christ's teachings. I'm proud to boast that Erin produced more missionaries than any other country in time.

And while I'm gettin' full of meself, I might as well add that it's my children what preserved civilization and all its records, while the barbarians did their barbarian best to destroy it during the Dark Ages. 'Twas to Erin in that Golden Age of Knowledge and the Book of Kells that the nobility of continental Europe sent their children for education. Why, 'tis the subject of the whole book, *How the Irish Saved Civilization* by Thomas Cahill!

BIBLIOGRAPHY

'Twas the followin' books that spawned me story of the comin' of Christianity to Ireland and to my dearest Maire of Gleannmara. So if your appetite has just been whetted by all these interestin' facts and lore, take a gander at the following titles.

Bonwick, James. *Irish Druids and Old Irish Religions.* New York: Barnes and Noble Books, 1986. If this were any more fascinatin', I couldn't stand it! Certainly an eye opener regarding the druids of Ireland in particular. Many of these fellas got a bad rap, take Camelot's Mordred, for instance, but that's a whole 'nuther story, 'nuther place, 'nuther time.

Cahill, Thomas. *How the Irish Saved Civilization, the Untold Story of Ireland's Heroic Role from the Fall of Rome to the Rise of Medieval Europe.* New York: Doubleday, 1995. An interestin' peek at just what the world owes me children, preservin' light and knowledge in a darkening world.

Curtis, Edmund. *A History of Ireland.* New York: Routledge, 1996. Full of historical information in a scholarly presentation, comprehensive.

Cusack, Mary Frances. *An Illustrated History of Ireland from 400 to 1800.* London: Bracken Books, 1995. Sigh. 'Tis hard to pick a favorite out of so many fine books, but this has to be among the best, written in an academic approach, but with true bardic flair.

Daley, Mary Dowling. *Traditional Irish Laws.* San Francisco: Chronicle Books, 1998. A delightful peek into me past with the entertainin' and informative Celtic law before Patrick got his saintly hands on 'em, also referred to as the Brehon Law.

Laing, Lloyd and Jennifer. *Celtic Britain and Ireland: The Myth of the Dark Ages.* New York: Barnes and Noble Books/St. Martin's Press, 1997. Ye'll never confuse non-Roman with uncivilized again.

Lea, Henry C. *Superstition and Force: Torture, Ordeal, and Trial by Combat in Medieval Law.* New York: Barnes and Noble, 1996. What can I say? After witnessin' such as this, I can't help but think that some of the folks in these pages just missed the whole point of the faith they professed, and sadly, it's still bein' missed today by some of our most pious o' professin' saints.

Macalister, R.A.S. *Ancient Ireland, A Study in the Lessons of Archaeology and History.* New York: Benjamin Blom, Inc., 1972. An arrestin' plethora of early Irish information, quite scholarly in its presentation, combining the knowledge from historical record and that confirmed by archeological digs.

MacManus, Seamus. *The Story of the Irish Race.* Greenwich, Connecticut: The Devin Adair Co., 1971. Ach, what soul with Celtic blood flowin' through his veins couldn't fall in love with this rendition of me children's story? 'Twill tickle the funny bone, move yer heart, and light yer fancy.

Mac Niocaill, Gearoíd. *Ireland Before the Vikings.* Dublin: Gill and Macmillan, 1972. We all need this kind of friend to keep us humble. 'Tis a bold and brash account of how things were in olden times, but I got the impression that, despite himself, this learned fella had to say some wonderful things about me and me children—all of which was true, o' course. No lore philosophizin' for this one, but full of spell-bindin' facts, some flatterin' and some, left to me, best forgotten—lessin' ye're writin' some academic paper or whatnot.

Mann, John. *Murder, Magic, and Medicine.* New York: Oxford University Press, 1992. Now I mentioned the Tuatha De Danaans were known as great healers, so gifted that they were considered to possess magic powers of healing. Read how some of the medicine of the past—that what didn't kill folks, that is—is being used again by our modern medicine. Magic?

Decide for yourself. Not only will ye be entertained, but enlightened as well.

Ó Cróinín, Dáibhí. *Early Medieval Ireland* (400–1200). New York: Longman Group Ltd., 1995. The man takes ye there and surrounds ye with all manner of information on what it was like to live in them times. 'Tis a veritable wealth of information and fascination.

Scherman, Katherine. *The Flowering of Ireland—Saints, Scholars, and Kings.* New York: Barnes and Noble Books, 1996. Another favorite! 'Twas the most inspirational of all reads to this soul, for it's the memory of how the Pentecostal Flame kindled in the hearts of saints, scholars, and kings. Praise be, I've not been the same since. Come to think of it, neither has the rest of the world.

Smith, Charles Hamilton. *Ancient Costumes of Great Britain and Ireland from the Druids to the Tudors.* London: Bracken Books, 1989.

Time-Life Books. *What Life Was Like among the Druids and High Kings: Celtic Ireland A.D. 400–1200.* Alexandria, Virginia: Time-Life Books, 1998.

Various Authors and Topics. "How the Irish Were Saved." *Christian History Magazine,* (Issue 60, Vol. xvii, No. 4). In keeping with the story of Maire and Christianity comin' to me green shores, this issue takes a look at Patrick behind the legend, the pains and pleasures of Celtic priests, and the culture clash of Celts versus the Romans. A keeper, to be sure!

Faith, I'd love to list the host of other books full of riveting fact and fiction that contributed to the tellin' of Gleannmara's story, but I'm runnin' out of time and space. Since this work was started, the numbers of works on Ireland and its past have doubled and tripled. Looks like the Golden Age of the Celts may not be over after all.

May the good Lord take a likin' to ye, dear hearts.

The Amazon wasn't at all what Jenna Marsten expected...

Not Exactly Eden
Linda Windsor

Jenna had come to this wild, exotic land of danger and wonder with one goal: to find the father she'd thought was dead. But the jungle has a mind of its own, and what she encounters there is a world beyond anything she imagined. For all its lush, tropical beauty, the rain forest is far from Eden—especially when it's inhabited by her father's partner, the ruggedly handsome Dr. Adam DeSanto. If ever there were a man in dire need of an attitude adjustment, it's Adam.

ISBN 1-57673-445-5

Kate's estranged husband has been missing and presumed dead...

ISBN 1-57673-556-7

Hi Honey, I'm Home
Linda Windsor

Kate finds herself face-to-face with her supposedly deceased husband! An obsessive journalist, Nick was reportedly killed in a terrorist attack five years ago, but there he stands, ready to take up where they left off. Well, she's not interested. But Nick and their precocious boys are determined to prove to her that God has truly changed Nick's heart.